THE PREDATORS
WANT HER...
THEY SHALL
HAVE HER.

PRETTY LITTLE PREY

A PARANORMAL SHIFTERS
REVERSE HAREM ROMANCE NOVEL

M.K. KATE

Cover Design by Meredith Hale

Cover Typography © Bookin' It Designs

Book Interior Graphic Illustrations by wanchana365, maxedoutmojito from sketchify and tmintco/Canva, Inc.

M. K. Kate - https://mkkate.weebly.com

Ebook ASIN: ———

Ebook ISBN: 9798215501733

Paperback KDP ISBN: 9798851319365

❀ Created with Vellum

For lovers of Damon, Spike, and all other sexy, selfish alpha men obsessed with one woman and black leather jackets

And for my mom, who did not get to read the last few chapters because of all the group sex

ALSO BY M. K. KATE

OUT NOW

PRETTY LITTLE PREY: A Smutty Paranormal Shifters Reverse Harem Romance Novel

COMING SOON

SUCCUBUS LESSONS: A Scorching Incubi Paranormal Reverse Harem Romance Novel

Pretty Little Prey is an extremely spicy paranormal reverse harem romance that contains omega-verse heat, light bullying from one of the harem members (in the enemies-to-lovers sense), dominant and dirty-talking alpha men, a basilisk shifter capable of hypnosis (so some dub-c0n), sexual tease-torture (performed by the love interests), actual torture (performed by the villain—not the love interests), betrayal (*no* cheating, just enough emotional betrayal to require some male groveling), murder, and explicit sex. But, yay for happy endings full of group sex!

PROPHECY OF THE TWO KINGS

Of the shifters, the king of light and the king of dark shall share a mate.

If they cannot share, they will lose her.

…

"They will most likely lose her." —Ye Ole Wise Seer

"*Fear the wolf in sheep's clothing.*"

Luna's mother had always said it before bed. Every night. All shifters labeled as *prey*—not predator—heard it. Rodent shifters, cattle shifters… Sheep shifters. "*Fear the wolf in sheep's clothing.*"

Truly, her mother should have said, "Fear men." Because how was sixteen-year-old Luna supposed to know that the first attractive boy who came sniffing around her—bringing her flowers and taking her on dates—was a vicious wolf-shifter?

How was Luna supposed to know he had found her and gained her trust, just so he could slaughter her family and the entire herd?

Because this was a world where prey shifters were hunted by predators. Taken as "pets" or killed for sport. Luna's kind, sheep shifters, were particularly rare.

Luna had cried and begged him to stop.

Rohan, the boy who had never *looked* like a wolf—the boy who had said he loved her, took her virginity, then brought his werewolf friends to kill her family—had chuckled darkly. "Pretty little prey. Look at you, already knowing your place. On your knees."

Rohan had sneered at Luna's mother while choking her to death. "It was too easy. One whiff of my alpha scent, and Luna followed me everywhere. The perfect little sheep. Dumb and addicted to predator cock."

The shame, humiliation, and raw pain Luna felt—after the men finished massacring her people in front of her—broke her. She laid on her knees by her families' bleeding bodies, sobbing.

She had led a wolf to them all.

She was the reason they were dead.

Fear the wolf in sheep's clothing.

She would fear every wolf after that.

Every predator shifter.

Every man.

She ran.

Through the woods, she ran from the hidden forest village of her herd, from the only life she had known. No longer feeling like a meek prey, she ran for her life as the wolves howled their amusement. *They love the chase.*

"You think you can hide from me, Luna?" Rohan's yell sliced through the trees and wind as she ran. "Prey were meant to be hunted!" His shouts sounded so close, but she dared not stop. She dared not let her legs slow or her heart beat any louder, for fear of being found. "I will find you," Rohan promised.

Luna had been on the run ever since.

CHAPTER 1

*S*ix Years Later

*I*s this rock bottom? Luna thought to herself as she took the fancy gold-embellished elevator up to the penthouse suite. Strangely, she was not excited to get called to clean up vomit from the floor of a bachelor party full of rich, mediocre-looking entitled men. Men of any kind—rich, poor, handsome, old, etc.—made her uncomfortable. *Wolf in sheep's clothing.*

She shook her head, clearing her thoughts as she strode up to the door to knock. *It's not like Rohan will be there*, she assured herself. Her fear of him being right behind her always lingered. It lingered along with the memory of the last words he yelled into the woods when she finally escaped from him and his pack, *"When I catch you, I will roast you over a fire and pick lamb chops from my teeth for weeks!"*

Lamb chop.

The main reason why Rohan's pack had hunted her for so long was because Luna was the rarest kind of shifter. A Duttur. A lamb shifter. No sharp teeth, or claws, or intense speed. She was born a prey. According to Rohan, she would die a prey by his hands.

She knocked on the penthouse suite's door.

Time to clean up drunk male vomit with a smile. After all, a smile meant a bigger tip.

She needed cash to skip town. She had already been in this city for two months. Three months was her limit. Her rule. *Keep moving and the wolves won't find you. Rohan won't find you.* She went by made-up names, bought fake IDs, and took jobs where no one cared if she was who she said she was.

Cleaning rooms in fancy hotels was her current career. Typically, over the span of six weeks, she could get enough cash to leave wherever she was staying, skip the next ten towns via bus, and start over somewhere else. For another three months.

She was tired of running, but she wanted to live. She had to live. *For mama.* If she lived by her on-the-run rules, Rohan might never catch her.

Might.

She shivered just before the penthouse suite door cracked open.

She expected to be met with the sounds of hooting and hollering and possibly catch glimpses of a naked stripper. Instead, the inside of the room was quiet.

For a moment, she thought maybe she had the wrong room.

Then, she locked gazes with the most handsome man she had ever seen.

Long, golden blond hair, ruffled with soft waves, hit just above the man's shoulders. Piercing light brown eyes; so bright, they were more like crystalized amber or dark honey. A dangerous, sticky sweetness.

Staring at him was like staring at the sun; Luna felt it could lead to lasting consequences. Definitely a form of blindness.

The man smirked and...*dimples* formed. And not the "*Oh, how cute*" kind of dimples. The little indentations in the man's cheeks taunted the obvious truth: *I can get whatever I want. Always. All I have to do is ask.*

He was...huge. So tall, her neck craned to look at his face. Wide shoulders and meaty arms like he played professional sports. Like he enjoyed tackling and wrestling and dominating...

Luna swallowed hard as the man tilted his head and narrowed his golden-brown eyes on her, swiftly dragging his gaze from her head to her toes.

"You are—" He cleared his throat. "—not what I expected," the man murmured. He appeared in his early thirties. Luna was bad at guessing age—maybe because she had grown up, fending for herself, at sixteen. *Six years have flown by.* "And you're late," the man added. "He's been waiting for an hour."

Hmm. The vomit call had been placed just fifteen minutes ago. Again, Luna worried she had the wrong room, but the unbelievably handsome man took her elbow and pulled her into the massive hotel room.

The extravagant living room was empty.

This is not the bachelor party. Had it ended already?

"Um," she started to say, but the beautiful man cut her off.

"I'm digging the maid costume, but maybe wear something that shows more skin next time or people will get confused," the man said.

Ah, the first sign of major *uh-oh* territory. "Um, I am here to clean—"

He held up a tan hand with long, large fingers. "You can save the act; I'm not your client. Though I have to say, the more you look at me with those twinkling blue eyes of yours, the more I'm wishing that was not the case." He winked.

Winked. At *her*. She blinked in surprise.

He continued, "The man you were hired to *please* tonight is waiting for you in the bedroom just through there." He waved to a door down the long hallway. "When you're done, you can collect the money here." He gestured to a briefcase on the coffee table.

Okay. Many details to unpack. Clearly, she had the wrong room. Also, the man had mistaken her for a prostitute hired to pleasure another strange man in the master bedroom of the penthouse. In addition, there was a briefcase full of money.

Luna's first thought was, *How much money?*

Should she have instantly mentioned how she was not the hooker they hired? Maybe. Instead, she said, "And what if I want to renegotiate the price?"

The man's dirty blond eyebrows shot up in surprise. His smirk deepened along with the dimples. "Is the ten thousand not enough for one hour of your services?"

TEN thousand dollars? For one hour? Luna tried not to let her face show her absolute shock. That kind of money could sustain her for months on the run. It would be... It would literally be a life saver.

She swallowed again. Could she really do it? Sleep with a stranger for money?

If the man was as sexy as his friend who answered the door, maybe.

Her teeth sank into her bottom lip.

The man's smirk fell into an expression of genuine curiosity as he squinted at her. "I don't think I've ever seen a woman have second thoughts about sleeping with him. I hope you know, your hesitation is something I will tease him mercilessly about for days to come."

The man was paying ten thousand dollars for one hour with a hooker. How attractive could he be?

Ten thousand dollars, Luna.

She needed the money to stay hidden, to stay running.

"He is just through that door?" She pointed at it.

"Yes," the blond man said, his voice deep and rumbly and again sounding curious and intrigued.

She nodded and walked on jerky legs as she approached the bedroom. The hallway felt especially long.

She was really going to do it. One hour of sex with a stranger.

Maybe it won't be so bad.

She had not had sex since losing her virginity to Rohan in a not-super-pleasurable experience six years ago. Mama had warned her about wolves and about selfish lovers.

Maybe I can just close my eyes, spread my legs, and count to four thousand.

Taking in a shaky breath, Luna stopped just in front of the master bedroom's door.

She knocked.

CHAPTER 2

*P*acing back and forth in the bedroom, Daxton growled, impatient for the woman to show up so he could get back to matters that *mattered*. He had suppressed his base, sexual urges as best he could over these past few months. Becoming king of the light shifters was stressful and required all of his attention. Even now the dark shifters, those ruled by the moon—werewolves, basilisks, vampires—threatened his rule. He had no time for women or courting or anything over the span of one hour.

However, he was an unmated dragon shifter in his early thirties. He had lasted as long as he could.

His cock ached for release. Even now, it throbbed with each of his strong heartbeats, confusing him. He had never felt such *tension*. His father warned that being so pent up could cause a dragon to make a mistake. Such as breathe fire in human form or slip up in battle. *Always another fucking battle.*

Daxton's mother had awkwardly inserted herself into

the conversation and stated that dragon shifters sometimes experienced increased levels of sexual frustration before meeting their mates.

Ridiculous. He had no time for a mate. Not with a war approaching among the hot and cold-blooded alphas. The Light and Dark Ones.

Daxton crossed his arms, attempting to ignore his erection, and checked his watch. *She's late*. He was a newfound king, damn it. He had much more important things to do than wait for a woman to slate his arousal.

Finally, a knock sounded.

He grumbled his frustrations under his breath as he whipped open the door. "You're late—"

Oh.

Oh, wow.

Big blue eyes gleamed at him, like jewels in the bottom of a treasure chest. Dragons loved jewels. Anything expensive—gold, rubies, and sapphires—decorated homes of dragon shifters. The practice dated back to cave times where the winged creatures protected treasure and passed time by watching it sparkle.

Dragons were simple, hedonistic creatures at heart. They liked to *own* everything. No one was more possessive than an alpha dragon.

Daxton stared at the beautiful woman and fought the desire to own her as well. *She looks like sunshine*. Her hair was a shocking, white-blond color. The pearlescent strands fell smoothly around her face.

"H-Hi," the woman stumbled to get the word out between those perfect, lush lips.

Daxton continued to stare at her silently, taking her in

with each ragged breath. She shifted closer, inside the bedroom, and her delicate scent wafted over to penetrate his nostrils. *Melted sugar.* Marshmallows dripping from firewood. The smell of youth and innocence and happiness and sheer pleasure.

He took her scent deep into his lungs, wanting to brand them with it.

The king of the Light Ones had found a woman who smelled like home.

His mate? *Only one way to be certain.*

He might never let her go.

*L*una waited for the sexiest man alive to say something. Anything. After her lame attempt at "Hi."

His nostrils flared at her; his dark eyes seemed to grow even darker. His pupils grew even larger. He breathed for a minute before rasping out, "Your smell…"

Oh Gods, when had she last showered? It was not like she did anything but work and hide in her small, cheap apartment. She had no reason to shower, put on makeup, or wear anything but her uniform. *I must be disgusting.* A hot blush claimed her cheeks as she looked down to the floor. What hooker didn't wear any makeup? Would he turn her away?

Why would it feel heartbreaking to be dismissed by this man I don't even know?

Something about him shook her to her core. Maybe his lonely, heated eyes. Or his muscular build that screamed, "*I will protect what is mine. Always.*"

I wish I had someone to protect me that ferociously, she thought to herself. No! What a meek, weak, traitorous thought. Turning to a man was the reason her family was gone. *She* needed to be strong.

"Um, y-you paid for an hour?" she confirmed softly.

A growling noise came from the man's chest. Guttural and deep. "Not enough," he replied huskily.

Her mouth dried up as she again tried not to ogle the obvious muscles straining behind his fitted button-down shirt. "Huh?"

"One hour will not be enough with such a stunning creature."

She looked over her shoulder. Had the real hooker shown up to replace her?

"You," the man said, a pleased purr rumbling his chest. "You are stunning. How much for the entire night?"

What was the normal going rate? She had no clue. So, she tipped up her chin and feigned the confidence of a professional. "Double." She cringed at her leap.

Without hesitation, the man replied, "Done."

Twenty. Thousand. Dollars. To sleep with this sexy male? *Okay, no arm twisting needed.* "Why do you need to pay at all?" Her dumb mouth spurted right as he took a step forward to reach for her.

He pressed his lips firmly together into a thin line before admitting, "Because I do not have time to court someone. Or to snuggle afterwards."

She pretended to hold a pen and write on her hand, noting, "*No snuggling.* Got it."

He huffed out a rusty chuckle.

She had *amused* him. Her deep blush returned.

"There is another reason why I must pay as well."

Here we go. Did he have a scary fetish?

"I am very…strong," he said it as if it were a major flaw.

"Okay."

"Because I do not wish to hurt you, we cannot touch."

Her mouth fell open, and she caught herself feeling major disappointment. "Oh."

"You look very delicate," the man said. "I fear losing control."

"Of your strength?" Was the man…a predator shifter? Luna's fear spiked; her heartbeat accelerated. Could he be a wolf? Could he have a pack? Could he know Rohan? "Oh."

He tilted his head to watch her reaction. "You fear me?"

She bit her lip, her gaze darting for the exit.

"No," the man grated. He stepped forward, caging her with his wide physique. "You will *never* need to fear me."

"I—I'm just not used to this. I don't understand what we'll do if we cannot touch."

A slow, mischievous smile spread across his face.

*D*axton gestured for the beautiful woman to lay on the mattress. "I want you on the bed. Now."

She swallowed hard but followed the instruction. Her lithe body crawled over the thick, white bedspread. She turned back to face him as she settled against the pillows.

Fuck, his cock was so hard. Pre-cum slicked the tip of him behind his boxers. "Pent up" did not come close to describing it. Staring at the woman, he felt like he had been injected with pure lust.

"Your name," he demanded, reduced already to only a

few words. When he was this aroused, his vocabulary went out the window.

"Um, Luna," she replied.

"Strip for me, Luna."

Her scent grew heavy in the air, lingering in the corners of his brain as he grinned.

"Mmm, I scent your arousal, little Luna."

She stiffened. "Scent," she repeated numbly. "You—you're not human? You're a shifter?"

The question threw him because it meant *she* was not human. "I am of the dragon clan," Daxton replied evenly, not revealing his new "king" status. *I would like to know a woman who wants me for more than my title.*

"N-Not a wolf?" she stuttered out, and he could hear the way her heartbeat quickened.

Had a wolf hurt her? He would kill it. *Slowly*. "Not a wolf," he said.

She nodded, seeming to reassure herself of something.

Daxton was about to ask her exactly who had hurt her in the past—full name, address, any known allergies—

She began unbuttoning the front of her white blouse. Daxton forgot how to do anything but watch and *want*.

Want her.

Her tiny fingers moved slowly over the buttons, teasingly. The obvious painful desire on Daxton's face must have motivated her, excited her—because she transformed into a little seductress right before him.

Her pink tongue dabbed out to her bottom lip, wetting it, and Daxton held in a low groan.

Dragons were dangerous. When their kisses became passionate, their fire was harder to control. Their grip was unnaturally strong and possessive, their talons spiking out when they felt overwhelmed. He feared hurting her.

But... *But dragons are incapable of hurting their mates.* Upon first kiss, their mates became fire-proof.

But if she is not yours, she could be fried, he reminded himself. Watching would have to be good enough for the night. *How the fuck will I resist touching her?* Dear Gods, he wanted to snuggle her afterwards and burn her scent into him.

He wanted to mark her as his.

His cock pulsed with excitement. "Please," he groaned to her.

Her fingers quickened as she removed her top, revealing her white lace bra.

"Faster." His hands balled into fists at his sides as he restrained from touching himself. "Want to see you."

She shoved down her black pencil skirt, kicking it off the bed. More white lace. A small triangle between her curvy legs.

The strong scent of her arousal hit him; a freight train breaking through a brick wall.

And his instinct—the ancient link between him and his dragon—came roaring to life.

Mate. Needs release. Must pleasure her.

His control fell with an audible ping to the floor.

As she spread her legs, he saw how her wetness made the thin white lace transparent.

Mate needs to be fucked. Hard.

Yours. Take her. Before another male does.

CHAPTER 3

*L*una shivered as the dragon shifter strode closer to stand at the end of the bed. The mattress she reclined on was massive—it could fit at least five people. Not that there were four men interested in sleeping with her. She shook her head at the silly thought.

The dragon shifter's black pupils had grown serpentine-like, featuring new golden flecks that glistened in the dim light of the bedroom. His skin seemed to shimmer, shifting between tan skin and ruby scales like he fought for control over his human form.

Luna bit her lip again. "Um…"

The man looked ready to pounce. Tendons strained in his neck. Each of his breaths shook his chest. His erection was a large bulge in his slacks. Very large.

"*Neeuck,*" he whispered in amazement.

"What?"

He moved so close, his knees hit the edge of the bed. "It means '*queen.*'"

More liquid heat swirled low, beneath her stomach.

That familiar aching echoed between her legs. The way he looked at her…like he wanted to eat her up.

In one paranormally fast move, the man stripped himself of his shirt, ripping buttons, and pushed off his slacks and boxers.

His bare cock swung up, slapping against a hard, toned stomach. His long, thick length pulsed before her eyes.

She gasped. He was perfect. She had no real experience to compare him to, but even she knew what perfection was when she saw it.

"Can *feel* your pretty gaze on me," he rasped.

The bulbous head of his erection was practically purple with pent up desire. Two thick, prominent veins lined the shaft. The girth of him… *No wonder he thinks his touch would hurt me.*

"Luna," he grated through clenched teeth. "My dragon is fighting me to touch you."

"B-But you said you could hurt me." Even as she said that, she could not resist the waves of heat radiating from him. Her skin *hummed* for his touch. She had grown slick between her thighs, her pussy weeping for him.

"Never. Never hurt you." His gaze fell to where her legs were spread open. "Want to pleasure you."

Gods, how she wanted to be pleasured.

"Touch yourself for me," he instructed in a low, deep voice that barreled through her and had her hips bucking up off the mattress. As if the sound of his voice was an invisible caress. *He would make a killing as a phone sex operator.* "Drag your fingers over that wet, needy flesh for me," he commanded.

Her hand obeyed. Her fingers dipped between her

thighs and gave a tentative stroke over her panties. At the mere touch, her head fell back to the pillow and her white-blond eyebrows scrunched as if the small touch was nearly overwhelming. With another stroke, a soft whimper spilled from her lips.

"*Fuck*," the dragon cursed. He loomed closer, his shadow engulfing her on the bed. "Panties off. Want you bare. Want to see you getting even wetter for me."

She panted as she struggled to shove her panties down her slender legs, before kicking them off as well.

He grabbed them from the air.

Her heart stalled at the sight of the heartbreakingly handsome man raising her panties, clenching them in a tight fist, to his nose.

Darkness washed over his face, his eyes big balls of tantalizing black. His lips curled like an animal as his nostrils flared for her scent.

A loud growl pierced through the hazy mist of lust in the room. And it came from *him*.

Self-control. Gone.

He snarled and sprang onto the mattress, holding himself above her. He fisted the sheet beside her hips, balancing his face over her stomach as he peered down at her. "Rub that swollen little clit for me before I lose control and suckle it for hours," he dared her. "Want you soaking these sheets by the end of the night. I want to fucking swim in you."

She was so hot at this point, she had to be on fire. Her skin from head to toe was a flushed pink. Sweat slickened the back of her neck, matting her platinum hair.

Her thoughts were nothing but a constant loop of, "*Oh Gods, Oh Gods, ohgodsohgodsohgods.*"

With a shaky hand, she settled her fingers firmly over her throbbing clitoris, stroking it hard and fast. She hissed as more wetness leaked from between her legs. Her core throbbed and clenched around nothing. She had never felt so empty. So...*hungry.*

"*Mmmmm,*" the dragon shifter's chest rumbled with approval. One of his hands left the mattress to wrap around his erection and give it a firm stroke up and down, before releasing himself. The flushed head of his cock glistened. His tortured expression spurred her on as she masturbated for him.

Watching her pleasure seemed almost too much for him.

"Fuck," he cursed again, closing his eyes for a moment. "My dragon wants...a taste."

"B-But you can't touch me?"

"Shouldn't. Feeling very—" another animalistic growl shot out of him, and he lowered and thrust himself against her hip, skin to skin.

His hot shaft seared her, wetness rushing uncontrollably between her legs at the direct contact of their bodies touching. His dick throbbed noticeably against her, so pent up with arousal for her. She moaned for it. For him. For *more.*

"If—oh—if you can't touch me, can I touch you?" she asked, her breath hitching on the words as her fingers sped up their strokes over her sensitive bundle of nerves.

"You wish to...touch me?" He looked surprised. Like he

21

was used to holding back. Like he had not felt the touch of a woman he desired in a long time.

"What if you lay back?" she asked. "I—I could move on you."

With impossible speed, she found herself straddling him. He must have turned them on the bed in half a second, positioning her spread legs over his hard stomach.

His eyes were entirely black now. Predatory.

But he is not Rohan.

There was no fear in her. She had never felt so…desired.

How was she going to leave him at the end of the night? Twenty thousand dollars, but never knowing this man's body and touch and passion again?

"Ride me," he demanded.

She began lowering herself to where his reddened, engorged cock strained toward her body.

He shook his head, grabbing at her hips to stop her descent. "No. Here." He tapped his mouth. "Ride my lips and tongue. It is time for my taste, little one."

*D*axton's dragon instinct was taking over him. Still, he pushed it back, trying to capture it in its cage so he could enjoy this for himself first.

His first taste of his mate's needy, quivering quim. *Drench my tongue, beauty.*

She ever so slowly moved to straddle his face. Biting her lip, she appeared hesitant to put her full weight on him. *Need her.*

He gripped her thighs, splaying them open and

throwing her onto his face. She hastily grabbed at the bed's headboard to balance herself.

Yes.

The first taste of her wet honey was ecstasy. The sounds of her moans were pleasure unequaled. How had he gone his entire existence without this woman?

Mine.

With each teasing lap of his tongue over her swollen clit, Daxton lost more and more control over his dragon. His instinct to align his cock with her entrance and thrust inside her tight sheath grew harder to ignore.

He didn't want to hurt her. Didn't want to scare her off.

Mate.

His dragon wanted to fuck her into submission until she knew she was his, forever.

Because he was hers.

Her hips jerked back and forth, grinding her pussy onto him.

As her moans grew louder, his hands fell from the tops of her smooth thighs to fist the bed beneath him. His claws sliced through the sheets. As he laid on his back and she rode his face to an orgasm, he bucked his hips. His cock rubbed against his own stomach, wanting her. Needing her.

Control slipping…

Chest heaving, he clamped a large palm around his shaft, gripping it tight and stroking—trying to push away the rising madness. If anything, his control over his dragon slipped further with each jerk of his cock. Yet, he couldn't stop. *Reaching a point of no return.* He jerked himself faster. Harder.

Fuck. *Fuck. Must fuck.*

His rising growl vibrated and hummed against her hypersensitive clit. She shrieked, so close to release, he could basically *taste* it.

That's it, just a little more, little mate. Feel my tongue? It wants inside you, just like my rock-hard cock.

"Yes, yes," she cried out, approaching orgasm.

He would be the only man to make her come ever again. *This, I vow.*

No matter what the prophecy says, this woman is mine and mine alone.

He jerked his hard dick faster, the tip growing slicker.

Tonight, my dragon will rise and pump my seed into her. Claim her.

Just at the thought of coming inside his mate, Daxton's balls tightened, his tongue flattened to her clit—

"GET THE FUCK OFF HIM," a male voice yelled.

CHAPTER 4

*C*onrad had paced the length of the large penthouse suite ever since the pretty woman stepped inside King Daxton's bedroom quarters. She was…different from the usual women who were sent to him.

For one, none of the women had ever made King Daxton moan like that. Dear Gods, the walls were thin. Conrad had heard every single growl, rumble, moan, sigh, and hitch of breath since she first walked inside and left his sight.

And he was goddamn hard from those sounds.

The lion shifter's cock ached behind his dark jeans. Just as his king had gone without sex for so long, Conrad had done the same.

In the privacy of the living room, Conrad palmed the hard bulge between his legs. The woman with the platinum blond hair came to mind as he squeezed and hissed out a pleasured breath.

He wanted her too.

King Daxton and Conrad had shared women before.

Maybe he could join them. Kiss the back of her neck as he guided her hand to stroke him…

Knocking sounded at the front door of the suite.

Odd. They were not expecting anyone else.

Conrad strode to the door, cautiously looking through the peephole to see a curvy brunette wearing the shortest dress ever made. He cracked open the door. "Yes?"

"I'm here to *serve*." The woman winked, jostling her large breasts at him as if the action were a secret handshake to be granted entry.

Conrad frowned. They had only ordered one woman. "Excuse me?"

"The company sent me for one hour," the strange woman said. "Sorry I'm late, I—"

Shit.

Conrad slammed the front door closed as the realization settled.

The pearl-haired woman in a maid's uniform had not been the hired "help."

She was a stranger. Without a background check.

Conrad had left his king alone and vulnerable. She could be a paid assassin.

He ran.

☾

"GET THE FUCK OFF HIM!"

Luna's thoughts were in a lusty haze as she neared the brink of orgasm on the dragon's gifted tongue. Mid-way through his devouring of her pussy, he transformed his tongue to be split at the tip like a serpent's and teased her clit unlike any sex toy ever could.

He sucked the needy flesh into his mouth. Licked. Worshiped.

"*Ahh,*" she cried out again, writhing on his face. So close. *So close.*

Suddenly, large, warm hands closed around her hips and *tossed* her across the room. She landed against the plush carpet but still winced at the impact. Her elbow throbbed in pain. No doubt a bruise would appear there the next day.

"I said, get off him," the male voice yelled again. It was the blond man who had greeted her when she arrived at the incorrect room.

The next two things happened in a blur.

The dragon shifter clamped a hand around the blond man's throat and threw him down on the bed. "*You DARE to touch your queen?*" the dragon bellowed.

Luna flinched away from the anger.

"She wasn't sent by the company," the blond man revealed.

Luna's eyes widened. *Time to go.* Considering the men were distracted, she hastily grabbed at her clothing and slipped it back on, though the dragon had placed her panties in an unknown location. The thing about being a prey: *we may not have super speed, but our ability to scatter has no equal.*

"She is a stranger who walked in here," the man choked around the hand on his throat. "She could be sent to spy for them—"

"She. Is. *Mine,*" the dragon shifter roared.

27

The dragon's back was to her and the open door of the bedroom as she slipped out of the room. Trying to be as quiet as possible, she quickly grabbed the briefcase full of cash from the living room's coffee table and sprinted out the door. Instead of waiting for the elevator, she ran to the stairwell, taking two steps at a time in a rush to get out of there.

Never had she ever felt such strong sexual magnetism. Such chemistry. The way the dragon had made her feel— from barely even touching her.

Dangerous, she thought to herself. *You trusted a predator before, and see how that turned out?* She was still running from him six years later.

I will never trust another man again. Especially a predator shifter.

This briefcase full of cash was enough to start over somewhere new. *The run continues.* Rohan would not find her; she would make sure of it. Or die trying.

But she would never see the dragon again. Forcing down the rising regret and sadness, she told herself it was for the best.

Finally, she exited the hotel. She ran right into a hard chest, nearly ricocheting off the man. Thankfully, his arms surrounded her and prevented a harsh fall. She looked up and made eye contact with striking green orbs. Green that swirled and swirled and… *Pretty*.

Her mind went blank as she stared into the eyes. There was a…a spiral in his eyes that just kept turning and turning. Churning. Her world tilted on her axis, her knees weakening.

"Very good," the man purred. "Entranced so easily. You can't look away, can you?"

A soft whimper escaped her. Why would she want to look away from such pretty eyes? Such pretty spirals. She wanted to fall deeper under their spell.

"Bastille, quit the hypnosis shit and help us figure out what room he's in," a random male voice said in the distance.

Everything sounded so far off as she stared into those pretty green eyes.

Then, the eyes darted away from hers, focusing on someone behind her.

She blinked. Spell broken. What the hell was that?

Fear spiked as she tried to walk around the stranger, but he blocked her from escaping him, keeping her caged in his arms. Maybe it was the fact that, moments ago, she had been denied her first earth-shattering orgasm, but his touch had her skin overheating and tingling for more.

What has gotten into me? It was like she was an animal in heat.

The more a prey is around predator shifters, the higher likelihood of her going into heat. She needed to get as far away as possible.

"He is in the penthouse," the green-eyed man, called Bastille, remarked to the person behind her in the same tone as *"Duh, you stupid idiot."* "King of the Light Ones *and* a dragon? He is materialistic narcissist central. Gotta be staying in the penthouse."

Oh no. The men were looking for her dragon shifter? *Not my dragon shifter,* she corrected herself, shaking her head.

"Please let me go," she squeaked out.

Bastille glanced back down at her in surprise, as if he forgot he still held onto her. Black hair, sexy slanted eyes, and a plush mouth. Bastille resembled the stereotypical motorcycle, black-leather-jacket-wearing bad boy all grown up. Traces of snake tattoos sprouted from under the neckline of his black shirt, stealing her attention.

She shivered as another wave of lust crashed over her. What was happening? Had the dragon triggered something in her and now she couldn't stop thinking about being touched? Caressed… Stroked…

His lips thinned as he scanned her face.

"Let me go," she requested again.

Bastille frowned at where his fingers encircled her arms, appearing lost in thought. "Why do I not want to?" Instead of sounding cocky or flirty, he sounded confused.

I so do not have time for this. Luna did the first thing that came to mind.

She slapped him.

The sound seemed to echo as the action shocked both of them. Bastille's mouth fell open; his hands released her.

A loud masculine laugh came from behind her. "*Daaaaammmmnnn.* Am I in love?"

"Is that briefcase basilisk leather?" another of the men asked. Basilisk? As in a snake shifter? She shivered in horror.

Luna then realized three large men surrounded her, including Bastille who looked like he could break through a brick wall with his muscular shoulders if he wanted to.

"What would a woman like you be doing with a basilisk skin briefcase?" Bastille asked.

Uh-oh. "Y-You can take it if you leave me alone," she lied. She needed the money; no way would she part with it.

"Wait," one of the men moved closer to her. The first thing she noticed was his red eyes. Double *uh-oh.* The tall, pale man licked his lips and tilted his head as he examined her. He moved so quickly, she had no time to react as he leaned in and nuzzled his face to her throat.

He hissed and pulled away, stating, "You smell like dragon."

What if they could smell she was a prey? Dread and fear ruling her, Luna took a step back, but the third man was right behind her. *Please let the dominating dragon scent cover my prey scent.*

"Get her in the truck," Bastille said ominously. "We're taking her with us."

She struggled to resist them, but the tall, pale one scooped her up into his arms and walked her to the large car, slamming a hand over her mouth to muffle her screams for help. His forearms bulged in front of her eyes, yet he acted like lifting her was nothing. He set her down on the backseat of the spacious car.

Though he kidnapped her—or whatever it was called when the victim was twenty-two years old and not a kid— his hold, his touch, was gentle.

When will this confusing night end?

As the strange men drove away with her, a loud gut-wrenching roar pierced through the skyscrapers of the city.

The dragon had realized she was gone.

CHAPTER 5

"*T*o be clear, I am her biggest fan after she slapped you across the face," Sly said as Bastille drove them to their off-the-grid cabin. "But I still don't understand why you wanted to bring her along with us."

Bastille did not know either. His gaze darted to the rearview mirror, which he had positioned so he could catch glimpses of her in the backseat. Something about her was…off. Her bright blue eyes were innocent yet emotionally scarred. Her creamy skin called out to him. His fingers twitched to touch her cheek, to stroke a thumb across it.

She intrigued him. But obviously, he could not tell Sly that. The man would bring it up once every hour in a thinly veiled joke. *Fox shifters can be so goddamn annoying*, Bastille thought to himself.

"Why do you have a basilisk leather case full of money?" Bastille asked her from the driver's seat.

The men had opened the case as soon as they pried it from her small, slender fingers. She just looked so *delicate*.

Skin and bones. Breakable. *When was the last time she ate?* Bastille wondered. Not that he planned on feeding her. He just kept her around because he wanted answers. Not for any other reason. His fingers tightened over the steering wheel.

Luna stared out the window of the car, watching the trees whirl by on the drive. She appeared uneasy while looking out at the woods.

Bet she's a city girl who has never been anywhere without indoor plumbing and air conditioning. Bastille smirked, imagining her walking into their wooden cabin and cringing at the lack of marble floors. After all, they had caught her coming out of the swankiest of hotels and with a case holding ten thousand dollars. Not to mention she wore a white blouse and black pencil skirt like a preppy woman of high society. Though a bit disheveled.

"Excuse me?" Bastille asked, trying to get her attention, but she still stared out at the woods. Her expression appeared haunted. *She fears something.* What?

And now you want to protect her, Bastille? He shook his head at his inner thoughts.

"Blondie," Nikolai called to her from the backseat beside her, taking her from her self-induced trance. "The boss asked you a question."

"He's not my boss," she replied coolly. "Now, will you drop me off somewhere in *civilization* with my money or will I need to get the cops involved?"

Mortal cops? As if they could take her away from them.

"Nikolai said you smelled like dragon," Bastille reminded her. "Did you take the case from him?"

"Him, who?"

"Daxton Dragomir."

She scoffed. "*Dragomir* the Dragon? Lame name."

Sly chuckled loudly in the passenger seat beside Bastille. The red-haired fox shifter stared at the woman like he was smitten. *Hearts* in his eyes.

Hiss. "Do you know the Dragon or not?" Bastille grated, feeling agitated over the way Sly grinned at her.

"Not," she replied.

Nikolai frowned and leaned in to smell her again. "The dragon scent has faded now, but I can't place her scent." He tucked a piece of her hair behind her ear and dragged his nose along her neck. She let out a startled whimper and crossed her legs.

"You smell…" Nikolai's frown deepened. "I've never experienced anything like it before."

"I get it," she snapped at him. "I need a shower. I've been busy." She refocused on Bastille, their gazes connecting in the rearview mirror. "Now, will you let me go already?"

He shrugged. "We're only fifteen minutes away from home now."

"So?"

"So, we left Kobe home alone. He's probably ripping up the couch or pissing on the carpet as we speak."

Her nose wrinkled in distaste. "Next time, hire a dog-sitter."

Sly laughed for a full minute at that.

She probably thought they referred to a dog, of the human pet variety.

Little did she know, Kobe was a werewolf with separation anxiety.

When his vampire sense of smell gave him zero answers as to what she was, Nikolai asked her outright, "What are you?"

"Pissed," she said.

Bastille fought off a rare smile. "Give us answers, and we will let you go." *Maybe*.

"I don't answer kidnappers who manhandle me," she replied.

As Bastille focused back on driving the curving paths of the road, Sly turned in his seat to study the woman. "Bastille will get you to answer our questions whether you want to or not," Sly told her. Instead of sounding threatening, he sounded excited.

"You plan to torture me over a briefcase?"

"Not torture." Sly snorted, nudging Bastille. "He is a rare kind of shifter. A basilisk. Able to entrance anyone, make them confess to things, make them see things that aren't there…" Sly slapped Bastille's shoulder proudly. "My boy has talent."

"Do not call me 'boy,'" Bastille grumbled, turning the steering wheel sharply as they approached their hideaway.

"Sorry, my *man* has talent." Sly turned back to face the pretty woman. "You don't want to tell us the details now? That's just fine. Bastille will get them out of you whether you want to or not."

☾

*N*ot good. Luna was trapped. Trapped by a *basilisk* shifter, one of the most dangerous and feared paranormal species. She was fairly certain the man referred

35

to as "Nikolai" was a vampire, considering his penchant for smelling her neck, his pale skin, and startling red eyes. The man called "Sly" had way too much confidence around the other two men to not be a dangerous creature as well.

Surrounded by predator shifters. It had not happened to her in six years, since she lost her family and learned to stay away from them. All of them. Especially alphas.

Alphas tended to be hostile, prone to rage and high emotions compared to other shifters. Alphas also had a mysterious draw to them, one meant to lure young, impressionable prey like her.

The alphas who did not hunt and kill prey for sport kept them as "toys." Pets. Trophies to prove they could lull a prey into submission—often of the sexual variety. After all, prey were easily entranced and seduced by predators. Humans did not stop eating cake and cookies even though they knew sugar could kill them in the end. Predators had an unfair, evolutionary allure to them. Pheromones.

Rohan used to tease her about how his predator scent drove her wild. *"You can't stop following me around, can you?"*

Biting back fury, Luna admitted now that he had been right. Alphas emitted some kind of hormone that made prey want to be near them. Want to serve them. Want to…

She shook herself.

Just like predators, prey emitted pheromones. Luna spent the last six years trying to suppress them, fearing a predator realizing what she was. Around these men, she needed to remain calm, as pheromones released from spikes of emotion. Such as arousal.

As long as they did not find out she was a prey—a lamb

shifter—they would probably leave her alone after getting their desired answers. *If they find out I'm prey, they could hunt me, kill me for my sheep's skin, or worse...keep me as a pet.* She knew her kind was rare. It was dangerous to be a commodity in the paranormal world.

When Bastille stares into your eyes and hypnotizes you for answers, do not *tell him what you are.*

The large vehicle parked in front of a medium-sized log cabin. Fall leaves littered the ground, a golden-brown sea. *If I try to run, they will hear the crunch of the leaves and know exactly where I am.* Deep sigh.

Luna unbuckled her seatbelt, cautious to lose any additional safety around the predators. Just as she was about to open the car door, Bastille opened it for her on the other side. He must have moved *fast* to do that. Very fast. *Another strike for attempting to run from them.*

Bastille led her and the others into the cabin, his hand a constant pressure on her lower back. Domineering and dominating and *gentle? He's a predator, Luna,* she reminded herself. Still, she shivered at his touch.

He glanced down at where his palm laid against the dip of her spine and hastily pulled away his hand. Those fingers rubbed against the front of his black shirt, wiping away any remnants of her.

The second the door of the cabin creaked open, a burly man nearly tackled Bastille in a hug.

"Finally!" The large man's voice rang out, deep, low; damn, did she mention deep? The pitch of his voice was a pure rumble, resembling a beast's guttural growl. "Why leave me at home? I could have helped."

"Kobe, you literally chased a mailman in our getaway car last time," Nikolai commented.

"Did not. You're so dramatic."

This was Kobe? She thought they had referred to a dog ripping up furniture and scared of being left alone. Kobe was a man?

Bastille shoved Kobe off him, dismissing the overjoyed hug of the well-built man.

Kobe slapped at the arms of the other two men in greeting and turned, catching her gaze. His stunning gray-blue eyes widened. "Brought home a woman?" he asked with such pure, innocent excitement, she blinked in confusion.

Then, he threw his large arms around her and pulled her to his chest in a welcoming hug.

Everything went downhill after that.

Because Kobe leaned his face into the crook of her neck and sniffed. His body stiffened; his hands slammed to her hips to keep her close to him.

But Luna recognized his shifter scent.

Wolf. Alpha wolf. *Like Rohan.*

Her lungs clamped, shutting off her air supply as terror flooded her entire body. A frightened shriek came from her, whimpering sounds of absolute dread and fear poured again and again from her lips as his arms tightened around her.

Alpha wolf.

Beware the wolf in sheep's clothing.

Mama's bloody body.

My herd's camp on fire.

The smell of burnt flesh.

Before she could release a full scream, Bastille ripped her from Kobe's arms, tucking her behind him as if he was ready to battle his friend for her.

She hyperventilated. Her heart pounded so hard, she wondered if they heard it.

Nikolai lifted his hands to his ears—trying to block the loud sound of it?

"What the fuck?" Bastille yelled.

She couldn't stop hyperventilating as she stared at the wolf-shifter with wide agonized and terror-filled eyes. He was somehow bigger than Rohan. Broad shoulders and a sharp jaw. *He could break my neck with a jaw like that.*

"What did you do?" Sly asked Kobe, all the men appearing utterly confused at her horrified reaction to the hug.

"I—I just hugged her." Kobe stared right back at her; his eyebrows furrowed in worry. In hurt. "And I, uh, smelled her."

"If you don't start breathing correctly, you will faint," Bastille informed her, clutching her wrist and still maneuvering his body between her and Kobe. "Breathe, damn it," he commanded her.

"You're so good with women," Sly remarked. "Yell at her louder, and I'm sure she'll calm down."

Kobe took a step forward to be closer to her, but Nikolai shook his head, warning him away.

Breathe.

BREATHE.

Black dots took over Luna's vision. Fear still trampled her, clutching her throat in its terrifying grip.

"Breathe normally!" Bastille shook her, demanding it.

As she fainted, he grabbed her just in time to prevent her from falling to the floor.

CHAPTER 6

"*D*o you know her or something?" Nikolai asked Kobe a few minutes after Bastille glared at everyone and carried the passed-out woman out of the living room.

Kobe stared at where Bastille had disappeared from sight with her. "No. Never met her before." *But she's my goddamn mate*, he thought to himself. Wolves could identify their life-long mate through smell. Though he could not tell what creature she was, he knew she was not human.

The scent of her produced an instant reaction. She smelled like home. She felt *right*. But for some reason, *he* had not felt right to *her*. His mate's reaction to him had been blood-curdling terror. *Why?*

Even now, he ached to follow where Bastille took his woman.

"Why would she react like that?" he muttered.

"She is a very confusing creature so far," Nikolai replied.

"And hilarious," Sly added.

"Where did you find her?"

"Outside the Dragon's swanky hotel. She was carrying a briefcase of cash."

Sly shrugged. "Once we get answers, I'm sure Bastille will let her go and you won't have to worry about women fainting over your hideousness ever again." He elbowed Kobe and headed toward the kitchen.

Hideousness? Kobe was far from hideous. Though, he did have a scar that ran from near his nose through his bottom lip. Could she have feared how he looked? No. It was his touch that triggered something.

Will my mate ever want me?

Kobe was painfully familiar with rejection. Abandonment. His family, his pack, had left him behind when he was not yet ten years old. They simply…forgot about him.

His entire life, he had prayed to the moon to give him a mate to love and cherish.

She is mine, and she fears me.

"Will never leave me," Kobe growled.

Nikolai's eyebrows quirked, and Sly popped his head back into the living room in curiosity. "What are you saying, big guy?"

"She sleeps in my room tonight and every night after."

Sly blinked slowly. "Dude, do you have selective memory loss? First off, I already called dibs on her—"

Nikolai frowned. "When did you—?"

Sly continued, "Secondly, your presence frightened the girl so bad, it knocked her out cold. You think she'd sleep in your room?"

"I will show her she has nothing to fear." Protect. Cherish. *I will show her I can do such.* Mates were sacred to werewolves. They were like a full moon, calling them, drawing them near. Granting strength. He would die before hurting her. He would die *for* her.

"*Blanket*!" Bastille's panicked demand cut through the rooms of the cabin.

The men hustled to him.

C

*B*astille had just been trying to wake her. Water did that for many sleepers. After he sat her limp body onto a plush chair, he grabbed a water bottle and splashed it over her face.

No reaction. From her face at least.

But her body had shivered at the liquid's touch.

And her white blouse had grown transparent.

Bastille dug his nails into his palms as he watched two firm points form and stiffly poke the see-through fabric. Her white lace bra was visible. As was the dusky pink shade of her nipples.

Fuck, those perfect, suckable nipples.

His cock twitched behind his dark jeans, shocking him. He had not grown aroused in a long time. Cold-blooded shifters had no inkling for sex—that desire was replaced with bloodlust—yet, he had an erection over the *outline* of her breasts.

I've gone mad, he thought to himself. Aroused for the first time in a century over this clothed mystery woman? *How inconvenient. How unexpected.*

How annoying.

A little breathy noise came from between her lush lips,

the pink pillows of flesh pursing on a silent sigh. Her chest moved up and down with her soft breaths, chafing her hardened nipples against her wet bra and white blouse. The dusky tips tightened before his eyes.

I want to suck them. Just a soft suckling.

Lave one with my tongue.

"BLANKET," Bastille yelled. She needed to be covered. Immediately. No more nipple gazing for him. No more distractions.

Seconds later, Nikolai and Kobe barged through the doorway, both of them fighting to step inside the office first. Nikolai held a thin blanket. Kobe held seven various coverings ranging from thin to thick, from wool to fuzzy fluff.

"Is she cold?" Kobe asked, his question rumbling with desperation to warm her.

Sly stuck his head inside the room and grinned when he saw the transparent white blouse. "Did you guys have a wet T-shirt contest?"

Bastille took a mental note: *I will punch him later.* "I thought water would wake her up," Bastille replied.

"It woke up *part* of her," Sly joked.

The three men glared at him.

"What? What did I say?"

Kobe's hungry gaze locked onto her chest and moved over her neck and face. "*Perfect*," he whispered. Kobe sounded entranced, and Bastille knew better than anyone what that sounded like.

"Shit man, get control of yourself," Sly cursed, looking at Kobe's sweatpants.

The thin, gray cotton material did nothing to hide the

growing bulge between Kobe's legs. Kobe clenched his fists and glared down at himself. His erection appeared painfully hard. "I…can't control it."

"Take a walk," Bastille said, ice in his tone as jealousy prickled the back of his neck. *Kobe wants her.* Too bad, *he can't have her.*

Once Kobe and Sly left the room, Bastille focused back on waking the woman. Nikolai leaned back in the corner of the room, crossing his arms. The vampire was always content to observe.

Instead of ordering him to leave, Bastille thought begrudgingly, *Best not to be alone with her.*

"Wake up," he demanded.

The woman did not obey, still slumped over from fainting.

"I know something that might work," Nikolai offered.

Bastille was about to ask him his idea, but Nikolai moved with super vampiric speed. One moment, he stood in the corner of the small office. The next, he leaned over the woman and dragged his tongue from the bottom of her neck to her chin, licking her throat. His fangs flashed just before Bastille launched him off her. Nikolai's body slammed into the walled bookshelf, shaking the many leather-bound pieces of literature.

"You're not fucking biting her!"

Shaking himself off, Nikolai rubbed the back of his neck after being thrown into the sturdy bookshelf. "Why not?"

"Because she's not *yours*." Shit, that made it sound like he wanted her to be Bastille's.

Nikolai opened his mouth to reply, but the woman groggily asked, "What happened?"

She blinked several times before those heart-stopping blues connected with Bastille's mystical green.

No more playing around. Game time.

Bastille strode forward and cupped her neck—as if to choke her, yet his dominating hold was gentle. He steered her head to meet his gaze.

"You are going to answer some questions."

CHAPTER 7

*T*he green spirals pulled Luna in instantly until she was unable to look away.

"Very good," Bastille purred. "Keep staring."

The low voice's approval made her body quiver in the chair.

The pretty spirals just kept eating up all of her attention. All of her focus.

"Such a good hypnotic subject," the voice complimented her.

A soft little moan of pleasure came from her. *Want to please him.*

"Lose yourself in my eyes. Let your mind rest and listen to my words."

Her expression went blank as his eyes began to flash along with the spiral. *Flash. Flash.* Every one of her thoughts popped away.

"Good girl," he praised her, and heat swirled low in her stomach like an internal spiral, dragging her down, down, down… "What's your name, pretty girl?"

"Luna." The word came out in a dreamy monotone.

"Age?"

"Twenty-two."

Was she swaying in the chair now? It felt like she was swaying. Floating. *Mmmm.*

"How did you get the case of money?"

She licked her lips, zoning in and out as she gazed into those hypnotic green eyes. "I stole it from two men in the hotel."

A sharp snort came from the male voice in front of her, but those spirals kept her attention. "Stole?"

"Needed the money," she said.

"For what?"

"Skip town."

"You were planning to leave?"

"Keep running…won't get found."

A soft growl almost distracted her from the peaceful spirals. "Someone is after you?" the voice demanded.

She blinked, her eyelids feeling so droopy. So tired.

"No, no, keep looking in my eyes. That's it. Good girl."

Such pretty spirals…

"Who is after you—"

"DUDE," a different masculine voice shrieked, cutting through the hypnosis.

Luna blinked several times in a row. Oh…no. Bastille had done his hypnosis on her. She racked her brain for what she may have said. Nothing about Rohan. Nothing about being a prey. *Thank goodness.* Surely, they would let her go now.

Sly stood in the doorway of the office, holding out his

phone. "The dragon sent out an immortal-wide announcement. He found his mate."

Bastille's head shot to the side so quickly, his neck made a cracking sound. *He needs to do yoga*, Luna thought to herself. *Too tense.* Then again, how would she know? There was no time for yoga when she worked cleaning hotel rooms all day and night to save up money to keep skipping towns, always on the move.

"The dragon—" Bastille spat the words out in disgust. "—found his mate?"

"And," Sly added, "Get this—he lost her already."

"Lost?" Bastille repeated.

"He put out a forty-million-dollar reward for whoever brings her to him."

"Why should I care what the dragon does?" Bastille sneered.

"Because of this description." Sly read from his phone, "Blue eyes like sapphires on fire. Hair like moonlit pearls. She may or may not be carrying a basilisk briefcase with ten thousand dollars."

All three men turned to her.

Luna swallowed hard. *Shit.* Did this mean they planned on keeping her? Or "selling" her to the dragon?

What if Rohan saw the description? He would know her eye and hair color. White hair was not common in paranormals—it was a common trait of Duttur, sheep shifters. *The dragon just sent my location to the entire shifterworld.* For the first time in six years, Luna no longer had the advantage. *Rohan could find me and finish the job.*

She needed to get out of there. Fast.

49

Jumping up from the chair, she rushed to the doorway, but the three men blocked it easily with their large, muscular bodies. *Darn it.*

"Let me go," she demanded.

Sly smirked. "When you just became interesting?"

"The dragon's mate," Nikolai repeated slowly, tasting each word. He glanced at Bastille. "But that means she's your—"

"She's not *anything*," Bastille bellowed and stormed out of the room, slamming the door like a teenage girl during a temper tantrum.

Luna pursed her lips and pretended to check an invisible watch on her wrist. "Is that the time? I must be going."

"You're not going anywhere," Sly replied.

"I have many appointments."

"A lie."

"My schedule is quite packed."

Sly grinned at her. "Another lie." He sauntered closer. He laid his palms on either side of the armrests of the chair she sat on. He loomed and leaned down to speak in front of her face. "Part of being a fox shifter is knowing who is lying."

Luna grew desperate. *You want the truth, foxy?* "If I stay here, I will be dead within the week."

A loud noise sounded from somewhere else in the cabin. Like Bastille broke through one of the walls with his fists.

Sly chuckled again, but it sounded crazed. The laugh was false. With little amusement, he asked, "You think you will last the week?"

S he was Daxton Dragomir's mate. Of course, she was. Bastille bitterly thought to himself, *Daxton always gets whatever he wants.*

After drilling his fists into the most intact wall of the cabin, Bastille threw himself onto his bed. His black silk sheets did nothing to calm him.

The dragon's mate.

Someone knocked at his door, and he knew it was Nikolai. Without waiting for a response, the vampire glided inside, no invitation needed. Though Nikolai was not a shifter, Bastille had welcomed him into his group. The Dark Ones were any who were labeled as outsiders or "evil" by the Light Ones. Many in the immortal world saw vampires as parasites. Meanwhile, Bastille trusted Nikolai with his life.

"We have her," Nikolai said, as if that was all that needed to be said.

"She belongs with him."

"Not *just* him," Nikolai reminded him as he leaned against the door. "The prophecy says the king of the Light Ones and the king of the Dark Ones share a mate." He gave Bastille a pointed look.

Because Bastille was the king of the dark shifters. "Maybe I don't want her." If a part of her belonged with Daxton the dragon, Bastille could not see wanting any part of her. "If she's his match, she's probably a materialistic snob just like him."

How would he ever want someone befitting *Daxton?* And to *share* with the dragon?

He did not share.

And he fucking hated Daxton Dragomir.

"Are you so sure you do not want her?" Nikolai asked.

Bastille glared at his bloodsucking friend.

"Even I am…intrigued by her," Nikolai admitted, licking his lips absentmindedly as if he longed for a taste of her.

Bastille hissed at him, flashing snake-like fangs.

Nikolai chuckled, appearing much too smug in the face of Bastille's temper. "Right. You don't want her at all."

More glaring from Bastille. "I *don't* want her. Have you seen her? She's small, and delicate, and bright. She's *light*, Nik." Bastille wanted to punch something again. "Her and Daxton deserve each other."

Nikolai let out a heavy sigh. "Having cold blood does not make you evil, Bastille."

It might as well. King of the "dark." Dark may have meant night shifters, but to every paranormal, the Dark Ones were not "good" or righteous like the Light Ones: royal dragons, charismatic lion shifters, etc. Whatever.

Dragons are overrated. Throw something sparkly in front of them, and they'll be distracted for hours.

"What do you want to do?" Nikolai asked him.

Bastille laid back on his bed and stared at his ceiling.

"Do you want to sell her to the dragon? Throw her out? Keep her?"

Bastille pressed his lips together in contemplation. *She has met Daxton. She will never want me.* "She said someone is after her. She had been planning to skip town."

"So?"

"So, we find out who is after her and give her to them.

That way the dragon doesn't get her and she is out of our hair."

There. A plan.

In a matter of days, Bastille would never have to see the pretty girl with striking eyes and perfect breasts ever again.

Fantastic.

CHAPTER 8

*L*una's heartbeat pattered in a series of ragged thumps as the man neared.

"Please don't faint," the deep throaty voice requested.

Kobe. The wolf.

She took deep breaths to calm herself. If she let her fear rule her and she fainted, she would have no defense against him. *The second he finds out I am a prey, he will slaughter me for sport.* Just like Rohan. "Wha—what are you doing in here?" she asked.

The men had left her alone in the office after dropping the bomb that she was the dragon's mate. Rohan could be on his way, after having read the clear description of her. *Need to get out of here. Fast.*

"Please do not fear me, Moonbeam," Kobe said softly as he moved into the room. Gods, the man was so big, he took up all of the space.

Alpha wolves were always breathtakingly attractive. Strong and muscular, yes. But also sharp cheekbones, wild hair, and bright soulful eyes. Ruggedly handsome. The way they moved—with animalistic confidence—could make any woman's panties evaporate.

The fact that predators—especially, alphas—could emit a sexual pheromone to madden and lure prey was severely unfair. Though they did so without trying or meaning to, she despised them for it.

Rohan's words still rang through her mind, *"One whiff of my alpha scent, and Luna followed me everywhere. The perfect little sheep. Dumb and addicted to predator cock."*

Never again. All predators were monsters.

"Are you hungry? Thirsty?" Kobe asked her. His dark gaze flicked over her body from head to toe, as if scanning for injuries. The subtle act of protection warmed her. No. Maybe he was checking what parts of her he wanted to tear off first with his wolfish jaw.

Do not soften to him or any man.

Her stomach growled with hunger, interrupting her thoughts and betraying her in front of the wolf.

The excitement lighting up Kobe's eyes confused her. If he were in his wolf form, Luna imagined his tail would be wagging back and forth, hitting the furniture.

"What do you want to eat?" Kobe asked, waving for her to follow him to the kitchen. And she did follow. Slowly.

The cabin was much larger than she had originally thought.

The second she saw all of the kitchen appliances—a large oven, a toaster, a panini press, an air fryer—she bit back a moan. Six years on the run with little money meant living on microwavable just-add-water noodles. When was the last time she had access to a real kitchen? To real food?

Her gaze also locked onto the display of kitchen knives. *If I can just snag a few for protection…*

"We have steak," Kobe said. "Would you like steak?"

"I do not eat meat." *Duh.* She *was* meat.

He frowned. "No meat?"

"No."

The wolf glanced around the kitchen, as if struggling to think of anything else. *Typical predator.*

Luna inched to the massive refrigerator. Upon opening its door, she bit back another moan. It was so lusciously full. Her eyes skipped over all the red meat and focused on the produce. Broccoli, green peppers, and *cheese*. She loved cheese.

Grabbing at random ingredients, she turned to set the items onto the counter and gasped at how Kobe stood directly behind her; his alpha scent slammed into her hard. *Strong pheromones.*

The wolf smelled like sex in the woods before dusk. Pine and sweat and sweetness unparalleled. Her knees weakened, the tips of her breasts tightening beneath her bra as the powerful scent overwhelmed her senses. She grew slick between her legs.

"G-Get back," she stuttered out through a wave of lust.

Kobe frowned again, flinching at her dismissal. "I only wish to help, Moonbeam—" A small step forward was all it took.

Thump, thump went her heart.

Alpha pheromones licked up her bare arms and up the curves of her legs. An invisible sexy smoke that hovered over her, vibrating against her body and turning her on within seconds.

How was he producing so much? What strong emotion was he feeling to produce such thick waves of pheromones?

Her stomach twisted. Her core clenched. She stumbled, clutching onto the countertops. She hoped to Gods Kobe did not notice the little jerks of her hips, her body seeking pressure. Seeking *thrusts*.

The dragon had gotten her so close hours ago, and she had not orgasmed in so long. Not to mention how the longer she stayed around these predator shifters, the bigger the chance she could go into heat. She had never before needed to worry about her heat. It only occurred if a prey had prolonged contact with predators, serving as a "defense" mechanism. It was meant to draw predators to her and "entice" them to protect her rather than kill her—as was in their nature, considering Rohan.

If she went into heat, these men would figure out what she was: a rare prey. *They could kill me or eat me.* And if her heat started…they would fuck her. The predators and her would be overcome with lust—not being able to fight it.

"B-Back away," she said.

Kobe growled, "No. I must prove to you I will not hurt you. You must not fear me, Moonbeam."

More of his alpha scent flooded her nostrils. Her toes curled. The junction between her thighs dewed with moisture. The dragon had kept her panties, so she had nothing there to catch her wetness. If she kept breathing in his alpha scent, if he kept looking at her like he would do anything for her, her arousal might start dribbling between her legs.

What would he do if he noticed? Lap up her wetness with his tongue?

"I don't want you near me," she yelled at him, his pheromones pounding into her brain and coating it in a horny fog.

This time, his flinch was all the more pained. When the large man recovered, he lost his tender *I-just-want-to-help* façade and moved his face incredibly close to hers. Trying to intimidate her? But there was no coldness in his expression—only hot desire.

She fanned herself.

"You, sit," the wolf told her. "Now." This was a side of him she had not yet seen.

Hard. Stubborn. Dominating.

Sexy alpha.

But she denied his request. "I'm hungry."

"I will make you food." The wolf pounded a hand to his chest, over his heart. "*I* will provide for you. Sit and rest. I will bring you food."

She worried her bottom lip with her teeth. "I don't want steak."

"I will make you a grilled cheese."

Grilled...cheese? Had his alpha scent just gotten stronger or was her arousal spiking?

Her mouth watered at the prospect of melted cheese over toasted, buttery bread. *Stay calm or your prey pheromones might come out to play.*

"Sit. Now." The wolf stared right into her eyes, daring her to disobey him and suffer the consequences. What would he do? Spank her?

Oh Gods, now his pheromones were messing with her brain.

She stepped over to where a stool sat beside the kitchen island counter.

"You're, uh, making me food?" She struggled to understand him. Wolves were selfish, violent creatures. Was he planning to feed her to fatten her up so he would have more to devour later? *Once he realizes I am prey, yes.*

Kobe cooked in silence, but never went more than a couple of minutes without gazing at her.

The predator watches me as he cooks. Because she reminded him of food?

I need to get out of here.

Breathing through her mouth to wane off some of the alpha-induced lust, she relaxed into the stool, cautiously watching him. His muscular back stretched the fabric of his fitted, navy-blue shirt. The cords of his forearms became more noticeable as he flexed and moved around the stovetop.

Just as Kobe finished searing both sides of the grilled cheese sandwich, Bastille strode into the kitchen along with Nikolai and Sly.

"Is the princess settling in?" Bastille mocked her, speaking to her in a harsher way than he had before. Just because he found out she was the dragon's mate? Did he hate the dragon so much? "You do realize Kobe is not your servant?" Bastille asked her in a condescending voice that reminded her of the rude hotel guests who left her a fifty-cent tip and a snide remark about how she should have gone to college if she wanted to make real money.

Luna scowled and ground her teeth at that. Yet another

example of a predator looking down on a prey—though he did not know what she was. *Alphas are assholes*. Exhibit A.

First, the wolf had scolded her into sitting down and letting him cook for her. Now she was being scolded for letting him?

Kobe ignored his friend as he plated a piping hot grilled cheese and walked it over to her. He slowly laid it down in front of her. She reached for it, but he gently swatted her hands away. Confused, she blinked up at him.

He lifted half of the sandwich to his lips and *blew on it* for her, cooling it. He then held it out for her to take a bite. He wanted to feed her like a pet?

"I can feed myself," she grated, anger and hurt pride leaking from her.

Still, her prey instincts purred at being taken care of by this man, *damn it.* Prey instincts were to cater to predators. To be meek and submissive. Luna had learned the hard way to never be those things again.

Kobe grunted and continued holding the amazing-looking sandwich before her lips. "Just a little bite, Moonbeam."

Leaning forward and eating from the wolf's hand had to be some kind of trick. *He wants me to trust him.* And thus, she was even more suspicious.

She glared. "Are you going to make airplane noises while feeding me?"

"Would that make you eat?" he asked. "You are thin. Want to feed you."

But she knew more than anyone that wolves always had ulterior motives. "Maybe I like being thin." Her stomach was rude enough to growl, announcing her as a liar.

Kobe narrowed his eyes on her, silently daring her to eat.

"Maybe I'm hungry for something else," she attempted a soft growl, trying to sound threatening.

Instead, she sounded suggestive. Like what she meant was that she was hungry for *him*. Damn it.

Kobe's eyes blazed as he stared at her with more intensity than she previously knew was possible. The back of her neck began to sweat, and her thighs clenched together in reaction.

"I—I meant, I'm hungry for freedom," she said.

He pushed the sandwich closer to her lips. Gods, it smelled *so good*. "Eat, Moonbeam."

Sly watched the interaction, amused. "Should I be jealous that Kobe hasn't hand-fed me before?"

Kobe moved the grilled cheese right in front of her lips, but her stubbornness peaked and she quickly dodged it.

"You have *got* to be kidding." Bastille gaped at them. His angry green eyes darkened to a vicious emerald. "Of course, the dragon's mate is a spoiled little princess just like him. Sorry, we don't have any lobster for you. Melted cheese on bread must be beneath you—"

Luna's face shot forward as she took a bite from what Kobe offered her. She had been unable to resist any longer. After going so long without, she could not imagine any meal being of greater luxury than this homemade grilled cheese.

"*Mmmmmm.*" A broken moan clawed out of her throat and echoed around the kitchen, seeming to bounce off each wall and shiny metal appliance.

She could not help it. After being around alphas for

hours now, tired from having worked all day cleaning hotel rooms, and indulging in a bite of pure cheesy perfection, Luna's moan rang out, loud and clear and *loud*.

As she slowly chewed, cooing noises of pleasure came from her and she forgot where she was. Forgot who was watching her.

Forgot that predators had just heard her overtly sexual noise.

CHAPTER 9

*A*ll of the men froze at the sound of her moan.

Kobe's shaft was stiff as it pressed against the seam of his sweatpants. He had been hard since the first moment he breathed in his mate's scent. It acted as an aphrodisiac, awakening every part of him.

She moaned around another bite of the sandwich.

He had fed his mate. *Provided* for her. Happiness infiltrated him. He would *always* provide for her.

Meanwhile, Bastille's jaw ticked with barely controlled rage. The sound of the strange woman's pleasure...did something to him. Each little lush sound gripped at his chest and squeezed around his internal organs—like a boa constrictor hugged his ribcage.

His heart pounded harder than ever before. As a cold-blooded basilisk, Bastille's heart never quickened past a slow, constant beat. This was brand new to him. She was brand new.

And she's the dragon's mate, Bastille thought. Which meant, according to the prophecy, she was also his.

His dick twitched beneath his pants when she again moaned through *another* bite of the sandwich. Bastille glanced over at the other men, and his anger spiked higher at the way all three of them stared at Luna—with unconcealed lust.

Bastille yanked a chair back from the table, allowing the scraping sound to interrupt the moment. "Enough," he demanded loudly. "You moan over simple food?"

She blinked, pulling away from where Kobe held the grilled cheese sandwich for her. Pressing her pretty pink lips together, she glared at Bastille.

"We know it can't taste *that* good," Bastille added. "The fake moans are obnoxious."

"I'm sure you're used to women faking moans around you," Luna said, carefully taking time with each word. "But mine are real."

"Over a sandwich?"

"It's a *really good* sandwich," she shot back, maintaining eye contact with Bastille as she leaned forward and took a huge bite from the grilled cheese. The challenge was obvious.

A tiny woman was challenging the king of the Dark Ones.

A dab of melted cheddar clung to the edge of her lips. This time, as she chewed, her back arched and her eyes rolled back, her expression going slack. A loud moan escaped her trembling lips, "*Mmmmm.*"

Fucking orgasmic.

Kobe echoed her moan with a soft one of his own, a low rumble matching the sound of thunder. The werewolf was clearly taken with her. Why did that make Bastille so fucking mad?

She defiantly took another bite, practically swallowing Kobe's fingers in the process. Her tongue flicked against his fingertips; the smooth pink flesh dragged against his skin. Bastille knew all of his men were captivated by the appearance of that wet, flexing little tongue. Probably imagining it running over their cocks, circling the head. Flicking the hypersensitive slit at the tip to catch all of the glistening pre-cum. *Damn it*. Bastille's hands fisted at his sides once more.

The werewolf let out a broken groan at watching Luna and maneuvered a hand down to his lap to shift his erection in his sweatpants.

Fuck. Bastille slammed a solid fist to the table, rattling the salt and pepper shakers and startling them all. "Everyone out. Everyone but her." As a king, Bastille was used to people immediately following his orders, but the hesitation shown by the three of them stunned him. Kobe, Sly, *and* Nikolai. "Out. Now!"

Kobe glared at his king and let out a wolfish growl.

Disobeying his king? Over a woman?

Bastille's eyes flashed threateningly, and Kobe quickly looked down, breaking eye contact. The werewolf knew basilisks were capable of several things when they made direct eye contact: hypnosis, petrification, and death.

"I wish to talk to her alone," Bastille commanded.

Sly and Nikolai slowly strode out of the kitchen, leaving them.

Kobe stood from the table and approached Bastille, still only looking at the man's chin instead of his eyes. Before leaving as instructed, Kobe had the audacity to tell his king, "Do not hurt or scare my Moonbeam."

Pet names already? Bastille shook his head in disgust.

Once alone, he focused back on Luna, who practically inhaled the rest of the sandwich. That hungry? *She truly is thin. We'll need more groceries…* Bastille stopped his train of thought. *No, she'll be out of here in no time.* Hell, he would throw her out himself. The dragon's mate was no friend of his. It did not matter if she was supposedly Bastille's mate as well.

Bastille took a seat across from her as she feigned indifference toward him. He interlocked his fingers on the table and leaned forward. "You are the dragon's mate," he said.

She shrugged as she licked her finger and trailed it along the plate to get any of the crumbs. *That sexy little tongue.* "So you tell me."

"Are your loyalties with him? Do you love him?"

She snorted. "I knew the man for less than an hour." Though, the indifference left her face as she gazed dreamily at her empty plate. "He was…kind."

"Kind?" Bastille fought the need to crush something.

"Nicer than you so far."

Bastille did not like that. "What did the dragon do that was so *nice?*" He spat out the word like it was a personal affront to him.

Luna's head dipped, her hair falling forward, but Bastille could see the rush of blood to her cheeks. At her blush, Bastille's own body heated. Then, he remembered she blushed over the memory of the dragon. He grew cold once more.

"He, uh, made me feel good," she replied.

Bastille did not like that *at all*. "Made you feel good? So, he fucked you?" *Do not flip over the table.*

Her mouth fell open before she muttered, "N-No."

"How did he make you feel good if he didn't fuck you? Did he give you shiny gifts? Dazzle you with jewelry and compliments?"

Instead of responding, Luna did the one thing that couldn't have aggravated Bastille more. She remained silent and tilted her head, surveying him. Examining him as if *she* had all the power in the room.

"What?" Bastille gritted out.

"Jewelry and compliments? Thinking I expect lobster. Why do you want me to be shallow so badly?"

Smart, sexy little thing. "I want *nothing* from you," he growled back.

"Except for information about the dragon shifter from the hotel."

Damn it. She was right about that. "You said you were with him for about an hour. What happened in that hour?"

Her blush deepened into a darker red.

He wanted to throttle something. "He *did* fuck you!"

"He did not," she said.

"Then, please, enlighten me," Bastille rasped in that low, dominating voice. "Or, I can hypnotize you to tell me the truth again," he threatened. "You choose."

*L*una scowled at the basilisk predator. Threatening to hypnotize her unless he got what he wanted? Typical asshole alpha. *Knew I shouldn't trust any of them*. Still, if she risked fighting him

on this, he could hypnotize her, and she could accidentally let it slip that she was a prey shifter. *That cannot
happen.*

So, she told him the truth. "He… He licked me."

Bastille's dark eyebrows quirked at that. "The dragon
licked you?"

"Yes."

"*Where?*"

Her cheeks blazed with heat.

"Your pussy?" Bastille guessed. "He lapped at your clit
with his tongue?"

Did he have to word it so…crudely? So sensually? "Y-
Yes," she stuttered, her thighs clenching at his words.
Bastille was the epitome of an alpha, and his dominating
scent rolled over her in waves. Even from across the long
table, the intensity of his dark gaze tingled over her skin.

"You knew him for less than an hour and you let him
eat your pussy?" He sounded…jealous.

She hated that her cheeks grew even hotter. Could
someone faint from blushing too hard? "There were
circumstances," she replied.

Curious, Bastille crossed his thick arms over his chest
and leaned back in the chair. "Please," he said. "Tell me
more."

No way would she tell him about being mistaken for a
hooker and going forward with it for the money. It would
lead to more questions—questions she was not willing to
answer. So, she said the first thing that came to mind, "I
was horny, and he was hot. What more do you want me to
say?"

Bastille's eyes narrowed on her, the edges of his mouth

turning down in anger. "You were horny, so you let a stranger at a hotel eat you out?"

"Is this the part where you slut shame me?"

His lips pursed, sipping in a small breath.

She had surprised him again. Good. Trying to get back the upper hand in the conversation, she added, "He was good at it too."

Those dark eyebrows rose again. "Was he?" The two words sounded like a death threat.

"A real talent if you ask me." Did she sound confident? She hoped so. Maybe he would stop asking her about the dragon and let her go now. "His future mate will be *very* happy. Unlike yours, filled with disappointment."

Bastille's palm slapped hard against the top of the table, startling Luna.

The sound seemed to echo as they sat there in uncomfortable silence.

Those alpha predator pheromones were rolling off him in thick invisible clouds, clogging her lungs. Such potent, dominant masculinity. Virility. The man was infuriating but damn sexy.

He said evenly, "I can assure you, my future mate will not be disappointed with my skillful tongue."

She cleared her throat. "Oh?"

"You want to know something dragons and basilisks have in common?" he asked before opening his mouth and showing her. "Forked tongues."

Bastille's tongue transformed in front of her very eyes —growing long and thick, separating at the tip. A normal-sized snake tongue was small and thin, but the sheer thickness—the breathtaking girth—of Bastille's tongue insinuated just how big his basilisk form must be. *Huge freaking snake.*

Bastille flicked out his long, wide tongue, and it fluttered in such a way that mesmerized her. He spoke slowly, "I could vibrate my tongue directly over your *sssensitive* little clit. I could curl it inside you while I fuck you with it. Tell me, did the dragon *ussse* any *tricksss* like that on you?"

Luna's heart beat loudly in her ears; more blood rushed to her face. The room had gone thick with electricity, and, as a result, she found herself fighting her arousal. She blamed the predator pheromones, of course. And the way that tongue flicked and vibrated in the air. The fast rhythm of a hummingbird's wings. *What would it feel like against my clit?*

She needed to calm down. As long as the men did not trigger her heat, there was hope of her getting out of this without them knowing she was a prey.

As long as they did not scent her prey heritage through a spike of emotion, such as arousal. She needed to cool off. Fast.

Bastille leaned forward again, laying a hand on the table. He brushed his thumb back and forth over the wood. Back and forth. She couldn't help imagining that consistent stroking between her legs.

He fueled the raging sensual fire as he said, "Even without my talented tongue, I could make a woman come for me on command."

"O-Oh, really?" she questioned.

"Would you like me to demonstrate?" Bastille moved too quickly for her to see until he loomed directly over her.

He grabbed the back of her chair and tipped her back

until she had no choice but to lock gazes with him. Instantly, his green eyes became…coils. Coils that twisted and spun. Spirals. Pretty spirals. Her thoughts were silenced. *Nothing matters but the spirals.*

Luna mindlessly stared into them, helpless to look away. Hypnotized instantly.

"When I put you under a trance, I can make you come without even touching you. You wouldn't be able to fight the compulsion. I could just say 'come' and you'd obey, wouldn't you?"

Those spirals stole every one of her thoughts as she repeated back to him in a monotone, "I would obey."

"I could tell your pussy to get wet for me. To ache for me. And what would you do?"

She whispered, lost in his eyes, "Obey."

Bastille blinked, and the hypnotic spirals faded away. Luna was left staring at his cocky face as he smirked.

She scoffed, coughing a few times. "As if I would be turned on by you." As much as she hated to admit it, she *was* turned on by him.

"You were horny enough to let the dragon taste you after less than one hour." His lips curled sinisterly. "I wonder how long it would take you to beg for my cock."

Her breath hitched. "Excuse me?"

"You thought I was shaming you for letting him pleasure you, but maybe I just want the same chance. You act disgusted by me, but I bet if I kneeled between your quivering legs, I'd find you slick, soaked, for me. Wouldn't I?"

"Incorrect."

"No? You're sure?" He leaned down, pressing his mouth to her throat as he ran his tongue up the length of her neck, flicking against the exact erogenous zone there. "Maybe I want to see what a good girl the dragon's mate can be for me. Maybe I want your thighs to clamp and quiver around my head as I devour your swollen clit. Maybe I want to watch your eyes roll back in your pretty little head when the pleasure of my cock overwhelms you."

Her body jolted and quaked as a muffled moan poured from her lips.

"Look at you, already trembling for touch. So responsive. You like dirty words purred in your ear, don't you?" Keeping his face to the delicate curve of her throat, he… inhaled her.

Shit! What if she was emitting pheromones? "I NEED A BATH," she shouted, shoving him back. The truth was, his tantalizing words had made her wet enough that she worried she might leave a stain on the kitchen chair.

If he scents that I'm a prey… "I stink," she stated just as loudly and awkwardly as her previous shout.

Bastille frowned at the change in her.

"I need a bath," she demanded again.

He rubbed a hand over the lower half of his face before he replied, "Sorry, Princess. We don't have a porcelain tub here for you in this cabin in the woods. No bath bombs or bubbles."

"A shower, then. Now." She needed to scrub her skin raw until the scent of her arousal was gone. Until any chance of emitting pheromones was annihilated.

Tilting his head, Bastille stared at her in curiosity. After a quick moment of what appeared to be deep thought, Bastille dropped his hold on the back of her chair, causing it to tilt back to the floor with an audible bang, jolting her upright.

He turned on his heel and walked down the hallway, gesturing behind him to a closed door. "Bathroom is there. Try not to use up all the hot water masturbating to the thought of my tongue on your needy little clit."

CHAPTER 10

*L*una quickly stripped off her dirty, torn work uniform in the privacy of the bathroom. Steam poured from around the shower curtain as she prepped for a much-needed cleaning. She had wondered for a moment, when Bastille led her to the bathroom, whether he would stay there with her and watch her shower. He'd had this intense, possessive expression on his face. When he had left, the expression had turned sad and full of longing.

She shook her head to get rid of the image. *Just because he is a* sexy *monster does not make him* not *a monster.*

Her attraction to him was just due to prey instincts, of course. His dominating presence and dirty words did nothing to help dampen the arousal she felt around him. She needed to eliminate her prey pheromones if she did not want them to realize what she was.

She had worked on controlling her pheromones over the years—mental exercises, overworking/exhausting herself, and scrubbing her skin helped. But lust over sexy alphas had never been a factor. *What if I go into heat around them?*

Even now, stepping under the hot water, the tension in her abdomen did not wane. If she dared to touch herself now, they might smell her. Her pussy *dripped* from Bastille's words. His power was just so…delicious. Decadent. Dark and dangerous. He had an arrogant, sinister confidence that should have scared her—yet, instead, it frustratingly made her crave him more. She had never craved someone like this before.

She wanted the basilisk, so how was she the dragon's mate? *Oh Gods, I'm a slut.*

The water streamed from the showerhead and pressed wet kisses against her hard, tingling nipples. Her small hands crept up, up, to cup her breasts. *No!* If she touched herself, any scent she left would linger in the small bathroom. *No way to take the edge off.*

I need to calm the heck down and stop imagining the basilisk holding my throat as he fucks me against a wall. She needed to scrub her skin raw. Abrasion to the skin or a serious injury could mute her prey pheromones for a time. It had something to do with her supernatural healing not being as fast as predators' healing. If she were shot, she could die. If a vampire or basilisk were shot, they might laugh it off. *I need to remember who I am dealing with.* In her life, she had found that those who had the highest pain tolerance often enjoyed doling out the most pain.

She needed to cause herself pain to control her pheromones, but the vampire would scent blood.

She grabbed a loofah and a bottle of body wash, trying not to think about which guy it belonged to. Biting back whimpers of pain, she scrubbed at her skin with a male body wash that smelled way too good and scrubbed and scrubbed until the layer of her skin left was something pink that stung when the air touched it.

Her body would be too focused trying to heal itself instead of releasing any kind of pheromone.

For extra effect, she turned the hot water off and jolted her body with freezing liquid that burned at her raw over-sensitized skin.

When she finally stepped out of the shower, each step caused a little spike of pain. She would have to keep doing things like this until she managed to escape them.

I have to escape them.

She wrapped a towel around herself and glanced at her tattered uniform. *I so do not want to put that back on.*

Summoning all of her daring and confidence, she stormed out of the bathroom and into the living room where she heard the men speaking to each other.

Water dripped from her onto the hardwood floors.

She weaved down the long hallway to enter the common room. Kobe and Sly sat on either end of a wide sofa while Bastille sat in a regal-looking, black vinyl wing-back chair with brass nail-headed trim. Nikolai stood—or maybe it would be better to use the word "lurked"—by the grand fireplace. The flames cast shadows and golden light around the room—considering the sun had gone down hours ago, it was the only gleam that made the four dangerous men visible.

At the sound of her bare feet slapping over the hard-wood, the men looked up, stopping their conversation as she entered the room.

Kobe shot up to his feet as soon as he saw her. Sly and Nikolai's eyes widened before narrowing on her.

Bastille, cool as a sexy cucumber, sat on his elegant chair and gazed at her bare thighs, revealed by the short towel wrapped around her. His expression may have remained indifferent, but his stare burned into her skin. He hungrily brushed a thumb across his lower lip as his gaze raked over her.

They *all* gazed hungrily at her. *Thank goodness I won't be producing any prey pheromones for a bit.* Because arousal twisted low in her stomach as they perused her dripping body.

"Do you need help toweling yourself dry, Princess?" Bastille asked. "You're dripping water all over my floor."

"I'm sure this is the first time a woman has been wet in front of you, Bastille." Feigning confidence and power, she tipped her chin up and demanded, "I need clothes."

The men did not reply for several seconds. In fact, the four of them glanced at each other then went back to ogling her. Sly grinned like all his dreams were coming true, amusement pouring from his bright eyes. Her damp hair continued to drip water on the floor, which she did nothing to stop because: screw them, they were keeping her hostage.

She repeated, "I need clothes."

"Do you?" Bastille shot back.

"I vote 'no' on clothes," Sly remarked.

Meanwhile, Kobe began to strip himself. The muscles in his thick arms strained as he pulled his dark blue shirt over his head, revealing a set of abs that took Luna's breath away. The werewolf was made of pure muscle. Broad shoulders, meaty arms, and…wow. Luna wanted to explore the dips and ridges of his torso with her tongue.

But he was a wolf like Rohan. *Stop lusting after him!*

Still, Kobe *had* made her a grilled cheese and been the nicest to her so far.

Kobe cautiously took a few steps closer to her, reaching out to offer her his shirt. She hesitantly took it from him, trying not to stare at those sexy as hell abs. The warmth from the fabric of the shirt seeped into her. Surprisingly, something about his scent comforted her. He smelled like a run through the forest—pine and earth and crisp morning air. Familiar. Home.

Sly snorted. "Damn, Kobe, you going to give her your pants too?"

Kobe looked down at himself then back at Luna with a questioning expression. His fingers dipped to the waist-band of his sweatpants, and she choked out a gasp.

"N-No. This is fine." She clutched the shirt to her chest. Kobe was a large man, and his shirt was sure to cover a huge portion of her body. No worries about flashing the men if she bent over in it. "I just, uh, needed something to sleep in for the night." But would it just be one night? How long did they plan on keeping her?

"We should get her some baby doll nightgowns," Sly joked but was clearly scrolling on his phone as if he had just started the online shopping. "Do you prefer pink or light blue? We all know Bastille would prefer you in black lace."

Bastille still silently stared at her. His gaze flicked down to her pale thighs once more.

"Which bedroom am I sleeping in?" she asked.

The men glanced at each other again.

"Rock, paper, scissors?" Sly asked.

Bastille tsked. "Is the couch not good enough for you, Princess?"

"You can sleep with me, Moonbeam," Kobe offered.

She shook her head, trying to clear out the thoughts of slumbering beside the sexy shirtless man. She might end up grinding against him in her sleep with how horny she was. "To be clear, I will not be sleeping with anyone. I just need a bed. An empty one."

*N*ot sleep with his mate? That kind of thing was unnatural. Kobe already had a hard time not touching her or being in the same room as her. He had given her as much distance as possible after she seemed so scared of him upon meeting, but he was reaching his limit. His entire life, he had wished to find his mate. His true soul and heart match. He wished to not feel alone anymore.

When his pack left him behind so many years ago, he found Bastille and the others, but he still craved acceptance and love from a mate.

My woman finally stands before me, and I do not hold her? She does not sit on my lap? It was unheard of for a wolf to not be in constant contact with his mate. The protective urges were unlike anything Kobe had ever felt before. *Will die for her. Will kill for her. Want to hold her.*

"I will sleep with you, Moonbeam," Kobe grunted. He still stood only two feet from his mate, who wore nothing but a damp towel. Her wet white-blond hair was slicked back, giving the men their first clear view of her smooth, round face. Long light lashes framed big gray-blue eyes. Skin like coffee creamer. A nose that reminded Kobe of a button. Plush pink lips he imagined smashing to his own in a powerful kiss.

Beautiful. *So beautiful, it hurts.*

"I repeat," she said. "I will not be *sleeping* with anyone."

"You put extra emphasis on 'sleeping,'" Sly pointed out. "Are you meaning that sex is out of the picture? What about cuddling? Or staring dreamily into each other's eyes all night long? Or anal?"

Luna's jaw dropped, leaving her gaping there.

My mate fears anal? Kobe wondered.

Nikolai smirked at her reaction. "He is joking," the vampire assured her. "About the cuddling."

With a straight face, Sly said, "I never joke about anal."

"*No sex,*" she stressed.

"What about second base?" Sly asked.

"No touching," she replied, crossing her arms over the towel, still holding Kobe's shirt.

"Tell us, Princess," Bastille leaned back in his chair and let his hot gaze work over every part of Kobe's mate as he asked, "What do you have against sleeping in the same room as one of us? Considering you let the dragon eat your pussy after less than one hour of knowing him."

Sly choked out a snort. Meanwhile, Kobe and Nikolai froze, trying to absorb this new information.

My mate likes the dragon? Hurt sank into Kobe's heart. *Will make her like me too.* Maybe licking between her legs was the way to secure her heart. Kobe was talented at that.

Bastille smirked at Luna, who blushed furiously and glared at him.

"Do you have a reason for making me sound like a slut in front of your friends?" She clearly feigned confidence—the predators could tell by her racing heartbeat and the slight crack in her voice that her feelings were hurt.

With his impossible, paranormal speed, Bastille appeared in front of her, getting around Kobe somehow. The basilisk king wrapped a hand around Luna's throat, and she gasped in his grip. He held her in that threatening stance, and Luna instinctively raised both hands to cover Bastille's, to try to pull his fingers from her delicate throat.

Without Luna's grip on the towel around her, the fabric slipped and fell to the floor, leaving her damp and bare.

Everyone went still. The silence was deafening.

She shivered, the movement shaking her round breasts as the men stared at her. Bastille blocked most of the men's gazes, so Sly, Nikolai, and Kobe all took a step or two to peer around their king and see...her.

Deliciously naked with little trails of water droplets licking down her smooth body.

Kobe's wolf rose in him and growled a single thought through his mind.

MINE.

CHAPTER 11

*L*una gasped for breath even though Bastille merely cupped her throat—he was not applying enough pressure to threaten her airway. But his stance dominated her, leaving her breathless.

There she stood. In the nude. In front of alpha predator shifters.

Gods. Damn. It.

This was not the way to get them disinterested in her enough to let her go free.

"Well…" Bastille spoke softly against her cheek. "This was not what I had planned."

She cocked her head back to stare into those mesmerizing green eyes. "You didn't plan for the towel to fall? You don't actually expect me to believe that, do you?"

"I wished to punish you for your statement. Not strip you."

She was hardly listening to him. Shame and embarrassment clung to every portion of her revealed skin. She knew she looked like she suffered from hunger pangs—which she often did because she cheaped out on food to save money to skip town every few months, constantly on the run. She had just rubbed her skin to a state of irritated pink. She had also not fully shaved in…a while.

But when she dared to glance around at the men behind Bastille, she saw nothing but desire in their expressions. Hungry desire.

Frowning, she focused back on Bastille. "Are you going to keep holding my throat until I shiver to death or will you let me bend down and pick up my towel?" she asked him.

"You said something that angered me," he replied evenly. "Take it back, and I will release you without punishment."

Punishment? "What did I say?"

"You tell me. What did you say wrong?"

She wracked her brain. Before Bastille had turned all throat-hold-y, he had teased her about getting licked between the legs by the dragon. "You mean, when you slut shamed me?"

"I did not slut shame you. I mentioned that you let the dragon touch you, barely knowing him; yet, you refuse to sleep in the same room as one of us. Are we too low on the food chain for you, Princess?" Bastille shook his head. "That doesn't matter. Now, repeat *exactly* what you said."

"I don't remember."

"Why don't you use your pretty little brain and *think*?"

She scowled at him—mostly, because he was making it hard to think. They all were. Bastille held her naked body out for display in front of the other men. All of them emitted knock-your-socks-off level pheromones, which seemed to wrap around her and squeeze and buzz. Warming her. Arousing her.

There was something so tantalizing about being so vulncrable and bare in front of the powerful men. She should be terrified by them, but all she felt was indecent excitement.

"Don't remember?" Bastille asked. "If not, I will have to proceed with your punishment."

What the heck was he planning for that? "Why don't you remind me?"

"Nikolai has a perfect memory," Bastille said. "Nikolai, why don't you remind all of us of what she said right before I stood?"

The vampire licked his lips, his red eyes blazing as he replied, "She said, 'do you have a reason for making me sound like a slut in front of your friends?'"

"Right." Bastille released her throat and gestured for her to approach the couch. "Bend over the arm of the sofa."

She stood still, not obeying the alpha's orders.

"Accept your punishment, and it will be tame the first time."

"I don't deserve punishment," she said. "I've done nothing wrong."

As she refused him, he took a step closer to her. She stepped back. This continued until she stood close to the spot where Bastille gestured for her to accept her punishment.

Bastille rasped, "You implied having a normal, healthy sex drive makes a woman a slut."

She blinked. *Wait, what?* That was what he thought she

should be punished for? Not for talking back to him? "I—I... No, I didn't."

"Yes. You said I made you 'sound like a slut.' And I do not appreciate that term used in a derogatory way."

"Like you've never used that word before," she shot back.

He loomed over her, his gaze piercing hers. "I use it in the context of pleasuring a woman. Never to demean one."

She stepped back once more, the back of her thighs touching the arm of the sofa. "How is it different?"

"Because you used it like you should be embarrassed that the dragon tongued your pussy. You used it about yourself like you have something to be ashamed of."

"And that warrants punishment?"

Growing tired of her questions, he said coolly, "Bend over the arm of the couch, Princess."

Bend over? As in show him her bare ass? As in...was he about to spank her? "Um, I think you've got this wrong—"

"A slut is not a real thing. It's a phrase used to build shame. Or a phrase used to stoke arousal. One use is not allowed in this house. Can you guess which?" Bastille stretched his arms and cracked his knuckles as he nodded behind her. "Now, bend over the arm of the couch and put your hands on the bottom cushions."

She tried to back away again, but he had her trapped against the piece of furniture. "I—I didn't mean it in a bad way!"

He tsked, shaking his head. "The more you resist, the worse your punishment."

"This is getting good," Sly commented from somewhere, but Luna was too caught up in Bastille's intense gaze to look away.

She said, "I was only saying it that way because I thought that was what you were doing. Slut shaming me."

"Tell you what," Bastille said, tilting his head. "Let's play a game. Your punishment will only end once you admit that the word 'slut' fills you with nothing but lust."

"E-Excuse me?"

"Either that, or you can admit right now that the word 'slut' makes you wet. That the idea of being our dirty little slut, who gets teased and rewarded with our cocks, makes your clit tingle. I can smell your arousal, Princess. Best to just admit it now."

"S-Stop it."

"Fine. Game on, then."

Bastille clutched her arms, turning her in front of him so her bare ass grazed his front. He was so tall, the swell of her rear did not quite reach his crotch, which instead leveled with the curve of her lower back.

Luna now stood, completely captured by Bastille's alpha strength, nude in front of the others. Sly, Nikolai, and Kobe had formed some kind of half circle around them. The three men licked their lips as their gaze caressed down her neck, down her breasts, down, down...

"What are you trying to prove?" Luna asked, trying to summon more anger than arousal in her voice.

"Prove that you want us too. We're changing how you see the word 'slut.'"

"Just let me go!"

"Not until 'slut' fills you with nothing but lust," Bastille purred into her ear, his breath twisting strands of her snow-white hair. "No more shame, Princess."

This coming from the man who also enjoyed insulting her?

His mouth dragged down the side of her neck as he moved one of his hands from gripping her arm to fold around her throat once more. The dominating position should have filled her with fear, but damn if her nipples didn't harden.

"Shall I begin?" Bastille's other hand drifted down her arm to palm her hip. He may have been cold-blooded as a reptilian shifter, but his touch left an absurd amount of heat in its wake, shocking Luna.

"Moonbeam…" Kobe whispered, rubbing a hand over his jaw as his gaze devoured her body.

"You seem to have transfixed them," Bastille muttered onto her neck. "I am not the only one here with the power to hypnotize, am I?"

Was that a…compliment? "Just hurry up with the punishment if you won't let me go."

Bastille's hand shifted from her hip and trailed up to her shoulder with such a surprising gentleness, Luna went momentarily breathless. "How are we to let you go now?" Bastille asked softly.

She blinked and began to turn her head, needing to look at him and better understand his meaning, but his hold on her throat tightened.

"Fine, then," he said. "Gentlemen, why don't you sit back down and enjoy the show? It's about to begin."

CHAPTER 12

*W*hen you think of the word 'slut,' you think of shame. Judgment," Bastille commented from behind her as the hand not cupping her throat brushed over her collarbone and flattened over her chest, just above the swells of her breasts. "But what is a slut? A woman who enjoys sex? A woman with many partners to keep her satisfied? None of that is shameful."

"I—I get it," Luna said. "Being a slut means being empowered. Are we done?"

"That's not what I was getting at. I want your meaning and feeling behind the word to change."

"Can't you just—" Luna cut off on a gasp as Bastille's hand cupped her right breast.

His thumb swiped out over the lower curve of her breast, just below where her nipple continued to pebble for him. He stroked back and forth, causing waves of lust to crash over her from the mere anticipation of a firmer touch on the sensitive tip of her breast.

She involuntarily let out a squeak.

"Look at these pouty, *slutty* little nipples," Bastille rasped in her ear. "Puckered for a mouth. Begging to be touched." His thick fingers drifted further up, dragging over one of her nipples but not settling over it. The motion was a tease. A light caress with no promise of more.

It drove her a little crazy.

He pressed two fingers to her bottom lip, pushing her mouth slightly open. "And these slutty little lips," he cooed. "What were these lips made for, Princess?"

"T-Talking back?" she guessed.

"Mm, maybe you need to phone a friend. Sly, what are her lush lips made for?" Bastille asked him.

Sly grinned as he leaned back on the couch. "I'm going to go with, 'sucking cock.'"

She swallowed hard, but she could not deny his dirty words turned her on even more. Her abdomen twisted with arousal. With need.

"These lips are for sucking our cocks like the good little slut you are, Princess."

Her breath caught in her throat. His words should piss her off, so why were her hips beginning to rock?

"Lick my thumb," Bastille commanded. His finger pressed further into her mouth, making her open her lips enough for his thumb to enter.

Hesitantly, she flicked her tongue against his thumb.

"*Very* good," he purred his praise, and another shiver shook her. "See what a good girl you can be? A good little slut for us?" he asked.

She was about to elbow him over that taunt, but he pinched the tip of her tongue, pulling lightly and shocking her still.

"And this slutty little tongue? This is for licking up our cum."

She should have been rioting. She should have been overheating with contempt. Instead, she was overheating with thinly veiled lust. *I should hate the words he is using. Why am I feeling like this?*

He released her tongue and moved his hand back to her breasts. "But back to these perfect fucking handfuls." He squeezed the sensitive, curved mounds of flesh, and she bit back a moan. "What would you say if I said I wanted to fuck them? If I laid you back on the couch, pumped my hard dick between them, and fucked your soft tits until I came on your neck?"

She swallowed another whimper. The image he painted... It infiltrated her mind, corrupting it instantly. Like chocolate syrup dissolving into milk after someone aggressively mixed it with a spoon. She could see it clearly —Bastille's jaw clenched, his eyes screwed shut in pleasure as he thrust his cock between her breasts. Him telling her what a good girl she was to take it.

She had forgotten his question.

"Speechless?" Bastille chuckled. "Now we know what it takes."

Unable to form a retort, Luna held her breath as he captured her nipple between his fingers and gave a light tug. *"Bastille."*

"Mmm, a slutty nipple like this needs to be teased, doesn't it? You want a tongue caressing it? Maybe a mouth to pleasure the little peak?" Bastille pinched her tender pink flesh so hard, she cried out.

At the sound of her pain, Kobe twitched and jolted

upright. "Moonbeam?" Apparently, the werewolf was ready to intervene at any moment. However, his offer to help was overshadowed by the enormous bulge forming behind the crotch of his sweatpants.

"Aww, did that hurt?" Bastille chuckled; his fingertips continued petting her nipple. Blood rushed back to it after his harsh pinch, causing an erotic tingling sensation that just made her wetter between her legs. "Would you like me to ask Kobe to come over here to kiss it better?"

Breathless no longer accurately described her. She could no sooner take in a deep breath than she could stop blushing. Wetness rushed between her thighs at the offer of having Kobe tend to her breasts.

Since he received no response from her, Bastille continued. "How does it feel to have such slutty tits, Princess? Such slutty nipples, begging to be abused by my mouth?"

She bit her tongue so hard, it bled a little.

"Still not willing to admit the word 'slut' turns you on?" he asked.

She gazed at the other men for help, but they offered no assistance.

"Moving on, then," Bastille said. His palm skimmed down her stomach, which twitched as he grazed over it. He did not stop until the tips of his fingers hovered just above her slit. Just above where her bundle of nerves pulsed for him. "Should we talk about your slutty little pussy now, Princess?"

A broken whimper clawed out of her throat without permission.

"Did all the blood rush from your tits to your pussy, baby? Is that where you're aching? Tell us."

She pressed her lips tightly shut, not trusting herself with a single word right now. She was too turned on. She blinked open her eyes and bit back another moan at what she saw.

Kobe's right hand had fallen to the crotch of his sweat-pants. He rubbed the large bulge of his erection through the material as he gazed at her. Sly was doing the same, teasing his hard-on at the visual of Bastille pleasuring her.

Nikolai's red eyes burned from across the room as he licked a protruding fang in his mouth.

Luna jumped and squealed as Bastille slapped his hand sharply against her pussy.

"Focus, Princess. I asked you a question."

How was she supposed to remember what he asked when her body was lighting up like this? She felt like a forest fire—hot, uncontrollable, and about to be destroyed and left as ash.

"Oh no, is our little slut too far gone to speak? To do anything but moan?" Bastille rasped in her ear as he—ever so lightly—teased the top of her sex, his fingertips barely making contact with her throbbing bud. "Does our little slut need to be fucked?"

"*Uahgahuhhahh.*" The sound that came from her was utter gibberish as Bastille firmly gave a first stroke over her clit. White light blurred her vision before her head fell back against his chest.

"That's it... Melt for me like a good girl."

She followed his instructions, bucking her hips into his hand. He slid his finger further down to rub circles over the entrance of her pussy. The heel of his palm ground against her clit at the same time, and she moaned again.

"*Fuck*," one of the other men cursed, but she was too lost to lift her head and see who.

"Your drenched little pussy is soaking my hand, Princess." Bastille's evil grin was audible in his smug voice. "I think maybe you do like the word 'slut.' I think it turns you on to be made into a little puddle of foggy lust. You let your abductor touch you like this?"

"*Oh Gods*," she whimpered.

He pressed a long, thick finger forward until it pushed past the tight ring of her entrance. Her inner muscles quickly clamped down around the intrusion, squeezing the digit as if it begged for more. *Want him to fill me up.*

"This slutty pussy needs to be filled," he said, reading her dirty mind. "You want my cock to stretch inside you, don't you?" He plunged a second finger inside her and curled them until he stroked a special spot of sensitive ribbed flesh.

"*Ugahuhahh.*"

He teased her for two full minutes before slipping his fingers from her wetness. At the lack of his touch, she wailed with need. One of the men grunted in response, but Bastille made no quick move to finger her again.

Instead, he slowly lifted his fingers, damp with her essence, to his mouth. He licked her from his skin, and her entire body quivered. She did not even find it inside herself to worry if he could taste that she was a prey.

"*Please*," she cried out, desperate for release.

Using his super-predator speed, he dove both hands to her aching pussy, unleashing her throat from his grip. He pinched her clit and sank three fingers inside her, fingering her at such a ferocious pace, her vision blurred once more.

"*Fuck*," she yelled out, shaking so hard, she might have fallen if Bastille did not have her caged against him.

"Now, tell me," Bastille purred as her pussy convulsed around his fingers again and again, building up to a powerful orgasm that was sure to make Luna black out. "What is a slut, Princess?"

"*Mmmm.*" Her hips undulated, meeting every thrust of his hand. Electric currents invaded her veins as coils of tension swirled in her abdomen.

"Is a slut someone who feels good?"

"*Mmmm.*"

"Or someone filled with shame?"

She moaned again, mindless to whatever it was he said. Other male grunts of pleasure met her ears.

"You like being a good girl?" Bastille asked her, moving his fingers even faster now. So fast. *Oh, Gods.* "You like being a dirty little slut for me?"

"Yes!"

At her admission, Bastille dropped his hands from her and stepped back.

Her mouth fell open in shock. "Wha—What are you doing?"

"I told you the game only lasted until you admitted it."

Trembling with need, she fumbled over her words. "But I...I—"

"Need to come?"

She hated swallowing her pride like this, but her pussy wept for him to finish what he started. "*Please*, Bastille."

CHAPTER 13

*"P*lease, Bastille."

He shrugged coolly. "No."

She looked ready to cry.

Meanwhile, Nikolai stared at Luna's neck from across the room, barely holding onto his self-control. None of the men noticed how large his pupils had grown. How his fangs had lengthened. They were all too distracted watching her as Nikolai licked his lips.

The vampire had not told any of them about his not having fed in two weeks. Not a single drop of blood. His nightmares had been plaguing him—always fueled by taking another's blood—and he had tried to abstain and gain some clarity. Lately, his mind was always on the brink of madness—not that he let it show. *The more I drink, the more victims' memories haunt me. The less I drink, the more the hunger controls me.*

At that moment, the hunger gripped him. Hard.

"Bastille," Luna yelled at him for leaving her high and dry. Her overly-excited, thumping heartbeat was audible to

Nikolai. The unique, mouth-watering scent of her warm blood pumping under that smooth skin filled the living room.

Fuck.

His throat burned for a taste of her. She smelled so sweet, like flowers and chocolates. *Like Valentine's Day.* The month of red.

He licked his lips again, his fangs *aching* to pierce her skin. Her creamy, soft skin. Just sinking his teeth into her would be Heaven. Her breath would hitch in surprise; her nipples would pebble for him. She would instantly stiffen at the sensation of his bite, but the second he drank from her, her body would go limp and utterly relaxed for him.

His cock stiffened at the thought of biting her.

She is already turned on. Now was the perfect moment. *The pinch of my fangs would fill her with ecstasy.*

Unbeknownst to the three other men, Nikolai's mind underwent a raging battle. Shouldn't bite her. *Want to bite her.* Shouldn't. *Thirsty.*

It had been too long. For weeks, he had suppressed his hunger.

No longer.

His vampiric speed allowed him enough time to appear behind Luna, steal her from Bastille, dig his fingers into the locks of her pretty white-blond hair, and pierce his fangs into her neck.

One moment, Luna was vibrating with lustful need and fighting with Bastille. The next, her head was thrown back and a sharp pain erupted in her neck. Searing pain… And then…*Pleasure*.

Hot. Scorching. *Pleasure*.

"*Ahhhhohhhh, yes*," she moaned. She was already so close to the edge of ecstasy.

Strong arms wrapped around her front, forearms caging her chest as her back was yanked against Nikolai's chest. Her limbs were jelly as he held her, feeding from her neck. Warm drops of blood trickled down her throat, but she could not find it in herself to care.

Because nothing had ever felt so good.

Fingers caressed down her arms. Phantom hands trailed up her stomach and cradled her full breasts. She gasped as Nikolai gave a powerful *suck* at her throat. The suction reverberated around her nipples and between her legs—like little tongues teased her there and left her on the edge of orgasm.

Oh, Gods.

One of Nikolai's hands dropped to her lower abdomen.

Yes. Blood flowed out of her, leaving her weaker and weaker, but it was addictive. She floated in ecstasy. *Is this what it feels like to fly?*

She knew of women addicted to vampire bites. Was she about to become one?

Nikolai's fingers stroked down, down, down her trembling stomach until he dragged a finger over her slit.

At her wetness, Nikolai groaned onto her neck, biting her deeper and sucking harder.

Her eyes rolled back. *PLEASURE. Mind-numbing pleasure.*

His fingers settled right over her clit, swirling it, teasing it, stroking it.

Yes, yes, *YES*.

He gulped hcr down as he pinched her sensitive bundle of nerves. He still held her firmly against his chest, mashing her breasts into his forearm. She bucked into his embrace, seeking more. Her ass brushed against his large, hot erection, and both of them gasped.

*B*astille, Sly, and Kobe could not move. None of them knew what to do. How to proceed.

Nikolai fingered Luna's bare pussy in front of them as he drank from her neck. Her wetness glistened right before them. The scent of her arousal and the sight of her so mindless from need made the men…slow to react.

"Fucking stop," Bastille ordered, choking on the words.

The vampire ignored his king's demand. The vampire probably could not even hear the demand over Luna's loud as fuck moans.

"Make him stop," Bastille said weakly to Sly and Kobe as all three of them watched Luna's hips rock against Nikolai's fingers. This had not been part of the plan. He had meant to punish her. Take her to the brink of orgasm and leave her there.

Now, her face scrunched in ecstasy. Her mouth hung open as she gulped for breaths through her endless sounds of pleasure.

All the men seemed capable of hearing was the slick sound of Nikolai's fingers working over her pussy.

"Please," she begged, close to coming again.

This wasn't supposed to happen, Bastille thought as he dug his nails into his palms, fighting the instinct to touch her again. To *help* the vampire bring her to orgasm. And another orgasm. And another. Until she forgot all about Daxton Dragomir.

Kobe dropped to his knees in front of them, gazing at Luna's dripping pussy. "So lush, so *wet*," he groaned. One of Kobe's hands dipped to readjust his massive erection in his sweatpants. His face inched closer to the junction of Luna's creamy legs. Entranced and hypnotized by her wetness, Kobe muttered to himself, "Want a taste of you too, Moonbeam."

No. *Shit*. No. Bastille tried to shake himself. They needed to stop this. Nikolai had already drunk too much. The girl could… She could die.

"NO." Bastille summoned all of his resolve and grabbed Nikolai by the back of the neck, yanking him and his fangs from Luna. He threw Nikolai against the wall, the impact shaking the entire cabin.

Nikolai's red eyes were glazed over. Ingesting blood was a natural high only vampires knew. Typically, he always appeared regretful and angry at himself after feeding, but this time Nikolai's expression was pure, smug pleasure.

"Just a lick, love. Just one," Kobe whispered, still on his knees in front of Luna. Bastille turned to see the werewolf lean in and drag his tongue over her swollen, needy clit.

Fuck. Losing control of the situation.

Luna cried out again, her head falling back.

Bastille glanced at Sly for help, but the fox shifter stood

ram-rod straight, frozen, entranced, and squeezing a hand over the crotch of his pants.

Useless, Bastille raged. *They're all fucking useless.*

They thought they could touch her? Lust after her? She was *his*.

No, she was the dragon's. Bastille did not want her. He would never accept sloppy seconds or half of someone's heart. *All loyalty or none.* He just enjoyed…teasing her. And her sassy comments. And the way her chin rose when she spoke defiantly to him—something no one else would dare to do.

"*Please, pleasepleasepleaseplease*," Luna stuttered again and again.

Bastille's eyes were wide as Kobe continued to eat the fuck out of her pussy.

The werewolf let out an animalistic growl and shook his face between her thighs, using his lips, tongue, nose, and teeth to tease her. Kobe's chin was damp with her as his hand dove inside his sweatpants.

By the looks of it, she held on by a thread.

Kobe's arm jostled, performing jerky movements, as he stroked himself and feasted on her. Luna's fingers tangled in his dark, unruly hair. The werewolf's tongue flattened and swiped over her—a vicious, feverish rhythm.

"Just a little more," she begged. "*Please.*"

It was the "please" that got him. Bastille moved around her, standing at her back once more. He reached around her, his hands shaking for a second before he gripped her perfect tits. *They burn in my palms.* Exquisite handfuls. Kneading her mounds of flesh, his fingers clamped her nipples as he demanded in her ear, "Then be a good little slut and come for us."

She shattered into a million pieces, screaming with her release. Back arching so sharply, her spine might have snapped. Lost in rapture, she seemed to splinter apart.

Kobe groaned, lapping up her orgasm as he jerked his cock harder, faster—coming onto his fingers in a rush.

Nikolai still swayed against the wall where Bastille had thrown him, a dreamy expression haunting his face and an obvious bulge taking up room in his slacks.

Bastille grunted in painful arousal as his cock continued to throb for attention. The point had been to tease her, not leave himself with an insistent erection. *Going to fucking strangle it once I get to my room.*

Even after her mewling moans stopped, her sweet pheromones filled the air, messing with the predators' minds.

"What…What was that?" Sly broke the silence, speaking over the heavy gasps for breath. "It was like I couldn't think through her lust."

"Pheromones," Bastille muttered.

"She is a prey." Nikolai licked his lips of Luna's blood. "Tastes like…lamb."

Luna gasped and threw a protective hand over where she had been bitten. Fear sparkled in her eyes.

I do not want her to fear me. What was Bastille thinking? Fear was the best way to ensure power. Of course, he should wish her to fear him.

But a prey? "Impossible," Bastille mumbled.

"Duttur are extinct," Sly said softly. "Sheep shifters were the first to be hunted. There is no way."

"It's true," Nikolai said, licking his lips of her as well. "A prey."

Kobe stood from his kneeling position and tucked a strand of her pale hair behind her ear. "A pretty prey."

Luna backed away from them. "You—You're wrong."

She backed up, right into Bastille's chest.

He peered down at her, tilting his head. "A prey? Truly?"

"Not just that." Nikolai smirked, knowing more about the girl from tasting her blood. "A prey who is days away from going into *heat*."

CHAPTER 14

The men had locked her away. Like a pet. *I don't think so*, Luna thought to herself.

The first skill she learned on the run from a wolf pack: how to pick locks.

A few wiggles and a *click*. Boom. Freedom.

Luna snuck away from the bedroom the men had locked her in to sleep for the night. *No sleep for me.*

The cabin was pitch black, just like the night sky outside. Through the windows, trees blocked the moonlight, leaving everything...extremely dark. She tiptoed, praying not to run into anything and make a noise.

She needed to get out of there. Now.

Not only did the four predator alpha males know what she was, but the vampire had said she was days away from going into heat. If she went into heat around them...she would have no choice but to throw herself all over them.

How would it be any different from what you let them do to you already? She had let Bastille touch her, the vampire feed from her, the werewolf...devour her.

She pressed a palm to her forehead.

Predators were *killers*. Now that they knew she was a prey, they would kill her.

What if these men are different? She shook herself. *One orgasm and you want to trust them?* Weak. She hated feeling this weak. Predators did this to prey: made it easy to feel you could lean on them, trust them. *Then, they slaughter your family for sport.*

And yet, she let a *wolf-shifter* lick her to orgasm. *Damn it.*

Wolf packs knew each other. There was a chance Kobe knew Rohan. A chance they were friends. Or related. She fought off the wave of nausea.

She had to escape them before she went into heat and became mindless to her hormones, begging for them to touch her and fill her with their cocks—*stop thinking about their penises!*

Predators were not meant to be with prey. A pair like that would always end in death. And Luna had not worked so hard for so many years to survive, just to throw away her life on some alpha shifters.

A muffled male voice rang out through the office door, which Luna slinked past in the dark hallway, unbeknownst to her abductors. "Prey shifters have been hunted for centuries," one of them said. "How could she even be alive? Sheep don't have any abilities. No protective instincts."

"And you're sure she is a lamb shifter?" Another male voice. Bastille.

"Tasted like lamb chops," Nikolai—it had to be the vampire—commented.

Lamb chops? *Asshole.* She paused to listen to their

conversation but knew the longer she listened, the higher her chances of getting caught before she could escape. *Just one more minute, in case they say something relevant.*

"She said someone was after her."

"Maybe a farmer?"

She frowned. A farmer? Was that a joke?

"Farms have been forbidden for years," Bastille said.

Were they talking about a farm for prey shifters?

"Last I heard, there was one, close to the border, working on a serum to, well, to…"

There was a short silence. Luna held her breath.

"What?" Bastille demanded.

"A serum to increase obedience in prey. Basically, it makes them shift or do whatever they are told. Like shifter slaves."

Hair stood up on the back of Luna's neck. Someone—a "farmer"—was collecting prey shifters and injecting them with a brainwashing serum?

So, Rohan will now be co-starring in my nightmares.

A creak came from inside the room. She needed to leave before they discovered her. On her next step, the floorboard beneath her creaked as well. The men's conversation inside the office stopped.

All of them seemed to wait for another noise.

"She's locked in her room," Nikolai said. "It's just the old cabin making noises."

I know how to pick locks, bloodsucker. Luna flipped off the closed office door, her barely visible middle finger raised to the ceiling in the darkness.

A sigh came from someone through the door. Deep and

aggravated. Bastille. "Kidnapped and locked up in one day. She really is helpless, isn't she? A Duttur prey."

Helpless?

She flashed her second middle finger to the door as she moonwalked smoothly across the hardwood floors down the hallway.

They thought she did not know how to do anything for herself just because she was a prey? Bastille had mocked her when Kobe made her dinner, acting as if she wouldn't know how to make a bowl of cereal. Like she was pampered her whole life. *Not even close, buddy!*

A part of her wanted to see Bastille's face when he realized she had broken out of the room and escaped the four alphas. *He thinks I'm just a weak, meek prey who is incapable of taking care of herself.* She wanted to revel in his disbelief and regret when he found out she had been on the run, scrubbing bathrooms and living off noodles, and sleeping only four hours each night on an air mattress in a closet.

Too bad, she would be long gone before any of them noticed.

With aching slowness and special attention to every creaky floorboard, Luna moved to the doorway in the kitchen. *Almost there.* She would leave this place, skip town, and never see the predators again.

Skip town with what money?

She bit her lip and glanced behind her. If she could leave with the basilisk briefcase of cash she had gotten from the dragon, she could disappear. Safety ensured for at least a year of hiding. She could treat herself to more than microwavable ramen each day.

She wanted that money.

Dammit. Just before she escaped through the side door of the cabin, she turned around. The briefcase had to be in Bastille's room. It was clear that he was the leader. He was most likely to have the case.

She tiptoed back, passing the closed office door where the men spoke, and approached the bedrooms toward the back of the cabin. Bastille would have the largest room. Possibly black walls. *He seems like a man with a mirror on his ceiling.* Someone who knew how perfect he looked. Someone who preferred to watch his own face during sex instead of a partner's. *Stop thinking about Bastille's sex life,* she chastised herself. It was just his potent alpha pheromones messing with her mind.

She paused in front of the bedroom door at the very back of the cabin before slipping through the doorway.

Black silk sheets on a king-sized bed.

A bookshelf of only dark-colored, leather-bound books.

A long mirror on the freaking ceiling perfectly reflected the entire bed, proving her assumption true.

The room smelled like him; like sunlight basking over pine trees and earth. Like baked nature. Luna used to roll her eyes at the way women described the perfect man smelling like sandalwood but now she understood. Bastille smelled like sex in the woods. Rough, hot, dangerous... A fantasy.

The basilisk case sat on a dark wood dresser beside the closet.

Yes.

She grabbed it and started for the door, but her heart stopped as she heard heavy footsteps trotting down the hall. Walking toward her.

Damn it. Could she not catch a break?

The footsteps did nothing but grow louder as she glanced around and assessed her situation.

Closet. Hiding spot. *Run.*

By the time Bastille strode into his bedroom, she was hidden in the darkness behind his various coats and shirts. The closet door was still slightly ajar—just open enough for her to peek through and see when he left again.

Please let him leave the room before he catches me.

Please have him only come in to grab something and go.

astille let out a frustrated breath before pacing back and forth, in front of his bed. The king of the motherfucking Dark Ones, the most dangerous of shifters, was attracted—*mated!*—to a Duttur prey? A sheep shifter. When he first beheld her pale as snow hair, he thought of her as a little lamb, but Duttur were thought to be extinct.

Earlier, she had said someone was hunting her. *Bastille* had said he would give her to the hunter.

That was before I cupped her tits and watched her come on my friend's mouth.

Even now, the memory seared his brain. The way Nikolai had fed from her neck and fingered her wet pussy. The sounds she made when Kobe knelt between her legs and attacked her clit with his tongue like it was a popsicle and he was trapped in a desert. Bastille had clutched her luscious breasts in his hands and demanded that she orgasm for them. And, like a good, obedient prey, she did as she was told.

Fucking flawless. It was annoying as hell. She didn't seem to notice how stunning she was. So delicate, yet her eyes screamed war. A fighter's soul stuck inside a princess' body. Unbelievably sexy.

The way she moaned...

The pheromones she had put off...

Fuck, I need to come, Bastille thought as he sank back onto his mattress. His cock had remained hard for her—hours after finding out what she was. It had been hard to think, brainstorm, or plan with the rest of the guys due to his hard-on.

Even now, just the thought of her soft white-blond hair made his breath hitch and his chest tighten. *Want her so fucking much.* He wanted her on her knees for him, submitting to his pleasure. He wanted her gripping the headboard of his bed to support herself through his ruthless fucking.

He wanted her screaming for him, screaming *his* name, and coming all over his cock.

He wanted to kiss her neck before giving her his claiming bite—one that would remain visible to all paranormals, proving that she was his. Forever.

Clearly, he was not about to claim her forever. It was already agitating to want the same woman as Daxton. To share a mate with the man he hated? He was capable of a lot—mostly violence—but he was not capable of that.

Just need to work her out of my system and forget about her, he thought to himself. *It's just been so long since I've felt sexual desire.* He was pent up—that was all. All of his twisted thoughts about the stray sheep shifter would straighten themselves out after he relieved himself of his arousal.

The image of Luna's head thrown back, her mouth open and forming the perfect O as she came on Kobe's tongue, pierced through his mind again.

Shit.

He still remembered pleasuring her pussy and tasting her on his fingers. Utter sweetness.

Bastille stood—only to whip off his shirt and unbuckle his pants.

Going to fuck my fist until I stop thinking about that little lamb.

CHAPTER 15

No way was he about to… He couldn't just…

Luna stared, wide-eyed, shocked, and turned on as she watched Bastille strip from where she hid in his closet. His hands moved in a rushed urgency to unbutton his black shirt and push it off his shoulders.

Abs.

Rock hard, defined abs and muscular pectorals lay beneath various tattoos, most of which looked to be artistic snakes slithering over his smooth skin.

His fingers battled to unbuckle his belt and rip down his pants' zipper. His clothes were shoved away, no barriers left to hide the stunning taut skin.

Luna's breath stalled as she beheld his thickness.

Bastille's enormous erection looked painful. The reddened tip of his cock appeared wrathful as it slapped his hard, muscular stomach, demanding to be touched. Her gaze leisurely ran over the dusky, tantalizing color of his sensitive flesh and the veined lines that angrily pulsed along the length of him.

Bastille raised his right palm to his mouth and a serpentine-like tongue unraveled and laved over the skin of his hand, dampening it. Then, he used that same hand to wrap around his stiff cock.

Oh. Oh no. *I'm not supposed to be watching this.* Luna clenched her eyes shut and bit her lip. Two seconds later, Luna's eyelids fluttered open once more—the temptation too strong to resist.

Though she knew Bastille to be an asshole alpha, there was something about watching him pleasure himself that made her mouth dry and her throat constrict into a slow swallow. The way he had touched her earlier... His filthy words... She had never been so turned on.

And now, this?

Luna was no stranger to watching porn or reading dirty books, but the way Bastille gripped himself was different from what she had seen. He did not simply "pleasure" himself.

His jaw was clenched, like he was pissed off to an ungodly extent. His green eyes were narrowed and spewed hatred and anger as he stared at his hand on his large shaft.

He settled into his spot, sitting on the edge of the bed with his spine tilted back toward the mattress. The position was one of tension—not allowing him to relax or fully lay back. His left hand violently fisted the black silk bedsheet at his side.

At the first downward stroke of his right hand on his stiff cock, Bastille released a pained, guttural grunt. His eyes shut tightly, and his breath grew ragged as he proceeded to...*attack* himself.

The strokes were so fast, so demanding and desperate,

Luna had to hold back a whimper just from watching. His fingers were wrapped firmly around his shaft as he jerked himself. The pace—the frenzy—was so furious, his motions were a near blur. Yet, still, he did not quiver, moan, sink into the mattress, or reveal any emotion on his face other than bitter rage.

As if the action of jacking off his flushed, aching cock made him angry. As if he took no pleasure in it.

"Fucking...lamb," he muttered under his breath, cursing as his hips gave a slight bucking motion. "Goddamn dragon..."

Lamb? Was he thinking of Luna and the dragon shifter?

Bastille was so aroused, each of his palm's strokes emitted a slick sound of flesh meeting pre-cum. As he savagely fucked his hand, his lips parted, but no sound escaped—like he used all of his might to hold back a blissful groan.

Luna's body clenched. Overheated. Flushed.

The room filled with his alpha pheromones from his arousal, choking her from her hidden position in the closet. How was it that, for years, Luna barely had a sex drive to worry about, but ever since she met the dragon and these predators captured her, she was constantly squirming with unadulterated desire for them?

"*Uhgh*," Bastille grunted with each harsh thrust of his hips into his hand. "*Uhgh*." His fingers, fisting the sheet, tightened as he jerked his hand faster. "Fucking—prey."

His body finally fell back onto the bed, his spine meeting the soft mattress. Yet, none of his tension seeped away. He growled as he angrily stroked his throbbing cock.

His free hand fell to caress his heavy balls, and Luna bit her bottom lip even harder.

Her thighs clenched together again as new wetness rushed between them. Her breasts ached for touch. Her clit pulsated with need. *Damn it, I was not supposed to see this.* As much as she tried to deny it, after the men had pleasured her, a part of her almost wanted to stay to see what it might be like—to stop running and live for sexual urges. To stay in one place, with them.

She held her breath as she watched him pump his shaft into his hand. Then, Bastille surprised her.

He looked right up into the mirror above his bed, and his eyes turned to hypnotic spirals.

She fell into trance but was able to blink herself awake since his gaze was not focused on her. He stared into his own eyes as he stroked. For a moment, she rolled her eyes at him, thinking he was admiring himself. But then, he spoke.

"You can feel her. Sinking onto your cock," he told himself. Was he…hypnotizing himself while he mastur-bated? *My Gods.* Others could fantasize, but he could convince his body to *feel* his fantasy.

Such power.

"Feel her tight pussy fucking clutching you. So fucking tight. Fuck." His breathing became ragged as he kept up his fierce jerks, the anger on his face slipping as the pleasure trickled in. "Feel her ride your cock. *See* it."

Bastille groaned, and one of his hands lifted to a spot of air over him. The way his fingers moved… Was he imagining stroking her hair? Suddenly, he grabbed her invisible hair and twisted it over his fist, pulling it back roughly. Luna's own head fell back as if she could feel his fantasy.

"Fuck me," he growled to his fantasy girl. Was it her? "Fuck me, Princess. Like I know you want to." His hips bucked up into a hard thrust—she could practically feel it between her legs. His phantom cockhead so deep inside her, it rubbed a hidden spot of pleasure she had never been able to reach on her own.

Shit. Luna's hand sank between her legs as she watched him lose control. *He is thinking of me.* Her fingers circled her throbbing clit in time with his thrusts and grinds.

His thighs fell open as his stomach hollowed rhythmically from the pleasure. "I want you to come all over my cock, Princess," he rasped to his invisible fantasy. "Will you be a good girl and do that for me?"

Fuck. She fought to swallow down her moan as her fingers sped up between her legs. If she came, would he be able to smell her? Find her in his closet? What would he do if he did? *Punish me again?* Just the thought pushed her closer to coming.

She was so close. She knew it from the insistent pulse on her clit and the continued contracting of her pussy around her fingers.

"Come for me. Fucking squeeze the life out of my cock before I fucking—" He began to roughly thrust into his hand with each word. "—fill—you—up. *Come for me.*"

She could not hold it back. Mouth agape, she cried out in pleasure as she came around her fingers for him.

Instantly, Bastille let go of his hard erection—not having come yet—and looked at his ajar closet door.

He heard me.

And he is still hard.

Something about that detail made him seem all the more dangerous. As if, due to his erection, he might be thinking with only his most savage animal instincts. He slid from the bed and inched toward the closet.

In all his naked glory, he ripped open the closet door, towering over her where she kneeled. In that position, her mouth was even with his engorged, reddened cock, which jutted up against his stomach in painful, pent-up sexual frustration. Her lips pursed on a hissed breath, which blew directly over his glistening cockhead.

Bastille let out a violent growl and grabbed her by her hair. *Not so gentle now.* He pulled her to his bed, tossing her onto it as he stood before it. "What the *fuck* are you doing in here?"

"I—I…" Her orgasm had muddled her brain. She was still rolling through the aftereffects, her pussy still lightly spasming.

"I locked you in Kobe's room, so what the fuck are you doing here?"

Could he tell the pink in her pale cheeks was from a fresh orgasm? "I—I broke through the lock."

Bastille blinked, his eyebrows flying up in surprise. "You *what?*"

Was he going to continue standing there naked and aroused? His broad chest was slick with sweat. The dusky tip of his shaft shone with barely contained pre-cum.

She tried to remember his question. "I picked the lock."

"You know how to pick locks?"

A question she should not answer if she wanted to keep her upper hand, her element of surprise. Bastille thought her to be some spoiled prey, not a girl who lived on the run for years—he would not expect it when she escaped them.

"You were trying to escape," Bastille said, putting together the puzzle even as his cock twitched against his stomach, begging to come. "And you came to my room... For the briefcase? You needed cash. You were going to disappear."

How was this man capable of figuring it out when his dick seemed to throb with each heartbeat? Luna could hardly focus. Her front teeth sank into her bottom lip as her gaze darted down once more to his massive erection. The fat mushroom tip was purple and glistening. *Hypnotic.*

"Tell me, did you like the show you witnessed?" Bastille asked her, but instead of sounding smug, he sounded irritated. Because now she knew he fantasized about her?

"It was nothing," she swore. "I didn't see anything!"

"Ohh, not enough for you? You want to watch some more?" His right hand flattened against his muscular chest and slid down, down, down his light dusting of a happy trail, down to wrap around his shaft. He gave it a firm stroke. "Need to see the grand finale?"

"W-What?" Her mouth was so dry as she watched him give himself another slow stroke up and down his cock.

"I can smell you. Your arousal. Did you come with my name on your lips?" He stroked again, his fingers squeezing the base of him. "You touched your pussy while you watched me jerk off?"

She could not deny it.

He licked his lips and let his green gaze tease her skin. "Take off the shirt," Bastille instructed.

"What?" She wore the large shirt Kobe had given her.

"Why don't you hypnotize yourself to see a woman's naked body? You don't need to see mine."

He growled again—the sound so threatening. *A real predator stands before me.* "I want to see *you.*" He sounded so angry about it. Frustrated with himself. "Take off the shirt."

She fiddled with the hem, which sat mid-thigh. She couldn't tear her gaze from his hard length. His thick shaft strained up, toward her on the bed. Like even that part of him knew she was the cause of his pleasure.

"Take off the shirt before I rip it off you and make you walk around naked for the rest of your time here," Bastille said.

She glared at him but…she wanted to follow his order. Her body ached to watch him lust for her. Second by second ticked by as she calmly removed the shirt, pulling it over her head and holding it beside her. After coming while watching Bastille, her nipples were still perky, hard little peaks for him. Her stomach contracted as cool air brushed over her bare sex.

"Happy now?" she asked him.

The pleased, masculine rumble that came from his chest made hot sparks roll over her revealed skin. Her body squirmed, not satisfied with only one orgasm. *Greedy bitch.*

Bastille loomed over the edge of the bed, near where her feet sat on the end. He grabbed her ankles, shackling them with his fingers, and pulled them far apart. She inhaled sharply at how he spread her legs, opening the view of her slick pussy to him. Another pleased sound came from deep in his chest. Something that sounded like a…rattle.

Weren't basilisks supposed to release a rattle sound before they were about to strike? Luna cursed herself for not paying attention in shifter school when she was a teenager. Little had she known she would be a runaway with so little education and a dire need to know how to handle predator alpha shifters.

"Watch my hand on my dick, Princess." He grasped himself, letting out a little hiss at his firm grip, and slowly stroked from the base to the sensitive, leaky tip. "You liked watching me before."

Yeah, when she was allowed to touch herself in private and not reveal to him how attractive she found him.

Still, her gaze locked onto his hand. He jerked his cock over her, taking his time as if the appendage wasn't red and engorged from not coming earlier. Instead of the angry, fast strokes she had witnessed from him, he now touched himself with a sense of leisure. Patient pleasure instead of anger.

As if touching himself in her presence made the act more enjoyable.

He sucked his bottom lip while he dragged his dominating gaze down her delicate neck, down her chest, to focus on the wetness between her legs. "You have the perfect body, Princess. Do you know that?"

She rolled her eyes, unable to help herself. She had been on the run for years. She was too thin. Very little curves—hardly any, if she was honest with herself. It was the life she had to live—not enough money for three meals a day.

"You don't believe me?" he asked, still slowly stroking his cock in her direction, right between her legs, at the end of the bed.

"Is there a point you're trying to make?" she asked, her voice defensive.

"There's only one *point* here." Bastille smirked at his erection. The basilisk was capable of jokes? "And it seems to be pointed right at you."

She swallowed again, trying and failing not to look at him as he pleasured himself.

His palm performed a twisting motion on the tip of his shaft, and his stomach muscles twitched at whatever sensation it caused.

A low grunt fell from his mouth. "Touch yourself for me," he said as he pumped.

She exhaled and gasped at the same time, resulting in a "*puh*" sound.

"You clearly liked watching me jerk off. You came. Why not again?" He waited before adding, "Touch yourself. Pet that pretty pussy for me, and you will be rewarded."

CHAPTER 16

"*Touch yourself. Pet that pretty pussy for me.*"

A squeaking noise came from her as her body shuddered on the bed. His dirty words snaked through the air and invisibly caressed right between her legs.

He moved closer to her, allowing his legs to brush against the end of the mattress. His hand moved over his cock in even, jerking motions. "I want to watch you tease your little clit."

She took in a deep breath, trying not to obey even as her hand sunk toward the junction of her thighs. She felt dizzy, though she laid down. Something about the powerful basilisk shifter unnerved her and unleashed something in her she had never experienced. Something dark, raw, ancient, twisted…and so damn sensual.

Her hand jerked closer to her aching core again.

"That's it," he cooed. "Touch yourself for me. Show me how you get yourself off."

She blamed her prey instincts for her helplessness in obeying him.

She barely held in a moan as her fingers slowly moved to her throbbing wetness. Even fresh off an orgasm, her body wanted more. Her sex drive lit up within seconds, her pussy begging for his thick cock. Hot pulses and tingles overrode her brain. Her eyelids drifted to half-mast as she skimmed her fingers over herself.

"That's it," he purred his approval. "Good girl."

"*Mmmm.*"

"Fuck, I love the sounds you make," Bastille cursed, stroking himself faster as he watched her fingers move more fervently between her legs. "Rub it good, baby. Tease it. Tell me how good it feels."

"Bastille," she cried out as her fingers spun around her pulsing bundle of nerves at the top of her slit. Her pussy convulsed before a new rush of wetness slickened her between her legs. Gods, she was just so *wet*. He made her this way. Inexplicably. Undeniably.

Her back arched as she inserted a finger while continuing to manipulate her clit the way her body wept for her to do. Bastille's jaw ticked at her passionate gasp, the muscles in his neck straining as if he struggled to control himself.

"Is your pussy nice and wet for me, lamb?" His voice rolled out so low, it rivaled gravity for what it was capable of pulling down with it. His green eyes were ablaze with lust as his hand blurred on his cock, gliding in fits of frantic speed. "I can hear the slick sounds of your fingers moving on it. Fuck, that's so sexy."

"*Bas...*" She whimpered as she felt his free hand clamp

around her left ankle. His touch just made her body tremble for more. More of his dirty words and commands. More touch. More pleasure. *More.*

"So smooth," he whispered to himself as his thumb stroked her ankle. "Fuck, what are you doing to me?"

He released her but threw himself onto the bed, over her, crawling up to meet her gaze. He held himself up, above her, his forearm tense. Mere inches separated their naked bodies.

Tremors rolled over Bastille's stomach as he gripped himself tightly and tugged. "What the fuck are you doing to me?"

"W-What?" she asked breathlessly.

"The dragon's mate. A prey." He shook his head. "Can't stop thinking about you coming for me. Again and again."

Her back curved off the mattress. Her hips bucked and caused her soaked pussy to grind against where he squeezed his arousal. *Sweet, bare contact.*

"*Fuck*," Bastille gritted out between sharp, white teeth. His hand fell from himself and suddenly his weight was on her, his cock aligned to her damp slit. He ground his hips down on her, pressing his shaft over her aching clit. Back and forth. Back and, *oh*, forth.

"Please," she begged, unsure what she begged for.

He held himself with one arm, his free hand moving to fold around her throat like a collar. "Why can't I stop thinking about you? Want to fucking consume you."

Her head turned mindlessly from side to side on the pillow as he continued to surge forward, urging her to rock against his erection.

Her thighs trembled as her body went pliant and obedient for him. "Please, please."

Abruptly, an agonized roar shook the cabin.

CHAPTER 17

*T*he roar pierced her eardrums, echoing around and bouncing off all the hardwood in the cabin.

Bastille and Luna froze on the bed, their wide eyes meeting. Hand still around her throat, Bastille turned his head to glance at the door. Two seconds later, the door slammed open as Kobe bellowed, *"She is gone!"*

Silence. Silence as Kobe saw Bastille and Luna's naked bodies on the bed.

"Moonbeam?" Kobe asked softly, the tension in those broad shoulders easing.

Bastille and Luna were still frozen. His hand still around her throat.

"You found her?" another voice trailed into the room just as Sly poked his head inside. The fox shifter grinned from ear to ear at what he saw. "Oh, snap. Orgy time?"

"Get the fuck out," Bastille ordered harshly from the bed.

Casually, Sly leaned back against the doorway and crossed his arms over his chest. He nodded at Luna. "Does this mean we're keeping her?" he asked. "Keeping the dragon's mate would be an act of war."

Bastille's breaths grew heavier as his jaw clenched.

"Plus, you know the prophecy," Sly said with a pointed look.

"Prophecy?" Luna asked.

But Bastille's expression was a prison meant for only the most evil of villains—meaning his every emotion went on lockdown.

Letting go of her throat, he pushed himself off her, leaving her shivering and exposed on the bed. "Of course we're not keeping her," Bastille loudly remarked. "I was simply…sampling. The dragon deserves my sloppy seconds for once."

Sloppy seconds? She felt something crack in her chest and grow cold.

"She's a meek, weak prey," Bastille insulted her, his back to her while he spoke to his friends. "She doesn't belong with us."

Meek. Weak.

I nearly let a predator have sex with me. Use *me*. Again. Had she learned nothing after Rohan? Betrayal, a broken heart, a lost family, and life on the run had not been enough to drive the lesson home?

Trust no one. Ever. *Not with your heart or body*. Especially a predator.

In that moment, she might as well have been a reptilian shifter because her blood went cold in her veins. Rage set up a home in her heart, decorating it with angry red. Frantically throwing on the shirt Kobe had given her to sleep in, she rose from the bed. Her bare feet slapped against the floor as she trudged to the door where Kobe and Sly stared at her.

Shoving her middle finger out toward the basilisk, she sneered, "Screw you, Bastille! Like I'd ever want to belong to you or be kept by you."

He smirked and turned from her. "You wanted me just fine a few minutes ago."

She replied, "Don't flatter yourself. I'm a prey surrounded by predators, and my *protective* instincts are pushing me toward my heat as a *defense* mechanism. I was horny, and—if I can't have the dragon—I figured you were a mediocre stand-in."

Bastille's spine stiffened, obvious from how he stood shirtless with his back still to her. He ever so slowly spun to look at her. Wrath rolled from him in waves, invisibly slapping her skin and making it sting.

His fangs began to become noticeable when he opened his mouth to speak. "What *the fuck* did you just say?" he growled. His eyes narrowed to serpentine-like slits.

"Shit," Sly muttered. It was the first time Luna had heard the comedic fox shifter with actual concern in his voice.

"Let me summarize in less words for your *itty bitty* snake brain to understand," she remarked haughtily.

"Oh, *shit*," Sly repeated.

"The dragon was *better*," she said simply. "And his dick? Bigger."

"You FUCKING—" Bastille shot forward but Sly caught him, tackling him to the wall before he could get to Luna.

Kobe quickly grabbed her by the waist and began

127

pulling her from the room. "That's enough, Moonbeam. Bedtime now."

"I will fucking *filet* you!" Bastille hissed as Kobe yanked her away.

Nikolai appeared just outside in the hallway, his red eyes wide. "What's going on?"

There was a loud crashing noise, and Bastille emerged in the hall. Clearly, Sly had not been strong enough to hold him back. The basilisk glared at where Kobe's hands secured Luna by the hips.

Bastille strode forward as he threatened, "Maybe I should send the dragon one of your pretty fingers in a box."

"Try it," she growled back. Her fierce anger and hurt pride did not allow her to realize the repercussions—the danger—of threatening a creature like him. She just kept thinking about that feeling of being thrown away. Used. Destroyed by Rohan. *Predators are monsters.*

"Maybe sending a finger is too small of a gesture," Bastille said. "What about a whole hand? That way he could at least jack off with it—romantic, don't you think?"

"Fuck you!"

His dark brows rose, and he smirked. "You were begging me to fuck you minutes ago." His hand fell to grip his bare cock. "I bet you're still wet for me."

"Come near me, and I'll chop your dick off," she threatened him—one of the most dangerous creatures in existence. Her "flight" instinct had taken a backseat in this fight.

Bastille gazed at Kobe, Sly, and Nikolai, making eye contact with each as he yelled, "No one touches her!"

Sly put his hands up in the surrender pose. Yet, Kobe did not remove his hands from her sides.

"If she wants the dragon, then she only gets the dragon," Bastille added, scowling at her. "We don't touch her no matter how much she begs."

She glared back, opening her mouth to state that she would never beg, but he continued.

"And you will beg." Bastille's voice dripped with contempt. "Because just like you said, you're a prey. We're predators. Sooner or later, our pheromones will trigger your heat. You think you'll be asking for the dragon then? No. You'll be mindless to get fucked by the nearest cock, and I will enjoy watching you rolling around in need —unsatisfied."

Sly scoffed, stealing Bastille's attention.

Bastille belted at him, *"What?"*

"Bastille," Sly said. "We... If she goes into heat, there's no way we'd be able to resist it. Her pheromones would—"

"Shut the fuck up, Sly."

He shut his mouth.

"Wow, what woman could resist your charms?" Luna mocked. "You really are so nice to your friends."

His hands balled into white-knuckled fists at his sides. Bastille tipped his head back and roared with boiling anger. He breathed heavily, exhaling his rage before stating evenly, "She picked the locks on your door to escape, Kobe."

Sly, Nikolai, and Kobe blinked in surprise before glancing at her.

"From now on, someone always remains with her. So she can't escape."

Well, shit, she thought to herself. But she would find a way to slip out. She had to.

"Kobe, she'll sleep in your room. No touching."

Kobe's expression was one of pure heartbreak. He wanted to touch her that bad? *Maybe I can use that to my advantage*, she thought. After all, why was the werewolf loyal to such an asshole basilisk?

"And if any of you dare to touch her, dare to make her come, I'll fucking know it." Bastille stared through her. "I know what sounds she makes."

As Luna was escorted back to Kobe's room for her lockdown, she heard Sly comment under his breath to Bastille, *"Just a meek, little prey, huh?"*

CHAPTER 18

*L*una did not see herself as impulsive, but if any emotion led to her making thoughtless, dangerous choices, it was anger. Hatred. And she *hated* Bastille. His words of *"sloppy seconds"* kept echoing in her mind, zig-zagging back and forth in her skull, as she laid on Kobe's bed, eyes closed in the darkness.

The werewolf slept on the floor per Bastille's orders of "no touching." It made her want to slink down and join him, seduce him, and touch him all over—until Bastille heard her come around the werewolf's cock. *What kind of thought is that?* Dangerous!

As much as she feared werewolves due to Rohan, she had to admit Kobe was utterly gentle with her. He had given her a small tour of his room, shown her which blankets were the softest, and offered her hot tea and hot milk to help her sleep. Though Bastille had given an order, Kobe looked at her like he wanted nothing else but to touch her.

When she had glanced down...his erection bulged the front of his gray sweatpants.

She let out a deep sigh and turned in the bed. It really was a massive mattress—though Kobe was a wide, broad-shouldered man, so she supposed maybe there was *not* room for both of them without touching.

At the sound of her shifting, Kobe whispered from the floor. "Moonbeam? Are you alright?"

She cleared her throat. The pet name he gave her filled her with…*not* anger. Not fear. Instead, it was something warm and bubbly. *Dangerous*, she repeated to herself.

"I'm fine," she told him. "Just wired."

Silence blanketed the dark room once more. She opened her eyes, staring into the pitch black.

"Do you fear him, Moonbeam?" Kobe asked softly.

"Fear Bastille?"

"I would never let him hurt you," he promised.

But could he stop him even if he wanted to? Basilisks could kill just from eye contact.

"Will protect you with my life," Kobe said.

She sucked in a breath. "Why?" Leaning up on an elbow, she peered over the edge of the mattress, but she was unable to see him in the dark room.

"You are my mate."

Oh Gods, another predator male who thought she was his mate? What the heck was going on?

"Are you sure?" she asked, doubtful. It was rare for a predator to be mated to a prey. And for a prey to be mated to *multiple* predators? Unheard of.

"When I first saw you, my wolf growled, '*Mine.*' My heart seemed to grow in my chest, to make room for you. With my every breath, I will protect and provide for you."

His words softened Luna. *For so long, I have wanted to*

hear something like that. Wanted to be protected, instead of always having to protect myself. "What are we going to do about Bastille?" she asked. "We'll need to run away to be together."

She hated using the werewolf's feelings for her own purposes, but Bastille had threatened her. She needed to get out immediately, and if she could find an ally in Kobe on the basis that she would stick around with him after she escaped, so be it. Even if it might be a lie.

"We cannot run from him," Kobe whispered, his low voice so gravelly and rich, it made her squirm on the bedsheets. "He will get used to you, Moonbeam. He will not always be so mean."

She was just supposed to "*wait it out*" for Bastille to be less cruel? *No thanks.* She raised an eyebrow at that. "Um, are we talking about the same hyper-raging, murderous lunatic? There's no way I can be around him. He'll kill me."

"He will not hurt you. He will threaten but never hurt you," Kobe said.

Had he not heard the *I'll-cut-your-hand-off* threats? "You're a lot more confident about that than me."

"You are his mate," Kobe shared. "He will not hurt you. Shifters are incapable of harming their mates"

Luna froze on the bed, flat on her back. "What? I'm the dragon's mate."

"The prophecy says, 'the king of light and the king of dark shall share a mate,'" he grunted. "Bastille is king of the Dark Ones. If you are the dragon's mate, then you are also Bastille's."

King of the Dark Ones? No… *No.*

Bastille was king of the Dark Ones? The leader of the

dark shifters: werewolves, basilisks, vampires, every big bad go-bump-in-the-night monster ruled by the moon? He was *that* infamous basilisk shifter? Kobe, Nikolai, and Sly were his retinue? Shit, now she really needed to escape. How had they not murdered her already?

"Your heartbeat races," Kobe said. "Do you need hot tea?"

"N-No."

She was Bastille's mate? Had anyone informed Bastille of that yet? Because the only warmth she got from him was lust. The rest was all cold front—like a harsh winter. If insults were snowflakes, he blew a blizzard at her.

"Sleep, Moonbeam."

"The king of the Dark Ones will never accept a prey shifter as a mate. People would revolt." Then again, the king of the Light Ones would never accept one either. Predators ruled the paranormal world. There was a reason why prey were near extinction. "Kobe, the only way I live through this is if you get me out of here."

"You will live through anything because I will always be there to protect you. You will never know fear again. Now, sleep, Moonbeam," he repeated. "Dream of me as I will dream of you."

There was no way she would sleep tonight.

She needed to form a new plan.

☾

"*M*oonbeam," a masculine moan broke through her sex dream. "Please. Do not tease me," he rasped, sounding tortured.

She blinked open her eyes, her sight adjusting to the dark of the morning. Her hips rolled, rocking her aching core against something firm and hard. Like warm steel. *Mmmm.* Her eyelids drifted shut once more.

"Moonbeam," the deep, sexy male voice repeated.

"*Mmmm.*"

"Moonbeam, please." The masculine pleading tore her from her dream-like state, fully waking her.

First, she became aware of the firm muscular pecs her palms warmed. Then, she noticed the thick thigh she ground her pussy against like a cat in heat. Finally, the hot bulging erection pressing against her stomach as she laid on Kobe.

Her mouth fell open. Had she rolled completely off the bed and onto him on the floor?

"Awake now?" he grunted. His erection throbbed against her like it wanted to ask the same question.

She had shifted in her sleep, moving the hem of the large sleep-shirt up her belly, so that her bare stomach and pussy touched the werewolf. "I…"

"My mate sought me in her sleep," Kobe said softly, in awe, almost sounding proud of himself. As if her cuddling him in the night was a gold medal. It was…adorable. This predator was friends with the king of the Dark Ones, yet he was adorable?

"And her body wakes, hungry for me." She could *hear* his grin. "I am a very happy wolf."

"What about your king's order not to touch me?"

"*You* are touching *me*, little mate," he pointed out, silently chuckling. His chest moved up and down below her, jostling her so that her pulsing clit rubbed over his hard, thick thigh again.

"Is that a loophole?" she asked, trying not to pant out each breath as her folds grazed against that hard thigh of his. "I can touch you, but you can't touch me?"

"I could touch you," Kobe whispered into her ear, trailing his lips over her earlobe and neck. *Shiver*. "But Bastille would be angry."

"When is he *not* angry?" She rolled her eyes before sighing heavily. "So, you won't touch me then?"

Kobe blew a hot breath over her neck. "Moonbeam, I would die to touch you. The only one who tells me not to touch you is you."

She blinked. "You would disobey him?"

"I have waited a long, long time for you," he said. "You are everything. A light. My reason to live."

She pushed up on his chest, gazing down at him in disbelief. "You hardly know me."

"A mate is part of another—chosen, fated, and developed by life apart. I feel I know you as I know myself. We were made for each other. My mate would know loneliness. Maybe know what it means to feel abandoned." As he spoke, he lifted a large hand and played with a few strands of her pearlescent hair. "Or feel doomed by what she is, the way I have felt doomed. As my mate, you are sure to understand this, yes? You feel the same?"

Lonely, abandoned, and misjudged for what she was? *Yeah*. She felt the same. Her chest tightened with emotion. "What happened to you?" she asked.

"My family—my pack—did not find me worthy. When I was...young, they left me behind in the woods. Told me I was to wait for them to come back and to guard our hunting grounds until they did."

"They never came back?"

"Alone in the woods, it took my eleventh birthday for me to realize they never would."

Luna's heart wrenched itself in her chest. She felt his pain as if it was her own—some mate mumbo jumbo? He lost his family just like her, but not from any mistake he made to trust someone. Not like she had.

"How could they leave you? Or not find you worthy? You're a born alpha." She could scent the rare, dominant pheromones. "You're huge and, uh, muscle-y—" His chuckle shook her again. "I mean, you're strong, so few would challenge you as an alpha. And you are friends with the dark king."

"I was not big and 'muscle-y' then. I did not know the king. Bastille did not choose us for our connections or strength," Kobe replied cryptically.

"Then, why? Why the three of you?" They did not act like bodyguards or advisors. "Nikolai is not even a shifter."

Kobe shrugged, seeming more interested in playing with pieces of her white-blond hair than answering questions. "He collects outcasts," he said.

Outcasts? What was the story behind Sly and Nikolai? And why would Bastille find outcasts? That almost made him sound nice. Redeemable. Thankfully, she knew better.

"My mate smells of pure sweetness," Kobe groaned quietly in her ear as he rubbed his nose down her neck.

His erection throbbed, twitching against her stomach as she laid on top of him. The heat of him seared through his pants, pleasantly burning her skin.

"I think you need a, um, a cold shower. Or, uh, a hot one," she mumbled, blushing. Who wouldn't blush at the mere size of him? *My goodness.* She wouldn't be able to walk for a week. *No sex with Kobe. It would delay my escape plan.*

"A wolf stays hard around his mate. I could empty myself of cum, and the next second I saw you, I would be hard again," he purred into her ear, still dragging his big lips up and down the tender skin of her neck.

"That sounds painful," she commented. "And inconvenient."

"It is said that the first few years of matehood are spent pleasuring each other."

She gulped, unable to hide the way her hips rocked down, grinding herself against his hard thigh at his words.

"I do not know if years will be enough," he rasped. "Centuries of you would not be enough. Want to suckle your nipples while I rut into you."

"Kobe…"

"Sly says I can be intense. Did I say too much again?"

"I—I liked it," she said.

"Little mate, I like you very much. You have no need to feel lonely anymore. Our pain is in the past—used to shape us for each other. I would wander the woods by myself for years to be worthy of you."

Damn it. *Stay strong, Luna!* He was a predator wolf.

Kobe touched her hips and gently lifted her from his body. "Hungry? I will make you breakfast."

"No meat, remember," she called to him as he strode to the bedroom door.

He turned to grin at her, his face lit by the soft morning

light glowing behind the window curtains. "I remember. My mate is an herbivore." His wolfish smile and white teeth should have concerned her. Instead, her heartbeat sped up in her chest. "An herbivore who moans over grilled cheese."

She threw his pillow at him.

CHAPTER 19

"If she doesn't come out of her room in the next thirty minutes, I'm walking in there and fucking pulling her out," Bastille growled impatiently as he sat forward on his black wingback chair, fingering a few of the circular brass nails in it.

"Pull her by her hair?" Sly asked. "You always were the kinkiest of us."

"Kobe, you said she was awake hours ago." Bastille turned to the werewolf who guarded a plate of cold pancakes on his lap. Kobe had made them for *her*—not offering to cook for the rest of them. Not offering any pancakes to his *king*.

She sows discord between my men, Bastille thought bitterly to himself. *And I want a fucking pancake.*

"She was tired," Kobe replied. "Did not sleep much. She might have fallen back asleep."

"Didn't sleep much?" Bastille questioned. "You didn't touch her, did you?" Murder flared in his eyes.

"Gods, what the fuck is going on?" Sly threw his arms

up in frustration as he spoke to his king. "Dude, she's your *mate*. Your one and *only* mate. Why are you acting like this? Yelling at her, threatening to cut off her fingers. Don't you want to *win* her from the dragon? If so, you're messing it all up."

Bastille glared at him.

"You don't need to instruct us not to touch her. You need to give her a reason to stay. I'm not surprised she tried to escape last night."

"She will *not* escape."

Nikolai stepped forward to ask, "If you do not want her for yourself, why are we keeping her? If she goes into heat—"

"I don't want to hear it," Bastille said.

He had no idea what he would do once she went into heat. He talked a big game—saying he wouldn't let any of them touch her, saying he would watch her go unsatisfied. But he knew the stories about a prey shifter's heat. A prey's heat had once ended a war because the two sides had to stop and have an orgy until it was over. The scent and pheromones she would put off would be irresistible. The frantic lust that would ensue…

"If you're trying to win her *Beauty and the Beast* style, you need to start dressing her in ballgowns and finding her a library pronto," Sly commented. "She probably hates you right now."

She probably hates you right now. Finally, an emotion Bastille was familiar with. He was not about to try to win her from the dragon. What an insolent notion. To fall for his mate and know the pleasure of being with her, only for her to choose Daxton in the end… No.

Daxton would give her expensive clothes and jewelry and pamper her with bubble baths in luxury hotels all over the world. The light shifters were rich in money. The dark shifters were rich in fear.

I do not need to wonder which of us she will choose. I already know.

And he hated her for it.

"Ten more minutes," Bastille said through his teeth. "Then I go in there and drag her out."

"Miss her that much already? Awww," Sly mocked.

Nikolai's phone dinged, and the men glanced at him as he read the screen. "The dragon has sent a search team nearby for her."

Bastille clutched the arm of his chair so hard, it made a cracking sound. "They won't find her."

"They know we have a cabin in the woods."

"They don't know we have her," Bastille said. "Yet."

"There might have been a witness at the hotel," Sly said. "We did kind of kidnap her right off the street. Someone could point to our car and find us."

"What happens if they come knocking at our door, Bastille?" Nikolai asked. "Are we giving her to them or what?"

Bastille cracked his knuckles, staring his friend down. "I will die before I let him have an ounce of happiness that his mate would bring him."

"Still doesn't clear up what the plan is for her," Sly said.

Soft noise came from down the long hallway, and the men each sat up straighter in their seats in the living room, preparing to see her. Bastille ran a hand down his black shirt, smoothing out the wrinkles, and Sly smirked at him, noticing.

"Moonbeam." Kobe shot up to stand as she walked into the room. "I made you lemon blueberry pancakes. They are cold, but I will heat them." He strode back toward the small kitchen.

Bastille's lips pursed, and his eyes widened at the way Luna *smiled* at Kobe. Had he truly ever seen her smile? It lit up her entire face, stunning the basilisk from where he sat —as if she was the one with the power to petrify.

"Thanks, I'm hungry," she commented and sank onto the couch where Kobe had been sitting. Defensive, she crossed her arms over her chest as she glanced around at the other three men. "What's the plan for today?"

"You slept away half of it," Bastille grated.

She shrugged. "I was tired."

"Does the dragon know he has a lazy mate?"

She scowled, pointing an angry finger at him. "I am *not* lazy. You have no idea how hard I've worked—" she cut herself off, letting Bastille reel in the fact that he craved her to finish the sentence and share any morsel of information about herself. Not to use against her, but because he was curious.

Nikolai's phone dinged. He checked it as Bastille and Luna glared at each other, neither breaking eye contact. The vampire's phone dinged again. And again. And again.

Ding.

Cursing, Bastille broke the staring contest he had with Luna to look over at Nikolai. "What's going on over there?"

"The dragon's men are getting closer. Within fifteen miles."

Bastille cursed again.

"Should we head out and do a little slaughtering? I'm thirsty," Nikolai said.

Luna gasped and gaped at him.

"Unless you're offering?" the vampire smiled at her, tilting his head. "I love the taste of lamb chops in the morning."

"Rude."

"It was a compliment."

"A gross one."

Nikolai—a constantly stern, expressionless vampire— smiled. A half smile, but still a smile. *At her.*

Bastille stood, maneuvering between them to block her. Bastille positioned his back to her, as if he was able to ignore her completely. Speaking to Nikolai, Bastille said, "You, me, and Kobe." The dark king chose his team. "Let's send them in the opposite direction."

"I get to stay with the little lamb?" Sly smirked. "Best Tuesday ever."

"We could all go," she said, stretching out her arms and legs. Did she think of it as some kind of field trip? "I'd like to get out of the house."

"And try to escape and be reunited with the dragon? I don't think so," Bastille shot back. "Sly stays to ensure you don't make a run for it. He's a predator, so he's naturally faster than you."

She pretended to write a note on her hand with an invisible pen. "*Break his legs before making a run for it.* Got it. Thanks."

Instead of taking offense to the threat, Sly tipped his

head back and laughed, grinning at her again like she was the most entertaining thing he had ever seen.

Not finding her comment funny, Bastille growled under his breath, "Don't be idiotic and try something while we're gone."

She leaned back and smiled, looking so sure of herself, so full of pride. Almost…queenly. "Your majesty, when you all leave, you're taking all the idiotic in this cabin with you."

Majesty? *She knows I'm the king?* Bastille glared at Kobe as the werewolf re-entered the living room with piping hot pancakes.

*B*efore Bastille, Kobe, and Nikolai left to go on some mission in the woods, Bastille gripped Sly by the throat and said, "If you dare to touch her while I am gone, I will help her break your legs."

So, of course, Luna wanted to get Sly to touch her. It wasn't even the horniness—though that was getting quite strong after being teased last night by Bastille and this morning by Kobe's big, strong thigh.

She just wanted to unravel Bastille's self-control.

She wanted to make him so enraged, his head literally exploded.

How mad would he be if he came back to her seducing Sly?

Pretty Gods dang mad.

CHAPTER 20

She lounged back on the couch as Sly returned from making them both cups of tea in the kitchen. He set hers down on the coffee table and chose the seat across from her—in the fancy chair where she had only ever seen Bastille sit.

"Is that not Bastille's chair?" she asked, picking up her hot mug and holding it to her chest.

"While the parents are away, the fox shifter will play," Sly remarked with a sly smile, leaning back in the regal chair.

A predator willing to disobey his king? Perfect. *My escape plan gains hope!* "I feel like of any of them, you're the one more willing to break the rules he sets," she observed aloud.

"I believe you mispronounced 'brave' in that sentence. Not 'willing.' Brave."

"Why did he choose to leave you here with me?" she asked nonchalantly as she sipped her tea. She cursed, losing her calm façade as she burned her tongue on the hot liquid.

"Careful with that mouth," Sly said. "It's one of my favorite parts of you. Though, there are many."

A blush warmed her cheeks as she rolled her eyes.

Sly was rakishly handsome. His dark reddish-golden hair curled in long wisps to frame his face, where sharp cheekbones shared the stage with dimples and lips adorning a slight resting pucker. His narrow eyes and the mischief that shone in them made it look like he always knew someone's secret. And it was a dirty one.

"I burned my tongue," she explained her curse.

"Do you want me to kiss it better? Maybe sucking it into my un-burned mouth would help?"

She swallowed down her rising lust and crossed her legs, shifting on the cushion.

His smirk deepened.

She repeated her earlier question, "Why did he choose for you to stay with me?"

"A basilisk, werewolf, and vampire should suffice," Sly said. "Fox shifters aren't really known for their fighting skills."

Luna did not know much about fox shifters, other than that they could sense lies—maybe because they were so good at telling them. "What are fox shifters known for?"

"Stamina." He winked.

A surprised chuckle came from her as she shook her head, smiling softly at him.

His good-natured grin dropped from his face, leaving his expression more serious than she had ever seen on him. "That is a dangerous laugh you have," he said softly.

"What makes it dangerous?"

"It sounds like...eternal happiness. Like church bells and childhood. Redemption and love."

She blinked, not at all expecting words like that from the playful jokester.

He leaned over his knees, so his face was closer to hers from over the coffee table. "It's dangerous because of the thoughts it makes a man think."

Entranced by the beauty of his face, she mumbled, "What kind of thoughts?"

"Thoughts like murdering anyone for taking the smile off your face," he replied evenly.

She swallowed again. *Okay*. She needed to remember this cheerful comic relief was still a predator unafraid of murder. Now, how to use him to escape...

"What if the others need you and you're here?" she asked.

"There's this thing called a cellphone, where all someone has to do is call—"

She *hmph*ed and focused back on her hot tea. The rising steam stroked her cheeks as she breathed in the fruit-scented herbs.

"I can't wait to see how you try to escape while they're gone," Sly said through a naughty grin.

"I—I wasn't going to try to escape again," she replied. *Damn it*. Was she that easy to read?

"A lie," the fox shifter pointed out.

She tsked and re-crossed her legs again. "You know, it's rude to use your predator powers in front of a prey."

His lopsided grin widened. "Oh, I do so apologize."

"You're forgiven."

"So quickly?"

"I'm a very good-natured and trusting person."

His chest rumbled with laughter. "Another lie." He blew over his tea, momentarily stunning her with the lush curve of his pursed lips. "I think you want something from me."

"What?"

"An ally," he guessed. "Help escaping. Maybe my super sexy body."

She snorted.

"Bastille said none of us can touch you," he reminded her. "So, you should stop biting your lip as you look at me and clenching those thighs together to put subtle pressure on your aching clit."

Shit. She shivered from a new wave of arousal crashing over her.

His blue eyes burned like little flames as he commented, "I am a great reader of people."

"You ever try reading books instead?"

"You fascinate me," Sly said, tilting his head and leaning closer as he perused her. "Prey are known for being the weaker species, being driven to submit to and fear predators."

She sipped her tea, not caring now if it burned her tongue. She had a feeling injuring her tongue might be smart around such a wise fox. *Give him no answers.*

"But I watched as you cursed at the king of the Dark Ones. A little lamb against a fucking basilisk." Sly whistled, impressed. "I want to know why you're different from what we were raised to believe about prey."

"I'm not special or different in any way. I am terrified of predators," she half lied, half told the truth. "If I were wearing boots, I would be shaking in them at your mere presence."

She *was* scared of predators—because of what Rohan had taken from her. But, she had nothing left to lose anymore, other than her life. So, with fear came hatred and distrust. A desire to fight back against them, in the name of her slaughtered family. In the name of all mistreated and abused prey shifters. Yet, her self-preservation reminded her that a prey did not have the power or strength to take on a single predator, let alone the pack Rohan ran with. Currently, her only option was to keep running.

"Hmm," Sly made a noise. "Bastille said you once implied you were being hunted by someone."

Shit. Had she said something while under hypnosis?

"I can only assume it's a predator since you're a prey. The question is: why? Who?"

Shit. Shit.

"Bastille wanted to find them and give you to them."

Horror squeezed her lungs, suffocating her. Give her to Rohan? *Need to escape. NOW.*

"Tell me who is after you, Luna," Sly said.

She did the only thing she could think to do, to distract him.

She stood, grabbed the hem of Kobe's large shirt, and yanked it off her, leaving her bare, naked body on display for the fox.

Sly's dark red eyebrows lifted slowly on his face, those tempting lips curling into another smirk as his gaze trailed down her creamy skin. "Little lamb..." He purred a deep, guttural sound of approval. "I was hoping you would do that."

S he was tied to Bastille's chair. *How the heck did I allow this to happen?*

But Sly had moved too fast. One second, he sat in front of her. The next, he disappeared somewhere in the cabin and reappeared with rope. She had tried to run, but the predator was too darn fast. He moved in a blur. He had her secured to the grand vinyl chair before she could so much as blink.

"Damn it," she yelled, trying to rip her arms free of the rope.

He had her thoroughly bound. Ropes secured her wrists to the arms of the chair. There was a line of rope at her neck and shoulders, her bare stomach, and at each of her ankles, splaying her legs open.

"Let me go!"

"So you can try to use your feminine wiles against me? I'm only so strong," Sly replied.

"Tying me down, naked, is supposed to strengthen your resolve against me?" she huffed. "Just seems kinky."

He grinned. "Bastille has hypnosis, but I think I can get answers out of you in my own way."

She scoffed. "Good luck."

"You don't think I could get you to give me answers?"

"Not unless the answer is spelled f-u-c-k-y-o-u," she replied, glaring at him.

Sly turned and strode down the hallway, toward the bedrooms.

"Where are you going?" she called out after him. "You're just going to leave me like this?"

"Got to get my interrogation toys," he yelled back.

Toys? As in torture devices?

Shit. Shitshitshitshit.

She yanked on the ropes, wiggling and squirming to free herself, but nothing worked. The fox clearly had experience in tying people up. He was really going to *torture* her for answers? She had severely misjudged the jokester predator. Dangerous; diabolical; no remorse. She should have known.

Damn it, why did she have to keep getting reminded, in the worst ways, that all predators were monsters?

She was still fighting to free herself when Sly returned to the living room, holding a toolbox.

"Please, don't do this," she pleaded, hating that she begged a predator for anything. "My answers aren't even interesting. They have nothing to do with you or your king. I—I don't even know anything about the dragon!"

Sly calmly lowered the dark red toolbox to the coffee table.

"If you torture me, Kobe will be pissed. He thinks I'm his mate."

That caused Sly to quirk an eyebrow.

"A-And I'm your king's mate. Do you think he wants me to be tortured?"

"I thought we already established this," Sly said, petting a hand over his ominous toolbox. "I'm brave enough to disobey my king once in a while."

CHAPTER 21

"They're heading in the opposite direction. Our work here is done," Nikolai said as the three men watched the dragon's soldiers march farther and farther away from the cabin. "That was good thinking to plant her old clothes to the north. Her scent will draw them away. They won't think to search our area again."

Bastille examined the vampire's face. "You told Luna you were thirsty. Yet, you didn't try to feed off any of them when we got close." Typically, Nikolai did not fight his bloodlust. It was a part of him.

Nikolai looked away from his king, peering into the woods.

"We could have killed some of the dragon's guards. Why didn't you want to?" Bastille asked again.

Nikolai remained silent; his lips pressed into a thin line.

"She is changing you," Bastille stated, his tone one of annoyance.

"She is not."

"We need to get rid of her." Bastille kicked a large stick. "She is doing damage to us."

A light growl came from Kobe's chest.

Bastille gestured to the werewolf. "See? She's making Kobe—one of the most loyal of you—*growl* at me."

"Moonbeam stays," Kobe said.

"*I* make the decisions." Bastille slapped at his chest. "*I* am your king."

"The sun will be down soon. We need to head back," Nikolai commented.

Cursing, Bastille said, "We can't keep her."

"Then let her go," Nikolai said simply. As if it were *simple* and not utterly complicated.

Just the thought of letting her go drove Bastille crazy. His fists balled at his sides; his fangs lengthened in his mouth, feeling full of venom and *wrath* at the idea of returning to a home without her and her sassy, haughty mouth and adorable glares. "I *can't*," he bit out.

Nikolai sighed as he said, "Then, my king, *don't*."

"*P*lease don't hurt me," Luna begged as Sly fooled with the locks on the toolbox of his "*interrogation tools*." "I'll tell you things; it's really not worth cutting me up. I promise." What would telling him about Rohan really do? Worst case scenario was they gave her over to the wolf who killed her family. She'd be hurt either way. She had no reason to undergo torture.

"Aw, don't be like that." Sly pouted. "Don't ruin the fun by breaking before we've even begun."

"Sly, please."

"Mmm," he purred. "I like the way you say my name when you beg like that."

"You sick fuck," she exclaimed. "Let me go!"

Sly slowly slid open the toolbox.

She closed her eyes, not wanting to see the knives he would sink into her. Not wanting to see anything that would cause her harm. She talked a big game, but paper cuts made her curse. To be cut and left bleeding? Gaping wounds without any supernatural healing abilities?

Her entire body trembled with fear. If vampires were unable to lick and heal their victims' wounds, she would have still been bleeding from Nikolai's bite.

"Open your eyes, lamb."

"No," she squeaked out.

"Open them. Now."

Drawing in a long, deep breath, her eyelids fluttered open to peer into the box.

No knives.

Sex toys.

She released a yell of pure anger—her fear swooping out of her so fast, it left an absurd amount of room for rage. "Are you fucking *kidding me*?"

Sly tsked, shaking a finger at her. "You're the one being so dramatic."

She tried to break herself free again. "You are so ridiculous."

"We're going to play a game." Sly stroked a hand over one of the large vibrators in the box. Vibrators, dildos, a blindfold, a butt plug, and—were those nipple clamps?

She could kill him. "You're going to sexually tease me for answers?"

His grin deepened, flashing brilliant white teeth. "I love how smart you are. Picking up on context clues like that. Such a good little lamb."

She cursed him up and down, shouting and yelling obscenities as she thrashed in the ropes.

He chuckled at her dramatic display. "Smart and violent. My two favorite traits in a woman."

"Now, I'm so pissed at you, I won't tell you a thing," she remarked. "Go get some knives from the kitchen because that's the only way you'll find out anything."

"Don't tempt me. I would get them if I thought you were into knife play. But bringing those out would make Bastille *super* jealous."

She released another mini-roar of anger again—the sound so soft and meek compared to the roars a predator could release.

"Should we start with the nipple clamps or go straight to Mr. Vibrator?" Sly asked.

"Screw. You."

"Vibrator it is, then." Sly gently picked up a wand vibrator with a thick bulbous head meant for powerful clitoris stimulation.

"Why do you even have these?" she asked, trying to delay him as he balanced the wand in his hand.

"Made a rush order, but don't worry, we know how to use them. We like to thoroughly pleasure our women," Sly replied. "Our cocks do a great job, but there's something about fucking a woman with a vibrator strapped to her clit. The vibrations are so powerful, you can almost feel them on your dick with each thrust. Want a live demonstration?"

If Duttur shifters were capable of growls, she would have released one.

"Imagine being one of those women—their desires catered to by four men *and* sex toys. Sound like a dream?"

The four of them had shared a woman before? Luna had a hard time imagining where all the body parts went. But the thought still made her core tense, her abdomen hollow, and her cheeks bloom red.

"Is that something that would interest you?" he inquired.

"No," she replied through clenched teeth.

He snorted. "Another lie."

Moving forward, ever so slowly, Sly clicked on the vibrator. It thrummed to life, shaking in his hands. He lightly grazed her throat with the twitching bulb, dragging it down her chest and over her stiffening nipples.

"Let's see if I can get these into tight little beads for me," Sly whispered.

He brushed the quivering device over the peaks of her breasts, watching as her nipples slowly tightened and pebbled for him. The vibrations pounded through the thin skin there and seemed to send electricity through her nerve endings, all the way down to the wetness gathering between her legs.

Her traitorous clit began to pulse, hyperaware of the toy. "Y-Your king said you're not allowed to touch me."

"But I'm not touching you," he said. "The vibrator is."

"Damn it, Sly. What do you want from me?"

He leaned closer over her. His crystal blue eyes—the

color of exotic oceans Luna always dreamed of visiting—captured her gaze. His predator scent wafted over her nose, but she held her breath, trying not to inhale too much of his irresistible hormone-inducing crisp apple and woodsy scent.

"What do I want from you?" He swiped a thumb over her bottom lip. "Too. Many. Things."

He swept the vibrating head down her spasming stomach, down, down, to the top of her slit.

She gasped, inhaling a lung full of his pheromones. *Fuck*. Her hips bucked, trying to grind herself onto the vibrator he held just out of reach.

He snuck his face to her neck, nuzzling through her hair to speak into her ear. "I want to see how many times I can bring you to the brink of orgasm and stop and start again, before you forget your entire vocabulary."

CHAPTER 22

"*I*t's ironic, isn't it?" Sly smirked. "That you were trying to use your deliciously sexy body to distract me—use me to get what you wanted—and now, you're all tied up, quivering, and at my sexual mercy." He laughed at her glare. *Aw, little creature, how adorably violent*, he thought to himself.

Her cheeks were flushed, growing pinker with each second as he hovered the thrumming vibrator right over her swollen little clit. The tops of her thighs jiggled with anticipation. Her mouth fell open and revealed that perfect pink tongue he loved so much.

Fuck, she is perfection. Funny, vicious, mysterious, and dripping with sexual need. Sly's cock lengthened, hardening behind his slacks as he watched her shake, tied to the chair of his king.

"Any last words, lamb?" he asked.

"Screw. You."

He pressed the vibrator directly over her clit, and Luna's body froze. Her breath caught in her throat; her pupils dilated as she stared into his eyes. He watched, smiling, as the sudden pleasure overwhelmed her.

Her hips twitched, moving forward half an inch to press herself more firmly against the vibrating bulb. Her mouth was still agape as her back arched in the chair, her taut stomach tensing for a moment. "*Fuck*," she moaned.

"That's it," Sly cooed. "Grind that clit against it. It'll feel so good."

She sucked in a breath and closed her mouth, trying to glare at him but failing as he clicked the setting button up to a faster vibration. "*Ugh*." Her head fell back against the chair.

"Tell me who is after you," Sly said.

He pressed the button again, making the bulb move faster.

Her body jumped and began to squirm in the chair, fighting the ropes as her clit became more sensitive and her instinct was to close her legs to the aggressive sensation. Pleasure clouded her pretty blue eyes as she writhed.

"Stop this," she pleaded.

"Okay." He turned the vibrator off completely.

She cursed and thrashed against the ropes again.

"Tell me who is after you."

She breathed heavily but offered nothing.

The vibrator turned back on—this time at an even more powerful setting. She squealed as he pushed the bulb firmly to where she throbbed.

"You act like you don't like this," he said. "But watch what happens when I move it away." He lifted the vibrator so it no longer touched her, and her hips thrust upward at the loss. "Humping the air like a little slut in need of fucking." He moved the bulb back, massaging her clit with it.

She bit her bottom lip, but a moan still escaped her mouth.

"You're so fucking hot," Sly muttered under his breath as he watched her body writhe. "Who is after you?"

"L-Let me go, Sly."

"But you don't want to be let go. You want to be a good girl and come all over this vibrator. And come and come and come. It's all you want right now, isn't it?" He pressed the button again, intensifying the vibrations.

"*Mmmm.*" Her fists clenched the arm rests as she panted for more. He reveled in that glassy look in her eyes. Luna always appeared on edge, fearful, or angered. But now, Sly saw excitement and need lighting up her face. The sight lurched his heart in his chest. He wanted to see all of her possible expressions.

Especially her expression when she came.

"All you can think about is coming for me," he said. "Letting that orgasm take you away."

She cursed again, her hips jerking involuntarily as if seeking a real cock.

"Maybe I should get that butt plug out—stretch you so you're ready to take a couple of us."

"W-What?"

He kicked the setting up another notch.

"*Fuck,*" she cried out, quaking so hard, the bottom of the chair shuffled against the hardwood floor.

His free hand lifted to play with her nipple again, stroking it softly, rolling it between his fingers and giving it a slight pinch. He admired the slick sheen of sweat glistening over her chest.

"*Uhgah!*"

"Unable to form words already? That was way too quick." He turned off the vibe.

Even with it off, she shook in the chair. "Damn it, Sly!"

"Tell me who is after you, and I'll let you come."

*F*uck this mother-flipping fox shifter! She wanted to break free and slap him silly. Maybe ride herself on his hard cock while she was at it. Damn it, she was so turned on. Her pussy *ached*. Sweat dampened the back of her neck.

"*Why* would I tell you? Huh?" she shot back, breathless.

His expression became solemn and serious. His fingers released her hard nipple to gently touch her cheek. "Because I know what it's like to be hunted," he whispered.

She stopped fighting the ropes, growing still as he continued.

"Fox shifters aren't natural fighters," he told her. "We're an almost extinct breed."

"Hunted?"

"Families wiped out by the 'stronger' predators."

Families? Like his? She wondered. Maybe he did understand what she had been through. *Still shouldn't trust him.*

"Knowing who is after you will help us protect you," he said.

He turned the vibrator on high, shocking her, and she shrieked as he held it to her sensitive bundle of nerves at the top of her sex. Her body strained, her taut abdominal muscles jumping and jerking.

"Fuck, look at the way you tremble for it," Sly commented.

Luna moaned as Sly's hand fell to rub over the bulging crotch of his pants.

He hissed at the touch of his own hand. "Maybe I should fuck you with a dildo while it vibrates against your clit like that."

Her back kept arching, more and more, her spine fighting to push her pussy harder to the bulb. If he dared keep her in this agonizing state of dissatisfaction any longer...

Something coiled and tightened in her lower stomach.

"Ohh, there it is," Sly said as Luna's face contorted, her hips thrusting up again and again. "Close to orgasm?"

He turned it off.

In pent up frustration, she yelled, "Let me come!"

"But it's so fun *not* to."

On.

Her clit pulsated violently against the bulb. "*Oh, Gods,*" she moaned loudly.

"Trust me, little lamb, and I will reward you."

"J-Just let me come this time, okay?" She panted, her shallow breaths jostling her breasts, which Sly seemed to enjoy. "Please."

Sly's head shot to the side as he peered over to the big window, overlooking the woods outside. He pursed his lips, his eyebrows furrowing.

"What?" she asked.

He frowned, still gazing out the window. "I thought I heard something."

Were the other predators back yet? Would they watch her sexual teasing? Her torture? Would they join in?

He turned to focus back on her but then peered back out at the woods. He squinted, but shadows and darkness were all she saw. The sun had gone down and with the height of those old trees, the woods were nearly black. How much better was his predator eyesight?

He leaned the long wand of the vibrator against her stomach, using the rope there to secure the bulbed-end to her pussy. With the vibrations still on.

"What?" Her jaw dropped. "You're going outside and leaving me like this?"

"I'm going to check out that sound." Sly walked toward the door. "I'm sure it's nothing."

"Can't y-you turn off the vibrations while you do?"

Sly shot her a naughty smile. "Think of it this way, the longer I'm gone, the more of a chance you'll get to come."

She swallowed, watching him leave. She could still see him through the window, moving deep into the woods, until he became a shadow in the darkness.

The vibrator continued to run, massaging her hard clit. *Fuck, just come already.*

A creak of the floorboard caused her eyelids to flutter open again. She glanced around the room in alarm.

Then, she saw *him.*

CHAPTER 23

*H*er gaze connected with his.

It was the dragon's friend or guard or whatever he was. The blond-haired man who had interrupted her orgasm in the hotel bedroom by yelling that she was a spy—which, rude, by the way. She had been about to come then as well. So, the irony that he emerged in all black and went straight for the vibrator, trying to remove it from her, was not lost.

He went to his knees in front of her, his gaze falling over her naked form tied to the chair.

"W-Wha—"

The man threw a hand over her mouth, blocking her question. He put a finger over his lips, silently telling her to be quiet. She blinked, thinking maybe she had begun hallucinating. When he removed his palm from her lips, he refocused on working the ropes over her stomach to remove the vibrator.

Her eyes rolled back as her panting accelerated. That

heat swirled low in her abdomen, and her pussy began to spasm as she grew close to orgasm once more.

As soon as he grabbed the handle of the vibrator to remove it, she hastily shook her head at him.

He frowned, not understanding.

She whimpered and bucked her hips, rubbing herself against the bulb. Her teeth sank into her bottom lip as her clit pulsed more irregularly. *So close to orgasm.*

Realizing she wanted him to wait until she came, the man's lips separated on a puff of air. Surprise flickered across his face as he gazed up at her. Then, he shook his head right back at her.

"*Please*," she mouthed. "*Please, I'm so close.*"

He gaped at her. Clearly, this was not the rescue he had been expecting.

"*Just let me come*," she mouthed.

He blinked twice and glanced down at the way her pussy rocked against the vibrating bulb. As if pushing himself out of a trance, he shook his head again.

She nodded hers.

Head shake.

Nod.

Head shake. Nod.

He removed the vibrator. She let out such a tortured, heart-breaking whimper, he reluctantly pressed it to her clit again. He must have accidentally hit the setting button as well because the vibrations reached their peak speed and force, and her head fell back as she silently screamed.

She undulated against the device as the dragon's right-hand man watched her face contort in ecstasy. Her juices slicked the bulb and the chair as she rode out the waves and waves of convulsions and heat.

While she was distracted with her orgasm, the blond man cut through her other ropes until she was free from the chair. He turned off the vibrator and put it on the coffee table. He slowly rose, at a height that was so much taller than her.

Holding out a hand, he nodded for her to take it.

He was then tackled to the ground.

Sly sucker-punched him in the jaw the second he had the dragon's man pinned to the floor. The men rolled around, both with predatory super strength, throwing punches.

Luna quickly rose from the chair, grabbing Kobe's shirt from the sofa and wrenching it onto her body.

The predators continued thrashing each other. Sly's nose cracked from one of the hits; Luna winced for him.

Fox shifters are not natural fighters. Worry leaked into her chest even as she reminded herself that Sly was part of the team keeping her hostage.

Luna, this is the perfect time to make a run for it.

If the dragon's man won, she would just be held captive by a different group of predator shifters.

Time to run.

"Luna, don't you dare!" Sly shouted as he continued tussling with the blond man. "Don't run!"

She ran.

Sprinting to the exit, she turned the doorknob as soon as her hand came into contact with it. *Don't look back. Don't hesitate.* She slipped out into the night.

Free. At last.

She ran through the woods. If she were a predator, shifting into her animal state could have made her faster, but sheep were not runners. As long as the men did not return any minute and Sly did not immediately crush the intruder, she had a chance at freedom.

After a bit of running through the dark woods, she tripped over a hidden branch and cut her knees on something sharp. *Shoot*. That would help them scent her. Under the night sky, she couldn't see anything, but she brushed herself off and began to run again.

A wolf's howl pierced through the air.

She froze. Howls like that reminded her of the night Rohan and his pack hunted her for hours in the woods. She had just narrowly been able to escape.

What if that was Rohan right now?

What if he had finally found her? The dragon's guard had.

Run, Luna. She ran harder. Faster. Trees whipped past her.

The wolf howl sounded again, closer this time.

Just keep running.

Several branches snapped nearby.

Run.

A bone-chilling rattling sound came from behind her.

No. No. *No*.

Something thick and smooth wrapped around her waist, grabbing her from her running and yanking her back. The large appendage felt like a gigantic octopus arm as it continued to wrap around her again and again, coiling and constricting—squeezing her tight, but not so tight that she struggled to breathe. Yet.

The rattling sound calmed just as a pair of familiar serpentine green eyes appeared right in front of her face. In the darkness, all she could see were the green eyes of a massive fucking snake. She shivered at Bastille's basilisk form. They were one of the most feared shifter breeds for a reason.

Those angry eyes narrowed on her, but then the pretty spirals appeared over them, and Luna's body slackened, her fear slipping to the ground.

"*You thought you could run from us, Cotton Ball?*" Bastille's voice penetrated her mind as she lost herself in his hypnotic eyes. "*A slow, little prey. And you thought you could run from us? From ME?*"

His voice vibrated with malice, but Luna still calmly stared into the green spirals, utterly entranced. He had her right where he wanted her.

"*Were you headed for your beloved dragon? Be honest.*"

Luna shook her head. "No."

The green eyes widened and softened, losing a bit of anger behind the beautiful, attention-snaring spirals.

With aching slowness, the tail wrapped around her midsection eased, lowering her to stand on the ground once more.

Bastille shifted into his human form, still holding onto her tightly, as if afraid she might run again. He was also... in the buff.

Completely naked.

Luna could hardly see anything in the dark, but she felt

his bare skin brush against hers. His firm, muscular, tattooed chest heated her through the thin material of Kobe's sleep-shirt.

Bastille held her firmly against him and…

He was hard.

CHAPTER 24

*G*oddamn *brat*, Bastille thought to himself as his heart rate calmed with her in his clutches once more. *Thought she could run from alpha shifters?*

Did she have no idea that the *chase*, the *hunt*, excited alpha predators more than anything else?

In his case, *sexually* excited.

She makes me so fucking hard.

His cock throbbed against his stomach, completely erect after hunting her down in the woods. It twitched against her hip as he trapped her in his arms, and she gasped at the feel of it.

Shit. Now, she knew she had made him hard. Fantastic.

He ground his teeth and bit his tongue, but nothing dwindled his erection. Not when she breathed in short little pants after having run so far from the cabin. His face buried into her hair, close to her neck, as he breathed in her delicious scent.

Prey really do attract predators. That was why they were

hunted. *To want and to care for something is to have weakness,* Bastille reminded himself.

"How did you get away from Sly?" he growled into her ear.

"I guess I'm not weak and helpless after all," she replied haughtily.

Nothing but a sexy, distracting nuisance. "That remains to be seen."

"You are very hard right now," she replied, seeming as distracted as him.

Her breaths remained rapid and short. As a Dark One, Bastille was gifted with night vision. Gazing upon her shuddering tits and the flush of pink covering the tops of her cheeks and traveling down her neck... Fuck, as much as he didn't want to want her, he craved her.

Her soft scent was so alluring and sweet. A cherry glaze. Mouthwatering.

"A prey running from a predator?" He explained, "The chase gets our blood pumping."

"Hunting me turned you on?" she asked, ice in her tone, though her body remained hot to the touch. "Psychopath."

"You're lucky I was the first to find you," he said. "Kobe is probably hard as a rock right now, sniffing around for you."

"Hard at the idea of hunting me? Hurting me?"

Bastille frowned, his thoughts moving a bit slower due to his hard as fuck erection. "We do not hurt women."

"Sure," she replied sarcastically.

Had someone hurt her?

His heartbeat sped up again, and he clutched her

tighter. Her sweet scent messed with his mind, creating thoughts like "*Protect her*" and "*Keep her.*"

But she was the dragon's.

What if I fuck him right out of her system?

She let out a little breathy noise when his engorged cock brushed against the hem of her shirt, aligning directly between her legs.

The scent of her arousal infiltrated Bastille's nostrils. Sweet, sweet black cherries.

"Why act like you want to escape me now when your body betrays you?" he purred, leaning forward to breathe in more of that spicy, sweet arousal. "You want me."

"I—I do not."

"You want me to fuck you in these woods right now? Against a tree?"

"N-No."

His lips pulled up at the ends. "You're lying."

"You don't know that; you're not the fox shifter of the group."

Bastille tsked. "And here I thought a precious prey would not be caught dead in the woods, let alone willing to rut against the bark of a tree."

"I guess you don't know me."

Bastille's right hand dropped behind her, smoothing over the curve of her ass under the shirt. *Pert and perfect.* Palming the round squeezable flesh, he groaned into her ear, instinctively grinding his aching cock against her.

"You're supposed to be proper," he told her. "Docile. The dragon's perfect innocent mate."

"Fuck you," she shot back, and he suppressed a lusty chuckle.

"Mmm, you'd let me fuck you right here, wouldn't you, Lamb Chop? I can tell how bad you need it."

She scoffed a little too dramatically. A little too *lady-doth-protest-too-much.* "As if."

Bastille ran his smooth hand up her inner thighs, disappearing under the baggy shirt.

She sucked in a breath. "W-What are you doing?"

What *was* he doing? Thinking with his throbbing cock, that's what. "The guys will find us soon. If you're aroused, Nikolai might try to bleed you dry again. Bloodlust and lust get confused for him."

"But I'm n-not aroused."

"The scent of you thickens the night air," he whispered to her neck, his hand moving higher and higher up the shirt. Up her legs. So close to where she would have been wearing panties if this had been a normal night.

A second ticked by in slow motion just before he ran the backs of his fingers between her slit, opening her to the chilled night air and petting her there.

He bit back a curse. "Fucking drenched for me."

"Not for you," she tried to protest but her hard tone became flimsy upon his touch.

"If I have to fuck your mouth to get you to stop lying, I will," he threatened. She shuddered at his sexual words. Her hips flexed to his touch. His cock continued to throb with each of his erratic heartbeats. "Look at you, wet and pliant for my fingers." He groaned. "Want to feed my cock into you."

"*Bastille.*"

"Woman, *my name on your lips.*" He could come from the sound alone. He jerked his hips against her, rubbing his erection over her. "Be a good girl and touch my cock while I make you come on my fingers."

Another gasp of surprise. "Excuse me?"

"You got to come last night, while your little display in the kitchen left me hard as nails. If you're greedy enough to demand another orgasm before bed, then you should at least return the favor to one of us."

She bared her teeth at him even as she wet his fingers. His thumb circled her needy little clit, and her eyelids hooded. "I don't have to do anything," she replied.

"You hate me that much?"

"Despise you," she bit back.

Because he was so beneath the dragon, she did not want him?

I'm never good enough.

"I could make you touch me," Bastille mused darkly. The twin hypnotic spirals appeared over his green eyes once more.

"Y-You wouldn't," she stuttered, trying so hard not to be swept up in those entrancing eyes again. "Not against my will."

Damn it, she was right. He wouldn't. The spirals faded. But fuck, he wanted her to at least want him a fraction of how much he wanted her. Was he expected to finger her to bliss and receive nothing? Hand her over to the dragon and receive nothing? He wanted her to choose him.

Fucking choose me. Please.

His fingers explored her wetness, diving inside her tight sheath to stroke a special spot Bastille knew would drive her wild. *Choose me over the dragon. Choose me.*

"Close already?" he teased her as he felt her core

175

clamping lightly around his digits. "Such a greedy little pussy. Needs to be tended to."

"I hate you," she bit out through breathy intakes.

"Don't…say that," he growled.

Her mouth fell open as he stroked her g-spot again and again, settling into a rhythm that made her dizzy with pleasure.

Need her touch. Bastille grabbed her hand and pressed it against his bare shaft. "Put me out of my misery, and I will make you feel so good."

Her hand tightened around his cock, and he yelped with pleasure. Still, she hesitated.

He breathed into her ear, "My balls have been blue since the moment you bumped into me on the street. Damn it all, I *ache* for you. Please, little prey. Just touch me. Please."

And she…did.

*W*hat was she doing? Jerking the cock of the man she hated? Her captor. Was this a form of Stockholm syndrome?

Her small hand wrapped around the wide girth of his shaft, his skin scorching her with its heat. Weren't snake shifters cold-blooded? Yet, Luna felt as if she were burning up from the inside.

It was the tortured *"Please"* from Bastille that got her. The word took her legs out from under her and shoved her into a pool of lust for him.

His alpha pheromones bombarded her, but it was more than that. Had anyone ever made her so mindless? So angry and turned on all at the same time?

His fingers still curled inside her, rubbing a spot that made her cross-eyed, moving in and out with such precise rhythm, she wanted to cry. He was so *good* at that. A strange jealousy rose in her at the question of how he had gotten so good at it.

It must have been his alpha scent corrupting her brain because with that jealousy came a desire to make him forget anyone before her.

She gave a test stroke of her palm around his shaft. His reaction of a jagged breath and a buck of his hips spurred her on. She had only given a hand job once in her life. Rohan had asked it of her, his alpha predator pheromones enticing her.

Bastille had said *please*.

Even now, the way his green eyes locked onto her face was so different from Rohan. Like he was silently whispering, "*I would die for your touch.*"

Gripping his cock, she began to stroke it in rough jerks up and down. Her thumb teased the rising liquid at the tip of him and used it as lubricant for her strokes.

With his right hand busy playing with her between her thighs, he moved his left hand to grab at the flesh of her breast, kneading it in his palm.

"These tits kill me," he murmured and began pressing hot kisses down her neck as he fingered the life out of her. "Soft, perfect. Who gave you permission to be so fucking perfect?" When he alternated with fast-paced thrusts of his fingers, he made sure to grind the heel of his palm against her throbbing clit.

He had been right. She was already close to coming.

It made no sense the way she struggled to even give

herself an orgasm; yet, these predators had achieved it in so little time.

"Kobe is close by," he whispered in her ear, moving his fingers even faster.

Luna could not catch her breath. Her pussy fluttered around him.

"You need to either come in the next sixty seconds, or he will find you like this. Jerking me off, your pussy pinned on my fingers, soaking them in your sweet honey. He might want another taste."

Her broken moan rang out. Gods, she really was drenching his fingers. Her wetness ran down his hand.

He pressed his forehead to hers. "Make me come, pretty prey."

She moved her palm faster over him, both of them groaning out in unison.

"Going to come all over your fucking hand. Next time, inside you—your pussy, your mouth, till you're all mine," Bastille muttered to himself, like he didn't think she could hear him. "Never going to stop."

What happened to "*no one touches her*" or how he would let her go without if she went into heat?

His talented fingers drove away that thought. She wailed into the night sky. So close. So. Close.

"Kobe will be here in fourteen, thirteen, twelve, eleven, ten, nine—"

Her mouth gaped open, and his left hand shot up from her breast to muffle her scream. Her pussy clamped down around his finger, so hard she worried he would lose all feeling.

Colors dotted her vision, and she swayed from the

power of the orgasm, twitching again and again in his hold. Reveling in each all-consuming spasm. His cock jerked in her hand, and he grunted into her soft neck, pressing his lips against the tender skin there as he spurt jet after jet of his release.

She blinked, her gaze shooting up to connect with his.

"I want to try something," he said urgently. "Let me."

"Say 'please.'"

"Trust me," he commanded.

"When you've given me no reason to?"

He growled, glaring at her with enough heat to rival a bubbling volcano. "Please, I wish to give you more pleasure. Will you trust me?"

Trusting Bastille sounded like the dumbest thing she could do. Still, at the promise of pleasure, her traitorous, desperate body nodded her chin of its own volition.

His green eyes spun with entrancing spirals.

She fell under his spell so easily, already drowsy and dreamy from coming.

"You will obey everything I say."

"I will...obey..."

He smirked as she sunk into his hypnosis.

"Good girl. Now, come again," he said simply.

Her body vibrated from a new earth-shattering orgasm that came out of nowhere. "*Whaaaa...*"

His fingers kept moving inside her. What should have taken several more minutes, took one second upon his order.

Those spirals controlled her. "And again. Come again," he said.

Her legs turned to jelly, her spine arching back as she

shook from another powerful release. She panted out his name. "*Bastille.*"

"Love my fucking name on your lips."

He was *still* fingering her after three orgasms. She quivered, shaking so bad, he nearly lost his grip on her. "C-Can't take anymore."

"You will take all I can give you," he commanded. "One last time, come all over my fingers. Soak my hand so the others can smell what we did."

The spirals spun and pulsed in his green eyes.

"Come again, baby lamb."

CHAPTER 25

*K*obe came upon them just as Luna fell to her knees in exhaustion. The wolf pounced on his mate in his animal form. He ran his nose over her, searching her for any injuries. Instead, he found her panting from sexual release. He smelled her wetness on Bastille, and her aroused scent hit him like a cannonball. *Want her.*

The chase had never particularly turned Kobe on before, but this was his *mate*. Looking for her and finding her—finding her squirming after a fresh orgasm? He had never been so hard.

In seconds, Kobe shifted back to his human form, completely naked. He laid over her on the autumn leaves, warming his mate.

His thick erection pulsed against her, and she gave a tired moan.

"Shit, Kobe, control yourself," Bastille warned.

Kobe had a tendency of struggling to separate his

human-self from his wolf. His instincts always roared louder than any silly human or societal expectations. Right now, his instincts said to *rut*.

Kobe growled at his king and pressed his hips down onto his mate. His hands splayed open her legs, shoving up the hem of the oversized shirt. *Need to thrust*.

"Get the fuck off her—" Bastille started but Luna's arms whipped out and wrapped around Kobe, holding him close. One of her hands swooped down to push on Kobe's ass, grinding him between her legs. A dark, choked laugh came from Bastille. "Still not satisfied, little prey? How…intriguing."

Luna was reduced to a moaning mess. Kobe approved.

Because he was mindless for her.

Cock so fucking *full* for her.

Heart beating so fucking hard.

His wolf instincts took over as he jerked his hips over her, dragging his cock over her clit again and again—not penetrating her, but grinding. Rutting like the animal he was. Her back dug into the ground, but she made no move to stop him.

Need to come all over my mate. Make her mine.

"*Can't. Stop*," Kobe grunted into her ear as he thrust against her. His hand fell to pinch her folds around him as he shoved his cock to scrape over the swollen hood of her clit. Reduced to an animal. He feared hurting her, scaring her, but she seemed to…love it.

She dug her nails into his ass, and he moved harder over her, quickening his strokes.

"Moonbeam," he rasped as his hips jackhammered back and forth, grinding himself against her. "I am…lost."

She moaned out, "*More.*"

His mate wanted more?

A wicked grin stretched the werewolf's mouth. *Little mate, you do not know what you ask for.*

He gripped her waist and turned her to face the ground, so she was on all fours, her hands and knees on the ground of the woods. Her fingers clenched around leaves and grass and sticks, as if she needed to somehow hold on for the ride of a lifetime.

Kobe's large hands sank below her stomach, to her dripping sex. Fingers pinched and played with her hyper-sensitive clit. Other thick fingers dove into her wet entrance.

She shrieked her approval.

From behind, Kobe thrust his jutting shaft against his mate's ass, grinding and grinding, while fingering her with absolute precision and the kind of wild pace that only a man who was half-animal could produce.

"Want…inside you," Kobe bit out, his cockhead leaking pre-cum for her and trailing onto her ass cheeks. "Want to mark you. *Fill* you. Breed you."

She shrieked again, her pussy gushing over his fingers.

The thought of my fucking makes her wet. Kobe grinned.

"Fuck," Bastille muttered from somewhere beside them. Kobe was too distracted to look. Was his king touching himself while watching the two of them together?

"Moonbeam." Kobe's shaft rubbed against her smooth cheeks again and again. The feeling of her pussy wrapped so tightly around his fingers… "Will never get enough of you."

Her back arched to him, their bodies mimicking sex.

"Waited a millennium for my mate. You are *mine*," Kobe growled, caging her to his body. He matched the thrusting of his fingers to the quick rolls of his hips. "Mine. *Mine*. No one will take you from me. Mine. As I am yours—"

He came.

His head fell back as he howled to the sky, jerking his cock and coming onto her back. She cried out as her release claimed her as well, her pussy trapping his fingers inside her.

Their heavy breathing echoed in the woods. Kobe and Luna laid back on the leaves, beside each other, reveling in their satiation.

Meanwhile, Bastille reeled, still clutching his erection before aggressively asking Kobe, "What do you mean, *'your'* mate?"

The two men did not speak during the entire walk back to the cabin.

Nikolai and Sly had eventually found them after searching in the opposite direction for her. Both seemed confused as to why Bastille and Kobe emitted clear *don't-mess-with-me* vibes.

From what she understood, Kobe was a teddy bear of a person. A golden retriever personality stuck in a danger-ous, bulky, and unfairly sexy wolf-shifter's body. Though Luna was still wary of him—due to him being an alpha wolf like Rohan—she could not ignore the way he treated her. Even as they walked, Kobe held a hand on her lower back and directed her so she did not trip on a rock.

At one point, she almost walked into a low hanging branch and the wolf-shifter *punched* his fist in front of her to break the branch before it could scrape her forehead. He was protective in a way that made a woman like her—used to taking care of herself—swoon. *And his fingers...*

She needed to escape these alpha predators before she allowed herself to weaken. Prolonged exposure to alpha pheromones had to have lasting effects somehow. She could be losing brain cells. After all, what else could explain the way she came *eight times* for them within two days of knowing them. Embarrassment heated her face. She had known Rohan a month before he struck her family.

Cannot trust these men or any men. The sooner they got back to the cabin, the sooner the men would put on some clothes and be less distractingly nude.

Sly, Kobe, and Bastille—post shifting—walked naked. Ripping their clothes off before shifting did not exactly work for once they shifted back into human form. Still, they strode confidently, as if their penises weren't just... out in the open.

Shifters, she rolled her eyes.

Just before the five of them stepped into the clearing where the cabin was, Sly's arm shot out, warning everyone not to move. Kobe sniffed the air, then slowly guided Luna to stand behind him.

Curious and worried about a threat, she peered around the large man and saw it.

A group of men were walking in and out of the cabin. Two men, who stood just outside of it argued, and she recognized them.

The dragon, Daxton. And the blond-haired man who fought Sly...and watched her orgasm while tied to a chair and vibrator.

Her eyelids went heavy at the sight of Daxton. He truly was a princely male. He stood straight, doing so almost with conviction. His suit was disheveled, his black hair mussed—had he been yanking on it while searching for her? Her memory shot back to the way he had pulled her to straddle his face. The way his tongue—

Bastille wrapped a hand around her throat, distracting her.

At the threatening action, Kobe began to quietly growl, but Sly pressed a finger to his lips, expressing that they needed to be silent. The dragon's little army would be able to hear them.

If Daxton found her, she would be free of this group, only to become prisoner to another. *If Daxton thinks I'm his mate, he will never let me go.* After six years on the run, she could not imagine staying in one place with a predator shifter who could sneeze freaking fire. She wanted survival on *her* terms.

She nibbled her bottom lip, weighing her options.

Releasing her neck, Bastille pinched her chin and pointed her face to look at his. His eyes featured no hypnosis as he examined her expression. He scowled at her.

What had she done now? *Looked* at the dragon? *Sensitive male.*

Bastille seemed to wait for her to make a sound. To cause a scene so Daxton would find her and take her from them. It was an option. The dragon would have his guard down around her; it would be easier to run from him.

But Bastille glared like he *knew* she would choose the dragon. He challenged her with his gaze, waiting for her to give them away.

She thinned her lips, gazing right back with the confidence of an alpha predator.

Bastille blinked, his eyebrows furrowing in confusion.

He glanced at where Daxton stood fifty feet away then back at her. His eyes seemed to shout, "*Well, if you want out, here's your chance. Choose him, Princess.*"

Luna's pride never allowed her to back away from a challenge like that.

Fine. She would stick with the group of men who now knew she was a flight risk and would take better precautions than a locked bedroom door. Whatever. She would still escape them in the end.

She had to.

☾

She...wasn't choosing the dragon? Bastille gaped at her. Any moment now, she would scream out for him; Daxton would find her, take her with his army, and whisk her away to a fancy palace or penthouse or whatever the materialistic oaf called his "abode." *Pretentious ass.*

But she did not make a sound.

Maybe she does not want him, he thought. *Maybe she is still winnable. Maybe...she could want me*

For the first time in so long, *hope* blossomed and warmed his cold-blooded chest.

Suddenly, the prophecy of sharing a mate with Daxton did not matter anymore. *Because I will not let the Dragon have her.* Ever.

CHAPTER 26

*K*obe, Bastille, Sly, Nikolai, and Luna slinked further into the forest to hide from the dragon's search team. She still did not know whether she regretted not getting the dragon's attention and switching "kidnappers," but there was no going back now.

Find another opportunity to escape and do it.

After she did not call out to the dragon at the cabin, Bastille had cast her curious glances throughout the hike in the dark. Little *"who is this woman?"* and *"do I hate her or not?"* expressions from him. Occasionally, she flipped him off, and the sound of a rattlesnake's tail rang out.

But right now, she was exhausted. It had to be past two in the morning. She had barely slept earlier in the week due to nightmares of Rohan. They always got worse the longer she stayed in one place.

When she began swaying on her feet, her head unable to stay up much longer, Kobe snared a strong, thick arm around her waist and told the other men, "We make camp and sleep."

"We should keep moving—" Nikolai began.

"Camp and sleep," Kobe grunted, turning caveman and wolf-like on them. He gestured to Luna, who could scarcely keep her eyes open.

The men nodded. Camp and sleep, it was.

The four predators formed a circle, each one surveying a different patch of forest around them.

Kobe bent and quickly kicked away sticks and rocks. He gathered leaves to cover a rectangular shape on the ground. Looking at Luna, he pointed to it. "Sleep, *ma chekka.*"

She did not know what *chekka* meant and she did not care. It was as close to a soft bed as she would get.

"The dragon's princess won't be able to sleep on anything but feathers and rose petals," Bastille remarked, but the insult seemed to be delivered less harshly than normal. Like Bastille was testing out his ability to still read and understand her.

Princess? Feathers and rose petals? He has no idea who I am.

She all but launched herself down onto the makeshift bed of dirt and leaves Kobe made for her. She stretched on it, curling into herself, and prepped for sleep to overtake her. After years on the run with little money, she had slept on the cold, hard ground of the outdoors before.

She closed her eyes but could *feel* Bastille gaping at her.

Screw you, Basilisk. You have no idea who I really am.

She passed out within minutes.

☾

*K*obe stared at his sleeping mate's form on the ground. He wanted her on a soft bed made of clouds and silk sheets wrapped around her. *She deserves better than to sleep on dirt.*

"I can't believe she didn't yell out for the dragon," Sly said, staring up at the night sky through the overgrown treetops as he laid on his back. "I thought for sure that would be it."

"Just because she didn't choose him does not mean she chose us," Bastille replied.

Nikolai's red eyes burned as he assessed the forest for threats while the others relaxed. His thirst for blood had been utterly calmed after drinking from her the day before, his frantic mind finally back to normal after sipping from Luna's slender neck.

Nikolai...liked having her around. "What if she *did* choose us?" the vampire asked the group.

"Won't happen," Bastille said.

"Pessimist alert." Sly stretched out his arms and legs as he laid. "Kobe, why couldn't you make me a little bed of leaves too, buddy?"

Were they still talking? Kobe was focused on his mate's peaceful face. *So beautiful.* "Protect her."

Sly shook his head. "You're more caveman than normal."

"He thinks she's his mate," Bastille said.

Nikolai's head shot over to gaze at Kobe. There was almost a flash of...could that have been jealousy in the cold vampire's eyes?

"She is my mate," Kobe confirmed.

"What are the chances she is the dragon's mate, your mate, and Bastille's mate?" Sly pondered. "You'll need to invest in a bigger bed."

Kobe remained silent. Bastille broke a stick he found.

Quiet reigned in the forest before Bastille muttered into the darkness, "As long as I live, she will never be the dragon's."

"I wasn't the only one who saw her looking at him with *interest*," Sly added.

This time, Bastille broke multiple sticks when he punched the forest floor. The ground almost quaked at the force. "Her 'interest' does not concern me."

"So, if she did choose him, you'd just—what? Hold her captive?"

"Yes."

Sly scoffed. "Dude."

"Doubt your king again and see what happens," Bastille threatened.

More eerie silence.

"Maybe if you were nicer to her, she'd choose you," Kobe mused, less caveman-like as he laid down beside Luna's curled up, sleeping form. Keeping her safe calmed him. *Just wish I had a blanket.* Kobe was still in the buff after having chased her through the woods in his shifted form and being unable to go back to the cabin for clothes.

"Maybe he worries if he *is* nicer to her, she might still choose the dragon over him," Nikolai muttered. "Scared of vulnerability."

"Shut the fuck up, bloodsucker," Bastille barked.

The men quieted, listening to the soft sounds of the forest.

♭

"*R*ohan," Luna muttered in her sleep hours later, shifting on the bed of leaves and dirt.

Bastille's eyes shot open, and he sat up to watch her toss and turn on the ground. *What now?* He thought to himself, peering at her as she continued twitching in her sleep.

The other three men still slumbered, exhausted from chasing her in the woods earlier after so little rest the past week.

Bastille was used to no sleep.

"*Rohan*," she called out again in her sleep. Her legs jerked during her vivid dream.

Another man's name? Bastille's deadly eyes glowed in the dark forest; his fangs sharpened in his mouth. *She dares to be involved with another man?*

Kobe was one thing—though, Bastille could not deny the arousal he felt while watching Kobe finger her earlier. The dragon was an aggravation. But *another* man? This, "*Rohan?*"

He glowered in her direction as she repeated the man's name in her sleep. She whimpered. Was she having a sex dream about him? A sex dream about someone who was *not* Bastille?

Unacceptable.

Bastille moved until he loomed over her.

"*Rohan.*"

Jealousy ate him up inside. Had another man claimed

her? Had she been trying to run away from them to get to him? Rohan?

Note to self: kill all Rohans.

Luna continued to turn and twitch in her sleep.

"*Rohan, please,*" she cried out softly.

Rage. Absolute rage crashed over him, seeping into his bones.

He roared at her, forgetting that they were in a forest and the dragon's men could be nearby, "You *DARE* dream of another?"

At his loud yell, the men and Luna jerked awake.

She blinked several times, taking in her surroundings. She frowned. *Was she missing Rohan? Missing the luxury of a penthouse bed that the dragon could offer her?*

Why would she ever choose me?

More rage consumed Bastille as he clasped her shoulders and shook her further awake. "You dare have a sex dream of another right next to me?"

Kobe growled at his king's handling of his mate. *Oh well.*

"What are you talking about?" She acted innocent.

A liar. More rage. "You dream of touching another! Moaning out his name."

"I—I was not having a sex dream."

"You—" Bastille breathed in a sharp breath and froze. Luna's scent of arousal—which Bastille was quite familiar with by now—did not pierce the air. Instead, he scented…fear.

Kobe shoved at his king, and Bastille released her arms, stepping back.

Kobe nuzzled in beside her, wrapping his arms around

her to show he would protect her. To show he would deny his king and choose to defend *her*. A prey.

What has she done to him? A quick glance around revealed Nikolai and Sly also gazing at Bastille with wary expressions. No longer the expressions of men willing to follow him anywhere. *What has she done to all of us?*

"You had a nightmare, Moonbeam?" Kobe whispered, scenting her fear as well and trying to ease it.

She scowled at Bastille, keeping her lips shut in defiance.

This fucking woman, Bastille growled to himself.

"Want to tell us about the big bad in your dream?" Sly asked.

"Maybe I dreamed of being kidnapped by *you*," she replied sassily.

"Who is Rohan?" Bastille questioned. "You said his name repeatedly."

"Row hand?" she repeated, pretending she had no idea what he said. "Never heard of it."

"She just lied," Sly supplied the group with obvious knowledge. They could all hear the way her heart raced when Bastille mentioned the name Rohan.

"Did he hurt you? Rohan?" Kobe asked softly, still holding her.

She shifted, shrugging uncomfortably in Kobe's arms.

"Is he the one you're hiding from, Bo Peep?" Bastille's anger still ruled him at the way all of his friends gazed at Luna, at the way she clearly did not want to confide in him.

She sneered at Bastille, "You know nothing."

"Because you tell us nothing."

"Because you do not need to know."

195

"What *should* we know?"

She stood. "That I want to be set free," she said, stomping her foot to the ground. Her expression was full of such pride and confidence... *She looks like a queen.*

"Too bad, Woolly." Bastille could not control the sheep-themed nicknames. She did not need to know that nicknames were something Bastille gave only to those he liked. "You will never be free of us."

Her glare *pierced* him. "I should have called out and gone with the dragon," she said. "It will be my deepest regret."

The rage is back. Bastille's lips peeled up to form a sinister, bone-chilling smile. "You're going to wish you had not said that, Mutton."

CHAPTER 27

As they hiked through the forest, the sunlight barely breaking through the treetops, Sly moved ahead in his fox form, scanning the surroundings for threats. An hour earlier, Kobe confirmed that he still smelled the dragon close by.

Am I to always be hunted in the woods? Luna mused to herself bitterly. With the way Bastille clenched his fists and glared at her, she knew she needed out. Now.

But how to slip away?

A pang occurred in her left side, and she stumbled over a fallen tree branch.

Kobe quickly helped her up and brushed one of his large, warm palms over where she scraped her knee. Bastille chuckled at her mistake. *Snake bastard.*

A trickle of blood came from her scraped knee, and she cursed and wiped it away on her hand.

When she looked back up, Nikolai stared intently, *hungrily* at her shallow wound. Thankfully, Nikolai was the only one of the men not completely naked because he did not "shift" away his clothes. Yet, he stared at her now like *she* was naked.

The vampire would drink me down if he had the chance. Vampires were notorious for bloodlust, and Nikolai's red eyes meant he had killed before, unable or unwilling to stop until he sucked away all of the blood from a victim. *Does he feel regret over killing or is it simply in his nature?*

Luna still shivered at the memory of Nikolai's fangs in her neck and the suction of his lips. Yes, she had heard of blood whores: men or women who became addicted to the sexual "high" a vampire's bite created. But she had never thought it could feel like *that*. When he bit her, her mind blanked and her body stilled. It had felt like tiny tongues danced all over her skin. Her nipples had become hard little peaks; her legs had quaked with need. His bite felt like dirty, filthy sex.

She quickly looked away from the vampire, who still narrowed his eyes on her knee and licked his lips.

After a few more minutes of walking, another painful pang resonated in Luna's side. Like her organs were twisting inside her. She bit back a whimper when another pain came from her lower abdomen. Was this what contractions felt like for pregnant women? Her stomach *clenched*. What the hell? Was it hunger? The next wave of pain trickled up her spine, and she again stumbled—this time, against a tree on the path they walked.

"Forget how to use your legs, Q-tip?" Bastille mocked, but there was an edge to his voice that sounded like actual concern.

"Q-tip?" Luna remarked. Her random bits of pain

fueled her anger. "Because I'm a cotton ball? Duttur may be prey sheep shifters, but we still deserve respect in the paranormal world."

"You're right, Future Sweater," Bastille replied. "You deserve all the respect in the world for the way you can be sheared for a pair of mittens."

"Do you guys smell that?" Nikolai pondered aloud, interrupting the little power-play sass battle.

"What?"

"I thought…" Nikolai twisted his head to gaze around the forest but frowned. "Never mind."

Kobe touched her arm, leaning in to scan her face as he asked her, "Okay?" Caveman wolf speak for: *Are you okay?*

She ground her back teeth. Because *no*. "No, I am not okay. I have had roughly seven hours of sleep over the span of three days—"

The men's eyebrows rose at that, considering she had been with them for less than two days.

"—My feet hurt from running and walking in the woods for *hours*," she complained. "I have been *kidnapped* by four predators, one of whom endlessly seems to mock me and acts like he hates me being here yet *won't let me go*."

Another twisting sensation occurred in her lower stomach. A tightening in her chest also jabbed through her. Her ribs ached for a moment, but she ignored them. "And my body is feeling weird, probably from hunger and exhaustion and—"

She felt as if she had been zapped with four hundred volts, or knots, or whatever was a high amount of electricity. She fell to her knees, her spine arching as her stomach seemed to collapse. She gasped when the sharp pain ended but a new ache began.

"Shit," Bastille cursed, the sound of it bouncing off the trees around them.

"Fuck," Nikolai muttered, and Sly gave a foxlike howl in his shifted form.

Kobe closed his eyes; his nostrils flared, and his hands clenched into fists at his sides. His expression was one of failing self-restraint, as if he fought an inner battle but ammo was quickly dwindling.

Luna's mouth fell open, and a needy whimper clawed out of her throat. On her hands and knees, she shuddered, fisting random leaves and twigs on the ground. *Oh, Gods.* Her lower stomach rippled; her shoulders pushed back as her chest grew heavy.

Bastille gritted his teeth. "She's going into heat."

Heat.

Sly shifted back into human form, leaving him gloriously naked. Short, masculine, reddish-gold hairs decorated his chest and lightly dusted his muscular thighs.

Naked predators surround me, she thought to herself but instead of any fear, all she felt was *need*. Her body broke out into shivers, her limbs would not stop shaking.

"The dragon will scent her," Sly warned, blinking several times as he gazed at her on the ground. He bit his lip and tried to look away, but his gaze kept sliding back to watch her writhe.

"She'll draw in every predator within a hundred miles," Nikolai added through clenched teeth.

"We have to find some kind of shelter," Bastille said. "*Now.*"

"Walls won't stop her pheromones—"

"*Shelter.*"

☾

*I*n wolf form, Kobe ran ahead of them as the other men hastily carried her, looking for any kind of cottage or space with walls to muffle her cries of desire. She was growing feverish. Delirious. "*Please,*" she begged but could not finish the rest of her plea due to the constant contractions of her core.

Nikolai, Sly, and Bastille fought for control over themselves as they ran with her. While in heat, a prey's pheromones were like a pure aphrodisiac injected into a predator's jugular. It made thinking impossible. Made any movement but *fucking* feel wrong.

Whenever Luna emitted a fresh wave of sensual airborne chemicals, the men all stumbled, interrupting their fast running as their erections stiffened and throbbed between their legs. Running naked while turned on just meant their cockheads slapped up against their hard stomachs with each stride.

At least Nikolai wore pants; though, the fabric did little to disguise the massive bulge.

Finally, Kobe led them to an abandoned shack. The modest space was clearly used as a hunter's cabin on the temperate weekends. The house was one room, other than a bathroom—much like a city studio apartment where the living room was the bedroom. After breaking open the door, Kobe threw what appeared to be clean blankets down on the bed.

The men carefully laid Luna on the mattress and took large steps back.

"Fuck, she's...*strewing*." She was in heat, yes, but her chemicals were churning—strewing—into the air at a rate that would drive any predator in the damn city, maybe even state, in their direction. "The dragon will find us in no time."

Luna's spine curled back as she thrust her hips into the air.

Kobe shifted back into human form, but remained on all fours, gaze pinned to Luna. His face scrunched with concentration as his claws ripped into the wooden floors. He looked ready to pounce on her at any moment.

Brows drawn, Bastille bit out, "We have to sate her."

Nikolai's red eyes widened. "*What?*"

"What happened to 'no one touches her?'" Sly asked but already took a step closer to Luna.

"If her pheromones grow any stronger, it'll bring the dragon, his men, and any nearby predators right to us. If she is already strewing... We have to satisfy her for her pheromones to calm down."

"You *want* us to touch her?"

"It will take all of us," Bastille stated bitterly. "A prey in heat... The stamina alone will be too much for one."

"Says you," Sly muttered, hungrily watching Luna wiggle on the bed. "I'm the youngest of our incredibly old group; I can go all night."

"You've never experienced a prey's heat before," Bastille said. "It's not just sex—it's like she fucking drains your cock of cum."

"Moonbeam, say you want us to sate you," Kobe rasped,

fighting off the pheromones as best he could, but his body lurched forward inch by inch, pulled by an invisible force. "You must say it."

"*Please*," she cried out, vibrating on the bed with need. "I —I need…*Oh!* I need you."

Bastille's fangs lengthened in his mouth.

She has decided her fate.

CHAPTER 28

*L*una watched as her stomach *rippled* before her. Her body was betraying her. But, Gods, she couldn't think through the sensations. She *needed*.

"Please, touch me." Was that her voice? Her demand? Everything seemed to blur but the men standing around the bed. Their alpha scents had always gotten to her, but now, it was like nothing before.

She reached up with her own hands to remove Kobe's shirt from her body.

Kobe jumped onto the bed, crawling up to level his face to hers. "Forgive me, *ma chekka*." He ripped the shirt into two shreds of fabric, wrenching it from her.

She gasped as he nuzzled her breasts.

Another male's large hands trailed over her hips.

Kobe shifted to the side so he could cup her breasts and suckle her aching nipples. The sensations shot through her and gathered thickly below her abdomen. He laved the sensitive pink peaks of flesh with his tongue, then sucked and nibbled. Tears streamed down her face from how good it felt.

"No tears," Bastille's deep voice rang out, his thumb catching a drop of the saltwater. "We will make the pain go away, little lamb." *So much* affection *in his voice*, she noted, surprised.

A tongue dove between her folds, searching for and finding her pulsing clit. Nikolai's red eyes blazed as he looked up at her from his position between her legs. His fangs were distended, but he carefully moved his lips and tongue so he did not pierce her. Why did she *want* him to pierce her?

Other hands brushed over her body, caressing her hair, neck, hips, and thighs. She had never felt so…desired. Bastille, Kobe, Sly, and Nikolai all watched her every reaction to their touches, doubling up on whatever caused her to moan—which was almost everything. Her skin was hypersensitive, tingling like every pore opened up to receive more attention.

Feverish, she panted for breaths. Nikolai gripped her inner thighs, prying them as wide open as they would go, so he could devour her wet, pink flesh.

Her inner muscles clamped down around nothing and released, begging to be filled. *"Please."*

Nikolai removed his mouth from her to rasp, "She's *soaked.*"

"Please," she screamed as another round of contractions shook her body. "Please, please fuck me."

The men cursed. "She's too fragile. Even if she wasn't strewing, even without the pheromones, there's no way we could maintain enough control not to hurt her. She's a prey."

To distract her from their discussion, Sly slipped two fingers into her slit, entering her and stroking the secret spot deep inside her. "This what you need, baby?"

"More! *Fuck me, please.*"

Kobe cursed. "Could hurt you."

"Please!"

Bastille punched the wall, headbutting it as well for good measure. "Not only is she a prey—look at her. She's *delicate*. We can't. We're too fucking strong. We could grab at her hips and break her damn pelvis."

"She needs it." Sly curled his fingers inside her, continuing to stroke that hidden, ribbed flesh. Her chest flushed with a sheen of sweat as more wetness leaked from her. "There's no way she breaks through the heat and stops strewing pheromones until she's thoroughly—"

"Don't say it."

"Fucked," Sly finished. "Thoroughly fucked."

"*Fuck.*" Bastille rubbed a hand over his face. "I already feel like I'm going to die if I don't get inside her soon."

"Not the only one," Nikolai said.

"If any of us feels his control slipping, he taps out," Bastille commanded. "Understood? We have to go slow. If we lose control and use our full strength, we could break her. We go slow."

The men grunted in agreement.

. . .

ill finally have her, Kobe thought to himself, rubbing his face over her soft neck as the other men positioned themselves around her on the bed, making a nest of sorts. *Mine for the taking. Mine forever. Must make it good for her.*

"Who goes first?" someone asked, eliciting a deadly growl from Kobe.

She was *his* mate. Yes, she was also Bastille's mate, but wolves were more possessive than basilisks.

"Kobe, man, are you sure you can control yourself? You'll have to be gentle—"

Another dark growl came from the werewolf as he sank down between his mate's creamy legs, pulling them up to slink around his waist. She undulated for him, her face red and contorted in pleasure-pain.

"The growling is not giving us confidence that you'll control yourself," Sly said. "The wolf in you will want to rut her. You can't be too forceful. You're much stronger than her, you'll have to be soft."

"Will be soft," Kobe dismissed Sly, not wanting to hear anything but his mate's cries of ecstasy. His hand fell to the junction of her thighs and the pretty short patch of hair there. "Ready for me, ma chekka?" *My mate.*

"Hurry." Her head flailed back and forth on the pillow, her hair bunching into knots that he would soothe later. "Please."

Kobe aligned the tip of his shaft with her tight, wet entrance. After just slightly pushing the head inside, a groan was wrenched deep from Kobe. Her sheath gripped him so tight.

"So *hot*, like a tiny forge." Sweat trickled down Kobe's chest as he prayed for self-restraint. Sly was right; Kobe's instinct was to rut. To thrust—hard—with total abandonment. To jackhammer his hips with the pace of a hummingbird's wings. *She is too fragile for that kind of fucking.*

Her pheromones continued coming off her in strong waves, hitting the men who wrestled with their self-control. Sly was already stroking himself. Nikolai and Bastille each kissed, licked, and sucked at her tits.

Kobe's cock sank a little bit farther inside her, and Luna shrieked for more. He was just so big, and she was tighter than a fist. His heart raced in his chest, beating so hard it could have killed him. Slowly, he fed her more of his length. *So slowly.* Denying his basic instincts was like swallowing fire. Fucking painful; but, for his mate, he would do anything.

Tendons strained in Kobe's neck as he pushed in a little more. Her hot inner muscles clamped around him like nothing ever had. So taut. *How am I not to* thrust?

The wolf inside him growled. *NEED TO RUT.*

No.

He swallowed; his nostrils bombarded by her scent.

Suddenly, Luna's back arched off the bed. Her hips jerked up, impaling herself fully on the werewolf's thick cock. Kobe groaned, shaking over her with the need to move. The muscles of his arms twitched to keep him upright when they instead wanted to flip her over on the bed so he could take her from behind—the way his wolf was used to fucking.

In and out in punishing, fast thrusts.

Need to rut.

"*Ma chekka*, please control yourself," Kobe grated, fighting his wolf's instincts with all he had. "Need to go slow or will…"

"No slow. Fast," she moaned, rolling her hips to tease his cock in and out of her heavenly sheath.

Kobe's eyes nearly rolled back in his head.

"Fast. Hard," she pleaded.

Not good.

"Stay in control, Kobe," one of the men said. He did not care which one.

Must not hurt her. Must keep her safe. Must pleasure her. Must fuck her. Must RUT.

He shoved forward, digging his hard shaft inside her wet heat—hard.

"*Yes*," she cried out for more.

"Softer," someone said.

Then, Luna's stomach muscles contracted. Her pussy gripped his cock like a tight vise, trapping him inside her and seeming to…*pull*. To *suck*.

"*Ma chekka!*" Kobe's claws punctured through the mattress beneath them, just over her head, as his eyes went fully black. His hips thrust again and again, his strength driving her up the bed with each motion.

"Too hard, Kobe," someone warned, but he was past the ability to listen. Not with Luna's little nails digging into his ass as her pussy spasmed around him.

In a turn of events, Luna's pheromones spiked the air

until every breath of oxygen triggered the animalistic parts of the shifters' brains.

Heat.

"Oh, *shit*." The next wave of her strew hit them like a freight train, almost knocking the men down and off the bed. Their cocks swelled even harder, reddening and filling up for her as if she controlled them. And she did. The prey had become the predator.

The alpha men were reduced to a panting mess of lust. They purred and rubbed their faces and erections against her smooth skin. Their rumblings and whispered words of desire washed over her flushed, naked body.

"Little lamb," Bastille warned her, speaking directly into her ear. "You are about to get *fucked*."

CHAPTER 29

*L*una watched through hooded eyelids as the men lost their minds to lust.

Kobe's hips surged forward again and again, fucking her with his engorged shaft. It was so damn *big* inside her, taking up all the room. It breached against a spot she did not know existed—her fingers had never reached that far back to explore, and Rohan had never been this aroused and full for her.

It was a *revelation*.

All of the men's hands on her skin, their lips and tongues working her to orgasm.

And Kobe…

Kobe's original look of wonder, when he had first dipped inside of her, had fallen into an aggressive, animalistic, bared-teeth expression. His dark eyes were black holes, sucking her in as he urged his thick cock inside her. In, out. In, out. He moved so forcefully, his wide, strong thighs flexing with each movement. His large hands fisted the sheets on either side of her.

A new hand—Sly's?—snaked down her stomach to play with her swollen clit while Kobe buried himself inside her again and again.

"*Yes,*" Luna cried. "*So good!*"

"Touch," another masculine voice said—Bastille? It was hard to decipher anything over the loud grunts from Kobe and the whining from herself.

One hand captured hers and led her to a hard erection. He wrapped his fingers over hers, molding her grip over his shaft. "Touch me," the voice rasped.

Drowning in pleasure, she began to stroke it. Another hand took her free one and placed it onto another hot length of virile flesh.

There she was, the woman who hated predators, masturbating two men while another claimed her and having the mounds of her breasts licked, nipped, and her clit massaged in tight circles. *Who am I becoming?*

"More," she demanded.

Kobe shoved inside her even harder, hammering his hips to hers. Plunging and pumping himself into her. The fingers on her sensitive bundle of nerves sped up.

Luna's eyes crossed. "Going to… Going to…" Every time she meant to finish her sentence, Kobe thrust, and she lost her train of thought.

"Going to be a good girl and come for us?" Bastille teased her, tightening her grip on his cock. He kissed down her neck, his hand kneading her breast. "You're going to do a lot of coming tonight, Princess. No need to tell us each time or you will lose your pretty voice."

"Can feel you *squeezing!*" Kobe's head fell back, his pace growing erratic. "Will never get enough—*uhh.*"

Sly pinched her clit, causing a sharp sting, before giving it a sexy little *tug*.

Ecstasy. It rolled over her, making her breath catch and a long moan peal out of her. Her gripping pussy fastened around Kobe's shaft, almost as if the inner muscles wanted to suck him in farther.

As the orgasm wrung her, Kobe's seed rose, spurting from him as he bellowed with pleasure. He drove himself into her in a ragged, unsteady rhythm, plunging his cock into her spasming core.

"Too soon, too soon—*uhhguhh*." His thrusts slowed until he dropped down onto her, his cock still inside her.

Bastille yanked Kobe back by his neck, tearing his dick from Luna and tossing him onto the other side of the bed. "Did you like that, lamb?" Bastille asked. "Because I'm about to make you forget all about the fucking dog."

Kobe growled but moved to nuzzle her neck and replace where Bastille had been. Nikolai still masturbated as he focused on the pink tips of her breasts with his mouth. His tongue and fangs brushed over her in such a teasing, light caress, she cried out for more.

Luna moved her hand over Sly's erection, squeezing it as he kissed the crook of her shoulder and rubbed her soaked flesh between her legs.

"You still think you should have called out and gone with the dragon instead of staying with us?" Bastille gripped her thighs and wrenched them wide open, for him to position himself against her.

"*Please*," she moaned. Another contraction of lust occurred, her stomach rippling once more, *needing*.

The new waft of pheromones from her invisibly puffed

over Bastille's face. His green eyes went serpentine as he blinked, the black pupils growing larger. His girthy cock somehow became harder and thicker as a result. The tip was a dusky red, slowly turning purple and slick with pent up need.

"Fuck," he bit out a curse and aligned his shaft to her weeping entrance. "You need me that much?"

Luna should have said she did not need him, not after how he had called her weak and acted like she was gum stuck to expensive shoes. But she was lost. Everything was hot and achy. *Need him.* "*Yes.*"

His cock was beautiful. Lined with two prominent veins and a bulky thickness that should have scared her. The little slit at the tip of him already leaked with his excitement.

He claims not to want me, but his body betrays him.

"Remember to be gentle," Nikolai murmured against Luna's nipple, the warm puff of breath making her push her chest up to his mouth for more.

"Don't fucking tell me what to do," Bastille growled back.

"Please, take me. Hard," she begged. "Need it hard."

"If I gave it to you hard, you'd break, little prey," Bastille replied unevenly, trying to concentrate on his self-control as he sank himself inside her. Her wet heat engulfed his length.

Brows drawn over wide eyes, Bastille let out a jagged exhale through separated lips. "Oh, *fuck.*"

Sly moved Luna's palm over his own cock faster, squeezing her fingers around the tip. "What does she feel like?"

"Tight, wet heaven." Bastille pushed in slowly. Too slowly. "The deeper I go, the more she—*ughh*—the more she pulses around me." A loud rumbling came from Bastille's chest. "Shit, Princess, are you coming already?"

Luna's body arched up, off the mattress as he fully seated himself inside her. Kobe had made her even slicker. Sly surprised her by slapping the top of her slit, the impact reverberating through her clit and setting her off again.

She came with a scream around Bastille's shaft. He gritted his teeth, holding back as she clamped down, her pussy milking him.

More pheromones.

More rhythmic convulsions.

More damn pheromones.

And his control was gone.

"FUCK." Bastille grabbed at her hips, pulling his dick out and turning her on the bed until she was on her knees, her back to him. He pulled her up until he thrust back inside her from behind.

In this new position, every one of his thrusts rubbed against her g-spot. She wailed in surprise and pleasure as he pounded in and out, hitting that special spot each time. Perfect precision. Perfect pace.

In this new position, Luna faced the three men with raging erections. Apparently, Kobe was already ready to go again. *So, this is what a prey being in heat does to them.* The men jerked off right in front of her, no embarrassment on their expressions. In fact, their brows were furrowed and their mouths were agape. They looked to be painfully on the edge.

Luna's gaze dropped to Sly's cock. *So full.* The tip glistened with pre-cum. *Want to lick it.*

"Shit, she's looking at my dick like she wants to suck it," Sly groaned, jacking himself off faster now. That hand hypnotically smoothed over the length of him. Each time his fingers ran over the sensitive tip, his thighs trembled.

"Take her mouth," Bastille commanded as he rammed inside her. "Claim her. She's fucking *ours*. Forever." Their skin slapped loudly, as he anchored his grip on her narrow waist. "Never letting you go." Slowly, he brushed a hand down her stomach, down, down, to the swollen hood of her throbbing clit.

It's almost too much. But still, it was not enough.

Sly cupped her jaw, moving forward on his knees on the bed, to settle his erection before her face. "Please?" he asked.

Maybe it was her prey "heat" instincts, but she wanted to devour the funny, cute fox shifter.

Want to watch him drop his humor and sarcasm.

Want to overrule him with mindless lust.

She opened her mouth and gave a long lick from the base of him to the tip, flicking around the head.

Sly snarled and dug his fingers into her silvery white hair, yanking her mouth onto his aching cock.

"Such a good little lamb," Bastille kept whispering dirty talk into her ear. Saying how good she felt, how he could feel her pussy gushing around him, how they were going to make her forget all about the dragon… "Suck him deep, Princess. I want his dick brushing against your tonsils as you moan for more."

Why were his words just turning her on even more?

She closed her lips around Sly's shaft and bobbed her head as Bastille continued his punishing thrusts from behind.

"Fuck, she's—*ohhh*, she's really good at that." Sly's hips twitched as he restrained himself from mindlessly fucking her mouth. Sweat slicked his chest as he fisted her hair and prayed for control. His stomach muscles tensed as she sucked him.

"She's just getting tighter and wetter," Bastille announced in awe. "You like being our little slut in heat? You like taking two of us, pet? How about more?"

Luna felt a finger dip between her ass cheeks to rub over her back entrance, that hidden rosebud. In surprise, her pussy seized Bastille's cock, gripping him so tight he paused his movements and groaned.

"So. Fucking. Tight." He punched forward with his hips, beginning a new pace that had her toes curling in the sheets. "Yeah, you like the idea of taking three of us at the same time, don't you? Don't you, you perfect—fucking —woman?"

He pressed then eased then pressed then eased a finger at her back entrance, teasing her with what could be. She had never felt dual sensations before, never been with more than one man. *That's about to change*. She wanted it. To be held by multiple strong men, to be protected and pleasured by them.

"You want to be filled to the brim with two cocks like a good girl?"

Sly howled when she hollowed her cheeks on a strong suck of his cock, tonguing him as well.

Someone cursed loudly. Nikolai. He was slipping down

a path of no return as his red eyes burned on Luna's bare, flushed flesh. She was hot everywhere, her blood pumping quickly and pinkening her creamy skin.

"Need *a taste*," Nikolai grated through his lengthening fangs.

"No," Sly said but was distracted by her pliant mouth. "She's too weak for you to bite her, man."

Nikolai slid closer, licking his lips. "*Thirsty.*"

"No," Sly reminded him.

Luna lashed the tip of Sly with her tongue.

"Fuck!" Sly bucked, his cock sliding deeper in her mouth, causing her to gag for a second.

Nikolai's red eyes blazed as he once more rasped, "*Need a taste.*"

"Nik, no."

"Sit back, vampire," Bastille commanded as his king.

The vampire shot forward.

In the last second, Nikolai grasped Sly instead of Luna. His long, pale fingers tangled in Sly's short reddish-gold locks as he tugged Sly's head to the side, baring his neck.

"Shit, man, don't do it—"

Nikolai sank his fangs into his fox shifter friend, biting hard on his neck and giving a loud *suck*.

"OH, FUCK," Sly shrieked, his head falling fully back and offering more of his neck to the vampire.

CHAPTER 30

*N*ikolai slurped noisily from Sly's neck, one hand wrapped in his hair, holding him like a puppet master and the other sinking down to play with his own erection. Nikolai firmly stroked himself as Sly carelessly bucked into Luna's mouth.

The fox shifter cursed, "*Shit, shit, shit, shitshitshit.*" His cock surged with semen, filling up until it was painful. The vampire gave another heavy pull from Sly's neck, and Sly shuddered from the unexpected pleasure. The blood high from the bite, the blowjob… Nothing had ever felt so good.

Luna bobbed her head faster, noisily slurping and teasing Sly until his eyes rolled back in his head. He shuddered, his stomach hollowing.

Nikolai snarled into Sly's neck, continuing to suck his lifeblood.

"Going…to come…a bucket's worth," Sly warned through heaving breaths. "Never felt like this—oh, fuck, oh *FUCK—Uhgnh!*"

Nikolai dragged Sly's back against his front, yanking his

cock from Luna's mouth. Sly came in endless, strong spurts, some splashing on the bed and others whipping up and clinging to his hard, muscled stomach.

But…

"How—How am I still fucking hard?" Sly could hardly breathe through the lust.

Nikolai still sipped at his neck. That was how. Vampire bites were known for sexual endorphins. Combine that with a prey's heat pheromones…

"Shit, I—I—" Sly could not form words as his cock slapped back up against his stomach, fully hard and *aching* like he had not just come a second ago. "Nikolai, you've got to stop. I can't—you've got—oh shit, *never fucking stop.*"

Nikolai needed to appease his prey. A grateful parasite, Nikolai moved his hand from his own shaft to wrap around and jerk Sly's length. The vampire's fingers were cool yet electric on him. The grip was perfect, possibly because Nikolai had grown up knowing exactly what felt good on his own cock. Easy to replicate on another man.

With incredibly fast vampiric speed, Nikolai vibrated his fingers over the tip and base of Sly's shaft.

"*Shit!*" Sly yelled to the rafters of the shack. His entire body trembled to come again.

Kobe maneuvered around them to kiss at Luna's chest and knead her breasts with his hot palms.

At the sight of the two men, her pheromones grew stronger.

.   .   .

*B*astille throbbed inside Luna, fighting off another orgasm as she moaned in ecstasy again.

Shit. He had pushed her over the sexual edge at least four times now, and her feverish heat was still not breaking.

Don't know how much more I can give. At the same time, he thought, *I will give her everything*.

As he continued to tease her back entrance with his finger and fuck her from behind, he whispered into her ear dirty praises and cooed to her about what a good girl she was, soaking his cock. All the plans he had for her… How badly he wanted to watch his cum dripping out of her.

"You think the dragon could give it to you like this?" Bastille grated. "He would be too scared to pull your hair or slap this perfect fucking ass."

He slammed a hand against the side of one of her ass cheeks and it shook before him. She moaned out and ground herself back against him, as if begging for another strike.

"And you *love* this. You like it rough," he said it in such an amazed and grateful voice that she squeezed him with her inner muscles, choking his dick inside her. "*Good girl*," he praised. "Squeeze my cock again, and I'll keep petting your needy little clit."

She cried out, moving against him. Luna was not simply taking her fucking but delivering it right back to Bastille.

She is a queen, he thought to himself.

Bastille's rod grew thicker inside of her, filling more and more for her. His mate.

221

Will never let the dragon have her.

Will ruin her for him.

He expertly twisted his hips, driving deeper, and she *quivered.*

Her legs shook so hard, he had to support all of her weight so she did not collapse.

Bastille thrust harder, pistoning between her legs. "Say you are ours."

She murmured unintelligible sounds.

Bastille pulled harshly on her hair, making her head shoot up. "Say you are ours. Forever."

All of the men stared at her now, wanting to hear those words.

Nikolai released Sly's neck, licking up the traces of blood. Sly came again, groaning out and slumping onto the bed in exhaustion.

"Say it, lamb. From the moment I come inside your perfect little pussy, I will never let you go. Say you are ours, and I'll let you come." Bastille removed his fingers from her clit, and she hissed. "Say it, and we will protect you. Pleasure you. Always."

"But, I—I am a prey."

"We are your predators," Kobe whispered tenderly as if his mate was not being fucking *railed* in front of him by his king.

Bastille drilled into her with each word. "You will be our pack's little lamb," Bastille said. "Now, say you're ours, and you will come harder than you ever have in your life." He licked the length of his finger and pressed it slowly inside her back entrance.

His finger rubbed against his cock inside her through a thin wall.

The double penetration had her shrieking.

Her vision blurred.

"Say you are ours, and next time, it won't just be a finger. It'll be Kobe's hard as fuck dick, with three of us filling you at the same time," Bastille promised, speaking and moving in a way that had her clit pulsing violently. "We will give your greedy pussy what it needs. Always. So, say it."

"I—I'm yours! *I'm yours!*"

She came. She came so hard, with Bastille's cock and fingers inside her, that her heat broke. Her pheromones waned in the air.

She screamed; Kobe leaned in and muffled the sound with a kiss. Her pussy clamped down hard around Bastille, who hissed and gave a loud, long groan as he pumped his release into her. Even as they came down from their orgasms, Bastille stayed inside her. He cradled her on the bed, cock still semi-hard.

All of the men cuddled up against her, each laying a hand on her flushed skin.

"How often do prey go into heat?" Sly joked.

Bastille's arms around her tightened.

☾

*W*hen Luna woke in the middle of the pile of alphas, she closed her eyes once more and gave a silent scream to the ceiling.

Dear. Gods,

What had happened?

She had never gone into heat before; it only happened to a prey who was exposed to predators for prolonged periods of time. She had no idea it would happen so quickly. She had no idea it would be so…

Even now, wetness trickled between her legs at the memory.

The way Kobe and Bastille had thrust so *deep*. The way Nikolai had bitten and masturbated Sly in front of her.

She would be having wet dreams for the rest of her existence, all starring the four men.

Bastille had promised to *share* her next time. To have three of the men fill her at once… What would it feel like to be so desired by all of them at once?

She needed to get out of there. Already, she fought off the instinct to cuddle deeper with the men, to sink into their hard chests, stroke their hair, and admire the curves and edges of their faces as they slumbered.

They helped her through the heat. For that, she was grateful.

But to stay around alpha predators who had originally kidnapped her off the streets? *Danger alert*. She needed out before she started to trust them, before she got attached. *Before they destroy me*. Rohan had taught her a very important lesson: predators did not belong with prey. They were two different genres. Two different species.

It would never work.

Alphas required someone obedient, quiet…and weak.

She never wanted to be weak again.

Every moment I spend with them, I grow weaker. She had developed a thick skin, a harsh work ethic, and an expectation for nothing above surviving. Grilled cheese sand-wiches and orgasms were luxuries she could not get used to. Because once the predators tired of her, she would be thrown out on her own again, with no protection but what she could provide herself.

The predators might want me now, but in a year? Two? In a week? Luna did not allow herself to assume the best-case scenario. *Prepare for the worst case, and you will BE PREPARED.*

She needed to escape, for real this time.

Slowly, she extracted herself from the pile and puzzle of male limbs. Each of them had somehow maintained at least one hand on her throughout their slumber. The second she left the bed, the four men shifted in their sleep. Bastille's mouth curved down as if his dream had suddenly turned dissatisfactory.

Already, they sensed her absence. How was she supposed to get away?

Throwing on Kobe's old shirt, she tied the ripped fabric together. She tiptoed to the only window the shack had and peered outside. *A motorcycle.* An old motorcycle, from the looks of it. If the engine ran, she had a chance at escaping the predators before they could get her.

New plan was made. *Time to execute it.*

She held her breath, praying not to make a sound and wake anyone up as she slowly opened wooden drawers in the kitchen area. One had to have either a key or possible supplies she needed to hot-wire and steal the motorcycle. All she really needed was a screwdriver and maybe a hammer. She had only ever hot-wired a car, not a motorcycle, but she believed she could do anything with the right motivation.

Creeeaaaakkk. One of the drawers made noise, and she bit her lip and glanced over her shoulder at the bed. The men laid still. She exhaled.

This "studio apartment set up" of the shack made a silent escape trickier.

Finally, she located a screwdriver.

So close.

She eased the front door open and closed. She continued to tread lightly on her feet—careful to avoid stepping on leaves or branches—until she reached the old motorcycle.

So close.

She quickly got to work at hotwiring the bike. Her small hands worked the screwdriver into the ignition barrel. Just unscrewing some things, connecting some wires, and she'd be out of there.

Once the motorcycle purred to life, she jumped up and down and did a happy dance. *I am that good.*

Now, she just had to ride it to the closest town and—

"What the *fuck* do you think you're doing?"

CHAPTER 31

"What the *fuck* do you think you're doing?" Bastille's voice pierced through the air, causing Luna to drop her screwdriver to the ground.

All four men now stood around the motorcycle, blocking her escape from all angles.

Nude.

Shit, she thought to herself. *Did the engine wake them? Did they see me do my humiliating happy dance?* She blushed but raised her chin with confidence. They did not know her. She could fool them.

"I was going to go grab some breakfast for us, in town somewhere," she replied, trying to keep her heart rate as even as possible. "We worked up an…appetite. I was going to bring food back." Wasn't that what predators thought of prey? Obedient servants. Lovesick weaklings. Predator groupies.

But fox shifters knew when someone lied.

She looked at Sly, waiting for him to reveal her fib to

the group. Instead, his gaze focused on the old, running motorcycle.

Sly's head tilted, his eyebrows furrowing. "Did you hot-wire that thing?"

Bastille scoffed. "How would she know how to…" He glanced at the screwdriver.

The basilisk appeared…*impressed?* Not that she cared.

"Hot-wire vehicles often, Fleece Machine?" Sly asked, his joking manner always in place, but real curiosity sparkled in his blue eyes.

"I do what I have to."

"And you think we're going to believe that you were planning to drive to the closest town to pick us up *breakfast,* wearing a shredded T-shirt?" Bastille questioned, his eyes narrowing. It seemed he had not forgotten her most recent escape attempt. Well, plural. *Attempts.*

Time to act like the perfect prey. Obedient, docile, giving, selfless, etc.

Dick whipped.

Luna blinked several times, trying to flutter her eyelashes. She also looked down instead of making direct eye contact—something most prey were known for as it was an act of submission. *If they are led to underestimate me, I will be able to get away from them sooner.*

She continued her lie, "I was, um, hungry after so much —well, um—I've never experienced such…"

"Fucking?" Bastille gracefully supplied.

"Y-Yes, sir," she replied, trying to sound like a smitten schoolgirl.

Bastille raised a dark eyebrow at *"sir."*

Was she laying it on too thick? Alpha predators tended

to be too self-centered to reject an ego-stroking. "I j-just thought it would be nice if I got us some breakfast. There was no food for me to try to make something for us here." *Ha*. Like she would ever waste her time making *them* something to eat.

"Why not wake us up to get you breakfast?" he asked, still suspicious.

"I thought it would be a nice surprise to, um, to reward you after all you did for me yesterday." *Oh, please*. Was it the best sex of her existence—past and future? Yes. But it was not as if *she* did not rock their world right back at them.

Funny how the second you let men gangbang you, they decide they would like to keep you.

Bastille still appeared suspicious, but Kobe moved forward to wrap his arms around her.

He smelled like *man*. Luna scolded herself for taking in several deep breaths of his alpha scent and relaxing into his embrace. "*Ma chekka*, you should never go out on your own," he said.

"I've been on my own for six years," she muttered bitterly, without thinking.

"Six years?" Nikolai frowned. "On your own since you were sixteen?"

The hair on the back of her neck stood up. "I don't remember telling you my age."

"I tasted you," Nikolai said. "Much like a talented sommelier, I can tell how aged my wine is."

"Gross."

"Effective."

Sly's stomach growled loudly.

229

Peering at her with curiosity, suspicion, and undisguised interest, Bastille said, "Breakfast, then. We will take our new pet out for breakfast."

☽

*S*ly drove the motorcycle to the closest town and returned with an expensive-looking black car to fit the five of them.

The men found flannel shirts and other miscellaneous male clothing to wear from the dresser inside the shack. Meanwhile, Luna had Kobe's dirt and sweat-covered shirt. When she gestured to herself, Kobe took off his borrowed clothes and offered them to her. The red flannel bagged on her, but she tied it to keep it from slipping off her shoulders. Kobe found a different pair of gray sweatpants and a black T-shirt to wear on their way into town.

Sly drove them to a local diner—the kind that always had "Mom" or "Pop" or "Pancakes" in the name.

Luna crossed her arms, wanting to feel annoyed that her escape plan had failed yet again, but this would be the first time in years that she ordered off an actual menu. That *she* was waited on and served. A little part of her could not help but vibrate with excitement.

I will escape from these men after *they buy me breakfast.*

Bastille continued to stare at her, shooting her looks of intrigue and suspicion. He was always trying to put her in some kind of box to better understand her. So far, he had always chosen the wrong box.

"Have anything you want," Kobe whispered into her ear, where he nuzzled his face into her neck.

The man was touchy. She wanted *not* to like it. Any other clingy man might have been annoying, but Kobe was like a sexy protective beast with the personality of a caveman and a friendly golden retriever.

Upon looking at the lengthy menu, nearly every item appealed to Luna. Why not overdo it before heading home to packets of expired gum and microwavable noodles? Her evil grin flashed so quickly, Bastille almost missed it.

His green eyes narrowed on her again from across the small table.

"Hi, y'all." A buxom waitress stopped in front of their table. Upon seeing the stunningly attractive men, she swallowed her tongue and stuttered out, "Will you be having me? I—I mean, what will y'all be having?"

Luna waited, glancing at the men. Bastille waved for her to speak and said, "Little lambs order first."

Luna rolled her eyes but proceeded to list every vegetarian option on the menu. Stacks and stacks of pancakes and waffles and toast and hash browns.

Kobe, Nikolai, and Sly gaped at her as she kept listing item after item. Finally, she finished her long order with a "*Please.*"

Thinking she had just ordered for the entire table, the waitress began to walk away but Luna stopped her. "The guys still need to order."

"You can't possibly eat that much," Bastille commented.

"Maybe I'm famished from yesterday," she shot back, daring him with her eyes to challenge her.

"Two dicks in you at the same time and you need three orders of chocolate chip pancakes? What will three cocks do?"

The waitress choked.

The men ordered meat. Sausage, bacon, ham, chicken—basically anything meant for a carnivore.

Once the waitress walked away with a notepad full of entrees, Bastille remarked, "I didn't realize how pampered you're used to being, Princess. Were you trying to break our wallets with that lengthy list of orders, or do you simply never think about money and cost?"

Ha! She nearly laughed out loud. No one thought more about money and cost than her. Fluttering her eyelashes and feigning innocence, she said, "I guess I assumed since the dragon could afford a penthouse, you could at least buy me breakfast—"

The terrifying noise of a rattlesnake's tail came from Bastille. Anyone else with a familiarity for how deadly basilisk shifters were might have frozen in fear. She ignored him.

"We're just as rich as the dragon," Sly said after a sip of his ice water. "We just happen to prefer living modestly instead of obnoxiously. No castle for us."

Her eyes bugged. "Castle?"

"The family home. The Dragomir dragon line comes from old money. Lots and lots of gold."

Hmm.

"Where did you learn to hot-wire a motorcycle?" Sly asked her out of the blue.

She blinked again and deadpanned, "What? Like it's hard?"

Sly chuckled. Nikolai smirked. Bastille frowned—nothing new there. Kobe seemed distracted, playing with a piece of her hair and gazing at her adoringly.

"When you said you'd been on your own since sixteen, what did you mean?" Nikolai asked another question.

Uh-oh. Her rule of *"Tell no one anything"* came into play. She shrugged. "Doesn't every teenage girl feel alone?" *Bob and weave, baby.*

Nikolai nodded but pursed his lips.

The more she piqued their curiosity, the harder it would be to slip away.

When the food came, Luna elbowed the men and threatened to stab them with her fork if they took a bite from one of her many plates.

Bastille watched her carefully as he lazily bit from a strip of bacon. "You do not eat meat?" he asked.

"Might be something about being meat, myself."

"You've never had a rack of lamb? Out of curiosity?"

"Screw you." Luna flipped him off with her left hand as she shoveled hash browns into her mouth.

Dear Gods, they were delicious. She moaned lightly around her fork, licking it clean. Her tongue flicked out, scooping the potatoes reddened with ketchup. Another moan of taste bud heaven came from her.

The lush, lusty sound leaving her lips…

Nikolai gripped the edge of the table so hard, it cracked.

"Maybe try not to moan around us when you eat," Sly said.

"Why?" Luna feigned ignorance. "It's just so *good*," she moaned loudly, teasing the men as she fit a large bite of pancake into her mouth. The syrup she drenched it in dripped down her chin lewdly. "*Mmmmmm.*"

Kobe growled softly beside her, reaching between his legs to adjust his erection.

"That's a lot of syrup, lamb," Bastille said.

"Mmmm, it *gushes* in my mouth." Did that sound seductive? Luna had little experience in trying to be seductive. "See?" She drizzled more syrup onto her bite and made sure to have the sticky substance shine on her lips as she licked them.

Why was she teasing them? She was not sure. But it felt like defiance. It felt...fun. When was the last time she'd had fun?

A second after she sexily consumed the dripping pancake, Bastille reached across the table, clasped a hand around her neck, and pulled her so her torso leaned over the plates of food. He pinched her chin, lifting it up, before *licking* her jaw and lips of the syrup.

His hot, thick tongue swiped from the bottom of her chin to the seam of her mouth, lapping up the syrup and lapping up *her*.

She swallowed hard, her heartbeat stuttering—which of course the four alphas could hear. A pleased rumbling sound shook Bastille's chest as he finished his lick up with a hard, passionate kiss.

Luna had never been kissed like *this*.

His lips slammed to hers, claiming and possessing. Like he wanted to eat her, ruin her, and cherish her all at the same time.

The kiss sucked the air from her lungs.

It turned her stomach upside down.

Made her skin break out into over-sensitive goosebumps.

Abruptly, Bastille let her go and sat back down.

Try to appear indifferent, she told herself. She shrugged as though the kiss had not just left her horny as heck.

He saw right through her and smirked. "Utter sweetness," Bastille commented, whether on the syrup or her lips, she was not sure.

Clearing her throat, she glanced over and saw Nikolai also smirking at her. Confidence and smugness rolled off the sexy as hell men. Their expressions were very: "*How could she* not *want us?*"

Sassily, Luna asked the vampire, "How is your blood sausage? Taste better than Sly's neck?" With how taboo vampire bites were, she had basically asked, "*Do you prefer the taste of your sausage or Sly's cock?*"

Nikolai's jaw dropped.

Sly sucked in a loud breath.

And Kobe and Bastille burst into hearty laughter that felt so foreign yet so welcome against her ears.

Sly shook his head and pointed an accusatory finger at Luna. "That shit was not fucking funny."

"You liked it," Nikolai remarked.

"You bit me!"

"And you came. Twice."

This time, Luna joined in with the laughter. At the melodic sound of her surprising giggles, the men's smiles grew until everyone at the table grinned idiotically at each other.

Sly pointed at Luna, "You're one to talk, Ms. I-Don't-Eat-Meat-But-I-Suck-Cock-Like-A-Champion."

Luna's mouth gaped as she guffawed.

"She doesn't eat meat because she has ethical standards

—same reason she'll never fuck you, Sly," Bastille shot back.

"Damn," Nikolai snickered.

Sly chuckled, not taking any offense. In fact, the fox shifter seemed delighted to hear such a humorous dig from his typically cold king.

Luna rolled her eyes. "I don't eat meat because I relate to being seen as a commodity. Being seen as only good for what I can be used for. Hunted, slaughtered…" She blinked when she realized she had just shared a little too much information. Too much *realness*. She tried to laugh off her statement but when she glanced at the predators, they all wore serious, solemn expressions.

Bastille's fist clenched on the table beside his plate. He growled, "No one touches you or hurts you ever again."

Kobe nuzzled his face into the crook of her shoulder, laying a sweet kiss to her collarbone. "Protect," he grunted, promising all she had ever wanted with one word.

"We know what it is like to be hunted for what we are," Nikolai stated softly from across the table, staring at her with his intense red eyes.

Luna frowned at Nikolai's comment. *Prey* were the hunted ones. "But you're predators."

"You'll learn in our world that dark shifters tend to be the 'outsiders' *not* by choice," Bastille said. "Those of us who didn't lose their families—" Bastille's gaze flicked over to Kobe. "—were abandoned by them."

Kobe shifted closer to Luna in the booth, his large thigh warming the side of hers under the table. "Will never leave you," Kobe vowed to Luna.

"If you wish for us to eat less meat…" Bastille dragged a

finger over his fork and met her gaze, stunning her with those bright green irises. "I would be willing to try a…salad."

Shocked, Nikolai turned to gape at him.

"Wow, king of the Dark Ones willing to eat salad," Sly remarked. "Your pussy is magic, Luna."

In a smooth move, Bastille stabbed his fork into Sly's hand. Luna guffawed again, breaking into surprised giggles. *Gods, I am a sick person*, she mused to herself but cracked up at how innocently straight-faced Bastille was after just stabbing his friend.

"Aw, fuck," Sly cursed, pulling out the fork and rubbing the back of his hand as it healed up.

"Only *I* get to refer to her pussy as magic," Bastille rasped, gazing at her with enough heat and longing to make her fan herself.

For a moment, Luna realized she may like the predators —a little bit.

And they liked her.

And she *really* needed to leave them behind or life was about to become messy.

CHAPTER 32

"I've got to use the restroom," Luna said as they finished up breakfast.

The second she slipped away from the table and was out of hearing range, Nikolai said, "We're keeping her."

Kobe grunted in agreement.

Bastille replied, "We already planned on keeping her."

"No. I mean, we are keeping her for us—not due to some feud between you and the dragon," Nikolai said.

Bastille pressed his lips together in a thin line but nodded.

"When she hot-wired that bike…" Sly sighed. "I don't know if my dick has ever been that hard before."

Bastille rolled his eyes.

"I'm serious."

"She is…" Nikolai dragged a fang over his plush bottom lip. "Fascinating. Not at all what I expected for the mate of the kings."

Bastille nodded slowly. "She is not a typical prey."

"But she *is* a prey," Nikolai reminded him. "She's weak and prone to...*not* immortality."

"Prey are worse than humans in life expectancy," Sly added, causing Kobe to stiffen and scowl. "Humans are delicate, yeah. But prey are delicate and *hunted* because of how rare they are."

Through a mouthful of bacon, Kobe promised, "Will protect her."

"She'd be easier to protect if we made her less...prey."

"What are you suggesting?" Bastille asked.

"Nik's a vamp," Sly said. "He could turn her into a predator like us. She'd be stronger. More protected. Less—"

"Fragile?"

"Yeah."

Sly was not wrong. The men had immortality, but Luna? Nope.

But to turn her into a predator—to change her species—that was something drastic. She could end up hating them for changing her, even if they did it for her own protection.

"Shit, she could literally trip in the bathroom and crack her head open." Sly painted the scene. "She could be washing her hands and slip and just...die."

They all flinched.

At hearing Sly's morbid imagination, Kobe shot up from his seat—abandoning his food—and jogged to the women's restroom to check on her.

"Great job," Nikolai commented sarcastically as Kobe entered the women's bathroom to search for his mate.

"Now Kobe is going to give some little old lady a heart attack."

Then, came the sound of Kobe's roar.

The alphas staggered up from the table, shoving at each other as they rushed after him.

Upon entering the small women's restroom, they realized Luna was gone.

"She...left us." Bastille's throat hurt. "She ran?"

"Wait," Sly sniffed the air, but Kobe beat him to the punch.

The werewolf's eyes went black as he grated, "She was taken. By a wolf."

Bastille scented the last trace of her in the room, smelling her fear. "A dead fucking wolf."

☾

One second, Luna washed her hands at the sink. The next, a large, calloused hand fastened around her mouth, muffling her shocked scream.

In the bathroom mirror, she met the gaze of Rohan. Six years later, and he was still sinisterly handsome. A real Ted Bundy; sick and horrific. She wanted to curse at her younger self for falling for his act. *Should have been smarter. Should not have trusted him. Anyone.*

Rohan was nothing but a killer.

"Pretty little prey," he whispered into her ear, his teeth grazing her flesh and making her shiver with hatred and— she hated to admit it—fear. "I told you I would find you again."

After all of her running, all of her hard work, after

everything, Luna's hard shell broke in half. Her sass fell to the floor. Rohan finally had her, and he would kill her. His promises to filet her—to rip her limb from limb—still rang in her ears.

Hot tears streamed down her cheeks. *Still so weak. Still just a prey.*

This was it. She was going to die.

"I have plans for you," Rohan sneered before shoving a needle into her neck and injecting her with the contents.

Her vision went black.

$$\mathfrak{C}$$

A hard slap against her face woke her. She tasted blood as she blinked her drowsy eyes open. *Rohan.*

He got her.

Assess the situation. Rope chafed her stomach, holding her still. She was tied to a tree trunk in the middle of the woods. A pack of predator werewolves stood around her; at least twelve of them. Large, tall males.

There's no way I can outrun them this time. No escape. Only death.

But I don't want to die.

She wanted more breakfasts at diners and homemade grilled cheese sandwiches and laughter. She wanted to break more locks and hot-wire more motorcycles to see Bastille blink in amazement and wonder at her. She wanted fun and a normal life.

"You did a good job at hiding, little prey," Rohan taunted her. "But the second the king of the Light Ones sent out that description, you should've hightailed your ass to a different state."

I tried, she thought bitterly. The four predator men had been her downfall, just like she thought. When would they notice she was no longer at the diner? After Rohan played with her entrails?

Deep sigh. "If you're going to kill me, hurry up and get it over with," she said.

Rohan's eyebrows shot up at that. "Has little Luna grown a backbone?"

The sixteen-year-old girl he had known had only cared about boys and flavored lip-gloss. She had been meek and shy. When Rohan first showed interest in her, she thought she would finally know romantic love. No one had ever been so wrong about anything, ever.

He added, "I'm going to enjoy ripping that spine right out of you."

"Then, do it and stop fucking *talking* about it." She was done with the fear. It had surfaced when she first saw him, but she would not let him see any more of her tears. Six years changed her.

I'm stronger now. I've had to be.

No more running.

"We have a bit of a decision to make," Rohan said, sinking onto the ground before her and crossing his legs. His alluring predator scent leaked into her nose, and she tried to hold her breath. "My pack can kill you and triumph in eliminating the world of your weak fucking race. Or we can be paid an ungodly amount of money to sell you to a farm."

A farm. Luna remembered Bastille or Nikolai

mentioning it. Something about keeping shifters in their animal state and an obedience serum. *No, thank you.*

"Both options sound bad to me," she muttered. "How about letting me go and becoming a better person?" She burst into fake laughter at the thought of Rohan being kind. She laughed and laughed and laughed, until tears streamed down her face.

Rohan stood and stepped back, brows furrowed as he gazed at her like she was the crazed one. "You are different now."

"Wow, you should be working for NASA with that big ole brain of yours."

The hard palm of his hand collided with the side of her face again. This time, the impact caused her teeth to chatter.

"I think the little prey forgot her place in the food chain," Rohan joked to his pack. Several of the men hooted with excitement, hungry for blood. For pain. *Hers.*

Another hit. This time, an actual punch that would leave a black eye. *Perfect.*

"Maybe I'll beat you within an inch of your life and *then* sell you. After all, do you know how much of my time you wasted running from city to city for the past six years?"

He kicked her in the stomach, and the pain exploded through her. She bent forward, gasping for breath.

Her ribs ached. Burned. "Why?" she cried out. "Why me? Why did you choose me?" If she was going to die, she wanted to know. He had chosen her, manipulated her, and slaughtered her family and friends…

Rohan tsked and grabbed a handful of her white-blond hair. "Because you, little cattle shifter, have no idea how rare you are." To be called *cattle* was the worst insult to a prey shifter. To be equated to domesticated farm animals. "You may just be the last of your kind."

She spat at him.

Another hard slap.

"You used to be so...soft," he said. "It was almost too easy to get you to take me home. Remember how you spread your legs for me, Luna? Remember how I took your virginity under the stars?" He leaned in to whisper into her ear, "My favorite part was making you bleed all over my dick."

Luna glared at him, her blue eyes flashing with hellish retaliation. "You're going to bleed for hurting me."

"Aw, did someone forget that Duttur don't have claws?" Rohan snorted. "So helpless." He smirked and ran a hand over the crotch of his jeans. "Maybe you can help me decide what to do with you. After breathing in some of my alpha pheromones, I bet you'd be panting to suck this dick."

She snapped her teeth. "Go to Hell!"

Rohan stepped closer to her, beginning to unzip his pants.

"I am the *mate* of the shifter kings," she said, finally admitting it to herself. "If you dare touch me—"

His wide, strong hand slapped harshly across her face again. She tasted blood in her mouth. "I've never pitied the kings before. But being mated to a *prey?*" Rohan sneered. "Disgusting."

She pulled at the ropes tying her to the tree trunk.

"Our world will never accept someone like you as a

queen," Rohan added, chuckling with the other men. "Not unless you're covered in steak sauce."

More male laughter. It ate away at Luna's patience. Heat rose to her cheeks, her neck. *Rage.*

"Dude, Rohan fucked the kings' mate." Another chortled, seeming to just now realize it. *Dumb fucking wolf.* "Broke in that prey pussy—the basilisk should send you a 'thank you' card."

More laughter.

Then…

Shrieks of pain sounded around them. Male screams of horror. Several, *"Please, no! I have a family."* Then, gurgling sounds, as if the men choked on their own blood. Thuds as their bodies hit the ground.

Wide-eyed, Rohan was yanked away from her by the back of his neck.

Luna blinked, her mouth opening as she saw her four alphas covered in the blood of Rohan's pack.

Kobe stayed in wolf form, ripping one man to shreds.

Nikolai licked his fingers of the dark red blood from several of the bodies.

Sly leaned against a tree, crossing his arms and smirking at her. Blood coated his face, the red matching his hair.

They all wore the same expressions of: *"Yeah, I'm* that *good."*

Bastille held Rohan up by the neck until the wolf-shifter's feet no longer touched the ground. The basilisk acted like Rohan weighed ten pounds and not over two hundred pounds of pure muscle.

Bastille, the closest of the men to Luna, squinted at her,

scanning her for injuries. He noticed the red rim forming around her right eye, where Rohan had punched her. A murderous gleam overtook his green eyes as he looked back to focus on Rohan.

"What the fuck?" Rohan's gaze darted around the forest floor to where his pack bled out. "What the *fuck?*"

"You took something of ours," Sly replied.

Bastille shoved Rohan against a tree, still choking him with a single hand on his throat. "You hit her?"

At his words, Sly and Nikolai stopped smirking. They took several steps forward, recognizing her injuries. Kobe dropped the leg he'd been biting into and began growling a low, vicious growl at Rohan.

Glancing around at all of them, Rohan asked, "Who the fuck are you?"

Luna rolled her eyes. Of course, all had *heard* of the king of the Dark Ones, but no one knew what he looked like. That was part of the fear: never look at a basilisk shifter unless you are ready to die. Amused, she could have snorted to herself. Rohan had no idea who threatened him.

Bastille tightened his grip around Rohan's throat. "You did not answer my question. You—hit—her?"

Rohan glanced at Luna, who remained tied to a tree. Kobe moved to bite her bonds from her. The rope had no chance against his sharp wolf teeth.

"Yeah, I hit her," Rohan admitted with no remorse. "Look, whoever you are, you don't know what you've done. She was *my* prey. I've hunted her for six fucking *years—*"

"Please, keep talking," Nikolai dared him.

"I've *earned* her," Rohan declared through bared, sharp teeth.

Bastille spoke to Luna without separating eye contact with Rohan. "Lamb, what did he plan to do with you?"

She swallowed and looked down at her feet. It was embarrassing how he planned to chop her up and literally eat her, all because of her animal form.

Sly nudged her chin up as Nikolai stated, "You don't look down anymore, love."

She inhaled. "He planned to make me shift so he could —so he could roast me. And eat me—"

Sly's enraged gaze zeroed in on Rohan. "Fucker!"

"I would very much like to be the one who kills him," Nikolai said.

Kobe growled and circled where Bastille held Rohan.

"We aren't going to kill him," Bastille said.

The men revolted. Sly and Nikolai shouted over each other, "*The fuck we aren't!*"

Bastille's green eyes began to swirl into spirals as he used his hypnosis against Rohan.

The werewolf fell for it instantly.

Rohan's expression blanked; his eyes went glassy.

"You are going to do to yourself what you planned to do to her," the basilisk said. "That includes cutting yourself into pieces. I say you start with the legs and work your way up. Roast your feet first and enjoy the taste of them as you consume yourself—"

"No," Luna yelled.

The men turned to her with shocked expressions. "*No?*"

"I want this over with." *Finally.* "Quickly. No endless torture."

"But he deserves—"

"I want it over," Luna shouted, her emotional meltdown just beginning. She had gone from certain death by her hunter of six years to the deadly hands of her protectors.

"You'd take orders from cattle?" Rohan asked, incredulous.

Bastille ignored him, raking his gaze over Rohan like he needed to choose the best place to injure. Then, he noticed the fly was down on Rohan's jeans.

He flexed his jaw and slammed Rohan into the tree behind him so hard, the thick, old oak shook. "Why the fuck is his zipper down?" he asked Luna.

"He…He wanted to see if his alpha pheromones could make me…" She blushed deeply and looked down to the ground again. The implication was clear.

Kobe shot forward in his wolf form, the size of him causing Bastille to let go of Rohan's neck. In half a second, Kobe's jaw clamped down around Rohan's throat. The sound of bones popping and blood gushing still haunted Luna when she closed her eyes.

It haunted her because a part of her *liked* it.

As Kobe flossed his fangs with Rohan's body, Luna began to breathe again.

She didn't have to run anymore. How was she going to spend her life now that she didn't have to run anymore? She could get back her real identity, get a real job, have a real future…

For the first time in six years, she would not have to fear the dark or constantly look over her shoulder.

Free.

She was finally free.

CHAPTER 33

"*W*here is your family, lamb?" Bastille asked softly.

Luna continued to stare at Rohan's maimed body. "Dead. H-He killed them a long time ago."

"He said six years," Sly reminded everyone.

"You have been running from him for six years? All alone?" Bastille took a step closer to where she stood, frozen in place as she processed her hunter's gruesome death.

"Never stay in a place…longer than three months," she stated unevenly.

"Running since you were sixteen?" Nikolai repeated in a voice of disbelief. "Alone for six years?"

All of the men glanced at each other.

Bastille's cold heart hammered in his chest. *She's…just like me*, he thought to himself. Lonely, misunderstood, and a tragic past. Bastille's family had been hunted by the army of Light shifters. Basilisks were thought to be so dangerous, dragons had once killed any that could be found. Adults. Children.

The king of the Light Ones, Daxton's father, had been responsible for killing Bastille's mother. Bastille had been a young child at the time—only a year old—and Daxton's own mother had taken pity on the new orphan. She took him in and raised him, trying to convince everyone that she could teach the "evil" out of his natural species.

Funny thing about being raised around people who all assumed him to be naturally evil—it made him want to be.

He had grown up with Daxton, watching him get anything he ever wanted with the snap of his fingers. Yet, everyone there, in the palace the queen and king resided in, watched young Bastille with eerie unease, as if expecting him to strike. They called him "snake boy" behind the queen's back. They left dead rats in his room. No one ever met his gaze.

Luna had experienced prejudice from what species she was born as—no control of her own. She had lost her family. She had been alone.

Just like him.

At least Bastille had found Sly, Nikolai, and Kobe when he rose to power. He chose them—outcasts of their groups. Kobe had been abandoned by his pack as a child for "delayed development" of his inner wolf. Sly was a rare kind of fox shifter whose family was hunted. Nikolai was a vampire who hated his species and struggled not to hate himself. All of the men understood each other. They had become their own little family.

My lamb had no one. Bastille's hands clenched into fists at his side before he stretched out his fingers, flexing them.

He took another step closer to her. *She will never be alone again.*

From the second she had walked into Bastille on the street outside of the dragon's hotel, he would have never been able to let her go.

My mate. I have finally found you. Bastille's heart released a cooling sensation as his blood pumped anew. *She is mine.*

He stepped closer once more, her sweet scent caressing his nostrils as he breathed her in. The wind tussled her smooth white-blond hair, gleaming with a sheen of icy silver-blue, the color of moonstone. Her beauty made his heart ache.

Then, his mate burst into tears.

*L*una sobbed incoherently as she stared at Rohan's lifeless corpse.

He is finally gone. I am free. Free to live. To have anything I ever wanted.

Tears flooded her cheeks, and she could hardly breathe as her brain processed the drastic change in her life situation.

"Make it stop," Bastille grunted to someone, but she was hardly able to hear him over the violent sobs wracking her body.

"Why do you cry?" Nikolai muttered to her right, suddenly appearing beside her with his paranormal speed.

"No more tears." Bastille wiped some of the droplets of saltwater away from her face as he stood at her left. The two large male forms, on either side of her, cocooned her into a cage of heat, of comfort.

Kobe, still in wolf form, barked and yelped and whined at the sight of her tears.

She continued to shake with gut-wrenching sobs.

"Stop crying." Bastille lightly shook her shoulders, seeming utterly bewildered as to how to make her feel better. "You wish for more pancakes? We will get you more pancakes."

"I—It's done," she cried out through her tears.

"He is dead, lamb," Bastille said. "Do not cry. *Please*." The basilisk sounded pained—as if he felt sorrow multiplied at the sight of her tears. "You are safe."

"I—I'm finally free," she stuttered out through choppy breaths. The tears streaming down her cheeks began to drip away and dry.

"You have us now," Sly said.

Her palm warmed as Kobe nuzzled his wolf snout into it and licked her hand. A broken laugh slipped through the sobs. Until, suddenly, she could not stop laughing. Laughing and laughing—struggling to breathe.

The predators gaped at her.

"She is in shock," Nikolai informed them. "Her little brain is breaking," he said in a tender, not-condescending way. Like he worried her prey brain really could break. Like a normal mortal's might.

"So fragile," Bastille whispered, reaching up to stroke her hair, trying to calm her.

"Vulnerable," Nikolai said, meeting Bastille's gaze over Luna's head.

She did not notice as the men nodded at each other, seeming to telepathically agree on something.

"Little lamb, we are going to keep you, care for you,"

Bastille cooed to her, still petting her hair. "You will want for nothing. My mate."

Her laughter faded until she frowned and stared up at Bastille in confusion.

The basilisk was being…kind to her? Gentle with her. Might she dare say he was being *loving* to her?

"You will never know fear or vulnerability again." Bastille cupped her face. "You will no longer be a prey. We will make you strong, make you immortal."

Wait…what?

"Do it," Bastille said softly, looking over her shoulder.

"I'm sorry, but it's better than losing you," Nikolai whispered.

Suddenly, sharp vampire fangs pierced the side of Luna's neck.

She gasped, her eyes going wide as Nikolai drew in mouthful after mouthful of her blood. Quick gulps. Too quick? She struggled, wiggling in his grasp to escape him before the strength left her completely. Oh Gods, was he killing her? Her vision blurred as he sucked. Her body quivered and clenched when the bite released its pleasurable high—but it was different from last time. Instead of being overcome with lust, her mind went blank. She floated, feeling drugged. Was he taking too much blood?

Then, a bleeding wrist pressed to her open mouth.

She blinked through her confused haze, trying to make sense of what was happening.

She tried to fight him, but she was too weak.

Her body went limp in his arms.

And the world faded to black around her.

CHAPTER 34

"*Y*ou didn't have to turn her right then," Sly commented as he drove the men and a passed-out Luna to a hotel in the city to spend the night—considering the dragon had found their secret cabin in the woods.

The dragon's men would never expect dark shifters in the city. Werewolves hated being away from the woods; vampires hated the crowds; basilisks hated the people.

"We could have waited a bit before we decided to turn her into a vampire." Sly stressed, "Maybe, I don't know, *talked to her* about it."

"Rohan could have easily killed her before we got to her," Bastille said as he watched Luna slumber against his shoulder in the backseat of the car. "You said it yourself in the diner: she could have slipped in the bathroom and died. Prey are fragile. Predators are not. She is now immortal and safe."

"*Against her will*," Sly remarked. "I'm just saying, she had an extremely emotional day after her very first heat. She's not exactly going to be happy that we turned her without even talking to her first."

"We did it for her safety," Bastille replied.

"She will never have reason to be scared or vulnerable again," Nikolai added.

"Nik, you've always hated being a vampire," Sly said. "Don't you feel any bit of guilt for cursing her too?"

Nikolai remained silent.

"It was my decision." Bastille added, "Prey continue to be hunted. She is no longer prey—so, she will have no enemies."

Sly snorted. "Other than *vampire hunters.*"

"They won't touch her. We'll protect her."

An hour later, the men tucked Luna in under a heavy blanket and watched her sleep on the big, white hotel bed. Wanting to care for his mate and spoil her, Bastille had found the second-most expensive hotel in the city— knowing the dragon might stay in the most expensive one.

The fancy suite even had privacy doors between the grand bedroom and large living room. Plus, gold accents and fluffy rich-people pillows. Bastille smiled to himself. *Nothing but the best for her.*

Nikolai cursed after looking at his phone. "The dragon was spotted in the casino downstairs."

"In this hotel?"

"Spotted two minutes ago."

Sly cursed. "No one saw us bring her in here. He doesn't know she's here."

Bastille scowled at the wall.

"We need to leave her. Show our faces downstairs."

"Not leaving her," Kobe grunted.

Nikolai explained his thinking, "Conrad was at the cabin; he fought with Sly. He must have told Daxton he saw her, which means he thinks we have her. If we show up without her, he'll stop searching for us. We'll make him think she managed to escape us."

"We can't just leave her here alone," Sly shot back.

Nikolai shook his head. "She won't wake for several more hours. The vampire transition can sometimes take a full day; she might be asleep until tomorrow morning. She'll be fine here."

"Not. Leaving. Her," Kobe repeated.

Nikolai threw his hands up in the air in frustration. "We have to *all* show our faces, Kobe. Otherwise, he'll know one of us is guarding her and that we still have her. They'll never stop hunting us."

Sly chewed the inside of his cheek but seemed reluctantly agreeable to the plan. Kobe and Bastille both gazed at Luna's peaceful sleeping face, pained to leave her.

"It's the only way we throw off the dragon," Nikolai said. "He knows we have her. If we make him think we don't, he'll stop looking for us. If he keeps thinking we have his mate captive... Bas, it will start a war."

Bastille cracked a knuckle. His eyebrows furrowed, but he eventually nodded. "We show our faces for half an hour, maximum."

Nikolai nodded.

"If she wakes—"

"She won't," the vampire assured the others.

The king of the Dark Ones flashed one more look of longing at his mate before turning and grumbling, "Let's get this over with."

*L*una awoke slowly, blinking and rubbing her eyes. Everything was so...bright. And loud. She threw the blanket over her head, burrowing under it to hide from the invasive sunlight that streamed through the window.

Wait a minute... Where was she?

She poked her head over the blanket again, taking in her surroundings. A fancy bedroom? Was she in a hotel? Had the dragon captured her?

She could not imagine her predators in a place like this. *I used to clean places like this.* She jumped from the bed and hastily closed the window curtains, blocking out that annoyingly bright sun. Why did her eyes feel so sensitive?

Her throat was burning, her stomach growling. *Hungry. Need food.* She glanced around and found a menu. *Room service!*

She called in an order of fries, grilled cheese, a milkshake, and more fries. Waiting for the food to come, she left the bedroom and walked into the living room of the large suite. The men were not there.

She frowned. Where had they gone?

Bathroom was empty. Kitchen was empty. Closet was empty.

They had left her there. All by herself. Hours after she had been kidnapped by Rohan?

Goddamn men. She wanted to kill them. For some reason, her emotions ran on overdrive. Her hurt feelings simply transformed into betrayed rage. She remembered

Rohan's death, but everything after that was a total blur in her memory.

Why would they leave me by myself in a hotel room?

Had they abandoned her here?

All alone.

She wrapped her arms around herself and shivered, feeling so damn cold. Why was she so cold? She pulled the sheet from the bed to wrap it around her shoulders, but she pulled so hard, the expensive fabric ripped. She stared at it in disbelief. She was not strong enough to rip a bedsheet. What the heck was happening?

She must have stood there confused for a while because there was a knock at the door. Her room service order.

Mmmm. Food. I'm starving.

She had just eaten a large breakfast hours before but for some reason she just…craved.

Hopefully, the milkshake soothes the fire in my throat.

"Thank you," she told the worker with a smile as he wheeled in several silver platters.

Thump, thump.

She frowned at the sound. A low, rhythmic thrum.

"No problem, miss," the server replied. His smile stretched his attractive face, brightening a beautiful set of hazel eyes. "Can I get you anything else?"

"No, thank you, I—" She had begun chewing on a french fry only to choke and spit it out. "Oh Gods, gross." She wiped at her mouth.

The worker frowned. "Everything okay?"

"Yeah." She waved it off. "I'm sure it was just a bad fry or something. I'm fine." She nibbled on another, but it tasted like pure ash. Dust. She spat it out onto the napkin. Maybe a bad potato?

"Should I ask the chef to make a new batch?" the worker asked.

She shook her head. "No, that's okay. I'm sure the rest of it is good." She grabbed the milkshake and slurped down some of the thick, cold liquid. *So thirsty.* But the ice cream soured in her mouth. Why did everything taste so bad?

Thump, thump.

And what was that damn *sound*? She looked over at the TV—off.

Thump, thump.

"Um, do you hear that?" she asked the worker as he turned to leave.

"Hear what, ma'am?"

Thump, thump.

"That sound."

"I don't hear anything."

Thump, thump.

Was she going crazy? "It's low and it's like a...like a...heartbeat."

Her gaze fell to his neck. To his pulse point. Somehow, she could see the skin there pulse with the *thump, thump* of his blood.

Oh my Gods.

She swallowed in horror as the desire to bite into the man's neck overwhelmed her senses. What was happening?

She stood deep in the living room, the worker at the door—but, suddenly, she appeared right in front of him. He let out a sound of surprise at how fast she moved. *Like a blur.* Like a predator.

"I—I'm so thirsty," she moaned out in pain, her throat on fire.

Thump, thump, thump. The sound became irregular. *He is nervous. I am scaring him.*

She bit her lip, not knowing what to do or say. Trying to hold back the impulse to wrap her arms around his neck and sink her fangs into his neck—Oh gods, she had *fangs*!

Her tongue slid over them. Her mouth fell open in a gasp. They *throbbed* in her mouth.

Pain. So much pain. So. Thirsty.

"Ma'am?"

"I—I'm so sorry," she whispered before sinking her teeth into his neck.

CHAPTER 35

"WHERE IS SHE?" the dragon roared as he clamped a clawed hand over Bastille's throat.

"Fuck. You," Bastille growled back, squeezing his own hand around Daxton's meaty neck.

"I know you have her. Give her to me," Daxton demanded.

"*Had* her. She escaped us," Bastille replied.

"You *lie*," Daxton shot back. "All you snake shifters do is fucking lie."

They continued to choke each other.

Kobe, Nikolai, Sly, and Conrad—the dragon's right-hand man—all watched their kings fight. None too worried, as they had all witnessed this before.

"She is *my* mate," the dragon said.

"Mine too," Bastille gritted back.

More mutual choking.

"Look, clearly we don't have her anymore," Sly said,

breaking the dramatic silent tension. "Do you see her with us now? No. She's long gone."

"I don't believe you," Daxton growled.

"I don't care what you believe," Bastille said. "I could kill you where you stand."

"That threat gets old." Daxton tightened his grip, and Bastille coughed. "I know you have her. You are keeping her from me. And what of the prophecy? If the two kings cannot share their mate, *'they will lose her.'* You would risk that? Her life over your own stubbornness?"

Bastille gritted, "Fuck the prophecy."

Daxton sneered, "It must kill you to know she is technically mine. To know her soul isn't completely happy without my being near her."

"She seemed happy enough riding my cock during her heat."

Daxton froze. His nostrils flared. His eyes flashed to narrowed slits like that of a reptile. "Her heat?"

"Did you not know she was a prey? She went into heat from being around us." Bastille smirked. "We all got a taste of her."

"I WILL RIP YOUR HEAD FROM YOUR BODY."

"My king," Conrad interrupted, touching Daxton's shoulder. "Remember the prophecy. Sharing. Or you both lose her."

Daxton cursed before tossing Bastille away, both ending their choking grip on one another. "You do not know her whereabouts now?" he asked the Dark Ones.

"No," Bastille replied.

"And if you find her, will you contact me?"

"Absolutely I will not."

Daxton glared at the basilisk. "I do not understand how you act this way. You were raised as my brother," Daxton remarked, his voice dripping with anger and betrayal.

"I was *never* your brother."

"As much fun as it is to hash out the complicated past between the two of you," Sly said, "I would like to do some gambling in this casino. Are we dismissed?"

Bastille and Daxton glowered at each other.

"We're done here."

☾

*H*is *blood tastes...so...good.* Luna's body trembled with pleasure as she drank from the neck of the hotel worker who had brought her food. The second her fangs slid into him, his whole body went rigid; then, he released a loud, yearning moan.

Luna remembered how good, how pleasurable, it was to experience a vampire's bite, but to be the vampire? She was flooded with ecstasy.

Heat crashed over her with each sip she took from the man's neck. His blood was like rich, liquid chocolate. It flowed through her, warming her, scorching her. Her cheeks flushed from it. Her nipples hardened and tingled, begging to be caressed.

Feels so good. As she fed, the burning in her throat moved down to her aching slit. Something ignited inside of her—a raw, ancient need. Her stomach clenched and wetness trickled down her thigh. Her clitoris pulsated and swelled for touch.

Can't get enough of this.

And neither could the hotel worker.

"Shit," he hissed as he arched his neck up to her, trying to give her better access to his blood. His dress pants bulged at the crotch, his erection thickening more and more as she sucked his neck. "Fuck, that feels...feels...oh, *fuck*," he moaned, his hips rocking forward to grind against her as she stood in front of him.

There was a loud thumping sound as she pinned him to the wall of the fancy hotel room. Her fangs dug deeper into him, and he reacted as if she sucked on his cock.

"Oh God, *it's so good*," he groaned.

SO good, she agreed, slurping more and more of the hot liquid.

"Don't stop," he begged.

How could she? It felt too good, too addictive. Oh Gods, was she... Was she going to drink him dry? Was she going to kill this man?

Her mind blanked as he cupped her breasts and squeezed them in his wide palms. *Feels so fucking good.*

He swayed a bit, his knees weakening, until they both slid down to the floor where she sat up over his lap and continued to feed from him. He wouldn't stop moaning and thrusting up against her, right between her legs.

Yes. His warm blood flowed so freely into her mouth as she sucked and rolled her hips over him. Finding that perfect alignment, that perfect spot to grind and *grind* and GRIND against. *Yes, yes, yes!*

"*Fuck*, please fuck me," the man pleaded. "I—I need... *Oh, shit.*"

Desire overrode her brain as her hands moved down,

between them, to unbuckle his pants. Impatient, she rubbed a hand over his hard cock, trapped by the fabric.

"Yes," he cried out, his face red as he panted each breath. "I—I'm so, oh, so hard for you."

She hissed and impatiently ripped open his pants, using her new vampiric strength and freeing his cock. She shoved down the sweatpants Kobe had given her and gyrated her soaked, quivering pussy over him. His body shook under hers with anticipation of his shaft sinking into her tight, wet heat.

Just as she was about to ease herself down onto him, her hair was yanked back.

Her fangs were torn from the server's neck, a firm grip on the back of her own, as she was pulled to her feet. She blinked rapidly, surveying her attackers. The fresh blood pumped through her veins, making her jumpy and scattering her thoughts.

"What. The. Fuck," Bastille yelled into her face.

She bared her fangs at him and tried to fight his grip as she wiggled to fall back onto her victim and suck more of that delicious, addictive—

"Luna," one of the men shouted.

"I don't believe this." Nikolai cursed and tangled a hand in his dark hair. "She should have been asleep, in transition, for hours."

"How did this guy even get in our room?" Sly jerked the worker up by his collar.

All of the men's gazes fell to the server's bare cock, which was out in the open due to his ripped crotch—courtesy of Luna.

Kobe released the deadliest growl any of them had ever heard from the tender wolf.

"She—she would be experiencing mindless lust while feeding," Nikolai explained calmly, as if he expected the wrong statement might cause Kobe to snap and rip the server's head off for touching his mate.

Everyone stood, frozen.

"Did you fuck this man, lamb?" Bastille grated into her ear.

The longer he held her away from the blood, the more her mind began to clear.

But then, he shook her. "Did you fuck him?" he shouted.

"N-No!" But she had been about to. A second away from sinking onto his hard cock and riding it into the waves of ecstasy as she drank his blood.

She tasted someone's *blood*. Drank it.

She could have killed him.

Her stomach turned. Her face went white.

"Oh shit, she's just now realizing what she is."

Rage. Inhuman rage.

She screamed as she wrapped her hands around Bastille's neck, trying to choke him.

"Lamb!" Bastille held her farther from himself, her arms too short to reach him. "You attack your mate?"

"*Want to kill him*," Kobe growled from where he loomed over the bleeding male worker. Considering Kobe's massive height, he would loom over anyone.

"Kobe, she didn't mean to touch him. Drinking blood—"

The werewolf's lips stretched to flash threatening, sharp teeth. "He smells like her."

"Agreed. Let's kill him," Bastille said evenly.

Gaining back her clarity, Luna quickly threw out her arms to try to slap against Bastille. "No!"

"He touched you," the basilisk king said. "I want to snap his neck."

"I want to snap *your* neck," she shouted back at him.

His mouth fell open. "What did I do, lamb?"

"What did you do? WHAT did YOU DO?" she shrieked.

"Fuck, her emotions are heightened due to the change," Nikolai said.

"I HATE YOU."

CHAPTER 36

*B*astille's heart froze in his chest.

"I HATE YOU," his mate screamed at him.

I hate you. He could not breathe. *She hates me?*

In his shock, his grip loosened, and his mate sank to her knees on the floor, sobbing.

She cries again? Because of me? Witnessing his mate crying was like cutting his own heart out with nothing but uneven shards of broken glass.

Nikolai quickly threw the server out of the room and shut the door in his face, locking it.

Kobe's chest rumbled with broken, muffled howls as he watched his mate cry. Pained expressions claimed the faces of each of the men.

I hate you.

Bastille fell to his knees in front of her, clasping the sides of her arms and holding her close.

"Ma chekka," Kobe pleaded, his hand clawing at his chest, over his heart—which broke at seeing her so sad. "Please do not cry."

"How could you do this to me?" she cried, tears glistening on her round, flushed cheeks. "You—You made me a vampire?"

"Prey are delicate; they are hunted," Nikolai explained. "We made you strong. Immortal. A predator."

"You thought so low of me, you changed my *species*?" she wailed through heaving breaths and streaming tears.

"We did it to *protect* you," Bastille said.

"Will always protect you," Kobe repeated, placing his palm on the back of her head and petting her. "Please. No crying."

"Your emotions are heightened right now," Nikolai said softly. "Once you calm down, you'll understand that we had to—"

"Food tastes like ash," she cried out.

That made the men pause. "What?"

"Everything I e-eat tastes like dirt."

Nikolai's lips parted, guilt flashing over his expression. "Vampires don't need to eat food to survive. It will taste wrong to you—"

"I lived *six years* off of microwavable noodles and gum," she exclaimed. "I—I wanted to finally try everything and—and enjoy myself and—and everything tastes like ash!"

Kobe stroked her hair and released calming, purring noises at her ear. He gazed around at his friends in horror. Horror for what they had done to her.

"The sun is too b-bright," she cried.

Nikolai stepped forward. "You will be very sensitive to sunlight, but it will fade with time. Though, the first century, you might want to only go out at night."

No sun for the first century? Bastille had not realized

that. Still, as a vampire, now she was strong and sturdy. *Safer.* "You will adjust," he promised her.

"I don't want to *adjust.*" She shoved at him as she cried harder. "I was finally going to be free. I was finally going to live a normal life, one by my own choices—and you took that away from me. You have trapped me for an eternity!"

"Not 'trapped' you—"

"I hate you for this," she promised.

Kobe again let out a dog-like whimper of pain.

"Undo it," she begged, grabbing onto Bastille's hands. "Please, undo it!"

"I—I can't."

Nikolai stated, "There is no way to reverse vampirism, Luna." A solemn look painted over his face as he said, "Trust me."

Their mate sobbed so hard, her face grew splotchy and her eyelids swelled.

"We will show you there are good parts to being a predator—"

Louder cries.

"You will like how strong you are like this."

"I—I fed from that man."

Nikolai said, "New vampires are very hungry. We don't blame you."

"*You* don't blame *me?*" Anger took over. No more tears. Only anger. Seeing red, she tackled Bastille to the ground, forcing the king of the Dark Ones to his back. She shouted at him, "I will never stop trying to run from you."

His heartbroken expression nearly gave her pause. She had never seen something so raw and vulnerable from him.

Bastille whispered, "Do not say that, lamb."

"I am not a 'lamb' anymore! I am a parasite," she shouted.

Nikolai flinched, stumbling back at her word choice. *Parasite.*

"Alrighty now, Luna," Sly said slowly. "Let's not say something you'll regret later."

"*You* want *me* to spend *more time* thinking about the choices *I* make before *I* make them?"

"That was a lot of emphasis in one sentence," the fox shifter commented.

Bastille tried again, still pinned by her. "Once you calm down, you will see that this is best for you."

His words seemed to cause nothing but rage in her.

*S*he could kill him. She wanted to kill him. *This* was what she knew of predator men. They did what they wanted, to whoever they chose, without regret or remorse or compassion or thought for the consequences to their actions. They had changed her biology—her species—without her consent simply because they wanted to.

Rage unleashed.

Red tinted her vision as she bared her fangs at Bastille and bit viciously into his neck.

Pleasure.

If she thought that human blood had tasted good before, she now knew basilisk blood was even better. Like a cold, thick chocolate milkshake.

"Shit," Bastille hissed as she sucked from his neck.

She wanted to cause him pain. Real pain. She wanted…

She wanted…

Oh gods, he tasted so good. She moaned into the flavor.

She felt someone's hands move to her hips from behind her, trying to pull her away from him.

"No, don't touch her," Bastille commanded, the sound of a snake's rattle humming in his chest. "I did this to her. I will feed her."

The hands left Luna's body. Instead, they were replaced by Bastille palming the sides of her waist and holding her as she straddled him on the ground. Luna clutched his head and shoulder, nuzzling her face into the crook of his neck where she drained him of blood.

He tastes like perfection. Like pure lust.

"That's it," Bastille rasped into her ear. "Take your fill of me." She dragged a mouthful from him, swallowing hard. "Fuck, you're a thirsty little thing."

His cold blood caused a change in her, hotwiring her body to only feel capable of lust—albeit angry lust. Her bite had a similar effect on him it would seem, considering she felt his dick thicken where her stomach touched him. The hot feel of his length stirred something animalistic and wild in her.

"Mmm, you're experiencing bloodlust," Bastille said. "I'll admit, your bite is having a bit of an effect on me too."

A bit? She wanted him mindless! She sank her teeth into him harder, and the answering throb of her pussy was impossible to ignore.

His blood made her so wet for him. She couldn't stop thinking about his hard dick inside her while she drank. Deep thrusts into her as she sipped deeply from him.

"Mmm, my mate loves the taste of me." Bastille's chest

rumbled with approval. "I can smell your arousal, pet. Drinking from me turns you on."

Damn him! Her hips were already rocking just above his crotch. She wanted to drop herself flush against him and grind to an orgasm.

She gasped against his neck when his large palms lifted to cup her breasts. He squeezed them tight, sweeping a thumb across the hard pink tips until they tightened to pebbles for him. Electricity sparked and crackled in her nerve endings.

"Love these perfect tits," Bastille groaned out, his own hips jerking up, his cock seeking her heat, as he roughly palmed her breasts.

She drank harder, the long pulls making Bastille grunt and flex his hips once more.

"You were about to fuck that worker," he reminded her gruffly. "Why are you holding back from me?"

Because you did this to me. Because I hate you.

"Let the lust rule you, pet," Bastille purred. "I'll make you feel so good."

"*Mmmm*," she moaned as his hands left her breasts and trailed down her stomach.

He tugged on the back of her thighs, roughly spreading them and forming a cradle for himself until the hard length of his cock twitched against her slit through his pants. His hand trailed back between them, to cup her pussy.

"Let yourself take what you need from me," he whispered into her hair. "Did you know, the more pleasure you give your victim, the better his blood tastes?"

CHAPTER 37

*P*leasure *him*? She did not care to do that. But it would seem he cared to pleasure her.

One of his hands continued to knead her breast and pluck at her taut pink nipple, while the other pet her between her legs, fueling the fire of need burning inside her. His thumb moved in slow, teasing circles over her swollen clit, making her body tremble at the sensation.

"That's it. That's my girl," Bastille cooed to her as he expertly strummed her erotic pleasure points. "Melting for my touch. Such a good girl. You take your pleasure so well."

She breathed out a heady exhale over his neck as he pressed harder down onto her sensitive bundle of nerves.

"You're a predator now, pet," he told her. "Take. What. You. Want."

The dam of resistance broke.

An animalistic growl vibrated her lips as she sank her pussy over his cock, grinding to her heart's content. Humping him again and again. *Feels so good.*

"It would feel even better to put it inside you," he whispered.

She knew he was not hypnotizing her, but she was under his spell. Like he spoke directly to her thoughts. Because she could not stop thinking about riding his cock. Her pussy spasmed for him, begging to be filled.

"It would feel so good to have my cock stretching your tight little pussy. I bet you're drenched for me. Practically dripping. Fuck, I would fill you up so good. Rub right where you need me to."

Her breaths were ragged as she ground over him. The pressure on her clit drove her head into the clouds and her thoughts into sticky cotton candy fluff. The delicious taste of his blood made her body hotter and hotter. Tighter. So taut, like she needed to explode. She needed release.

Need to come.

"Doesn't your greedy little pussy want to come?" he teased. "Think about how good it would feel to drain me of my blood and my cum at the same time."

That did sound good. It made her sound powerful. Like she could rule this alpha king by his dick. *Take* from him whatever she wanted.

One of her hands drifted down to shove at the waistband of his pants. Fabric ripped, and she maneuvered his bare, thick cock against her aching slit.

"That's it," he said. "Feed it inside you."

Her grip tightened on the base of his dick—so rough, he grunted in pain.

"Don't be mean, pet," he warned, that rattling sound echoing in his chest again. "Be a good girl for me. Take my cock. You know how good it will feel."

With painstaking slowness, she lowered herself onto him, sinking his cockhead inside her first before taking the rest of him. Bastille released a loud breath as she eased down onto his length. He sunk to the very hilt of her, the hot inner muscles of her pussy pulsing around his cock.

His eyelids fluttered closed, his expression scrunching into one of pained pleasure. "Fuck, you feel so good," he rasped. "Perfection."

"You've got to be kidding me," Sly scoffed, frowning at the display. Luna had forgotten the other men were there. Nothing but Bastille's neck and cock mattered to her. "She's pissed at him. Yet, *he* gets to fuck her?"

"Life isn't fair," Bastille shot back, before grabbing Luna's hips, lifting her a few inches, and bringing her down, hard, on his long, stiff cock.

She moaned loudly onto his neck, her fangs detaching from his skin for a second as her core adjusted to being filled so completely, stretching to his size.

"Fuck," Bastille cursed as he pulled her hips up and down, fucking her even though he was the one beneath her.

He controlled her movements, bouncing her on his hard length, pushing himself to reach the deepest parts of her. His thrusts were violent and feverish. Claiming. Harsh. Hot. Wicked. They sped up with each thrust.

Her mouth was agape as he rammed inside her again and again until his speed made her mind go blank. Her toes curled. Her muscles tightened and coiled with tension more with each passing second. His thrusts pushed her toward an orgasm she was not ready for. As a vampire, everything felt heightened. More intense. Too intense?

His hands felt everywhere, all at once. His palm slid over her ass; her breasts rubbed against his chest with every rocking motion. Her hard nipples scraped against the toned muscles of his chest.

Ripples of deep erotic pleasure ran through her, sizzling her veins with scorching heat.

He withdrew until just the tip of his cock stayed inside her, before pumping back in. His fingers sank into the flesh of her ass as the slick sounds of their bodies slapping against each other filled the room.

"Taking me so well," Bastille told her. "Such a good girl riding my cock. You're not mad at me anymore, are you, Princess?"

His question reminded her of what he had done. What he had made her.

She grabbed his hair and yanked it painfully until he hissed. Biting down hard, she pierced his neck once more, drinking from him.

Oh Gods. He had been right. Causing him pleasure while consuming his blood made him taste even better. The sweet, spiced flavor made her moan once more as she slammed her hips down on him, impaling herself fully on his hot length. In a frenzied anger, she scratched and clawed at his arms and the backs of his shoulders.

It was hate sex. Hot, hot hate sex.

Her back arched after he slapped her ass. His dick jerked inside her, and she felt herself on the verge of coming.

His strong arms wrapped around her, pinning her to his chest as he thrust up repeatedly into her heat. Then, he wrenched her face back by her hair, pulling her fangs

277

from his flesh so he could look at her face as he fucked her.

She bared her teeth at him, growling, and he smashed his mouth to hers. Her fangs nicked his bottom lip, and the kiss tasted of luscious blood.

Their lips tangled and battled.

Heat. Fire. Passion.

He mouthed "*mine*" onto her lips.

He tilted their bodies so his shaft entered her at a different angle. *Yes*. She jerked in his arms at the change in intense sensation. Her inner walls fluttered around his cock, telling him how close she was.

"That's it, come for me," he whispered.

She offered him a breathy curse, digging her nails into his forearms. "Screw you."

"You feel it too, don't you?" he asked. "The way we fit each other. Like we were made for each other."

She growled at him, a slave to her body as she rose up and down on his length.

"Because we were made for each other. You are my mate, and watching you ride my cock is one of the happiest moments of my long existence. I will always protect you, even if it means doing something you don't like."

"Fuck. You." She rode him harder. "I'm a person. Not a possession you can choose what to do with. Not a pet."

"You were a *delicate* person, and now you are strong. Immortal." Bastille clamped a hand around her throat, tilting her head so he could gaze upon her. "Look at your little fangs." He cursed, driving inside her more forcefully. "Sexy as fuck. Want to see them pierced into the side of my dick."

"I'd bite it off," she threatened.

"We both know you wouldn't." He smirked.

Damn him! Hate him! He feels so good.

Her pussy began to contract around him as something electric shot down her spine. Wave after wave of heat crashed through her. She screamed as she came, tight spasms wracking her. Her pussy convulsed around him, so tight it pushed him over the edge.

His lips parted on an abrupt exhale of breath. His stomach tightened, and his legs shook right before he threw his head back and drove himself so deep inside her, she felt every hot spurt of his seed.

Their breathing was a ragged mess for several minutes as they held each other close, their orgasms seeming to go on and on. She was too spent to remember to punch him or pull out of his embrace.

"Well, are you two done now?" someone asked, but Luna's eyes had slid shut.

"Sleep," Bastille whispered as he stroked a hand over her silver-white hair. "You did well for your first feed, my little mate."

"Hate…you."

"Do *not* say that."

"Will never…stop hating you." *Exhausted*. Dots of black claimed her vision.

CHAPTER 38

*D*axton glared up at the moon from his hotel balcony. *I know Bastille has her. I know it.* He cursed, his fists clenching on the railings standing between him and a long fall—though a dragon shifter had no worries of falling, since he could fly.

The past few days had been spent searching for her. He still remembered her sweet smell. Her sweet *taste* on his tongue. He had not been looking for a mate, but he had found his. Now, his heart panged at the lack of her presence beside him.

Maybe he should have been thinking about his kingdom and the pending war with the Dark Ones— always a war between the sun and moon predators—but all he seemed capable of reflecting on was the way her hair shone like moonlight. The way her sapphire eyes were treasures to him.

I hardly know her; yet, my soul recognizes her. I hardly know her, but she owns me. Was that what it was like for Bastille as well?

Daxton cursed again. How was he supposed to share her with the basilisk? Dragons were possessive, jealous creatures. *I would much enjoy spit-roasting him.*

He stared out at the other balcony rooms across from him. Gods, he could basically *see* her in his mind. Pale hair and skin. Glaring at the moon like someone had wronged her. Wait—that was her.

His eyes narrowed on the balcony room several floors below him on the other side of the massive hotel. *No other female has hair like hers.* Like moonstone.

His wings shot out from his back. As king, he was capable of partial shifts, meaning he could breathe fire or—when it suited him—fly while still in human form. *It suits me now.*

Flying across the stretch to where she stood alone on the balcony, the dragon swooped down. She was muttering angrily to herself and pacing back and forth. He pressed a hand over her mouth and gathered her in his arms as she flailed. Holding her, he flew right back to his room near the very top of the wide building.

She struggled, wiggling in his arms, but went completely still when he lowered them back to solid ground. His wings flexed and wrapped around them where they stood. The red scales provided a sort of sound-proofed barrier, hiding them from the outside world.

"D-Dragon?" she questioned.

"Little mate," he whispered, worrying this was a dream as he smiled down at her. "My name is Daxton."

He paused when he saw a flash of white in her mouth. Brows furrowing in curiosity, he gently pinched her chin and guided her face up to peer at her. He swiped a thumb over her bottom lip, peeling the lush, pink flesh back. Fangs. His little mate had fangs, which she had not had before.

Reeling, he asked breathlessly, "What did they do to you?" Pain speared his chest as her eyes watered.

Through unspent tears, she sputtered, "T-They turned me into a v-vampire."

"Against your will?"

"I—I was a Duttur prey and t-they—"

They had turned his mate into a Dark One—his opposition, the despised breed of immortals. Ones ruled by the moon and with a penchant for pain and evil. *They* altered *my mate*.

A loud, threatening rumble shook the dragon's chest. "I will slaughter them."

That caused his mate to cry. Silent tears fell down the smooth skin of her round cheeks.

"Ask me to kill them, and I will," he said, holding her tightly in his big arms, his wings still encompassing them both. "I will do anything for you. Anything you ask."

"I d-didn't ask for any of this," she replied.

"I could find a witch. Turn you back."

She blinked twice, peering up at him with wide, beautiful blue eyes. "What?"

"Witches are allies of the Light Ones. There could be a spell to reverse your…turning. Would you want that?"

"Yes!" She wrapped her arms around him now, holding him so close, he felt there was nothing in this world that could separate them. "Yes, yes, please. Truly? Please."

He kissed the side of her head, pressing his lips to her hair, her forehead, anything he could reach from his dominating height. "You are mine now, little one," he promised her. "I will keep you safe. They will never take you from me again."

*I*ncredulous, Conrad, Daxton's confidante, asked him, "You found her?"

Conrad's king grinned from ear to ear as he smugly informed his most trusted advisor that his mate was showering in the master bathroom of his hotel suite. "She told them she needed air and was standing on an outside balcony. I flew right down and picked her up."

"But they had her?" Conrad asked. "Even after they denied it in the casino?"

"Dark Ones lie as much as they breathe," Daxton shot back. Then he winced.

His mate was now a Dark One. A vampire. *Not for long.* She wanted to be turned back, and he would accomplish such for her. *Anything for her.*

Daxton stated, "We must return home as soon as possible. Call for the best witches around—we need a spell."

"They really turned her into a vampire?" Conrad shook his head, his lips curling back in an expression of utter disgust. "Monsters."

"She will be turned back to her original form; I know it."

"But could you love her if she stayed a vampire?" Conrad questioned.

Daxton's eyes flashed black. "She is my *mate.* I would accept her as any species."

"Even as a wendigo?" A sort of cannibal zombie—the thing of nightmares.

"I suppose she would devour me because I would not fight her off."

Conrad blew out a harsh breath. "So, the matehood thing is…a thing."

"I can hardly describe it. The pull to protect and touch her. To see her smile."

"The light shifters will not…" Conrad pursed his lips and sighed. "There may be conflict in making a vampire our Queen."

"Don't care," Daxton said, striding over to where his laptop sat on the living room table of the vast hotel suite. He sank onto the couch and opened the device.

"What are you doing now?"

"I wish to buy my mate clothes while she showers." He wanted to absolutely spoil her. Woo her. Win her.

"What happens when the Dark Ones realize she is missing?"

Continuing to online shop and ignore him, Daxton asked, "Would Luna look better in pink lace or red lace?"

"Daxton," Conrad said.

"Let them try to take her from me again." Daxton closed his laptop. A dark threat rang clear in his low voice. "I dare them."

☾

*L*una scanned the large bedroom, taking in her surroundings. *From one prison to another?* Just because these men thought she was their mate did not mean they were hers. Just when she had started to like them, Bastille, Sly, Nikolai, and even Kobe had betrayed her by changing her into a vampire.

But the dragon says he can turn me back. Thus, she was not looking to escape from him. She would stay with him for self-preservation.

Just self-preservation? She rolled her eyes at herself. Daxton was a large, imposing man—strong, handsome, and seeming to be ruled by his morals, unlike Bastille.

Had any man ever been as handsome as Daxton?

Perfectly slicked back dark hair. A striking angular face; features tall and prominent. The sharp rise of his cheekbones cast shadows. Tall and broad shoulders and bow-shaped lips. Daxton looked regal, like a rugged king.

He is a king, Luna.

She couldn't deny feeling a pull toward him. The last time they had seen each other was when he licked between her legs, urging her toward orgasm, while stroking himself. The memory of it made her nipples tighten and her skin flush with heat.

She had never forgotten his dirty rasps of *"Touch yourself for me"* and *"Ride my lips and tongue. It is time for my taste, little one."*

She could not help feeling a fierce attraction toward the dragon. *Am I a total slut for being attracted to so many men?*

Upon thinking the word *"slut"* in her head, her mind shot back to how Bastille had touched her in front of the other men. *"Does our little slut need to be fucked?" "Your drenched little pussy is soaking my hand, Princess." "I think maybe you do like the word 'slut.'"*

Maybe it was the newfound vampirism or how she had

experienced her heat for the first time just a day or so ago, but her body was constantly on the cusp of arousal. Of horniness. *Need.*

Calm yourself.

Stepping from the bathroom and into the closed-off master bedroom, she wore a fluffy white robe that Daxton put out for her. He, apparently, did not wish for her to put on *"another man's clothing."* She was not complaining. The robe was so soft, it reminded her of a luxurious spa day— something she had never had the chance to enjoy.

Rohan is dead and gone. I can do what I want. Other than eating and enjoying food—not blood. Her heart deflated.

"Why does my mate frown?" Daxton's low, velvety voice came from the doorway as he stepped into the large bedroom and closed the door behind him.

"Just thinking about how my entire life has changed so quickly over only a few days." *And how horny I am now, and how much I will miss pancakes.*

He walked over, cautiously approaching her as if not to scare her, and sat on the end of the bed. He patted the open spot beside him for her to sit. "Tell me."

"Tell you what?" This was a different way of getting information from her—far from Bastille's roar, threats, and hypnosis. Who knew simply *asking* could get results? "You want to hear about my life?" she asked in disbelief.

"Your life, your feelings." Daxton's lips curled into a heartfelt smile as she joined him in sitting on the bed. "Your hopes and dreams. I wish to know everything about you."

"Hopes and dreams?" she repeated softly, looking down at her feet as her cheeks warmed. Survival had been her only goal for six years. She had never allowed herself to have hopes or hobbies. "I—I used to like painting?"

His brows shot up, and his excited smile widened. "Painting?"

"One year, for my birthday, I begged my mom for a paint set." For the first time in so long, Luna relaxed beside someone and talked about herself. Something about the dragon made her feel safe. *Or maybe this is just what it's like to be a predator around another predator who does not throw threats and insults at me.* "Actually, I begged for one every year, but she stopped getting them for me because I started painting the walls of the cabin."

Daxton chuckled, and her chest grew warmer at the magical, melodic sound of it. "I'm sure you improved those walls, little one."

Her blush deepened. "I like to think so."

"Tell me more. Please."

"I—I went to an all-girls school for prey shifters. Most of the classes were on how to hide, cook, sew, and de-escalate conflict. I hated it," she admitted. "But there was this music class where I learned how to play a harp. I liked that." Gods, did she sound totally pathetic?

"An artist and a musician?"

Daxton's hand enveloped hers on the mattress, and the touch of his skin elicited sparks that raced through her bloodstream, making her heart skip and her stomach flip and her thoughts rhyme like stupid lovesick poetry.

"How did I get so lucky?" he whispered, seeming awed by her. His beautiful golden eyes burned with both longing and satisfaction as he gazed upon her.

She rolled her eyes at his kind, flirtatious comment, but a soft grin claimed her face as she glanced away.

"You do not believe me?" he asked, touching her chin and moving her gaze to meet his once more.

"You ask me about hopes and dreams, and all I can come up with is that I liked to paint and play the harp when I was in school." She bit the inside of her cheek and again tried to break eye contact. "Not very impressive."

He shifted closer, his scent of firewood and musky vanilla overwhelming her new vampire senses. *Roasted marshmallows and pine.* "Do you know what being a dragon's mate means?" he asked. "You could read the nutrition facts label off a heart-healthy cereal box, and I would listen with rapt attention. Everything you have to say is important to me. I want to know everything about you. I want to hear you play a harp. I want you to paint the walls of our home."

More blushing. Gods, how did his mere presence turn her into some kind of blushing, shy schoolgirl? *This is what it feels like to be treated kindly by an unbelievably attractive man who thinks I'm his mate.*

She thought back to Bastille's cruelty. He would *hate* that she spent time with the dragon. *Hmph, good.*

"In fact…" His grin was devilish yet still good-natured —like he planned to let her in on every secret he'd ever been told. Like they were best friends. "I have an idea."

CHAPTER 39

She was *laughing*. Luna. The woman who only knew about survival and escape and mourning and living paycheck to paycheck. She was laughing. More accurately, she could not stop laughing.

The dragon had called the hotel's room service. Twenty minutes later, a set of paints—a hundred colors—arrived at the door of the suite.

Daxton had grinned mischievously at her and said, "Let's improve this hotel's walls."

And they painted together. He turned on music with tempos and beats that were impossible *not* to dance to, and the two of them swayed around the suite, holding random-sized paintbrushes and colored the walls. Daxton described his art as "abstract" as he flicked paint against the wall.

Meanwhile, Luna expertly painted the rare lilac flowers that used to grow by her home. She painted birds flying freely in a perfect sky. She painted a herd of sheep on a hill, giving one of the animals her mother's eyes.

"It looks so real," Daxton would not stop complimenting her. Her cheeks were a constant pink. "You are a true talent." He grinned and wrapped an arm lightly around her waist. "My mate will be a famous artist one day."

She pointed to his *"masterpiece"* of paint specks and replied sassily, "One of us has to be."

His face lit up at her playful joke. He grabbed her and yanked her against him. She squealed with laughter as he pretended to nip at her chin and neck. She took her time with pushing him away.

"You know, most people know to tell a King that he is great at everything," he remarked.

"I won't lie to stroke your ego," she shot back.

He grinned fiercely at her. "Finally, someone to keep me humble. My mother will love you."

"Even though I am not a dragon?" she asked. *Or a Light One shifter?*

He tapped a finger to his chin, as he leisurely ran his gaze over her body. "I know," he suggested before shooting forward to drag a wet paintbrush over her neck. "We will paint dragon scales on you." He left a dash of red paint over her throat and stepped back to admire his work. "She will never know."

Luna snorted and shoved at him, rubbing her own wet paintbrush over the side of his face.

Daxton feigned a gasp and drew his paintbrush over the back of her hand.

She painted his muscular forearm and darted away.

They went back and forth like this, painting each other in random spots uncovered by clothing. Eventually, they moved to painting each other's clothing as well. The laughter pouring from both of them just made them laugh harder, with absolute abandon.

A sore loser, Luna tackled Daxton to the ground—something he allowed her to do considering he could have simply caught her weight. She pinned him to the floor and grabbed a full jar of yellow paint.

"Don't do it—" he started but cut off when she turned the jar and splashed thick globs of colorful non-machine-washable goop onto his chest. She expected annoyance or anger from him; instead, his chest rose and fell with laughter.

Covered in paint, he grinned at her with pure amusement and...something else in those sparkling golden eyes. A tenderness and fondness she was not familiar with. Pure adoration.

He appeared utterly smitten with her.

And for some reason, his warmth made her squirm from her position on top of him on the floor. The same position she'd had Bastille in while she fed from his neck.

Hesitantly and moving on pure instinct, Luna rubbed her palms over his chest, smoothing in the globs of paint and admiring the way the dampness made his shirt cling to the ridges and dips of his abs. *That is a strong core*, she thought to herself, blushing again, as she palmed his muscles, covering them in yellow.

"Does my mate wish to paint me?" Daxton purred.

She swallowed, still rubbing the wet shirt over his firm pecs. Maybe she didn't have to feel guilty about her attraction to him. *Bastille would hate this*. But Daxton was nice.

And sexy. And she wanted him. *And he didn't turn me into a vampire.*

While gazing up at him from under her eyelashes, she asked, "And if I do?"

He nearly ripped his shirt off.

*H*er arousal spiced the air, but Daxton reminded himself that he must be patient. The first time he had met his mate, he had thought she was a paid escort. They had fallen into a tangle of lust. Now, he was finally getting to know her and learn her—he did not want to ruin anything.

But, fuck, he was hard.

Her laughter and obvious talent with a paintbrush had aroused him to no end. When he first saw the detail she had put in the vignettes she painted, he had proudly thought to himself, *That right there is my fucking mate.*

So, when she tackled him—which he also found strangely hot, just like everything else she did—and began massaging his chest through his shirt, his cock became hard as stone. Solid as diamond. And when his mate implied she wanted to paint his bare body?

Fuck, I could come just from her naughty little smile.

Her tongue dabbed out to lick her lush lips as she stared down at his bare chest. Once the dirtied shirt was removed, she perused his abs and arms with patient admiration. She picked up her paintbrush and wet it in one of the open jars. She chose red, his favorite color.

Daxton shifted under her, trying to hold back his instinct to lift her by her hips, turn them over, and dominate her. He had to fight his instinct to carry her to the bed, spread her legs, and pound inside her tight pussy until she screamed his name…

She dragged the wet brush down his pec to circle around one of his nipples. He groaned at the teasing sensation, hissing at the cold temperature of the paint.

"You are…very strong," she said through a loud swallow —a gulp. Of nervousness? Or arousal? Daxton wanted to know.

"You like my muscles, little one?" He flexed, trying to be as nonchalant about it as possible. *I want her to desire me as I do her.*

"They're…nice." Her cheeks were as red as Daxton's dragon scales.

"My body is yours to explore and enjoy. Only yours," he replied.

She bit back a small smile and flicked paint over his eight-pack abs. She scooted back, plopping her round ass onto his knees as she made room to lean over him and paint more of his upper body.

However, from her new position, she now had a front row seat to the way his growing erection bulged the expensive fabric of his black dress pants. The lump continued to swell the more she stared at it. *Can feel her gaze on me. Like a real caress.* Daxton just barely kept his hips from rocking forward.

As she studied him, she swallowed audibly again, and he masked his amused smile.

"You're…big," she commented in a voice just above a whisper.

"Assuming you are referring to my massive cock."

293

She blinked, glancing away from it before settling her gaze right back on his full crotch like she just couldn't help herself. "Um, yes."

"Dragon shifters are extremely well-endowed," he explained.

She bit her lip and rubbed a hand over his firm pecs, spreading paint. Her touch made his cock ache and swell bigger behind the bulge of his pants. His blood heated in his veins at the feel of her.

She trailed that warm palm down, down, to the waistband of his pants.

"Luna!" Daxton's hips bucked up, jostling her from her seat on his knees. "Do not tease me, mate."

She lightly petted the top button on his pants. *Is my mate a professional seductress?* The answer had to be yes because she replied, "You said you would give me anything I want."

He released a little *"puh"* sound of air in his surprise. "You wish for my cock?"

She squirmed on his knees, and her arousal spiked the air once more. *Gods, the scent of her!* It could drive a dragon mad.

"I heard a rumor," he said softly. "That new vampires are particularly—" He paused, searching for the right word. "—*needy.*"

"Needy?"

"Tell me, little one." His large hands moved up the sides of her thighs, up to cup her hips, as he spoke. "Are your nipples tight? Breasts heavy?" He hummed, "Is your clit throbbing for touch?"

She gasped, her mouth falling open at his words. She

squirmed again, clenching her thighs together, but his big body between her legs stopped her. In an act of desperation, she lightly grinded herself against his leg, seeking out pressure.

His chest inflated with pride. *My mate likes my dirty mouth.* "I think my vampire is wet for me," Daxton rasped.

Her front teeth sank into her bottom lip, and he saw the flash of fangs.

He grabbed her waist and hoisted her forward until she straddled his hips and aligned her pussy to the bulge of his erection. With soft rocking motions, he guided her to grind against him, lifting the lower flaps of her robe, so she was bare and her wetness seeped into his pants.

At the pressure of her bearing down on him, his cock thickened to full length, filling with eager seed. *Want to claim her*, his dragon instinct announced.

"I heard that bloodlust and lust get entangled in a new vampire's mind," he said. "That every emotion and feeling is heightened. That the horniness is unimaginable."

She let out a broken moan as she rocked her hips to his, rubbing her soaked pussy over him.

CLAIM, his dragon instinct shouted through his thoughts.

Shit. Maintain control.

"The second you left me, I missed the taste of you on my lips," Daxton swore, jerking his own hips up to meet hers. His wide hands fell to her backside, cupping her rear and forcing her to grind harder against him. "I could not stop thinking about licking your sweet little clit to orgasm. Watching your face as you came for me. Watching you realize I wasn't going to stop at just one."

"*Mmmm.*" Her eyelids fluttered shut, and her brows furrowed, her hips seeking more pressure. *More.*

"I wouldn't have stopped eating my mate's greedy pussy until your legs shook and your throat grew hoarse from screams."

"Daxton," she cried out. "Please."

"Please what?"

The jerky movement of her hips grew erratic. Urgent. "Please fuck me."

"My horny vampire needs to be fucked?"

"Yes!"

His fingernails bit into the flesh of her ass. "You want my hard cock hammering inside you? Stretching you?"

"*Please,*" she whined.

"Mate, I would give you anything you want." He gripped her harder. "But I can't give you that."

CHAPTER 40

Luna gaped at Daxton. His erection was so hard under her, she thought he might explode. Yet, he just said he would not have sex with her.

Meanwhile, her new, crazed vampire horniness was completely real. And raging.

"What?" she asked him, sounding heartbroken over his rejection.

"The first time I am inside you, we must be married. Any children out of wedlock could be questioned for the legitimacy of their claim to the throne."

Her mouth remained agape.

"We will be married in days, little one. As soon as the witches turn you back," Daxton promised her. "In the morning, we will return to the castle—"

"Castle? A real castle?"

"Of course. With a grand ballroom for your coronation celebration."

She had not fully thought this through. Her thinking was: *Daxton is nice, sexy, and says he can reverse my vampirism. I'll stay with him until he does.* Now, it was: *Oh gods, he is going to marry me, and I am going to become queen of the Light Ones, and the idea of it might...excite me?*

It would certainly piss off Bastille.

Lost in her thoughts, Luna echoed dumbly, "Coronation?"

"We will marry as soon as you are back to your original state. We will perform the mandatory ceremonies, and you will become Queen. Then, with my ring on your pretty finger, we will fuck for days, *Neeuck*." He had used that word before and explained that it meant *queen*. "You will forget what it was like to not have me inside you. To not come every hour." A rumble shook his chest. "I will keep my mate utterly satisfied."

"Marrying seems, um, fast." Yes, she was angry with the Dark Ones for turning her into a vampire against her will, but that did not mean she was ready to sign up for being a gosh darn *queen*.

"Dragons marry the second they meet their mate."

"What if, later on, they don't like them?"

Daxton chuckled loudly as if she was jesting. "They are *mates*," he said like that explained everything.

Mates can hate each other and fight, she thought to herself. *Just look at how Bastille felt about me.* She shook her head. *Stop thinking about Bastille!*

"I know you are experiencing need," Daxton said, moving his hot, wide palms to her thighs, running them up and down. Squeezing at her tender flesh. "I may not be able to move inside you tonight." A slow, mischievous smile claimed his lips. "But I can still satisfy you."

Stunned, she watched as he picked up a paintbrush with

a long, wide wooden staff. He held the brush by its bristles, pointing the rounded, smooth cylinder end toward her.

"W-What are you going to do with that?" she stuttered.

In one smooth, impossibly fast move, Daxton rolled them until she laid flat on her back on the floor, and he loomed over her body.

He wrenched her thighs apart, flashing her bare, damp pink flesh at him, and settled between her legs so she could not close them. His fingernails lengthened to black claws as he shredded the sides of her white robe apart and revealed her heaving breasts and hard nipples.

"Perfection," he muttered while his dark, heated gaze raked over her.

Claws disappearing, he traced his fingers down her chest, grazing her hardening nipples, until his hands lingered at her slick folds. He lifted the wooden end of the paintbrush to circle her swollen clit. The bundle of nerves throbbed, making her pussy spasm in a direct response to the sensation of the smooth wood rubbing over her pulsing bud.

Daxton leaned down to suck one of her taut pink nipples into his mouth.

She cried out as he gave a hard suck and tapped the wooden brush handle against her clit. *Tap, tap.* "*Oh!*" Her head fell back, her spine arching.

Another powerful suction on the tip of her breast. Then, *tap, tap.*

"*Daxton.*"

He released her reddened nipple from his mouth. "Fucking love my name on your lips."

He kissed along her chest before dipping his head

lower. Lips pressing over her stomach, down her abdomen. Down, down, until his face was level with her wetness. He cursed as he examined the lush, damp heat of her. A blush darkened her cheeks as she watched his nostrils flare. As if a wave of pure lust crashed through him, the black pupils of his golden eyes grew narrow and serpentine-like. He licked his lips and breathed in her scent.

"My mate," he muttered in a hoarse voice. "My future wife. Queen." He rubbed the wooden paintbrush end over her swollen clit and purred when her thighs quivered. "This pussy is mine now," he warned, dragging the paint-brush through her slit, down to align with her entrance.

More wetness gushed from her as she witnessed his hungry expression. He pressed the smooth, hard cylinder in just enough for her pussy to feel the invasion of the tip— to crave the feeling of being filled—before he pulled it back out of her.

"My pussy," he repeated. "Say it."

"Y-Yours."

"Who do you belong to?"

Bastille had asked the same question. She bit her lip and gyrated her hips for more of his touch.

"Who do you belong to, Luna?"

What if she didn't *want* to belong to anyone? *A lie.* Because when Bastille and Daxton looked at her like that— like she melted their entire world—she wanted to belong to them. Both of them? Bastille would never allow it.

Daxton's eyebrows furrowed with displeasure at her silence. "I'll teach you who you belong to." His warm hands shifted under her knees. "Show me what is mine." He mercilessly parted her legs wide open for himself, leaning in to speak against her aching clit. "And watch me while I feast."

He sank his head down between her smooth, trembling thighs and gave a soft kiss over the hood of her clit. He released a guttural groan at the first taste of her, the vibration of it thrumming over her pussy. His fingers bit into her fleshy thighs as he held her tightly to his mouth.

His gaze burned into hers as he hungrily watched her reactions. In masterful, controlled strokes, his tongue dragged up and down the hypersensitive bud. Her breath caught deep in her throat as he licked and sucked and teased with that talented mouth. That skillful tongue. *How did he learn this so well?*

As he expertly executed flicks over her pulsing bundle of nerves, her hands shot down and grabbed at his dark hair. When her hips began to rock, pushing herself harder onto his mouth, he pulled back and delivered soft, teasing licks, caressing up and down.

She didn't realize she had been craning her neck to watch him work between her legs until he gave a powerful suck over her clit, and Luna's head fell back to the floor. Her back arched as her limbs shook from the rising orgasm.

Electricity. Throbbing. Something built inside her.

He just kept up that leisurely lapping of his tongue, around and around, and up and down, over her clit. The pink flesh yielded to the sensual force he used, twitching every time he pulled away.

He fed the staff of the paintbrush into her clenching core, using her slickness to ease it in. He slowly pumped it in and out of her. The handle was thicker than two fingers, but the girth was nothing compared to the size of his bulging erection.

He tilted the paintbrush, seeming perfectly aware of the angle required to rub the smooth head against that secret spot inside her, running it over the ribbed inner flesh.

At the sensation of being filled so skillfully, her head tossed and turned. Her moans were a long string of incoherent sounds emanating from her parted lips. Lights flashed over her vision. He sinfully coaxed her body toward an orgasm that had all of her muscles tensing in anticipation.

Caressing her slit with his irresistible tongue, he asked, "Do you know who you belong to now, little one?"

"*Ugahmhm,*" she moaned.

"That is not a word, Luna," he teased. "Did my silly little mate forget her words?" He pressed his tongue so firmly against the hood of her clit, swiping at it, before he curled the end of his tongue and *swirled* and *flicked* and *dipped*.

She cried out more incomprehensible gibberish, the back of her neck slick with sweat. Her breasts heaved and shook as the hot muscles of her pussy began pulsing around the piece of wood.

"Look at you, taking it so well," he rasped his approval, watching intently as the staff of the paintbrush disappeared inside her again and again. "In a few days, we will be married, and this will be replaced with my hard cock. It aches for you, Neeuck. Fuck, it throbs even now, weeping at the tip to sink inside your glistening heat."

Another broken sound spilled from her—pained pleasure. *Need to come so bad.*

"Unraveling for me like a good girl," he purred, his

voice so deep, it vibrated her bones, echoing throughout her body. "Beg to come."

"W-What?"

"Beg me," he demanded, his voice growing harsh and dominating. Why was that so damn sexy?

She should have despised the way he commanded her, writing him off as another self-centered alpha predator. But his demands were accompanied by intoxicating flicks of his tongue and consistent strokes of the brush. Her traitorous body went soft and pliant for him.

"Please," she whispered.

He hummed and pinched the sides of her clit with his free hand. "My mate can beg better than that." Using two fingers, he pulled back the hood of her clit and lapped directly over her most sensitive flesh.

Her toes curled as she pleaded, "*Please*, please, Daxton. Please."

"You will call me 'my king.'" He tapped at her bare clit, and her hips shot up, off the floor. "Say it."

"P-Please, my king."

"Fuck," he gritted, and she felt his hot length pulse against her where his lower body loomed over her. His own breaths were ragged, as if pleasuring her also pleasured him. As if he too was on the brink of orgasm.

She bucked her hips in an act of shameless yearning. "Please, my king, let me come. *Please*."

"I want you coming every day of your life. Coming on my tongue, my fingers, my cock…" He grunted, a blazing need shining in his serpentine eyes. "Fuck, just to look at you on the edge. Flushed. Slick. A wet little mess for me."

"*Please*," she squealed.

He guided the staff of the brush inside her once more. "Look how greedy you are for it."

"Daxton!"

"Come for me," he commanded. He gave her clit a slick, french kiss that ended in *suction*.

Heat erupted inside her as she felt a bolt of electricity strike her stomach and light up along her spine. Tingles. Flames. The orgasm hit her so viciously, so violently, that tears sprang from the edges of her eyes, leaking over the sides of her face and into her hair. Her entire body shook, as if experiencing a rapturous earthquake.

Through it all, even through her desperate scream, her dragon shifter watched her thrash as she came, her pussy clamping down hard around the staff.

His lips curled into a smile of triumphant male satisfaction.

There was something about the way he looked at her with so much adoration and pride.

She realized he could talk her into anything with more sweet gestures and a talented tongue like that.

She realized maybe she was in over her head.

She realized maybe, in a few days, she would be married and a queen.

And Bastille would rage war.

CHAPTER 41

"We are here, my king," Conrad announced, waking Luna from her sleep.

She drowsily lifted her head from Daxton's broad shoulder and glanced around the interior of the private jet. Bastille had not been kidding about the glamorous lifestyle of the dragon king. Bottles of champagne on ice, little TVs for every leather seat, all in a *private jet*—need she go on?

"Ready to see your castle, little one?" Daxton grinned at her.

Oh, shit. Her stomach turned, and her face drained of color. Correction: the color green made an appearance.

"Do not be nervous," Daxton reassured her as he took her small hand in his large one. Compared to her, he really was a big man. "My parents will love you; my people will love you—and we will be married by the end of the week," he promised.

She swallowed at the obvious heat in his golden eyes. His words from the day before slinked around in her head. "*With my ring on your pretty finger, we will fuck for days,*

Neeuck. You will forget what it was like to not have me inside you. To not come every hour." She fanned herself, the color red returning to her cheeks.

"You will meet my parents over lunch. Then, you will be prepared for the wedding announcement ceremony, where our people will meet their new future queen."

She nibbled her lip. "This is moving very fast, Daxton."

"You told me how many years you have spent running." He cupped her round face, his thumb stroking over the skin there. "So many years unable to dream and aspire to something. You have survived and persevered. Your drive to protect yourself will translate to protecting others who need protection. My people will be lucky to have such a strong, formidable queen."

More blushing. She looked over at Conrad from under her lashes and found him staring at her with a curious, perplexed expression on his face. Her blush deepened as she recalled when he had tried to save her at the cabin while she was tied up to a vibrator, and how she had begged him to let her orgasm before he helped her escape. *Does Daxton know about that?*

Thump, thump.

Luna sucked in a breath as her gaze fell to his jugular. To the pulse at his throat. *Thump, thump.* Dread consumed her as she realized she was hungry. For...blood. She cringed at herself and looked away.

The sudden lust for blood did not dissipate when she saw Daxton's gaze skim over her dark red dress—one he had ordered for her online and had delivered hours later before they flew in the jet to his family's castle. The low V-cut of the front revealed more cleavage than she was used to showing, and the king seemed particularly enamored with it.

Thump, thump.

She held her breath, trying not to smell the delectable man. The hunger made her throat sting.

Peering out of one of the port windows, she gulped.

Located in an area off the grid from regular civilization, the massive palace of white brick sat on a large cliff, overlooking the sea. The crashing waves and fog created a haunting mist over the bottom of the castle.

Didn't know places like this existed in real life. And it could be her *home*. Forever.

From a life on the run with shabby hotel rooms featuring leaky ceilings and yellowed walls to a castle as a queen? Her instincts whispered: *Too good to be true.* Meanwhile, her throat screamed: *Thirsty.*

"Come, little mate." Daxton lifted her to her feet and guided her to exit the small luxury plane.

She did her best not to smell him, listen to the beating of his heart, or stare at his thick, juicy neck.

"It is time for our future to begin," he said.

Two worries nibbled at the back of her brain.

Are the Dark Ones coming for me?

How much longer can I go without feeding?

❨

*T*he lunch with his parents was…awkward.

At first, they had welcomed her with open arms, gushing about how happy they were that their son found his mate. Then, his father sniffed her and reeled back in disgust at realizing she was a vampire.

"*Mated to a Dark One?*" his father had asked, aghast, like it was a fate worse than death.

"She was a prey shifter. A Duttur. But Bastille…" One Daxton's hands tightened into a fist before he released a heavy breath. "The Dark Ones turned her before I could get to her."

His mother had frozen, staring at Luna with wide eyes that seemed to flare with…guilt? "Bastille did this to her?" she asked unevenly.

"Yes."

Daxton's mother laid a hand over her heart, clutching a gold string of diamonds around her nape. "You poor thing."

"One of the witches will be able to turn her back," Daxton said in a rush. "There must be a spell."

"To reverse vampirism?" Daxton's father stated slowly, "I know of no existing spell."

"The witches will have to come up with something. She must be changed back."

Luna shifted all of her weight on her opposite foot as she assessed the situation. She had gone from a lowly, disrespected prey to a hated Dark One in the palace of light shifters where she was perceived as a monster. *Can no one accept me as I am?* She shook her head at the thought. She *wanted* to be turned back to her old self.

Eventually, everyone awkwardly sat at the long, wide grand dining table. Salads sat on beautiful porcelain plates featuring gold etchings. Luna picked up her fork, feeling hungry, then remembered what she was hungry for now did not equate to normal food. She frowned at the salad.

Daxton's mother took a long sip of ice water from her glass goblet before breaking the silence. "So, you can only, ahem, consume blood?"

"I used to be a herbivore," Luna stated sadly, swallowing down her sorrow. Her throat burned as thirst raged. "But, um, yes. N-Now food tastes like ash to me." *And I'm trying not to take a bite from your son's sexy neck*, she thought but kept that to herself.

"And how do you plan to feed while you are here?"

"*Mother*," Daxton scolded.

"What? It is an important question. If she gets lost in bloodlust, she could hurt someone. *Kill* someone—"

"She will feed from me," Daxton replied, his eyes narrowed on his parents.

They scoffed. "Be serious about this, Daxton. A new vampire? What if she cannot control herself? What if she hurts you?"

"She will feed from me," he repeated. "And only me."

"You would let a leech have your blood?" his father asked, incredulous. "*Weaken* you?"

"We strengthen each other. Like true mates."

"Gods, hopefully the witches answer our calls soon." His father blotted his stern mouth with a burgundy cloth napkin. "You are waiting to marry her until she is turned back, I hope? Not that being a prey is much better—"

"*Father*," Daxton growled back, baring his teeth. "She is my mate."

"And she is also *theirs*," his father warned. "The prophecy states, the king of Light and the king of Dark shall share a mate. And, if they cannot share—"

"I know the damn prophecy!"

"If Bastille has already claimed her, he will come for her. This union will start a war."

"She is MINE." Daxton banged a large fist to the table, and it shuddered under his wrath. Luna squirmed from her spot, suddenly aroused and thirsty. Lust and bloodlust.

Daxton added, "He will not take her from me again." His black pupils grew into slits over his eyes, anger and possessiveness ruling him. "I will allow *no one* to take her from me."

She should have shivered in fear at the dark power emanating from the dragon king, but all she felt was warmth at being so ruthlessly protected. Warmth and hunger.

Damn, this hunger.

Thump, thump. His heartbeat was so strong. Like him. So big and strong. Delicious. She bit her lip, not realizing her fangs had fully distended and sliced into the flesh. She licked away the trace of her own blood and almost groaned at the need to feed.

Unaware of her internal struggle, Daxton continued, "Bastille did not leave a claiming bite on her."

"Not *yet*."

"And what if he comes to the wedding? Or asks to visit the Council?" his mother asked softly. "The king of the Light and the king of the Dark shifters are members of the Council of Immortals. He must be invited as a common courtesy. To deny him at the door would be an act of war—"

"I would allow him to attend," Daxton replied, and everyone in the room—including Luna—gaped at him. "I would not turn him away."

"He might try to take her."

"Let him try."

"Daxton," his mother wailed.

He reached over to clasp Luna's tiny hand in his. "I am marrying my mate by the end of the week, if she will have me. If Bastille wishes to watch this happen, so be it. If he wishes to put down his moody, misplaced vengeance and join us for a night of celebration, so be it."

"But the prophecy—"

Daxton quoted it, *"If the kings cannot share their mate, they will lose her.* Yes. I know. I will allow him a chance to be close to her. To see if he is willing to put his vendetta and threat of war aside and join the shifter communities, light and dark as one. This could be a chance for peace. If Luna wishes to be shared and if Bastille is willing to share her, I will do so."

But the way he said it made it sound like he would prefer to eat shards of glass than share her with the basilisk.

He repeated, "I will do so. To protect her *and* our people. And his."

Luna thought to herself, *Bastille would never allow Daxton the same courtesy.* Not the possessive alpha basilisk full of hatred for the dragon. She was surprised Daxton was even able to offer such after all the times he growled at her: "mine."

He betrays his instinct to keep me safe. She tried not to swoon, steeling herself against the rising butterflies. And the rising hunger.

"I would not allow Bastille to take me," Luna spoke up for the first time since Daxton's parents began quarreling with him. "He turned me into a vampire against my will. Daxton has been the first predator to show me genuine kindness." *Other than Kobe*. "I…I would like to stay with him," she realized it to be true the second she said it. Maybe Bastille had been right before to worry about the dragon's ability to win her.

But, as much as I fight it, I desire both of them. How could any woman resist such potent, confident, sexy masculinity? Dominating and doting; the eternal irresistible mix.

"And being the queen of the Light Ones?" his mother inquired. "You believe you could get some of the most powerful factions of dragon, lion, leopard, sphinx, falcon, tengus—"

"I believe predator shifters would do well to have a queen who knows exactly what good *and* evil they are capable of," Luna replied. "Predators often forget that some shifters are not as strong as them. Some take advantage of that and prey on the weak. They forget that their actions have consequences. I believe I would be a fair queen. I would like to remind everyone that shape shifters are a rare breed of immortals. We should be *protecting* each other. Not warring."

Daxton's father stared at her from across the table, blinking as if he had just realized she sat there. As if he was seeing her for the first time.

Daxton's father said, "People forget that dragons were once a hunted species. Killed for sport; their murderers made into legends. To survive, dragons became vicious and slaughtered villages and melted kingdoms. In modern day, it is possible that the raw power has gone to some shifters' heads."

"*Possible? Some?*" Luna repeated, snorting in a very unbecoming, un-queenly manner. *I am hangry.* "Predators forget about prey shifters all the time." Her temper, which she had hid pretty well since leaving the Dark Ones, spiked. "Duttur, my kind, are light shifters too. Funny how you did not mention any prey light shifters in your list of who I would be queen of," Luna remarked to Daxton's mother.

Sitting up straighter, Luna continued, "Sheep shifters were slaughtered by Dark Ones *and* Light Ones for sport. My kind is so rare now, I may just be the only one left— possibly because I have hid from any predator shifter since I watched my family killed by a pack of them six years ago. No royal member or king of the light shifters helped us. No king protected us. No king *cared.*"

Luna held her head high as she glanced around the table at some of the most dangerous predator shifters to exist. Freaking fire-breathing dragons. *Don't care anymore.* "I believe your people—which include prey shifters by the way—deserve a queen like me. One who will care, who *will* protect them. As you all have failed to do."

The dining table was silent. Daxton's parents stared at her with no emotion on their faces. Well, maybe shock.

Beside her, Daxton held her hand so tightly in his that if she had not been a vampire, it might have hurt. Instead, it granted her strength.

He gazed down at her, his eyes blazing with pride and adoration. "Neeuck," he whispered. *Queen.*

Everyone looked to his father, who sat ramrod straight in the tall chair. He flicked his gaze over Luna, examining her face like he would analyze a map while discussing battle strategy. "My son just recently became king when I stepped down."

His words seemed to be a threat. As if what he really meant was, *I could take the throne from my son if you endanger it.*

But his father's head tilted as he stared at her. She refused to lower her chin, break eye contact, or shiver under the intensity of his power. Then, he said, "I give your union my blessing."

Luna, unaware just how immersed she got herself in this new world, felt her face break out into a wide grin. Daxton's expression mirrored hers as he squeezed her hand.

Daxton's father added, "As long as she is reverted back into a light shifter."

She stiffened but reminded herself to relax. It was a slap to the face that her species—what she was—meant more than *who* she was. *But, I want to be a prey again, remember?*

At the same time, she had not known she wanted the position of queen or any power whatsoever, but now she looked forward to not only being able to live but also evoke change for prey shifters like her. One of her best friends growing up had been a rodent shifter. *I wonder if she lives? I want to ensure she thrives.*

Luna squeezed Daxton's hand back as she let the idea—of marrying this intense and beautiful man and becoming queen of predator shifters—wash over her and settle.

My life starts now.

She wanted it. She wanted this. She wanted the dragon.

Bastille will hate me for it. Would Kobe? Sly and Nikolai? What if she saw them at the wedding ceremony?

Daxton's father warned, "Understand that our people have hated vampires for a millennium. We—they view them as parasites. They might never accept one as their queen. If you remain one for long, there will be an uprising."

Luna crossed her arms and leaned back in the chair. "Then, those witches need to start returning our calls, don't they?"

CHAPTER 42

"Ow!" Luna cried out as the manicurist chopped off a large portion of her overgrown fingernails, trimming them.

Luna tried to calm herself, but it was overwhelming with all the people huddled around her. Two manicurists, a makeup stylist, a hairdresser, a wedding gown designer who kept wrapping measuring tape around various parts of her body as she was "groomed" for the announcement of her engagement to the king.

Daxton had retired to his throne room to make preparations and left her to this crew for her "preparations" for the party.

"Ow," she complained again when the hairdresser tugged especially hard at her silky silver-white hair.

The hairdresser smirked and shrugged at her pain. *Maybe all Light Ones really do despise vampires.*

"Be gentle with her," Conrad instructed from his spot in the corner of the room. He stood and watched her get bombarded with hairspray, makeup, and nail polish.

"Why aren't you with Daxton?" Luna asked. "Doesn't seem like this would be very important for you to do."

"I have watched over the prince—the king—for many years. Now, the king treasures your safety over his own," he replied, his expression cool and unfeeling. Indifferent. "Thus, I am the only one he trusts to watch over you."

"You think I could be in danger?" she asked before cursing at the way the makeup artist jabbed at her eye with mascara. "Hey!"

"Leech," the woman mouthed, and Luna's jaw fell.

Conrad said, "We are hopeful that the faction of witches will attend the gathering tonight. With them here, they could perform the spell and reverse your vampirism."

"Goodie, goodie," Luna replied.

She did want to turn back—she missed food—but she hesitated at the idea of losing her now super strength and speed. She was immortal now, about to become a queen to some of the most powerful and dangerous shifters in existence. *Drinking blood may turn me into a horny mess, but being a predator after so many years of being a prey is kind of, well,* nice.

"Maybe once you are a prey again, the Dark King will not want you," Conrad said, *still* no emotion playing across his features.

"Why do they hate each other?" Luna asked. "Bastille and Daxton?"

The workers all held their breath and paused their work.

Conrad took his time in replying, "They grew up together. The queen—Daxton's mother adopted the basilisk when he was very young. His family had been killed, but she wished to let him live. Basilisks tend to become irritable and murderous as they age. Evil and irredeemable. Her choice was questioned many times."

"So, Bastille grew up in a castle full of people expecting the worst from him? Expecting him to turn evil?"

Conrad frowned at Luna's response, as did the workers around her.

"Basilisks are monsters," the hairdresser commented.

"Have you ever known one?" Luna inquired and got her hair pulled as a result. "That's what I thought."

"It is said that whenever the Dark King and the Light King shared a toy while growing up, the Dark King would break it just so our king could not have it. He would rather neither of them be able to play with it than let it give the Light King happiness."

"Seems to me, considering we are in a castle, that Daxton had plenty of toys and plenty of possible replacements of toys while growing up," Luna stated.

Had Bastille grown jealous? If he experienced the same negativity and prejudice she had so far over being a vampire, then maybe he had grown tired of it. Grown cold. She could imagine Daxton was seen as the golden boy compared to temperamental Bastille.

"You defend the Dark King?" the manicurist gasped.

"I'm just saying, when you treat someone a certain way, they can start to become—"

The hairdresser's fingernails dug into Luna's scalp so sharply, Luna sucked in a breath and hissed from pain.

"Enough," Conrad announced, and the women froze. "Leave us. Now."

The workers glanced at each other in confusion. "My liege—"

"Leave. Now," he snapped, and they rushed to exit the grand castle bedroom. Conrad silently glared at her as he leaned against the wall.

"What?" Luna asked.

He pushed off the wall and strode closer to where she sat. "Are you hungry?"

Random question, much? "I don't eat food anymore. Remember?"

Conrad scowled at her mouth. "I asked, 'are you hungry?'"

Did he mean….for blood?

"I saw your fangs flash in your mouth. They lengthened when the hairdresser hurt you."

She shrugged. "Maybe it's a defense mechanism."

He tilted his head, his long, blond hair flopping to the side as he peered down at her. "So, you do not need to feed?" he questioned.

"Can you not use the word 'feed?'" She cringed. "It makes me sound like a parasite."

He remained silent. No doubt thinking: *That's what you are.* She glared right back at him.

He informed her, "It is said that a new vampire must feed once every day."

"Wow, who knew I was in a room with a vampire expert?" she snorted.

"We cannot risk you going into bloodlust during the party."

"It's *my* engagement party. If I want to eat someone who attends, that's my right to do so," she joked.

Her joke bounced right off his fitted dark gray suit, leaving him unaffected. "It is said that bloodlust can overtake vampires, changing their personality and leading them to make choices they would never do on their own," he said.

He thinks I'm a monster. "I wouldn't hurt anyone," she snapped at him. She stood from her chair, so he didn't tower over her by so much. *He still towers over me by over a foot.* "Blood stains would ruin my pretty dress." They had put her in a silky dark burgundy gown. The deep, rich color made her pale skin glow like moonlight.

Conrad sneered, "You make jokes about such a serious matter?"

"What do you want me to do, Conrad?"

"Feed."

"Not thirsty."

His eyes narrowed angrily. "You're lying."

"You don't know that. You're not a fox shifter."

He stared her down.

"Fine, I'm a bit hungry, okay? A little peckish."

He nodded, appearing solemn. "You will drink from me."

She gasped out, "*What?*"

"You must drink from me," Conrad told her as her eyes grew into wide saucers of shock. Her gaze fell to the constant pulse in his throat. "Our king cannot be seen with bite marks on his neck," Conrad explained hastily. "The people will think he has been overthrown. Brainwashed by a pretty vampire."

Her white-blond eyebrows rose. "So, you want me to feed from you instead? To protect his image?"

"Not just his. Until you are changed back, it is dangerous to remind our people—including the ones currently in this castle—what you are."

Her jaw ticked. "A parasite?"

"I did not say that."

"But you're thinking it," she said, shaking her head. "You clearly cannot stomach the idea of my bite. So, why offer?"

"To protect him. And the kingdom."

She rolled her eyes. "So righteous."

"I do what I must. For him."

What he *must?* She tried—and failed—not to take offense. "I don't know if you know this, but vampire bites aren't some horribly painful act. It actually, um, it feels good." She cleared her throat.

His glower darkened. "I know the drugging effect the bite has."

"Have you ever felt it?" she asked, studying him with curiosity sparkling in those blue gemstone eyes.

His stern expression and unwavering, steady gaze did not correlate with the quickening of his heartbeat, which she could hear perfectly with him so close. *Thump, thump.* He appeared utterly calm and indifferent, yet his heart raced.

She added, "You know it can cause some—um, it can lead to—"

"Can we just get it over with?" Conrad asked sharply, his cold tone spearing through her.

Asshole. "I've met grilled cheeses and blood bags way nicer than you," she remarked.

"Am I supposed to act like I will enjoy feeding one such as you?"

"One such as me?" she echoed, her tone turning fiery to his cold voice. *So freaking tired of being judged for what I am.* Her hunger and bloodlust easily transformed into uncontrollable anger—a common symptom of new vampirehood. But knowing it was expected did not make it harder to fight.

Gods, she wanted to bite his head off and rage. "You snotty, royal light shifters are all the same." Her voice rose in volume more and more as her emotions spiraled. "I'm the king's mate. It shouldn't matter *what* I am. Just because I got turned into a vampire against my will does not make me a monster."

"You need to feed," he said again, ignoring everything else she told him.

"Screw you," she yelled at him, slapping his chest. "I'm *fine!*" She wasn't. Her throat burned with scorching pain.

He grunted and stumbled back. Apparently, she had slapped his chest a little *too* hard. *Little Luna* had hurt a predator lion shifter? Vampiric strength was no joke. *I...like it.*

He growled, "Do you plan to drink from the king? Even knowing you could drain him dry without meaning to? You have been a vampire for mere days. You have no control yet—"

"I won't drink from anyone," she swore, even as her stomach wrang itself and ached. "I'll be fine."

"Understand me, little girl," Conrad muttered threateningly in her face. "If you endanger my king, I will have no trouble finding a stake."

To drive through her heart? "You have no idea how

wrong you are about me. I would never hurt anyone, espe-cially Daxton."

"You've never been a vampire before," he said stiffly. "You have no idea what you would do."

CHAPTER 43

*C*rashing. *Growling. Ripping. Roaring.*

"He's, uh, not doing so well," Nikolai stated to Sly and Kobe as they listened to Bastille rage in the hotel bedroom. A set of thin doors muted the noises but not by much. It had been over a day since Luna had gone missing. The king of the Dark Ones was still…reacting

Kobe leaned forward from his seat on the hotel sofa. "Why do we wait? We should go to her."

"He is our king. We take direction from him," Nikolai replied even as he thought to himself that this temper tantrum delay was ridiculous.

Nikolai had turned Luna into a vampire. She was out there, in Light Ones territory, not knowing how to control her bloodlust. Not knowing what positive traits to focus on when she remembered her new aversion to food and sunlight. He wanted to be there for her, teaching her. Helping her.

Nikolai thought to himself, *I am no longer all alone.*

Kobe growled.

"We know the dragon has her. News of the, uh, the wedding—" More crashing noises came from Bastille's bedroom. "—has been announced to the Council," Nikolai said. "We are invited. We can go and see her right now, but we have to be smart about this. We can't just grab her and make a run for it."

Sly cracked one of his knuckles. The jolly comedic relief had not smiled since realizing Luna was gone. "Light Ones hate vampires. His people could kill her before the wedding. Or after. She is a sitting duck in enemy territory!"

"*Want to go to her*," Kobe grated.

"Our *king* is the one with the invite. We cannot go without him." No matter how badly Nikolai wanted to get to Luna, he knew Bastille had to accompany them to the Dragon's palace.

"Let's fucking go," Kobe roared to Bastille through the grand bedroom door.

Bastille burst through, entering the living room absolutely seething with rage. "He *dares* to invite me to their fucking *wedding*?"

"We need to fly there immediately, Bas," Nikolai said. "If we want to get there before—"

"Before they say their vows?" Bastille sneered. "Before they become unified in the eyes of the Council?"

"Remember what the dragon said in the casino just yesterday. Remember the prophecy," Nikolai stated. "He might be willing to share—"

"She is MINE," the basilisk roared.

"*And* mine," Kobe joined in, his fingernails turning to claws.

"How am I—the crazed, red-eyed vampire who is haunted by countless victims' memories—the one acting the sanest right now?" Nikolai shot back. "We need a plan if we're going to take her from him."

"We *can't* take her from him," Sly exclaimed, throwing his hands up to his reddish bronze hair. "We 'take' her, and we start a war. And maybe she doesn't want to be taken! Did you forget how mad she was at us for turning her into a vampire? She said she hated—"

"I know what she said," Bastille bit out.

"So, are we going or not?"

"Oh, we are going," Bastille said, storming toward the door to leave. "I'm going to kill that fucking dragon right before his wedding."

"And what if the witches turn her back and they get married before we get there?" Nikolai asked.

"I will make her into a widow."

Sly dropped his face in his palms and cursed.

"Luna is a new vampire. Her emotions are heightened, and the last thing she felt toward us was—" Nikolai choked out, "—hatred. She won't be happy to see us when we get there." He took a deep breath. "Young vampires are known for being needlessly violent. Experiencing raging tempers and spurts of bloodlust. If Luna hasn't fed since she left us, she could be on the brink of an episode like that."

"I like my mate feisty. So what?" Bastille shot back.

"So, if Luna accidentally kills a light shifter before we get to her…"

The Light Ones would have the perfect excuse to assign

her a death sentence. Not to mention what killing someone would do to her mental state. Luna was delicate. She was naturally *good*. Nikolai had spent centuries coming to terms with his nightmares, with his past. If Luna killed…

Kobe grunted, "We go now."

CHAPTER 44

*I*f Luna thought being a prey was bad, she had no clue how horrible vampirism would be.

She couldn't even enjoy stuffing her face with delicious looking hors d'oeuvres when she felt a hundred glares and narrowed gazes focused on her in the ballroom. Daxton had described the night as a long-awaited introduction of the new queen. He made it sound happy and exciting. Welcoming. Instead, she had been met with frowns.

Hated. Despised.

"Parasite," someone had whispered when she strode by them to move toward where Daxton charmed a group of people across the room.

"Leech," another one called Luna as she passed.

Each word was a hot poker, stabbing at her again and again, causing pain and annoyance. Anger. Luna just felt so *full* of anger. It was not like her. Sure, she got pissed at times in life, but this was an overwhelming haze of red over her vision. Prey or predator, why could no one accept her as she was?

Thump, thump.

Gods, there were just so many people in the room. And she was so damn thirsty.

Thump, thump.

And their heartbeats were so freaking loud. And their judgmental whispers speared through her ears, left and right.

"She was with the snake king."

"A bloodsucker as our queen?"

Luna scowled, her fangs peeking out from behind her lips as they protruded. Her teeth sensed a threat. Her throat stung.

The Light Ones were supposed to be the "good guys?" Other than Daxton, Luna had found them to be a bunch of pricks. As much as Luna claimed to hate Bastille, she better understood him now. If he had been raised in this type of environment, where people viewed him as a monster without ever knowing him, no wonder he turned out so rough. The basilisk shifter had trust issues, same as Luna.

"How much longer until the witches fix her?" one stranger asked at normal volume as Luna walked by him.

Fix me? She glared at the man and flashed her fangs. His quick look of terror calmed her rising anger—for a moment.

Thump, thump.

So. Hungry.

"I don't know what is worse: a prey queen or a parasite."

Luna's back stiffened. Her steps stuttered as she paused.

From across the room, Daxton met her gaze and smiled warmly—having no idea what these immortals muttered about her. He waved her over to join him.

Thump, thump. There was so much blood in the room. Hot blood pumping through immortal bodies. Powerful blood that would taste so good to her…

"Gods, imagine our king stooping so low. So many high-born dragoness shifters to choose from and he is fated to a leech."

"To share a mate with the snake," one exclaimed in horrified disbelief.

"Who is she going to feed from?"

"If our king wears a bite mark of a Dark One, I will retch."

More red fogged over Luna's vision. Her narrowed eyes could hardly squint through her rising haze of wrath. Her throat felt like she had swallowed flames that burned her sensitive inner flesh. She could not even drink hot tea to soothe the pain; it tasted like ash water to her.

"Monster," another murmured.

"Killer."

Thump, thump. Thump-thump-thump-thump-THUMPTHUMPTHUMP.

Luna glanced around the room for the accelerated heartbeat. It sounded as if some creature feared for its life. Her fangs throbbed in her mouth at what she saw.

A large, male predator shifter sat at one of the circle tables in the corner of the ballroom, lifting a mouse by its tail. Playing with it. Scaring it, as he pretended to dangle it over his mouth. Chomping his teeth—as if he would eat it whole.

And it was not simply a mouse.

It was a rodent prey shifter in its animal form.

Luna did not know what came over her. She imagined

the wave of bone-melting fury to be similar to being possessed by a ghost. Her vision glazed over. Her white fingers tightened into fists. Her teeth ached, needing to bite. To pierce.

And suddenly, with a speed she had never known before, she *launched* herself at the man. She broke his wrist as she freed the mouse shifter from the male's fingers. The animal dropped to the floor and scurried away.

Then, her fangs sank into his neck. She sucked so hard, the man nearly fell out of his chair. This time, her victim did not moan. Luna *wanted* to cause him pain, so no drugging venom was released in her bite. The man screamed in agony. And screamed. And screamed.

Maybe she should have felt guilty, but in her mind, she kept seeing him toy with the prey shifter. She kept seeing Rohan and Bastille do whatever they wanted to whoever they wanted with no remorse.

These predator men deserve to be put in their place.

She sucked from his neck harder, reveling in the pleasure she took from hurting someone who hurt others.

And chaos erupted around her.

☾

"She is perfection. An angel," Daxton was telling one of the oldest members of the Council of Immortals.

As a fellow reptilian, Orfus—a chameleon shifter who could turn invisible to the naked eye and remain in human form while doing so—was like an elderly uncle to Daxton.

"Ah, yes, I remember young matehood well." Orfus

smiled tenderly at the new king. "You must be ecstatic to have found her."

"I just wish I had been able to keep her from the Dark Ones. Turned into a vampire…" Daxton cursed. "It's despicable what they did to her."

"*AHHHHHH*," a shrill scream broke through the grand ballroom.

Daxton's wings shot out from his back at the potential threat. His gaze swung around the room, frantically searching for his mate—to protect her from whatever caused the scream.

But Luna was the cause.

Immortals swarmed around a corner of the room as his mate drank from the neck of a Council member. A sphinx shifter—rare and powerful.

Daxton raced to her side, pushing the guests back. His voice boomed. "*Get away from her.*"

"She's killing him," someone screamed.

"She'll drink him dry!"

Daxton cursed and motioned for Conrad to help him. Ever the trusted soldier, Conrad blocked the watchers from trying to separate Luna and the sphinx shifter.

"Someone get a stake," another bystander yelled.

A stake? Someone *dared* to imply killing his mate? *SCORCH them*, his inner dragon demanded. "ENOUGH," Daxton roared, and the room went silent.

Silent other than the greedy slurping sounds his mate made as she drank from the shifter. The man was slowly losing his grip on her shoulder as he tried to shove her off. The fact that a new vampire was strong enough to overpower a sphinx was enough to give Daxton pause.

"Get her off of him," a member of the Council demanded.

"Luna," Daxton said softly as he moved closer to her, placing a warm hand to her back. "Release him, Neeuck."

She did not listen. His mate was lost to bloodlust. How had he been dense enough not to ask her about her hunger? He had hoped the witches would be onto a cure by now.

One shifter moved forward to pull Luna off of the man, but Daxton shouted, "No! You do not touch her." His chest rumbled with the sound of a popping, crackling, kindling fire, scaring the shifter away.

Daxton wrapped his arms around her waist but did not pull her. Her teeth were too deep in the shifter's neck. "Little mate, you must stop. You will kill him."

"Just remove her from him, King Daxton," another commanded.

A king does not take orders. Daxton growled, "If I pull her from him, her fangs will take off his damn head. She is biting too deep."

His mate was about to kill for the first time. She did not deserve this. She did not deserve the guilt she would feel afterwards. Or the haunting memories and nightmares that followed ending a life. *I will kill those Dark Ones when I see them.*

"Damn it," Daxton cursed but there was nothing he could do. "Luna," he whispered to her ear as he blocked the others' gazes of her with his back. "Baby, let him go. You're going to kill him."

He stepped around her, so he could brush back her hair and look into her eyes. Gone were his mate's beautiful, innocent sapphires. Her pupils were blown; her irises were turning red. "Let him go," Daxton pleaded but there was a ferociousness gleaming in her eyes that he had no idea how to tame.

"She's killing him," someone shouted again. There was a soft shuffling noise in the crowd, as if someone prepared to jump in.

Scowling, Daxton informed them, "If anyone makes a move against her, I will roast you in flames." Though the threat was heated, it came out as cold as ice, freezing the onlookers where they stood.

"Luna," Daxton said, but it was too late.

The sphinx shifter's arm dropped, and his head lolled to the side.

Luna gave one final slurp at his neck, draining him of his lifeblood. Though her fangs retracted, her body sagged on top of the sphinx's and shivered. Daxton knew the old power in the sphinx's blood would be overwhelming to such a young vampire. *What will it do to her?*

"H-He's dead!" a shriek pierced through the ballroom.

As a new king, Daxton had no idea how to address his future wife—the light shifters' future queen—having murdered someone at their engagement party. In a way, he was saved by the bang of the ballroom doors bursting open.

The king of the Dark Ones walked inside. Bastille and his rugged followers.

The vampire, werewolf, basilisk, and fox shifter strode into the grand party like they were the guests of honor who enjoyed being fashionably late. Dressed in black and dark navy blue, the men oozed danger and power.

Bastille's dark, sinister gaze roamed the room, searching, until he locked eyes with Daxton. Though Daxton knew the potential threat of locking gazes with a basilisk, he did not look away. He matched the angry stare head-on.

Bastille moved forward, taking his time with each step. He did not yet notice Luna laying over a corpse behind Daxton's wings. "Where is my mate?" the king of the Dark Ones asked in such an ominous manner that the lights in the room might have flickered at the sudden chill.

"You can take her!" a woman in the crowd shouted.

Daxton made eye contact with the random woman and opened his mouth wide enough for her and the others to see flames swirling in it. Ready to turn them to ashes where they stood if another person commented about his mate.

"No music?" The fox shifter with Bastille's group tsked. "I thought Light Ones knew how to throw a party."

Daxton stepped to the side and retracted his wings into his back, so the men could see Luna's shivering form stretched over the dead man's chair. Upon seeing her, the Dark Ones shot forward.

"What happened?" Nikolai asked, blurring until he appeared right by Luna's side. The others were there a second later, placing a hand on her, checking her for injuries.

"Moonbeam?" the werewolf grunted into her hair as he nuzzled her. Nuzzled *Daxton's* mate.

Jealous, Daxton ground his teeth and spat out, "She has just killed." *Because of what you did to her.*

Nikolai cursed and petted her hair. Sly flinched. Kobe continued to hold her tight.

Meanwhile, cool and collected Bastille took in the scene and shot back, "Lynx the sphinx?"

"She drained him of blood."

Bastille snorted. "Good. The guy was an asshole."

CHAPTER 45

"This is your fault," Daxton bit out, glaring at Bastille as Luna slept off her "big meal" inside his bedroom chambers, just a few feet away from the men, on the massive bed.

The dragon's bedroom was expectedly over the top with dark wood and maroon and gold embellishments everywhere.

Bastille knew Sly would have his pockets full after swiping a few expensive baubles as the dragon focused his anger on Bastille. Even though the Dark Ones did not need more money, Sly was a shoplifter/pickpocket by heart. Fox shifters did what they had to in order to survive. So did orphan basilisks and abandoned werewolves and outsider vamps.

The king of the Light Ones knew nothing about striving to survive.

Bastille scowled right back at the dragon. "It's my fault you starved her until she slipped into bloodlust and killed someone?" He wanted to kill Daxton and carry Luna away from the palace that had caused Bastille so much strife when he was younger.

"Fighting like this solves nothing," Nikolai said. "She killed someone. She will now live with the instinct to do so again. She'll…dream of it for years to come."

Daxton stepped forward and jammed a finger into Nikolai's chest. "You doomed her to this."

Nikolai glanced down at Daxton's finger on his chest, not seeming particularly surprised at the accusation. The vampire's head fell forward as he nodded, accepting the responsibility and guilt.

Did Daxton not understand why Bastille had Luna turned? It was for her *safety*. She would live forever now. She was now as physically strong as she had always been on the inside. His mate was born a warrior. Now she could fight any battle she wanted, all by herself—with her deadly basilisk waiting, lurking, in the background in case she needed him.

"You said you might have some witches who could turn her back into a prey?" Sly asked, trying to abolish the tension in the room.

Daxton nodded.

Bastille groaned and threw his hands up in the air. "You would take away her strength? Her immortality? Over one little kill?"

"She doesn't *want* to be a vampire."

"Who cares what she fucking wants as long as she *lives*?" Bastille exasperated.

"Get him out," a feminine whisper came from the grand four poster bed. Luna was waking.

Bastille's heart galloped in his chest as he peered at his mate.

Kobe smiled from his spot closest to her, rubbing a hand over her back. "Moonbeam."

Bastille spoke tenderly, "Princess, don't feel guilty about—"

"Get them all out!" she yelled. The wretched pain in her voice was enough to silence the men into a stupor.

Blinking, Daxton turned to the Dark Ones and said, "Leave. She doesn't want to see you."

Bastille ignored the dragon and stepped closer to where Luna laid on the bed, her face hidden in a pillow as she laid on her stomach. "Princess—" he started.

"Get the fuck out, Bastille!"

He shook his head, steeling himself. "You don't mean that. Your emotions are running high."

"I don't want to see any of you," she cried into the pillow. "You did this to me."

"Don't feel guilty about killing the sphinx, Princess. I'm sure he deserved it."

"Get out!"

Daxton motioned for the men to exit the room with him. All of them hesitated but when Luna screamed for them to leave again, they did. With tortured expressions, they staggered out into the hallway where Daxton closed the bedroom door and looked over them.

Kobe clutched at his heart like it had been ripped from his chest.

"Why did you come?" the dragon king asked. "To try to take her from me? As you can see, she'd rather stay with me."

Bastille's eyes narrowed into slits. "And how has that been? A vampire living in the light shifters' castle. It didn't seem like your people were welcoming her with open arms."

Daxton scoffed. "She committed murder in front of them."

"She was starving, and she fed," Bastille corrected.

"Because you don't care at all about killing, do you?" Daxton asked pointedly.

Hurt and anger flashed in Bastille's eyes before he had the chance to mask it. Daxton used to know him better than anyone; they grew up together. *But he only sees me as a killer, just like the rest of them*, he thought bitterly to himself.

"When it comes to my mate's survival, I *enjoy* the killing," Bastille replied.

"Have the witches found any spells yet to turn her back?" Sly asked, trying to keep them on topic.

Daxton frowned at the red-haired fox shifter. "No."

"Luna needs to learn how to feed and pace herself, so she won't kill again," Nikolai said. Everyone turned to look at the brooding vampire. "She may not want to see us, but she needs to learn how to handle the bloodlust, and no other vampire would step foot in the palace of the light shifters to teach her."

Daxton flexed his jaw, considering it. "I will allow you —and only you—to see her for a lesson."

"We'll need a...food source as well," Nikolai commented. "For her to practice on."

"She will feed from me," Daxton said adamantly.

"She feeds from *me*," Bastille remarked. "I'm her favorite after all. I could hardly get her fangs out of my neck the first time." *Ha!* Bastille suppressed an outward grin. *A new way to cause the dragon pain.* "She loved my taste so much, she started riding my cock for more."

Daxton's nostrils flared as a thin line of smoke wafted from them. *Oh, fire breather.* Bastille smirked at his rival's jealousy.

"No offense but cold-blood is a different craving from warm-blooded victims," Nikolai said. "You and Bastille have reptilian origins. She fed from and killed a sphinx. It needs to be a warm-blooded light shifter to curb her new craving."

A warm-blooded light shifter who wouldn't try to hurt her? Everyone glanced over at Sly who studied a painting on the wall like he was devising a plan on how to sneak it out in his back pocket.

His red-brown eyebrows arched when he noticed their attention on him. "Hmm?"

"It should be Sly," Nikolai said. "Someone she knows. Any connection might help her fight the bloodlust."

"And if she can't and she sucks me dry?" Sly asked. "What then?"

Bastille strode up to the fox shifter and grabbed his arm, squeezing it. "Thank you for your service."

"Oh, fuck you," Sly snorted.

"Moonbeam won't hurt you," Kobe grunted.

"You have to trust that she can pull back in time," Nikolai stated. "Can you do that?"

"Trust the woman with major trust issues? Oh, sure, of course." Sly crossed his arms, trying to appear tough but Bastille saw right through him.

"She won't kill you, Sly," Bastille said.

341

"How do you know?"

Annoyed by the truth, Bastille huffed. "Because she likes you. You make her smile."

Daxton frowned at that and narrowed his eyes on Sly, seeming to assess him for the first time as a real threat.

Sly sighed and shook his arms out nervously. "Fine, she can drink from me."

Nikolai shrugged and deadpanned, "If you die, at least you'll enjoy it while it happens."

"Thanks for the silver lining, Nik."

"You're quite welcome."

CHAPTER 46

"*L*ittle mate," Daxton cooed to Luna as she dozed off into the pillow.

Gods, the bed was so soft. *What kind of sheets are these?* she wondered with her eyes still closed. *I never want to leave this bed or face the consequences of my actions ever again.* It was entirely possible that sphinx blood had kind of made her high. Or tipsy. Or whatever happened to new vampires hyped up on ancient, powerful juice.

"I need you to sit up for me," Daxton whispered to her, rubbing a small circle on her back.

She scrunched her nose but shifted on the bed, turning until she met his gaze. The memory of what happened slapped the sleepiness away. Guilt and fear claimed her entire expression.

Her lip trembled as she suppressed tears. *My emotions really are on the fritz.* "Are you going to execute me?"

"*What?*" Daxton exclaimed. "Gods, no! I would die before you were ever harmed."

"No one will want me as a queen now." She sniffled. "I—I'm a murderer."

"It was not your fault," Daxton said, trying to soothe her. He brushed a strand of her hair from her forehead. "It was the bloodlust."

No, it wasn't, she wanted to say. Yes, the bloodlust was what caused her to launch herself onto him and drink him to death, but the idea of hurting him once she saw the man toying with a prey shifter…

Horrified, she realized, *I liked it.*

Daxton would never want someone like her. She used to wonder how she ever got unlucky enough to be matched with someone as jaded and complicated as Bastille, but maybe this was why. She was not *all good* the way Daxton was. Righteous? Fair? She had killed someone at her engagement party. *He must be so embarrassed of me.*

"Daxton, what if I'm not meant for your castle? Your people hate me…"

"They hate what you are, not who you are."

She clenched the sheets in tight fists as she sneered, "But that's fucked up. Don't you see that? Why are all these light shifters so focused on animal origin? Or old prejudice. That shifter I k-killed, he was hurting a prey shifter in the middle of a party. In front of some members of the Council. They were all *laughing.*"

Daxton rubbed a thumb over her cheek tenderly. He patiently let her spew all her thoughts at him instead of interrupting her. *I like that he listens.*

"I wanted to hurt them," she admitted, shuddering on the bed. "I know the bloodlust is strong; I know my emotions are supposed to be heightened. But, I…I don't know that I regret it. Predator shifters only seem to understand violence and power." Luna blinked up at the dragon. "Someone needed to stand up for that prey."

Daxton pursed his lips but replied softly, "There are many immortals who have grown too…stubborn in old ways. But we could lead them into a new era, Neeuck."

"Daxton, they will never accept me."

"You will be changed back to your old state," he said confidently. "I promise. The witches are working on it now."

"Daxton…" Luna breathed out a sad little exhale.

Though she had never thought herself in a rush to marry, it hurt her that he would only marry her after she was a light shifter again. *It shouldn't matter what I am*, she thought. Bastille did not care "what" she was, only that she was safe and strong and immortal. The basilisk had changed her because he wanted *more* of her. Not because he wouldn't accept her when she was a prey.

"Luna, I am going to bring in the vampire and fox shifter. I need you to remain calm." Daxton rolled off the bed and walked over to the doors of the bedroom.

She sat up stiffly. "Wait, what?"

"The vampire can help you learn to control your blood-lust. Since it remains unclear when the witches will change you back, it would be wise for you to know about your hunger and how to sate it, safely." Daxton's large palm wrapped around the doorknob. "This will be good for you."

"I don't want to see them," she said. *They make me feel weak*. Being mad at them was easy when she didn't have to see them.

Daxton repeated, "This will be good for you."

Male alpha predators sure seemed all too comfortable telling her what was best for her. Making choices on her behalf without listening to her opinion. It made her fangs sharpen in her mouth.

Daxton opened the door for Sly and Nikolai to slip inside. There was a slight animalistic whine just outside, in the hallway, before the door closed again. *Kobe.*

"Did he explain everything to you already, babe?" Sly asked, unbuttoning his shirt.

"Whoa, whoa." She put her hands in the air, motioning for him to stop. "What's happening here?"

Nikolai moved so quickly, he blurred from across the room until he appeared right in front of her, beside the bed.

Nikolai had never shown her much emotion. He was the ever serious and logical one of the group. The one who showed the least feeling. But the vampire cupped her face and said with sad, regretful eyes, "I am sorry I was not here for you, Luna. I sired you; the death is on my hands. Do not allow the guilt to eat at you, pretty girl."

Luna blinked, her mouth agape, as she lost herself in the sincerity of Nikolai's burning red eyes.

"I will keep the nightmares away for you," he swore. "The way you do for me."

She kept his nightmares away? How? She had heard that vampires were haunted by memories of those they killed. Would that happen to her?

Nikolai stroked a finger down her cheek and chin until he drew a line down the center of her throat. The surprising, tender touch left her breathless.

"I will show you how to control the bloodlust," he told her. "How to drink without killing."

"And guess who your practice dummy is?" Sly shot her a nervous grin from across the room. "Spoiler alert: it's the yummiest one of the group." Sly gestured to himself.

He finished unbuttoning the first three buttons of his dark dress shirt. He pulled open the flaps of fabric, revealing the smooth skin of his neck and chest. She could hardly stop from licking her lips.

In a feigned Southern accent, Sly added, "Aw, damn, darlin'. You licking those lips for little ole me?"

Luna knew how Sly used humor to deflect and to mask his discomfort toward something. *He is nervous I will kill him, just like the other shifter*. Her heart twinged.

"Hey, now, don't look so sad," Sly said, moving forward to comfort her. "Nikolai can confirm how tasty I am, remember?" he joked to lift her spirits.

He comforts me as he prepares to feed me. Possibly sacrificing himself in the process. A little more of her hardened heart softened toward Sly.

"I'm a rare delicacy nowadays, baby," Sly continued when he noticed her stiff shoulders loosen as he spoke to her. "Fox shifters were hunted just like prey. Light shifters, dark shifters, they all wanted a piece of me. I may be one of the few left. But you understand how that feels, don't you, Luna?"

Her heart tugged her forward. She stood from the bed and took a step closer to him. She pressed a hand over his heart. "Sly, how did you end up with the Dark Ones?" He was a light shifter after all.

"I told you, Bastille adopted me," he said. "I may not be

some super strong basilisk, but everyone deserves a family, right, Luna?" The sincerity in his voice softened her even more.

I...have feelings for Sly. "I won't take you from your family, Sly," she promised. She would control her blood-lust. She had to.

"I'm not worried about that." A small smile stretched his plush lips. "I'm worried you will take *yourself* from my family. Don't give up on us, Luna. Not yet. Let us win you the way you deserve to be won."

Daxton cleared his throat from the corner of the room. "This was supposed to be a bloodlust lesson."

Nikolai nodded and moved to stand behind Sly, facing Luna. "Let's begin."

"No romancing, then?" Luna asked softly, her gaze locked onto Sly's pulse point as she drifted closer. "We just, uh, 'do the deed?'"

"Technically, I am buying you dinner first," Sly said.

"Focus on his heartbeat, Luna," Nikolai instructed. Tall, dark, and handsome. Imposing. Deadly. *He really does make a sexy teacher.*

Thump, thump. Gods, Sly smelled so good. Like summertime—sunshine, sensual sweat, and cold, refreshing coffee ice cream. Her fangs lengthened in her mouth, causing an ache of pain and thrill of anticipation. She still remembered the raw pleasure she felt while drinking from Bastille—a much different experience than when she wanted to hurt the other predator shifter. *What if I end up grinding myself on Sly too?*

She tried to clear her mind, shaking her thoughts from her head.

"Listen to his heartbeat before you bite," Nikolai said, curling a hand behind Sly's neck and bending it, so Sly's head tilted and his magnificent throat was on display to her. "That way you can recognize how much it weakens the longer you feed."

Thump, thump, thump.

His heartbeat was strong but irregular. *He is nervous.* She blew a calming breath over his neck, and Sly stiffened, preparing for the bite.

"Thank you," she whispered, before sinking her fangs into him.

CHAPTER 47

*S*hit, Sly thought to himself as her teeth broke through his skin and she began to suck. *Fuck.*

He was not the man to pine over another guy's girl—especially the mate of his friend and king—but this was *Luna.* Funny, pretty, sassy, guarded, soft, delicate, yet hard as stubborn rock, Luna.

Offering his blood to her was about as uncomfortable as it could be. Because he wanted her. Viscerally. He was just a fox shifter who the king of the Dark Ones kept around. How was he ever supposed to throw his hat into the ring for Luna? Compete against a basilisk, a dragon, and a werewolf?

And from the looks of how Nikolai stared so intensely at her—like she was his new favorite subject that he wished to become an expert in—it would seem the vampire was also a contender for her affections.

What if we could all share her?

Still, Sly felt a small sense of pride at being the one she

practiced biting. A welling sensation of desire ran through his veins at providing this to her.

It feels so fucking good, Sly thought. She sucked, dragging blood from him, and his shaft pulsed behind his pants zipper in response. Each pull from his neck felt like a tugging pressure, a luscious sucking on his cock.

Why did she have to tenderly whisper *"thank you"* just before this, making him melt for her? She was the king's mate. He shouldn't be feeling like...

His mind shot back to when he teased her with the vibrator in the cabin. Her naked body straining against those ropes, gyrating as she cried out to come... As she *begged* to come.

Sly's hands turned to fists at his sides, trying to resist the sudden urge to touch her. To cup her full breasts. To grab at her round hips. To *mold* himself to her.

The dragon might burn me to a crisp.

"See how you're making it feel good for him?" Nikolai asked softly from behind Sly. "Doesn't it feel good, Sly?"

She moaned against his neck as she drank deeply, and he went a little lightheaded—not because she took too much, but because her moan made his chest purr with approval. Hot little flames ignited in his bloodstream, pumping through his every limb, sinking to fill his cock, thickening it with need.

He became so hard, so fast, he groaned and ran a hand over his erection. Nikolai had once bitten him, but Luna's mouth sucking on his flesh... *Fuck.*

Her fingernails bit into the back of his shoulders as she clutched him closer. His chest smashed against her lush breasts as she pulled at him. Her firm, tight, little nipples poked into him, and his cock throbbed painfully as he recognized her new scent in the air—arousal.

He groaned in surrender as his head fell to the side, displaying more of his neck for her. His shaft pulsed violently for touch.

"*Mmm*," she moaned into his neck again, digging her fangs in deeper.

One of her hands fell between them and fiddled with the zipper of his pants.

"Neeuck," the dragon said from somewhere in the room. Sly could hardly focus on anything but this *feeling*.

"It is a normal part of the bloodlust," Nikolai stated.

"She didn't act this way before she killed."

"She *likes* Sly," Nikolai said simply.

Sly's heart warmed. Could he ever be lucky enough to be loved by Luna?

She pressed a palm to the bulge of his erection. Sly sputtered, but his hands seemed incapable of pushing her away. Not as her fingers stroked over his trouser tent.

"*Luna*," he gasped out. His hips rocked his erection into her hand, pleading for her to finish him, to offer him release. "*Yes*."

"Luna, what you're feeling right now is the effect of the bite," Nikolai said. "As you give your source pleasure, it feels better to drink from him. But that also means it is harder to stop."

She moaned louder as she slurped down more and more of his blood. Her hips rolled forward, seeking pressure between her legs.

Chill. Maintain a cool head, Sly thought even as the head of his cock wept for relief.

Lust and bliss overran his mind, drenching it like sticky syrup until all he could think and feel was the greedy need for more.

"Neeuck, you wish to…pleasure him?" Daxton asked, sounding astonished.

Her fingernails shredded the front of Sly's pants until he felt cool air brush over his hot, full erection. Then, as a predatory animal might, she mounted him. She gripped the back of his neck, leapt up, and secured her lithe legs around his waist, aligning her pussy with his bare cock. Her dress rode up to her hips from her position wrapped around him.

"*Neeuck.*"

"Luna, don't," Sly choked out but stopped himself from saying more. Because he wanted her. More than anything he had ever wanted. "Fuck," he growled, "Why did you have to be *his*?"

His resolve crumbled when she gave a long, wet suck on his neck as a response.

His large hands clasped her hips, rocking her against his aching shaft. She whimpered and moaned breathily against his skin.

"Fuck, you are so sexy," Sly rasped. "Wanted you since I first saw you. You slapped Bastille in the face, and I fell in love."

"*Mmmm.*"

Words flowed from Sly's mouth without him thinking them through. "Fox shifters don't have mates, but I do now, don't I? Please, Luna."

Nikolai squeezed a hand on the back of Sly's neck, reminding him of where they were. "Luna, you've taken enough. You must stop now. Your thirst should be gone. Retract your fangs."

But she kept feeding, making Sly dizzy with lust and...dizzy.

"Stop feeding now."

"She's not listening to you," Daxton said.

"Thank you so very much for pointing that out," Nikolai grated. "Luna, pretty girl, feel the hunger fade and stop. You don't want to hurt, Sly, right?"

Hurt me. Do anything you want with me, Luna, Sly thought to himself. *I'll let you do anything.*

Luna and Sly could do nothing but pant and grind and claw at each other in desperation.

"Hear how Sly's heartbeat is slowing? It's growing too weak. You must stop."

Sly fought a wave of disappointment as she rocked herself against his cock and threw her head back in ecstasy, releasing her fangs from his neck and interrupting the spell.

They both breathed so hard, their chests heaved from it. Blinking, bits of clarity returned to their anguished, hungry expressions.

Sly glanced over to where Daxton appeared ready to murder him. "Shit." Sly let go of her waist, causing her to tumble to the floor, hard on her rear. His cock sprang up to his stomach, jutting forward for more of her. "I, um, I'm sorry." He tried to help her back up.

Waving off his concern, Luna wiped the back of her hand over her mouth and hesitantly sat up on her knees. Wide-eyed and brows drawn, she appeared regretful as well. "I'm sorry that got a little, uh, out of hand. It was the bite," she explained.

"Not for me." Sly clenched his eyelids shut, scared to look at the beauty kneeling before him or the fire breathing dragon. "I—I wanted you."

Want her now. Always wanted her. Even now, Sly's cock throbbed for her, leaking to release inside her. His balls were laden with seed for her. The flush in her cheeks as she panted did nothing to wane his erection.

"Please forgive us, Luna," Sly said. "We made a mistake. We'll never take a choice away from you again—"

Daxton stepped forward, interrupting their moment. "Your vampirism will be reversed tonight or tomorrow, as soon as damn possible, and you will never need to feed from another again."

Luna flinched and nodded jerkily. But her gaze fell back to Sly's bare, jutting, reddened cock, which twitched in front of her face as she remained on her knees.

"Is your thirst not satisfied?" Daxton pointed out, "You're looking at him as if you want to eat him."

Luna shot back, "He's looking at me the same way."

Gaze at her as if Sly *didn't* want to devour her? Impossible. *So much want. So much desire.*

Lucky kings.

"You…want him too, Neeuck?"

"I…yes." She licked a fang, and Sly's cock jerked, bobbing between his legs.

"You already have two alpha kings and a werewolf," Sly said hoarsely. "No room for a measly fox shifter." *But a man could dream.* "It's okay, Luna. I'm used to being the guy who fades into the background."

She glared at that.

Then, she sank forward and took his cock in her mouth.

"Oh, fuck." Sly's head fell back at how she took his shaft deep in her throat. She bobbed her head once, twice, then pulled back.

She kissed the tip of his erection and whispered, "You never fade into the background, Sly."

Daxton moved to her and helped lift her from the floor. "You feel better, Neeuck?"

She blushed and nodded.

Instead of appearing angered like Sly expected from the king, Daxton nodded to Sly and Nikolai. "It's late. I believe it is time for the Dark Ones to retire to their rooms for the night."

Blinking in surprise, Sly asked, "We can stay here?"

Daxton's lips were pressed thin like he held back on saying something else. He said, "You are needed in case my mate gets hungry again."

CHAPTER 48

"I want to kill him," Bastille whispered low enough that the other paranormals eating breakfast in the large dining hall would not hear him.

Kobe sat at the end of the small table, eagerly watching the main doors for Luna to enter. Considering what happened the night before, Bastille doubted the blonde newbie-vampire would make an appearance. The members of the Council all watched the Dark Ones eat with caution.

Too many eyes on us.

"She doesn't appear to be forced into staying with him," Sly commented, sounding disappointed about the fact. "She seems to…like Daxton."

"Then, we share her," Kobe grunted, barely stopping himself from searching the palace for his mate. The werewolf would do anything to be close to her.

"You kill the king, you start a war," Nikolai warned Bastille in as quiet a voice as possible. Only Bastille, who sat beside him, could hear it. "Think of the prophecy. If you can't share, you lose her."

He knew he was *supposed* to share her. But the idea of watching Daxton's hands move over her body...

Bastille's fingernails bit into the flesh of his palms as his deadly fangs sharpened in his mouth. There was no way he could share her with the man he had grown to despise.

Each of the Dark Ones sat, stiff, in their seats. Until she entered.

The moment the grand doors opened, and Luna strode inside on Daxton's arm, the Dark Ones' necks craned to watch her glide into the dining hall in her stunning emerald green dress. In her presence, their shoulders sank back and the pressure in their chests eased. *There she is.* Nice and safe.

And inhumanly beautiful.

Bastille had mostly seen her in loose-fitting men's clothes and a dirty, ripped maid's uniform. This was something else entirely.

The porcelain of her skin behind the silky green gown glowed along with the bun and soft tendril curls of her platinum hair. Red colored her lips, making Bastille want to slam his mouth to hers in a kiss that might convince her not to marry the dragon.

She took their breath away. A collective unit of smitten and stunned predator shifters. So beautiful and delicate and regal in her gown. Soon to be queen of their enemies.

She strode in with her head held high, her gaze on Daxton and Daxton alone. It made Bastille's murder senses tingle.

Please forgive me, lovely, Bastille thought to himself as she walked by them without a glance. Was she still angry about them turning her into a vampire? How was she going to feel once Bastille killed her new husband?

His hands clenched into fists in his lap. He wanted her walking to *him* in that dress. Pledging her loyalty, her heart, to *him*.

Not the dragon, Luna. Anyone but the dragon.

Bastille looked over at Daxton's mother—the woman who raised him and banished him—but she actively avoided his gaze as she stared at the front of the room. *She does not wish to see her "failure" of a son.* The "bad seed" she had hoped to tame.

Those words she had screamed at him when she told him to never come back, *"Monster! I should have never stopped him."* Meaning she would prefer Bastille had died along with his parents, at the hands of Daxton's father.

All because he was a basilisk shifter.

How were they treating Luna as a vampire?

Unable to hold himself back any longer, Kobe shot up from the table and rushed to Luna's side.

"Shit," the others cursed and jumped up to follow him.

☾

*D*axton kept a comforting hand on Luna's lower back as they walked to the royal table for breakfast with the castle's guests. But she began to sweat as she passed Bastille and his men.

Last night, Daxton had spoken to her about her desire for Sly, and she had admitted to him that she experienced desire for…several of the men. *How did I end up here?* She was not some kind of femme fatale. Daxton, Bastille, Kobe,

Sly, and Nikolai. *I crave all of them.* Her hormones ruled her when they were around, and now she did not even have the excuse of being a prey surrounded by overwhelming alpha predator pheromones.

There was something about *them.* Yearning, lonely, misunderstood, twisted, dominating, doting. All of their traits seemed to blend together into everything Luna needed. Everything she related to and desired and... *Can I truly turn to putty in the hands of so many predator shifters?*

Her vampiric hearing picked up on the heavy steps of multiple men walking up behind her and Daxton. Anxious sweat slicked the back of her neck. She believed they would not hurt her, but they might hurt Daxton. And she liked Daxton.

In contrast, Daxton made Luna feel calm and comforted, like she could be utterly herself and always be cared for and protected. She literally committed murder in front of the man, and he waved it off. Meanwhile, Bastille made her blood run hot. He made her feel fiery and violent. And passionate. There was something about that dangerous-looking, tattooed man that called to her.

She stole a glance over her shoulder. Kobe quickly moved to her, weaving around various tables, through the dining hall. Meanwhile, the others followed him. Bastille appeared murderous, his jaw in a permanent lock as he scowled at the hand Daxton had on her back.

The Dark Ones looked *good.* Gone was the casual dark clothing the four men had worn in their time in the woods. They were each heartbreaking in their own suits—because they were in a castle? Trying to show up the well-dressed Daxton?

The four men appeared sleek and proper but just as dangerous. The first two buttons of Bastille's black dress shirt were undone, revealing a peek of his tattooed chest.

Devastating.

Yes, she was still angry about being turned into a vampire, angry they had made such an important choice for her, but a shiver ran through her at Kobe's expression of longing and pure excitement at seeing her. She had missed Kobe.

What would Daxton think? He never quite revealed how he felt about her touching Sly the night before.

Her cheeks darkened as she blushed. The second Kobe stood before her, Conrad appeared right beside her and Daxton in a protective, guarding stance. But Kobe would sooner die than hurt her.

"Moonbeam," Kobe whispered as he moved closer to cup her cheek.

Conrad lifted an arm, placing a palm over Kobe's chest, and keeping him from touching Luna.

"My mate too," Kobe growled, becoming aggressive at being held back from her.

Daxton's dark brows rose, and he glanced at Luna.

She brushed Conrad's hand aside and drew Kobe into a polite hug.

The werewolf was not one for "polite." He seized her in his arms, lifting her off her feet and holding her so close, she could feel his heart beating against her.

She had been so angry and hurt at what the Dark Ones did to her. Yet, now that it seemed reversible, she could not help softening to them. *Bastille is still an asshole though.*

Kobe's narrowed eyes connected with Daxton and

Conrad's over her shoulder. Kobe mumbled, "For her, I will share."

Eyebrows lifting higher, Daxton gave a small nod.

From what she understood, the light shifters took tradition very seriously. Matehood was like a religion. If someone was the mate of multiple paranormal beings, the connection had to be honored and the mate had to be shared.

It was hard to imagine the rugged and wolfish Kobe living in a grand castle with them, in his T-shirts, gray sweatpants, and flannels, but…

"I've missed your grilled cheese," Luna whispered to him, knowing the shifters around her would be able to hear her even if she meant it only for him.

Kobe pulled back to search her face. His own expression overflowed with pain and yearning. His furrowed brows and pursed lips silently screamed, "*Can you ever forgive me for allowing them to turn you into a vampire?*"

She petted his cheek in comfort, a silent acceptance, and his entire body trembled in relief.

"Missed you, Moonbeam," he grunted to her.

"You will forgive him but not me?" Bastille asked from behind Kobe.

Thus, the glaring exchange commenced. Glares from Luna and Daxton toward Bastille. A glare from Bastille toward Daxton. A glare from Conrad to Kobe as the werewolf continued holding her close.

Luna bared her fangs at Bastille.

Bastille stared at her sharp teeth, a glimmer of a smile on his face. Then, a frown. He spoke to Daxton while keeping his gaze on her, "Your people will hate her for what she is."

"The witches will find a cure in no time," Daxton said. "They should have something in less than a day."

"You would take away her immortality?" Bastille asked. "Leave her vulnerable to death?"

"We will protect her."

Bastille pressed his lips together, his gaze flicking over the dragon's face, as if searching for weaknesses.

"She does not want to be a bloodsucker," Daxton added.

Luna flinched at that word, and the others noticed.

Kobe held her tighter, pulling her slightly farther from Daxton and Conrad. Conrad tracked this subtle movement with tense, narrowed eyes.

"Tell me, lamb," Bastille rasped. "Have they hurt you for what you are?"

Daxton scoffed in offense. "Excuse me?"

"Your castle is full of outdated notions of dark shifters and vampires. I remember what it was like to live here." Bastille focused back on Luna. "Has anyone attacked you?" The genuine concern shook her.

She swallowed dryly and replied, "Not other than some hair-pulling by a feisty hairdresser."

Bastille nodded but still appeared sullen.

"We will speak of this hairdresser later." Daxton promised Luna, "She will be punished for hurting you."

"It could have been an accident—"

"She will be punished for hurting you," Daxton told her before looking back at Bastille. "I'm surprised you're still here, Bastille. Do you plan to stay for the wedding?"

Bastille cracked one of his knuckles before replying, "We both know she is my mate as well."

"I see no claiming bite on her." A claiming bite was when a predator bit its mate. Even when the mark healed, all unmated shifters could see the woman was unavailable. Like an invisible "*Do Not Touch*" sign.

Bastille grated, "She got taken from us before I could do so."

"Hmm, the same happened to me several days ago—my mate taken hostage by my enemies—but now I have her back." Daxton smirked. "And I shall remedy the lack of the claiming mark tonight."

Luna rolled her eyes at the show of testosterone but froze at the sudden animosity that washed over Bastille's features.

His eyes flashed black. "Bite her tonight and I'll kill you," he threatened.

Conrad took a step forward, but Daxton threw a hand up for him to stay back.

"She is my fiancé. It is my duty to complete the bond with a claiming bite."

Bastille shot back, "You'd 'claim' a vampire?"

"The witches will fix her soon."

Fix her. There was that word again. Luna's eyebrow twitched as she tried not to noticeably flinch. *Can no one accept me as I am?*

"Fix her?" Bastille repeated, releasing a disgusted sound in between a snort and a scoff. "She is perfection in any form."

"I was not implying that she isn't. But she doesn't want to be a vampire—"

"Have you asked *her* that?"

Luna rolled her eyes. So now Bastille wanted to act like he cared what Luna wanted?

"You have no business telling me how I should interact with my mate. I have satisfied her just fine on my own so far."

"Satisfied her?" Bastille bit out and narrowed his deadly gaze on the dragon. "You'll never be able to pleasure her the way she needs. You can thrust your dragon dick inside her all you want, but she'll be thinking of me when she comes."

Bastille smiled and continued, "We had her screaming for us and moaning with every breath. Our mate likes her hair pulled and her throat held. We were about to get her ready to take three cocks at one time—"

Daxton shot forward, appearing right in front of Bastille. Glaring menacingly, Daxton grated, "Say another word about her like that and you'll be a pile of ash."

Bastille shrugged, indifferent to the king. "Say another word about how she prefers multiple men to tend to her at once like the greedy little thing she is? Or maybe how absolutely soaked her pussy was when I fucked her with a finger up her ass—"

Daxton pulled his elbow back, ready to throw a punch, but Nikolai quickly caught his arm and prevented the hit. Conrad stepped forward to stop Nikolai.

"*Enough*," Luna hissed.

Her scandalized whisper did nothing to scold the men.

Bastille continued smugly, "What's it like to know I had our mate's pussy wrapped around my cock before you? The king who has everything."

Daxton replied, "At least my future wife knows I won't use hypnosis to get her to touch me."

Fury struck him as Bastille flashed his fangs at Daxton. "You dare court my wrath?"

"You are in *my* home."

Abruptly, Bastille stated, "I call for a contestation."

CHAPTER 49

"I call for a contestation," Bastille said suddenly, speaking the words loudly for many to hear.

All six of the men seemed to have palpable reactions. Heavy blinking. A stumble backward. A hitched breath—a form of masculine gasping.

Chills ran up the length of Luna's spine even though she had no idea what a contestation meant.

Daxton's face went slack with shock. "You *what?*"

"I call for a contestation."

Daxton shook his head, his perfect, slicked back hair staying in place, as he blew out a breath. "That is an archaic rule. A barbaric one."

"But it is a rule. An honored, ancient one. It must be followed."

But what does it mean? Luna wanted to ask.

Daxton took a step forward, closer to Bastille. "Think about this. Think about the prophecy. You *truly* wish for a contestation?"

Whatever it was, the idea of one made Bastille hesitate.

He inhaled. Exhaled. He glanced at Luna, gaze burning into hers, searching for something there. Finally, he replied slowly, "Yes."

"What does that mean?" Luna asked softly.

Daxton said uneasily, "It means the groom and the council member who contests the marriage enter into a duel." He pursed his lips on an exhale. "To the death."

"What?" Luna asked, shaking her head. "That's ridiculous."

"It is an ancient tradition. A true law."

"It started after rival shifters kept marrying their enemies' mates in retribution," Nikolai stated in a solemn, defeated tone. "Contestations are as sacred as matehood."

"It must be honored," Daxton whispered, appearing pained to admit such a thing.

"You're not just going to kill each other," Luna stressed, but each of the men's expressions had gone serious and grave, as if they already accepted that, by the end of the night, the Dark King or the Light King would be dead and gone. "*No*," she repeated.

"Do not worry for me, little mate," Daxton said, touching the tender skin of her arm.

"It will be over quickly." Bastille nodded, staring intensely at the dragon king.

"*No*," she exclaimed again. "No one is going to die."

"It's an immortal law. It must be honored," Daxton stated, speaking pointedly at Bastille as he added, "Unless the one who contests it takes it back."

Luna looked to Bastille, silently pleading with him to denounce his contestation.

Instead, the basilisk shifter shook his head and said, "Let's do this."

"Why?" She shoved at his chest, finally causing him to break his gaze from Daxton.

He peered down at her with indifferent, cold, green eyes. Bastille had looked at her in many unpleasant ways before—mostly with red hot rage—but never with such flippant indifference.

Luna said in a warning tone, "If you kill him, I'll never forgive you. I would never want to be with you after that. So, what would be the point?"

"That he never touch you again."

"Bastille!"

"I cannot sit back and watch you with him," Bastille bit out through bared teeth. A clear battle broke out over his expression—anger, sadness, doom, and dread all fought for time on his face. Like he hated to lose her, but he didn't see any other option. He whispered brokenly, "I *can't*."

"You will *not* hurt him," she demanded, slamming a fist onto his hard, muscular chest.

He shrugged off her hand, clasping her wrist and holding it. "You will forgive me eventually," he said, though uncertainty shone in those green orbs.

"No, I won't," she replied sternly. "And what about the prophecy?" She questioned all the men. "If you can't share me, you lose me. Does the chance of losing me not matter? You have to 'beat' him? Is your pride that toxic?"

"You say that as if you want us to share you," Bastille said. "But we all know who you will choose in the end. Even now, the only reason you are bringing up the prophecy is because you're afraid for your precious dragon."

"Stop that." She shook the arm that he still grasped, trying to jostle him—jostle some of his brain cells free to start thinking instead of letting testosterone rule him. "No one needs to die."

"Incorrect."

"Say something to him," Luna begged Sly, Kobe, and Nikolai. "Stop this."

The men, shockingly, stayed silent.

"You're just going to let them kill each other?"

More silence. She gaped at Kobe, and the werewolf broke her gaze to stare at his feet.

"Screw all of you," she exclaimed. "You don't care about me. Not really. If you did, you'd be worried about what a fight to the death means with the prophecy—aka my death sentence. You don't care enough to share me? Fine! I no longer want to be shared by any of you," she cried out.

Several royal guests and Council members glanced over at her, but the men had huddled around her in a circle to block the crowd's view.

"You may all be unfairly sexy, but I've dealt with prideful alpha predators before, and I have no interest in being seen as a toy or a trophy. I don't need someone making decisions for me about *my* future, and I don't need someone who wants to change what I am. If you'd rather fight to the death than share me for the *sake of my life*, then I want no part of this. No part of you."

Luna moved to escape the circle of men, but their broad shoulders and tall looming bodies prevented her.

Nikolai stated, "Let's move this somewhere else."

*L*ocked in a room by myself again. She scowled at the door, internally screaming in rage. *Kept like a damn pet.* Kobe stood on the other side, guarding the door to the bedroom while Daxton and Bastille began the contestation in the hallway outside of it.

With her vampire sense of hearing, she had an audible front row seat to the fight even though she could see nothing. *Damn door.*

"No powers. Let's do this hand-to-hand," she heard Daxton say.

"Afraid you'll meet my gaze and I'll petrify you instantly?" Bastille shot back.

"Basilisk, all I have to do is open my mouth and you would burn to a crisp."

"Fine. Hand-to-hand."

Meanwhile, she pounded on the door. "Let me out, you assholes!"

"They can't hear you," a voice said from behind her, and she gasped, turning around.

An older woman wearing a floor-length black cloak stood in front of the large bed. She grinned at her, flashing sharp, yellowing teeth. Her eyes glowed white and silver. A seer?

The woman said, "These are the king's quarters. A soundproofing spell has veiled this room for millennia." She whispered dramatically, "Due to all the sex. Did you know dragons roar when they come? Quite loudly."

Luna's hair stood on the back of her neck. Something about this woman's presence put her on edge. Maybe it was the eerie crooked smile. Or the way the cloaked woman flopped down on the bed and waved her arms back and forth as if making a snow angel. The intruder was utterly relaxed, like two shifter kings were not fighting to the death just outside the doors.

"Who are you?" Luna asked. "What are you doing here?"

"I will answer only one question." The woman's white and silver eyes emitted a flash of light. "Choose one."

Damn it. Luna wanted multiple answers. If this woman truly was a seer, then she would know who would win the contestation fight. She would know if Luna would ever get turned back into a prey.

Luna exhaled choppily, making a final decision, and asked, "How can I escape from this room?"

The strange woman threw her head back; the hood of her cloak fell from her as she cackled. She wiped at her eyes as if the question was hysterical. "Easy! You get captured and taken away."

Excuse me? "The only men who would want to capture me are outside the door, fighting."

The seer tsked, wagging a finger in her direction. "False."

A chill licked the length of Luna's spine. "Then, who?" Rohan was dead. No way he survived Kobe ripping his body to shreds.

"Prey are very hard to find nowadays." The seer sat up from the bed and took slow steps toward Luna. "Especially Duttur. All the sheep herds were wiped out."

Luna could hear yells and hits and bones breaking from outside the door. *Don't want to hear this.* Impatiently, she asked, "Your point is?"

"Do you wish to remain a vampire and stay with the men who chose their pride over a future with you? Or do you wish to escape as a prey?"

What kind of question was that? "Can you reverse the vampirism?"

Lightning struck outside, rattling the panes of glass in the room. The seer's eyes narrowed as her expression grew angry and vicious. Her lips curled over her mangled teeth as she admonished, "Your time for questions has ended. Now answer mine."

Luna shivered. She could feel the tingling electricity of magic—of dark power—swirling around the room. *What does this seer want with me?*

Lightning struck again, lighting up the dim room. "Answer!" the seer shouted.

"I—I wish to escape as a prey."

The electricity in the air waned, settling into nothing. The seer's glower turned into a sloppy, crazed smile. "You wish to be loved as you are. Do not fear. The kings will not kill each other...tonight."

A pang shot up Luna's side, and she gasped, clutching it. Her lungs twisted behind her ribs, which ached like the bones were bruised.

"They do care for you. Deeply," the seer said as Luna convulsed in pain. She moved closer, circling her. "But sometimes men need to lose a woman to fully grasp their true feelings."

"W-What are you doing to me?" Luna cried as she collapsed onto the floor, holding herself up on her hands and knees. She writhed as the pain moved up her body. As if knives were slicing through her every pore. Even her mouth ached—torturous agony—like a dental visit from hell.

The seer shrugged. "I am giving you your wish."

"S-Stop," Luna whispered, but darkness seeped into her vision, blotting out all color. Her mind blanked as she fell face-first to the floor.

"Oh, how they'll miss you," the seer gave a blissful sigh, holding a hand over her heart. "Don't worry, you thank me for this in about three centuries. At least…I think you do. Unless I'm confusing two futures again."

CHAPTER 50

Luna woke, her mind fighting through a groggy fog as she blinked and took in her surroundings. Pain. Pain in her ear. Harsh, wet pain. Her hand flew up to touch the area. Her fingers tapped against a triangle; the material of it felt like thick, hard plastic. It was also damp.

She moved her hand back to gaze at the red wetness on her fingertips. Blood. Her blood.

Someone pierced a fucking tag *through my ear?*

That damn seer! Luna jolted up, gazing all around for the woman. Yet, all she saw were metal bars and cracked, gray cement walls. She was no longer in the grand castle. She was locked in a cage. No windows. Underground? What the hell was going on?

Wait. Blood. She touched the throbbing wound again. *I'm not healing.* She swiped her tongue over her teeth. No fangs. *I'm not a vampire anymore.*

Her excitement was short-lived. Because she was now a prey—with no super strength or healing ability—caged in a mystery location.

"Ah, she's awake!" a male voice announced happily.

Luna followed the voice, standing on shaky legs, and wrapped her hands around the metal bars. He stood in the shadows, but she knew his voice was unfamiliar.

"Let me out," Luna shouted, trying to shake the metal bars, but they did not move. *Weak.*

The man chuckled at her demand, as if it was preposterous. "No."

She bit back a curse, attempting to get a hold of her anger as she tried to figure out her new situation. "Why is there a tag in my ear?"

"Because you are cattle." Cattle. The slanderous slur for prey farm-animal shifters.

Something about this sounded familiar, but she just couldn't remember.

"A little cattle shifter," the man muttered under his breath. She cringed at the awe and excitement in his blood-chilling voice. "You have no idea how rare you are."

"Oh, people have told me enough," she replied haughtily.

"Ah, but do you know the amount of money your wool goes for on the paranormal market? Or, you must know, some predator shifters love the taste of *real* lamb." The man stepped out of the shadows to appear in front of her seven-foot-tall cage.

By his crinkled eyes and the streaks of silver growing along with the black hair of his goatee, he had to be in his mid-fifties. The man's body was lanky, no big muscles like Luna saw on most predator shifters. Yet, something about him was intimidating. Threatening. Maybe it was his sunken beady eyes.

"Some simply like to have *pets*," he added in a suggestive manner that made Luna's skin crawl.

"Let me go," she demanded. "My mates are the kings of the shifters. I am queen of the Light Ones." Technically. Potential queen.

The man waved away her words, peering at her through the bars. He licked his lips as his creepy gaze perused her. Something he saw piqued his interest.

She glanced down and found that she no longer wore her fancy green gown. Someone had dressed her in a thin, tight white tank top—her nipples clearly visible—and matching white short-shorts. She quickly crossed her arms, trying to cover herself.

"Yeah," the man hummed. "You'll make me a pretty penny."

"I've heard of you," she shot back. "You're the farmer. The one injecting prey shifters with some type of obedience serum."

"You've heard of my little concoction?" The man preened, standing taller, his smile glimmering with pride. "Did you know it could keep you in animal form for the rest of your days? Unable to shift back to human. Just an obedient little pet."

Shit. She swallowed and took a step back from the bars, suddenly happy to have the barrier between them.

"But you need to shift into animal form first for the serum to keep you that way."

A breath of relief escaped her.

"So, why don't you go ahead and shift for me?" The man gestured for her to begin.

She scoffed. "How about 'no?'"

The man laughed off her protest and waved for her to get started.

She narrowed her eyes on him. "Why would I shift if you're just going to inject me with some kind of serum?"

He replied like it was absurdly obvious, "To avoid the pain."

Another nervous swallow. "Pain?"

The man dipped back into the shadows. Luna stepped forward, trying to see him in the darkness as metal clinking sounds and a rush of air pressure echoed around the underground cell. When he reappeared in front of the cage, he held a large hose, the metal circle end pointed at her as he gripped the switch on it.

"Wait, what—"

"Shift," the man repeated. "To avoid pain."

"No, wait!"

Ice cold water—with the force of five supernatural football quarterbacks—shot out at her from the hose, shoving her back against the sharp cement wall, causing her body to scrape over the rough cracks. Several bones snapped under the pressure of the hit. She cried out in pain as it continued pressing her harder and harder to the wall. *Too much, too much.* Her bones shook under the force, trying not to shatter.

Finally, he turned off the hose.

She fell to her knees, clutching herself, aching from the cold and the broken bones. "Stop, please," she begged.

"Aww, the cattle queen is begging?" the man mocked her.

Her rage spiked. "Fuck you!" she shrieked.

The hose erupted on her again.

◖

"*D*amn it, just stop fighting already," Sly yelled at Bastille and Daxton, who had been wrestling on the ground, punching, and breaking expensive vases over each other's heads for over an hour. "You're clearly equally matched without your powers."

"Fuck you," Bastille sneered back. "I have him."

Daxton elbowed Bastille in the gut and added, "Like hell you do, snake boy."

"If you kill each other, Luna will never forgive us. She's already pissed at us," the fox shifter said, for once the voice of reason. "She thinks we care more about the dark and light shifter rivalry than about her. Bastille, just revoke your contestation."

"No," he growled and slammed a fist into the dragon's jaw.

"Share her," Kobe grunted from his guarding stance in front of the bedroom they had locked Luna in for her safety. Knowing her, she might have jumped in the middle of the fight and gotten hurt. *Best to keep her safe.*

"I can't."

"Fuck, what is it with you two?" Sly threw his hands up in the air. "Why do you hate each other so much you're willing to lose your mate so the other can't have her?"

"I was willing to share," Daxton countered, spitting a trail of blood from his split lip.

"Liar," Bastille accused, tackling him to the floor once more while the other men rolled their eyes and impatiently glanced at the door where Luna was no doubt stoking her hatred for them.

"You act so high and mighty. So righteous," Bastille growled. "But there's no way you would have accepted my being with her. Be honest: when you saw she was a vampire, you were tempted to throw her out on the street."

Daxton roared, moving Bastille under him for a harsh blow to the ribs. "You are *wrong*."

"You hate dark shifters."

"I don't," Daxton replied.

"Your father killed my whole fucking family because of what I am."

"I'm *not* him, Bas," Daxton grated.

Bastille's eyes narrowed at the old nickname as he seethed. "Don't call me that."

"We were friends," Daxton held Bastille's hands down, pinning him. "Brothers."

"*Never.*"

"You were my best friend," Daxton yelled into his face. "Then, one day, you left me here without so much as a goodbye."

"Your mother *banished* me," Bastille shot back.

"You could have come to me—"

"I didn't belong here!" The basilisk shook off the dragon, shoving him to the side and standing. Towering in front of Daxton as the dragon remained on his knees, Bastille said, "You were the golden prince; you got everything you ever wanted. Everything I ever wanted. Everywhere I went, people treated me like a sewer monster."

Daxton's lips flattened into a frown as he stood. "You never told me that."

"You wouldn't have cared."

"I would—"

"I killed Sansa."

Daxton sucked in a breath. "What?" Daxton, Bastille, and Sansa had grown up in the castle together. Friendship led to more when Daxton pursued a relationship with her in their early young adulthood. But then she had...died.

"I killed her."

Daxton shook his head in disbelief at hearing Bastille killed his old girlfriend when they were teenagers. "They said her heart stopped."

"It was my basilisk stare," Bastille admitted, his frustration breaking apart in his chest and leaving emotional shrapnel. His head swung down, chin pressing to his chest. "It was before I knew how to control my powers. We made eye contact in the hall and she just...she went down. Your mother saw the whole thing."

"She *what?*"

"She told me you would find out," Bastille said. "And that you'd hate me for it. It was why I left."

"I never knew..." Daxton rubbed a hand over his face. "Bastille, I killed our nanny with an accidental fire-sneeze. It... Losing control is not your fault. We were so young back then; our powers were unruly."

"You loved her, Daxton. We both did. But it didn't matter. I ended up just how everyone said I would." Bastille exhaled roughly. "A killer."

"Bastille, we're all damn killers. We've had to be—either by accident or necessity. It doesn't mean you're evil."

Bastille grabbed Daxton by the throat but didn't squeeze. He held him like that, a silent threat and reprieve. "You don't get it," Bastille rasped. "As long as you live—the perfect prince—I'll never be worthy of her. She'll see that."

381

Daxton's claws extended, and he cut Bastille's hand until it bled and the basilisk let go of Daxton's throat. "No one is worthy of their mate. All we can do is try to be the best for them."

"I've already fucking failed," Bastille shot back, sounding agonized. Daxton's brows furrowed with, not pity, but *empathy*. "I turned her into a vampire and now she hates me, Dax. There is no sharing her because she'll never want me."

"Not unless you make it up to her and prove you learned your lesson," Sly commented. "And you'll have help with that," he reminded the kings that Luna had claim to more than Bastille and Daxton.

A tortured roar sounded several feet away, distracting them from the moment.

Kobe had thrown open the door to Luna's room and stood frozen, ramrod straight, just inside the space.

"What?" Bastille yelled to him.

Nikolai traced—blurring through the space with his inhuman speed—into the room to see what Kobe reacted to. The vampire cursed.

"What?" Daxton asked as well, echoing Bastille.

"She's gone," Nikolai shouted. "She's fucking gone!"

CHAPTER 51

*"D*o you smell that?" Nikolai asked as all the men scanned the room for clues as to where Luna had gone. There was no evidence of an escape. No rope to scale the side of the castle made from bedsheets tied to clothing.

"It smells like…"

"Prey blood," Bastille finished for him. "It's Luna's prey scent."

"The witches must have completed the spell to reverse her vampirism," Daxton murmured as he searched the room. "Where could she have gone?"

Kobe sniffed the air, growling at the obvious scent. "Fear."

"She was afraid," Nikolai confirmed. "Taken by someone?"

"Who the hell would have the balls to steal the mate of both alpha kings?"

"Hi there, handsome," a female voice whispered, and all of the men jumped in surprise.

They were used to sensing and hearing enemies from miles away. How had this cloaked woman snuck up on them?

The woman peeled back the hood of her cloak and revealed her aged, cracked, and grayed skin. The more witches dabbled in dark magic, the more their skin grew gray.

She winked and corrected herself, "Handsome*s*. Plural. *Meow*."

Daxton recognized her instantly. "Hag."

Sly gaped. "Rude."

"Her name is 'Hag,'" Daxton explained.

Hag grinned her twisted teeth at the men in a crazed stretch of her lips. "Hiya."

"Wait, *the* Hag?" Nikolai asked. "As in: the ancient, wise seer who wrote the prophecy about Luna?"

"I also do bar mitzvahs," she commented proudly.

The men blinked several times at the random change of subject. "*What?*" a dumbfounded Sly asked.

Daxton clarified for the group, "It's said that all of her foresight turned her a bit…"

"Don't you dare say 'loose!'" Hag scolded Daxton. "Just because I gave it up four times to that wolf pack back in the day—"

"Hag, where is Luna?"

"You mean the mate you didn't care to keep?" Hag tilted her head, her eyes flashing white-silver light as she smirked. "You lost her. Just as I foretold."

"But—"

"Unable to share." She formed fists and moved them through the air like she was playing the drums to build suspense. She tapped the invisible metal cymbal, finishing her dramatic drum roll. "And you lost her. Bye bye." She tossed her invisible drumsticks behind her back.

"*Where is she?*" Daxton growled, the threat clear from the low rumble at the back of his throat. Ready to produce fire.

"I told you. L-O-S-T. Lost." Hag rolled her eyes, snickering. "Gods, you dragon shifters might be well hung, but your brains are teeny weeny."

Bastille shot forward and clutched the arms of the seer so fiercely, the grip was sure to leave bruises. He bellowed into her face, "Tell me where my mate is NOW."

Though she had not been chewing gum a moment ago, Hag blew a big pink bubble of gum in front of the deadly basilisk's face before nonchalantly popping it and slurping it back into her mouth. "Or what?"

"I'll kill you!"

She yawned, the gum gone from her mouth. Had she conjured it? Seers weren't supposed to have the magic of witches, only the supernatural foresight. *What the fuck is she?* Bastille shook his head.

She shrugged, "That threat gets old. And anyway, you were the ones who couldn't share her. Why do you want her now?"

"WHERE IS SHE?" Bastille roared.

Hag wiggled in Bastille's grip and raised her fingers to her ears before promptly pulling out earplugs. "Did you need something, mister?"

"Hag, focus." Daxton took on the role of the calm, cool, and collected dragon when dealing with the crazed seer.

"Did you see where she is? Is that why you came to my room?"

"I see exactly where she is. Metal bars. Cold. Wet. No, wait, freezing. Freezing to death? Oh wow, a lot of pain. Good thing you two don't care about her anymore."

The alpha shifters could hardly hold back from thrashing the woman and shrieking up at the rafters.

"Pain?" Kobe growled.

"Freezing to death?" Sly asked. "What's happening to her? Where is she?"

"Well, you see, when a boy and girl fall in love, and the boy decides to be stubborn and not let his friends—enemy?—share her, the girl ends up being tortured because the boy didn't notice she was kidnapped by a prey-farmer."

More slack jaws. More clenched fists. More eyebrows drawn in anger and dread.

"Tortured?" Kobe echoed in a broken tone.

"If the farmer can get her to shift, he will shoot her up with a chemical to keep her in animal form—permanently. Spoiler alert: no witch spell will be able to counteract it. If he *can't* get her to shift, he will skin her."

"WHAT?"

"S-K-I-N," Hag spelled it out for the dragon. "Skin her. As in to remove the top layer of the body."

"But she's a prey now," Nikolai countered. "She won't heal from that."

Hag saluted Nikolai with finger guns and a first-place blue ribbon appeared pinned to his suit. "Duttur human form skin actually has very interesting qualities," she commented. "It can be turned into the *softest* material—as in, who needs cashmere? Or it has sleeping properties when consumed. Like those brain activity pills for the overthinker. Who needs to 'count sheep' when you can use the mystical properties of one?"

"Skinned? What the fuck?" Bastille raged. "Tell us where she is, specifically, right now."

She swooned. "So you can save her?"

"*Yes*," he hissed.

She mocked his tone as she replied, "*No*."

"Remind me why I shouldn't kill your seer, Daxton?"

The dragon scowled at Hag. "The reason is escaping me at the moment."

"Haha, aw, you babies think you could kill me?" She pinched Bastille's cheeks. "Adorable." She looked over each of the men, surveying them. "If you wanted her, you would have done anything for her. Instead, you chose past prejudices and pride. Jealousy. Ego."

"Well, we've learned our lesson."

She tilted her head. "Have you?"

"We're willing to share her," Bastille grated, glancing at Daxton. Both of them nodded stiffly at each other.

"Aw, too late," she said.

The men held their breath.

"Just kidding! You can find her at the farm located on the edge of the Mount Rancos cliff. She's in an underground cell there, impossible to scent her through the thick cement. But beware," the seer said as her eyes flashed with bright light again.

Lightning struck just outside the windowpane as she continued, "She is only there because of your choices. She was to become queen. Instead, she bleeds on a dusty floor, crying for her mother. She stopped begging for you to save her about five minutes into the torture. That was around the time she began to blame you for her capture. If you leave now, you might be able to get to her while she still has most of her skin."

"*Most?*"

"But, between us," Hag whispered. "I don't see how she'll ever trust or forgive you after this."

CHAPTER 52

*C*old. Broken. Hurt.

"*Please*, stop," Luna cried.

Pain. So much pain.

"All you have to do is shift," the farmer replied calmly.

Tears seared her cheeks as she laid on the cold cement floor, shivering and yelping with each quake of her chilled, mangled body. Her recurring thought, other than the obvious "*Make the pain stop*," was "*Stupid Luna. Learning again not to get mixed up with predators. Always ends in pain. Should have stayed on the run.*"

She imagined the men fighting to the death, wrapped up in their prideful egos and hatred for each other, while she lay broken and whimpering. All alone.

She had, incorrectly, thought having mates meant being protected and cared for above all else. They were supposed to do anything for her. Even get over a centuries-long vendetta. Or accept her as she was, without wanting to change things about her.

In that moment, as she fought to stay conscious

through the pain, she decided she might even hate them over this. *Never would have been taken by the farmer if they hadn't locked me up in a room by myself while they challenged each other.* Locked up in a room like a pet. Again.

They don't deserve me.

"Going to pass out so soon?" the farmer asked in a mockingly disappointed tone. "A little more torture, and your weak, little prey mind might break. Humans go into shock after enough pain. Shifters revert back to their animal form once they reach their breaking point. Thus, soon, you won't be able to stop yourself from shifting."

"Why are you doing this?" she asked weakly, her voice barely audible from her scratchy throat. *So much screaming.*

The man scoffed. "Money."

"I'm a queen. I can give you money."

"Not *this* kind of money."

The hose turned on again.

☾

*L*una did not know how much more of this she could take. She was getting closer and closer thinking: *Maybe life would be easier in eternal sheep form. If he just shears me, I might live a few years. If he cuts me up to sell as, in his words, 'prime lamb,' then death would be quick.* Still, she badly wanted to live. To experience things she never allowed herself while Rohan hunted her.

But this is torture.

She had no chance of getting free, not with so many injuries. She could hardly stand on her own.

The farmer had gone to "milk" one of his cattle—a

statement that caused her blood to curdle in her veins. During her short reprieve, she shifted into animal form. Though prey did not have the same supernatural healing that the stronger predators did, she would heal at least a little faster in that form than as a human.

It was only less than ten minutes, however, until the farmer returned.

The second she heard him, she began to shift back to human—not realizing her shifting would take longer due to her broken bones.

The farmer hooted with excitement when he saw her in sheep form. He grabbed at his keys, moving to unlock the cage.

Oh Gods, he's going to inject me. She thrashed her body on the ground, willing herself to shift through the pain. *Hurry up*, she begged herself. The farmer swung open her cage. *Hurry up!*

He pulled a thin rectangular box from his back pocket, opened it, and prepared a needle.

Dang it, hurry up and shift back, she begged her body. Her hands flickered between human fingers and hooves. Finally, just as he knelt beside her, her body convulsed and turned completely human.

She exhaled a harsh breath of relief.

"Damn it," the farmer cursed loudly, smacking her across the face and causing her to yelp. "Why can't you just stay shifted?"

"Don't...want to."

"Well, I'd rather have your special wool, but I suppose I could get started with reaping something for my efforts so far."

She blinked dazedly through the pangs of her suffering.

He dug into his back pocket again for something. He pulled out a switchblade.

No.

He settled onto his knees beside her as he moved the blade closer. "Your skin, even in human form, has useful properties."

"*Please.* Don't."

"Let's see how much skin I can get before your little mind breaks and you shift back."

And then...*agony.*

"**W**hich way?" Daxton demanded from Hag as he dragged the seer through the underground basement of the farmhouse. There were multiple tunnels. Already, they had passed a goat shifter in a cage. *Need to find my mate.*

The seer's eyes flashed white, and she pointed to the right.

The men hustled down the hall. The smell of dirt, rust, and blood made them move faster. Even with their super speed, they had to keep stopping to ask the seer which turns to make. So many intersections. So many scents of prey shifters overlapped, all hidden in different corridors.

None of the men wanted to split up to search. They were working together—for once—to find their mate. Their combined fear for Luna unified them. The idea of truly losing her...

Need to find her.

"Left," the seer instructed, and the men blurred down the dim, cement-walled hallway.

Then, a shrill scream echoed through the underground tunnels.

"*Moonbeam!*" Kobe growled, rushing forward to follow the sound.

The predators moved faster than they ever had, their hearts beating quickly as dread twisted their organs. Their breaths came in a rush as they worried over the state in which they would find her. *Please let her be okay. Let her not be permanently shifted.*

"Luna!"

A soft whimper was barely audible, but it speared through their ears.

Then, a male curse, and a crash, and the sound of broken glass.

Finally, Bastille, Daxton, Kobe, Sly, and Nikolai appeared in front of the metal cell holding their mate. What they saw shook them to their core. Blood—their mate's fucking blood—and bits of her skin and a red tag pierced through her ear.

An ear that was one of a lamb.

"Luna," one of them shouted in a hoarse heartbroken voice that all the men felt in their chests.

"*No*," another rasped, the tone gut-wrenching.

"Who the fuck are you?" The stranger in the cell stood and approached the men. "These here are my cattle! Get your own."

It happened in half a second.

Daxton's mouth opened, and bright red and orange flames covered the man from head to toe. He screamed in agony, again and again as the dragon's fire ate away at his skin, before he dropped down to the floor of the cell. Dead.

The men lightly shoved at each other as each one entered the cell, taking steps toward Luna's lamb form.

Skittish, she trotted back into a dark corner of the cell until there was nowhere left to go. A soft, nervous "*Baaaaaah*," came from her.

The men seemed to simultaneously collapse to their knees before her, clutching at their hearts or mouths or pulling at their hair as they saw her unfamiliar, beady light brown eyes—no emotion shining through. Just…blank.

"Luna, do you recognize us?" Sly asked gently.

Another monotone: "*Baaaah*."

Daxton slammed his fists to the floor, cracking the gray concrete floor. "Hag, how do we fix this?"

The seer crossed her arms and leaned against the metal bars. "Well, if you used context clues, you'd see he didn't get to inject her with the 'stuck forever in animal form' serum." She kicked at the broken glass of the small needle where wet liquid oozed from it.

Hope rose, only to dwindle. "Why can't she shift back?"

"Shift for us, Moonbeam?" Kobe purred to her.

Luna's lamb head tilted.

All of them held their breath.

But nothing happened.

CHAPTER 53

The seer pursed her lips at the little lamb. "She must have undergone so much pain that it broke her mind. Like the way humans go catatonic when they see a basilisk shifter in snake form. She would have reverted to animal form to protect her brain."

"But she's safe now—"

"Doesn't matter. Some shifters go catatonic, shift into animal form, and can never shift back."

The men froze at Hag's words.

"But she will heal eventually," Daxton assured everyone like he needed to say it aloud to believe it himself. "Even as a prey, she is a shifter and she can heal and—"

"*Men.*" The seer snorted. "It's not just physical injuries. It's called psychological damage. Pure pain, abandonment, and fear for her life made her this way. All of which you have experienced at some point in your lives."

All of the men winced, taking on that guilt and regret like arrowheads to each eye.

"How do we get her back?" Bastille whispered, staring down at the little lamb who watched him with blank eyes.

Hag's irises flashed with light again. "Give her the opposite of pain and fear. Show her she can trust you implicitly. Give her reasons to shift back to human form."

"But she hates us," Nikolai reminded everyone. "How are we going to get her to trust us?"

"Romcom movie night at Daxton's castle," Hag squealed with excitement, not matching the mood of the room at all. "I'll get the popcorn and you'll take notes during the grand gestures parts."

"Will you go home with us, little lamb?" Daxton asked her so softly, his voice might have been confused with silk.

"We're going to protect you," Bastille promised in just as gentle a tone.

"Feed you," Kobe added.

The men inched closer to Luna, stretching out their hands for her to sniff and lessen her fear.

Hag grinned her crazy smile in the background. "In this week's episode of *Sheep Whisperer...*"

☾

"*B*ut she loves my grilled cheese," Kobe growled at Sly when the fox shifter turned off the stove and stole his spatula. The werewolf had already made thirteen grilled cheeses; they piled up on a single plate.

"Yeah, in human form." Sly threw the cheese packets back in the refrigerator. "Sheep don't eat cheese. They eat plants and shit."

"My mate does not eat shit," Daxton grated from the kitchen table of the cabin.

"I didn't mean actual shit. I meant—" Sly stopped himself, rolling his eyes and groaning. "Whatever."

"I've never known an herbivore shifter," Bastille said. "Do we just get her grass from outside?"

Nikolai looked up from his phone where he sat beside Daxton at the table. "Google says lambs eat 'ground foods and tender forage.'"

Sly cursed, "What the fuck is tender forage?"

Nikolai clarified, "Forage that's been tenderized."

"Fuck you."

"Stop fighting," Bastille chastised the men from his spot on the floor.

Since the moment they had all settled in the Dark Ones' large cabin—after explaining to Daxton that a lamb would feel more overwhelmed in a grand castle—Bastille had not left Luna's side. His hands remained firmly planted in her wool at all times. Petting her. Calming her. Within the first few hours, she stopped shaking in his presence.

Of any of the men, Bastille's guilt was the most agonizing. If he had never called for a contestation, if he had trusted in the prophecy and let go of his hatred of the Dragomir family, his mate would have never gone through such pain.

Would take on all the pain for her, Bastille thought as his gut twisted, and he gently petted her shaggy, unbelievably soft wool. *Little fluffy ball of white*.

"Did the king of the Dark Ones just tell us *not* to fight?" Sly asked, incredulous.

Bastille was…changing. Almost losing a mate did that to a person.

For the first time in his life, Bastille was gentle. He had ever so slowly worked the red tag out of her ear and bandaged the bleeding area. He had tenderly bathed her with buckets of soapy, warm water. Sure, Daxton and Bastille had bickered about what temperature the water should be for their little lamb, but she sat patiently in the tub until they figured it out. He brushed her, pet her, and never left her side.

Days passed with her in animal form. The men tried not to convey their disappointment each morning when they woke and she was still the same. Bastille and Kobe took turns feeding her.

All of the men would spend time whispering promises to her. "Once you shift back, we'll do whatever you've been dreaming about. Travel the world. Eat at the finest restaurants. Or pancakes and grilled cheese. Whatever you want."

"Once you shift back, I have a full set of paints for you, little mate," Daxton would say to her. "You can improve these cabin walls. They drastically need it."

The men did everything they could not to fight as they tried to create a stress-free, relaxing environment for her. But there were some days…

"You won't even try it?" Daxton yelled at Bastille. "It could shift her back today!"

"I am *not* hypnotizing her. It may not even work."

"Then, why not try it?"

"Because I took her choice away from her before," Bastille shouted back at him. "I had her turned into a vampire against her will and she—" *Hated me.* "I'm never doing anything like that again. She'll take the time she needs to herself until she can shift back. We shouldn't rush her."

☾

*L*una stared at the kitchen counter, the men not noticing her fascination. Every day, Kobe made her a grilled cheese and kept it on a plate for her just in case she shifted that day. And she wanted it. She missed human food. She was stuck eating grass and ground corn all day.

The men would sneak around each other and hand feed her to try to get her to like them more. It was adorable. Sweet.

She wanted to tell them that.

She wanted to tell Bastille that she saw how soft and gentle he was with her. That she appreciated his constant comfort. She wanted to thank Daxton for shipping in some fancy as heck grass that admittedly tasted better than whatever they first fed her.

In fact, Daxton kept buying her random things, wanting to spoil her. His latest overspending habit was purchasing dresses for her animal form, which the guys had many thoughts about, consisting of: "Dude, we're taking your credit card away. You have a problem."

Luna wanted to laugh at Sly's jokes and tell him to stop being so serious—sometimes he would gaze at her with such an expression of dejection and pained yearning that she wanted to hug him. All she could do was poke her nose at his knees. She wanted to tell Nikolai to go hunting for blood because he wouldn't leave the cabin and he was clearly starving.

She wanted to snuggle with Kobe on the couch and watch the silly cartoons he put on every morning.

In her animal form, she had learned new things about her men. New quirks. They even had a game night and played cards on the floor—always wanting to be level with their mate instead of on the tall chairs—while Luna trotted around them in a circle and saw who had the best chance of winning.

Bastille kept losing because Sly figured out that Luna blinked twice whenever Bastille was bluffing. Sly kept that bit of knowledge to himself, winking at her throughout the game night.

She wanted to play them—annihilate them—in card games. And share meals with them. And travel the world like they promised.

"You will love Scotland," Daxton told her while holding a world traveling book. He would flip the pages and point to things for her. Whenever she nudged the page with her nose, he wrote down the area to visit in the future. "Stretches of wide green land for you to graze."

Nikolai scoffed. "We can't take her on a plane in her lamb form."

Sly defended Daxton, "But she's my emotional support animal."

"I have my own jet," Daxton added helpfully. "And plenty of money to bribe her into the country."

The men were adjusting. In the beginning of her animal state, they had clutched at their hearts and shed tears. Guilt and pain consumed their expressions every time they looked at her. Now, they were working together to provide for her, becoming a unit.

They made it known that they would be there for her in any form: vampire, prey, lamb…

They were not just being kind to her, but also to each other. When Daxton blew flames onto a marshmallow, Sly spent the rest of the night throwing random foods in the air to A) test the Light King's aim and B) see what the best torched snack was. Spoiler: it was marshmallows. Another spoiler: wooden cabins are flammable but thankfully, no real damage was done.

As angry and hurt as she had been from these predator shifters, she had begun to forgive them. Every day they stayed by her, with no promise of a future with her, and took care of her in this form, she fell a little bit in love with them.

Each night, the predators gathered all the pillows and sheets and formed a nest of cushions and warm male bodies around Luna.

Never felt so…taken care of.

They provided for her. They cooed their regret of how they had acted and promised to be better. She *witnessed* them being better.

Each morning, Bastille and Daxton would glance at each other and nod, as if they had a new understanding of what it meant to share a mate. Aka: to be civil and not act like spoiled, spiteful children.

One night, Bastille had pet her and whispered, "Even if you never turn back, this is enough for me. Just being near you will always be enough for me."

As the days passed, Luna felt more and more like

herself. She would poke her cold wet nose onto the men's cheeks. Kobe would purr, "*Moonbeam*," and hold her tight in his big arms.

"I miss your snarky comments, lamb," Bastille would whisper to her. "I know everyone wants you to turn back, but sometimes I worry that once you do, you'll hate us. And you have every right to. I don't deserve you." The basilisk stroked her. Petted her. "But I would do anything to make it all up to you. To start over."

Days passed of tender touches and words, until her mind felt clear.

Kobe sat on the ground while watching TV, and she jumped onto him, tackling him. Her hooves pinned his shoulders as he gaped up at her, on his back.

"Moonbeam?" His tone dripped with excitement. Anticipation. Hope.

She nuzzled her face into the crook of his neck.

"Moonbeam, please come back to me. To us." He burrowed his face into her wool. "Need you. Love you."

And she began to shift.

CHAPTER 54

*B*astille had finally taken a shower after all of the men's griping. Apparently, he had refused to leave Luna's side "long enough" because the men shoved him into the bathroom with a towel and a brand-new bar of soap.

He grumbled bitterly as he washed away the lather over his chest and meaty arms. Basilisk shifters did not often have to shower because they could just shed their skin for a new one. As fun as he felt it could be to leave the skinned shell of his body somewhere Daxton would stumble across it, he didn't want Luna to find it and have another reason to stay catatonic.

Loud shouting reverberated through the bathroom door, and Bastille quickly shut the water off to listen.

When he heard Kobe shout, "*Moonbeam,*" followed by a crashing noise, Bastille sprinted from the shower. Not taking the time to grab a towel to cover his naked body, Bastille splattered water all over the floors as he ripped open the door and ran for the living room of the cabin.

"What? What's happened?"

Bastille skidded to a stop, nearly slipping, as he saw Luna's human form shaking in Kobe's arms. Both of them were crying and clutching each other. Sly, Nikolai, and Daxton all burst into the living room as well. The intake of breath from all the men echoed around the space.

"Luna."

"Lamb."

"Little Mate."

The men fell once more to their knees, shuffling into a circle around Kobe and Luna, all reaching to put a hand on her, to verify this was real.

"We're so sorry, Luna," they repeated their apologies.

"So sorry," Kobe grunted into her neck.

"We'll never choose anything over you again."

"You are *everything*."

Bastille was one of the few not pleading out an apology. He sat on his knees, frozen. His heart beat anew in his chest. His cold reptilian blood warmed in his veins. *She is okay*. He could have cried.

When she pulled back from Kobe, the werewolf still firmly holding her to his body, she glanced at Bastille. Her beautiful blue eyes on him once more caused a cracking sensation in his chest. She reached out one of her small hands to him, and he leaned forward until she cupped his cheek.

"Bastille," she whispered.

"It was all my fault," the basilisk rasped in a broken voice. "All my fault. Acted like a bastard. I'm so sorry."

"Bastille," she repeated softly.

"Never felt so scared. Never wanted to lose you."

"*Shh*, basilisk," she cooed.

"Understand me, Luna." He grabbed one of her hands and squeezed it. "I have learned, in the harshest of ways, to put the past behind me. Daxton… I'm okay with it. We're all okay with it as long as we have you. Please don't leave us. I—I want to give you everything you ever wanted. I promise to be better. I promise—"

"I forgive you," she said, and his ragged exhale shook his entire being.

He closed his eyes and gripped her hand harder in his.

"They were all falling apart without you," Sly remarked.

A little smirk flashed across Luna's face. "But not you, right?"

"Who, me?" Sly scoffed. "I am far too manly."

"Who knew fox shifters were such liars?" she joked, and Sly chuckled—fifty-four percent from amusement and forty-six percent from relief.

"We were a wreck without you," Daxton purred to her, stroking a hand down her bare back. "You can truly forgive us?"

She shrugged, still held by Kobe. "If you ever act that way again, I'll just leave you all behind. And don't even *think* about locking me in a room again."

Bastille smiled wickedly with pride as he told Daxton, "My mate can pick locks."

"Our mate," the dragon corrected.

With a stiff nod, Bastille agreed, "Our mate."

"Wow, who knew I'd ever see you two agree on something—" She cut off and flinched, pulling fully back from

Kobe's arms and glancing down at her stomach. She dropped a hand over her side before trying again. "Watching you two agree on something is like—" She winced again, whimpering in what sounded like...pain?

"What's happening?" Sly asked into the void of concerned men.

Fear injected itself into Bastille's veins.

"I—Oh, gods," she cried out and clutched at her sides, stomach, and abdomen.

The men crowded around her, hastily shoving at each other as they examined her for injuries. They ran their hands over her, seeing no external reason for her pain. Being in animal form for so long had healed her past injuries.

Yet, she shuddered and yelped.

"What is it?" Bastille demanded, willing her pain away and wishing he could take it on for her.

"S-Something is happening." She whimpered again and clutched herself, turning into a little defensive ball as she curled up on the floor. She grimaced as pain appeared to stab at her stomach.

"What?"

Another whimper of pain. She pressed her lips tightly shut as her body convulsed.

"Why is she in pain?" Bastille asked the group in a rough, demanding voice, seeming just as tortured as she was, watching his mate writhe.

"I—I feel—" she trembled and grasped at her midsection. "Something else is happening. I think i-it's..."

"Oh, shit," Sly mumbled. "It's her—"

"Heat," Nikolai finished his sentence. "She's going into heat."

The men went stiff around her on the floor as the realization washed over them.

Running a hand through his hair, Daxton added not so helpfully, "She's been in human form less than five minutes!"

"Yeah, and she's surrounded by one, two, three, four, *five* alpha predator shifters at one time. That would trigger the defense mechanism instantly."

"How long do we have until she begins to strew the pheromones…?"

The male voice—whoever had been speaking, Bastille tuned him out—drifted off as the first wave of seductive pheromones wafted from Luna.

She finally uncurled her body and laid on her back as her first yearning moan came from her—the pain gone, nothing but raw craving in its place.

Her heat-induced scent seemed to puff out in steamy clouds of invisible smoke—choking the men, overriding each breath they took. As her body vibrated with need, the men's pupils dilated into large black spheres like they were high on her. Drugged by her pheromones. Their cocks swelled in their pants, thickening and lengthening further with each inhale of her scent.

"*Fuck,*" one of the men cursed in a raspy voice.

"It's…strong," Sly whispered in a tortured tone.

"*Please,*" she called out.

Sly reached for her, but Daxton growled, snapping his teeth at him, "*Mine.*" His primal expression suggested his mate's scent triggered his animal side—his possessive and aggressive fire-breathing dragon side. Even now, Daxton's eyes flashed serpentine. His expression was one of mindless lust—no recognition of the others. A rabid dog foaming at the mouth for her.

When Daxton's lips curled over sharp, threatening teeth, he appeared ready to bite off Sly's hand. Bastille warned, "Sharing. Remember, dragon?"

"*Claim*," Daxton snapped, nostrils flaring with her scent.

Throwing his arms up in surrender, Sly asked, "What's happening to him?"

"It's the impulse," Bastille explained through clenched teeth. "Alphas feel the overwhelming need to claim their mate. It can make us mindless. The only reason Kobe and I aren't shoving everyone away and pouncing on her is because we've claimed her once before."

Bastille slowly moved closer to Luna, watching Daxton uneasily. "He has yet to claim her for the first time, and dragons are especially greedy, possessive creatures. He's ravenous for her."

"*Claim*," the dragon repeated, flashing his sharp teeth.

Pink-faced, Luna whined a sound of yearning. Her hands fell mindlessly down her curves, cupping and squeezing and petting herself in front of the men who all remained frozen in place.

"Daxton, you've got to get control of yourself," Bastille ordered. "She's a prey again which means she is delicate. She can't take your claiming '*rutting*.'"

Daxton's hands ripped his dress shirt in half, shredding it from his body as he hastily unbuckled his belt and shoved down his pants. He growled with big black pupils, *"Rut her."*

Bastille blinked. "What did I just say?"

"Please," she cried, her hips bucking up from the floor and flexing in the air. All of them paused to watch her creamy thighs shake with need.

"We need to put her on a bed. Now."

Daxton swooped her up in his arms and rushed her to the closest bedroom. He laid her down onto the mattress, the others rushing in behind him. His body loomed over hers, about to mount her and fuck her into oblivion.

"Fucking stop," Bastille shouted, yanking Daxton's massive body off the bed by the back of his thick neck.

The dragon released a threatening rumble, like he was about to produce lethal flames.

"Calm the hell down. You're lathered up in a state that could hurt her."

"Never hurt her."

Bastille continued holding Daxton by the back of the neck. "Look, we all have to help her through her heat. One person isn't enough. So, when one of us touches her, you can't go all 'possessive alpha dragon' on us, okay? We all need to pleasure her."

Daxton narrowed his eyes on Bastille and growled again.

"Damn it, dragon. Maybe if you had sex before your wedding night you might have better control over yourself right now," Bastille said. "The more goddamn pheromones she pumps out, the less any of us will be able to *not* touch her. Understand? *Share.*"

Writing on the bed, Luna screamed for their attention, "PLEASE."

"Can you control yourself?" Bastille questioned Daxton as the dragon shifter pushed to get back to his mate. "She's vulnerable to injury, and the pheromones are only going to make the mindlessness worse. Can you be gentle with her?"

"Gentle." Daxton nodded, shoving at Bastille so he could join Luna on the bed again.

The moment Daxton held himself over Luna, she reached out and toyed with his bare cock. "Please," she gasped out, her eyes big and pleading. The dragon was instantly entranced. *Mindless need, back again.* She rubbed her palm over his growing bulge, cupping him. "I need you. Please."

At her touch, Daxton's pupils became thin, reptile-like slits. His skin flickered with red scales, shifting back and forth as his instinct ruled him. He began to mount her again.

"Shit," Bastille cursed, climbing onto the bed. The others hesitated to move closer, knowing a basilisk was the only true match for an enraged dragon.

Luna continued caressing Daxton's crotch, causing him to grate, "*Rut.*"

"Easy, big guy," Bastille said. In a turn of events, the basilisk stole Luna's other free hand and pressed it to his own erection. "You need to stop teasing the dragon, Princess. Want to play with my cock too?" At her touch, his trousers tented, his cock threatening to punch through the fabric. He thrust into her soft little hand. "Is this what you need?"

Even with hazy eyes and a lust-drunk expression, Luna narrowed her gaze on Bastille. She squeezed her hand over his pants tent and replied through her teeth, "Not a princess."

He grinned at her as he corrected himself, whispering, "Queen."

CHAPTER 55

*S*he felt like she was burning up with a fever—her skin so hot, someone could use her as a pancake griddle. A sheen of sweat glistened over her as her body quaked with each spasm and clenching of lust.

What the hell is wrong with these men? Mount her already! She felt her stomach ripple, and everything blurred. Her breath hitched, her back arched, and a new wave of pheromones emanated from her flushed skin. Her limbs and blood and heart thrummed with desire.

"*Hurry,*" she begged, and before she knew it, Kobe had pounced onto the end of the bed, shoving her legs apart and settling his mouth right between them. "*Yes!*"

The werewolf's lips closed over the top of her damp slit, tongue delving between her damp folds and darting to play with her throbbing bundle of nerves. In controlled strokes, he laved at her clit, performing expertly crafted flicks with the tip of his tongue. *Flick, flick.* Up and down. And up and down. *Yes.* She fisted his dark hair and moaned so loudly, it caused the men's oversensitive ears to twitch.

"Daxton, *calm yourself!*" She heard Bastille demand, but she was lost in Kobe's talented tongue.

The werewolf's fingers inched between her legs, probing her hot entrance. His chest rumbled with approval as he pulled away to growl, "*So wet.* Dripping for us."

"Hear that, dragon?" Bastille whispered into her ear even as he spoke directly to Daxton. "Your mate likes being touched like this. He's not a threat to you."

She let out a tortured whimper.

Daxton grunted.

"See her pretty little nipples? Look how hard they're getting," Bastille asked Daxton while trailing a finger down her curves. "Maybe you should play with one. Think about how good it would feel to suckle your mate."

Daxton grunted again. Suddenly, his hot palm fell over her right breast, clutching the flesh.

"But be gentle," Bastille reminded him.

After a faint growl, Daxton bent and pressed soft kisses over her right breast. He swiped his long tongue over her hard nipple, pebbling it further into a stiff peak that he suckled between his lips. Bastille did the same.

As Kobe sucked the swollen nub of flesh between her legs, the basilisk pinched her left nipple, making it sting, before licking away the pain. "You like having your tits sucked by us, lamb?" he asked gruffly.

"*Mmmm.*" Her head writhed from side to side on the mattress as Kobe flicked that perfect tongue over her and buried his thick fingers into her quivering pussy. In and out. *In. out. Lick. Flick. Suck.* "*Yes.*"

There was movement above her head, a shifting of weight on the bed, and she blinked up to see Sly smile and lean down to nuzzle and suck at her earlobes, one of her most powerful erogenous zones.

So many mouths on me. So many tongues. Hands stroking over her hips, her chest, her neck, her legs. Her skin was hypersensitive to each touch during her heat, the cells acting on the fritz.

"Please," she moaned out. "*Inside me.*"

She needed them inside her.

She tuned in and out, hardly hearing Bastille exchange low whispers with Daxton as Kobe's fingers dug into her fleshy thighs as he rhythmically sucked at her clit. His fingers inside her expertly prodded and rubbed that deep, inner ribbed flesh, causing every one of her breaths to turn choppy and desperate. More wetness rushed between her thighs, readying her for what was to come.

The tightness in her stomach gripped her, her pussy clenching around his digits and begging to be filled with something more. She flew one of her hands over and gripped Daxton's crotch again. "*Inside*," she cried out.

A new potent wave of pheromones emanated from her slick bare skin, sucker-punching the men. Luna could practically see the self-control in their expressions begin to slip. Nikolai and Bastille ground their aching erections against various parts of her.

It was Daxton who appeared to completely black out at the next airborne aphrodisiac-like cloud of pheromones.

He rolled onto her, launching Kobe to the other corner of the large bed, dislodging the werewolf's mouth and fingers from her pussy in one fell swoop.

"*Claim.*"

Her whine morphed into a moan as Daxton yanked her

legs up to wrap around his waist. Both his large hands settled at either side of her shoulders where his claws punctured through the sheets and mattress.

Bastille cursed somewhere in the background, but Luna could not hear him over the sound of her own frantic heartbeat as Daxton's cockhead nudged her slit, slipping through and grazing her clit. A guttural snarl vibrated Daxton's lips as he drove his hips forward and slammed his cock over her.

Panting, she undulated and rocked to try to position him at her entrance. He just kept thrusting forward, grinding onto her wetness and slicking his cock with it. *Preparing me for his size?* The long, thick length should have scared her; but, as a prey shifter in heat, all she could think was, *"Please."*

Considering Daxton's hands were practically inside the mattress—due to his *sharp*, sharp dragon talons—he could not reach down and align himself to plunge his raging cock inside her. His hips frantically rocked and churned against her, but all that accomplished was teasing both of them further and further into mindless lust.

"Damn it," Bastille grated, and Luna blinked her eyes open to see him move behind Daxton, kneeling on the bed. "To be clear, I'm doing this so you don't hurt her. So, don't get any ideas for the future," the basilisk mumbled bitterly.

Luna glanced between her spread legs, which Sly and Nikolai shifted to hold down and splay open across the mattress. Kobe sat behind Luna's head now and kneaded her breasts with his hot palms. His large erection pulsed against her ear, tempting her to turn her head and give it a lick.

But she got distracted.

Because Bastille's hand closed around the base of Daxton's thick cock.

"*Rut her*," the dragon growled, flexing his hips, but Bastille had him caged as he wrapped his free hand over Daxton's throat and held his shaft in the other from behind him.

"We're going to do this nice and slow," Bastille told them.

How he was still capable of orderly thought at this point, Luna did not understand. Red-faced and shaking from another round of contractions overtaking her body, her mind was lost.

On instinct, Daxton aggressively tried to buck Bastille's hold from him, but he was held in a choking grip both on his throat and cock. "Shhh," Bastille whispered to him like Daxton was a spooked horse lashing out. To try to calm him, Bastille ran his palm up and down in one firm stroke over the dragon's red-tipped erection.

Daxton's expression broke out into confused pleasure, his eyebrows furrowed yet high on his forehead, as if he wanted to resist liking the basilisk's touch but couldn't help himself.

Luna held her breath in anticipation as Bastille leaned Daxton back over her body and, with an unyielding grip on his length, slid Daxton's cockhead down to the entrance of her pussy.

Just before the dragon could slam his hips down and sink inside her for the first time, Bastille smirked at Luna from over Daxton's shoulder and shifted his cock right before any penetration occurred. Instead, the action caused

Daxton's hot shaft to swipe over the top of her slit again, scraping her clit.

Daxton snarled in lustful rage.

An evil, unamused chuckle came from Bastille's chest behind the dragon. He dragged Daxton's cock through her folds, up and down. Up and down. Teasing both of them with his utter control of their pleasure.

Luna squirmed, and Bastille tapped Daxton's cock against her clit. *Tap. Tap.* She whined, bucking her hips for more. She could feel Daxton's erection somehow getting even bigger.

Head flailing back and forth in sexual frustration, Luna shrieked, "Stop messing around and fuck me." Kobe pinched her nipples, and she moaned, growing even slicker.

"Did you hear that?" Bastille tsked, still playing with Daxton's cock in her folds. "So demanding. I think she needs a reminder as to who is in charge here."

She gyrated her hips and whined, "*Please.*"

"I don't know…" Bastille commented in a teasing tone. "Do you think she's wet enough yet, Dax?" He steered the dragon's erection once more, rubbing the sensitive tip directly over her swollen clitoris. Circling and circling.

She could hardly breathe.

Daxton's black pupils were ballooned, his nostrils flaring from inhaling his mate's aroused scent. Incapable of speech, the dragon bucked his hips forward, his jaw growing slack as more of her wetness clung to his shaft. *Thrust. Thrust. Groan.*

"Well? Is she wet enough, Dax?"

"I am. I am," she cried out.

417

"Hmm, are you sure?"

"Soaked. Now, please," she begged.

Bastille aligned Daxton's cock with her entrance once more.

Yes! Finally.

Daxton sank inside her by a single inch, wrenching a deep moan from the dragon's chest, before Bastille wrenched him back out and smacked his fat cockhead over her throbbing clit. The flesh slapped against each other, the force reverberating through her bundle of nerves. Daxton and Luna groaned in dissatisfaction.

"You don't like that?" Bastille taunted.

"No more teasing," Luna pleaded.

"You'll be a good girl?"

"Yes!"

"I want you to make him come quickly, Luna," Bastille added. "I want inside you."

She nodded and mumbled incoherent words as he dragged Daxton's thick shaft back and forth over her clit. "*Mmhmm.*"

Daxton's head had fallen to his chest at the sensations. The two of them were puppets—absolute sexual putty—in Bastille's hands.

"You think you can make him come within three minutes, lamb? That's how long I'm giving you until I'm inside you."

"Uh huh, uh huh," she nodded, though she hardly knew what she was agreeing to as her core clenched and her clit pulsed wildly with each stroke of Daxton's length over it.

"You're going to be a good girl and milk your pretty pussy around him? Suck every last drop of cum from him?"

Bastille's filthy words just stoked the fire building inside her abdomen. Swirling heat that rose and rose, getting hotter and hotter. Uncontrollable.

More pheromones.

Then, the sound of male teeth grinding and curses. "*Fuck.*"

"Three minutes. That's all I can wait," Bastille reminded her as he positioned Daxton at her pussy once more. "Make him come in three minutes or less. Or we'll both be inside you at the same time. Him in your pussy and me stretching that perfect fucking ass. Clock starts now."

CHAPTER 56

*B*astille's words echoed around in her skull as Daxton's thick cock sank inside her, inch by inch, stretching her flesh. *Clock starts now.* If she couldn't get Daxton to come in three minutes, she would have two men inside her at the same time.

The thought wildly excited her, causing her core to clench around Daxton's shaft. He growled with narrowed eyes as he fought to plunge fully inside her. Bastille gripped him in such a way that the basilisk had control over the pace of Daxton's thrusts.

Luna couldn't help thinking back to the dual sensation of back when Bastille fucked her with a finger teasing her ass. The tingles... The fullness... That had just been a finger or two. Bastille's cock was—*ahem*—big.

She lost her train of thought as a groan wrenched itself from deep within Daxton's chest. Sweat dripped from his wide, tense chest as he pushed—or rather, Bastille pushed—his cock farther inside her. The length of him eased into her, and her hot inner muscles clamped around him in such a tight, vise-like grip, it was difficult to feed his shaft any deeper.

So full.

"How does he feel, lamb?" Bastille asked.

"*Good*," she moaned out, her pussy pulsing around him again.

"And how does she feel, dragon?"

A low, rumbling growl.

As Bastille guided him inside her a little more, Daxton's thick muscular arms twitched and the tendons in his neck strained.

By the time his cock was fully sheathed in her, Luna's back arched off the bed, pressing her hips firmly to his. She was murmuring something that sounded like a dead language. Or made-up language. Or…it didn't matter.

Because Daxton filled her to the hilt.

She cursed, breathless and writhing on his shaft. In the midst of her heat, her stomach contracted, and her pussy tightened even more around him, seeming to try to suck him in deeper. Warmth and awareness prickled at her every pore. *So full.*

"Ready for your first round of fucking, lamb?" Bastille asked her.

Her hair tangled in knots at her head as she shook with pent up need. "Please, *please*, please." She clawed at Daxton's chest.

"Get her arms," Bastille told one of the men behind her, and someone secured her wrists and held them back, behind her head, toward the headboard of the bed. "You're going to take all our cocks by the end of the night, like a good little slut for us, aren't you, Luna?"

"*Yes!*"

"You like the idea of us thrusting inside you? Of being full of our cum? Of it dripping out of your pretty little pussy?"

Her eyes went crossed at his words, her sex squeezing tighter around Daxton.

"You want to be held down and fucked within an inch of your life—" Bastille cut off. Even Daxton's low grunts waned.

Because Luna's pheromones spiked the air once more. But this was…new. Somehow more intense.

Like a radio frequency that blanked out all ability to think.

This wave of her strew wafted out, knocked the air from their lungs, and spiced every breath with unbearable lust. Lips parted and nostrils flared. Their cocks swelled even larger, filling with the need to spend inside her. To *claim*. At some point, the men must have removed their clothing because now their bare erections brushed their hard, flat stomachs and glistened with pre-cum.

Something snapped in the brains of the predator shifters.

Reduced to grunting cavemen. Horny animals.

Bastille's eyes glazed over.

Daxton broke free of Bastille's grip and *rutted*.

He speared her pussy onto his reddened, engorged cock, pistoning in and out with such a frantic pace that each thrust launched her body further up the mattress. His thick thighs flexed with each harsh movement. His hips surged forward again and again, urging his cockhead to rub against the deepest parts of her. Mewls of pleasure seeped from her lips like pornographic music.

Under hooded eyelids, Daxton's large pupils were black holes, as soulless as a demon's.

"Mate. Rut. Need."

His constant, punishing pace drove her toward a powerful orgasm. A constant, steady pounding rhythm that made her teeth chatter and her limbs shake. Her head tilted back. Her mouth fell open on a silent scream as he just kept drilling into her again and again, jackhammering inside her. Her heart raced as heat expanded across her chest, flushing her skin. A sort of weightlessness began in her abdomen, coiling and twisting tighter and tighter. *Yes, Gods, yes—*

He was yanked out of her and thrown across the room.

She might have screamed if, in the next instant, Bastille had not appeared on top of her. He claimed the spot Daxton had been, his black eyes just as glassy. Just as mindless. A true predator, he wrapped a hand around her throat, collaring her, and licked his lips with a serpentine tongue.

Luna thrashed on the mattress, jerking her hips up to his, desperate for release. That dusky cockhead was near purple with desire, the veins so prominent, she thought she might feel each of his heartbeats with it inside her. He notched his big cock to her entrance and shoved inside, burying himself in her tight, wet heat. *Always the perfect fit.*

His grunt of pleasure echoed her moan of ecstasy. His free hand, not around her neck, dragged down her chest, playing with her pinkened mounds of flesh and pinching her nipple. Looming over her, he savagely filled her, tunneling in and out of her, eyes locked on hers.

All the while, Kobe, Sly, and Nikolai ran their hands over her body, stroking themselves while watching her.

Her mouth still hung open, incapable of speech or truly anything other than panting out every breath.

"Mine," Bastille declared through bared teeth.

He felt so good inside her. Too good? Her nearing orgasm was rising once more, a balloon about to pop. He rubbed the spot that made colors dash across her vision. He grabbed at her left thigh, moving it up and changing the angle to something earth-shattering. She quivered as he rammed away inside her.

"*Mine*," he repeated in an animalistic growl.

"Mine," Kobe joined in, suckling at her right nipple as Sly did the same to its twin.

"MINE." Daxton pounced onto the bed beside them and rolled them over, knocking off the others.

Bastille gnashed his teeth as his shaft slid from Luna's slick pussy. Daxton quickly secured Luna so that she laid on top of Bastille's chest, her body and legs stretched wide in front of where Daxton hovered over her on the mattress. With her back to Bastille and her front to Daxton, she was reminded of Bastille's earlier threat of double penetration. *Not a threat. A promise.*

She wanted it. She wanted all of them inside her. Touching her. She wished she had more hands.

Daxton buried his thick shaft inside her once more. Someone's hand sank down to play with her clit as the dragon resumed his addictive thrusts. "Mine," Daxton growled again as he hammered his urgent hips to hers. Hard. Fast.

"More," she cried out.

Daxton froze over her, and she blinked open her eyes to see he was being choked by a hand behind her. Bastille. The two men gazed at each other from over her shoulder. Daxton shot his own hand up and held Bastille in the same threatening grip. Both men already panted, but the choking led to tense, red faces.

A blood vessel made itself known on Daxton's forehead as—while being choked—he thrust inside her, slow and hard. Hard enough that her back was crushed into Bastille's chest with each motion. Daxton clearly could not breathe through Bastille's hold on him, yet he couldn't stop fucking her.

"Mine," Bastille said.

"M—uh—nah," Daxton could barely speak through the choking.

Shit, Bastille is really crushing his throat.

In a moment of coherent thought, Luna moved to distract the man at her back on the bed. She maneuvered her hand around her bottom, lifting herself up to touch the hard bulge at her lower spine. She teased his cock, stroking her thumb over the sensitive skin under the head of his length. That seemed to get Bastille's grip to loosen on Daxton's neck.

She continued her manipulations on Bastille's cock, rubbing and jerking him off behind her until finally his grasp on Daxton's throat loosened. His hand fell from him and moved behind her instead.

She gasped when his hot cockhead brushed against her back entrance. He teased the rosebud of flesh, pressing the tip inside her enough to have her sucking in two lungs-full of air.

"Mine," he repeated.

"Mine," Daxton shot back aggressively as he quickly jerked his hips, making the four-letter word seem to have multiple syllables according to his fast thrusts inside her.

"Yours," she whispered, taking every one of his savage thrusts and trying to get adjusted to Bastille's slow descent on claiming her virgin ass.

"Ours," another masculine voice growled. Kobe. The way she had been repositioned on the bed meant that— with her head fallen back at Bastille's shoulder—she saw Kobe crouched directly by her head. His hand swept up and down his flushed erection, the tip no farther than two feet away from her face. *Want him.*

She gazed at his dick and licked her lips. Even with the possibility of being filled by two men at once, she wanted three. *Go big or go home.*

But it wasn't just her heat. *I really do want all of them.* Smirks from Sly. Grilled cheeses and caveman grunts from Kobe. Snarky remarks and dirty yearning from Nikolai. The kindness and need to spoil her from Daxton. And the raw intensity and dominating magnetism of Bastille.

They are mine.

Keeping her gaze zeroed in on Kobe's hand jacking his cock in long strokes, she craned her neck, licking her pursed lips.

Reading her mind, Kobe sank closer, his knees on either side of her and Bastille's head as he lowered his shaft to her lips. With her head hanging back, her throat was level, a straight tunnel he could thrust inside. The perfect position for deep throating.

"Ours," he promised again in a low, throaty voice.

"Ours," Daxton echoed and slowed his ravaging of her.

"Ours," Bastille agreed.

Luna reached out toward Sly and Nikolai, offering her hands, and they took them. With their free hand, they touched her everywhere they could. Her stomach, hand, ankle…

All of them were connected.

Treasured. She felt treasured. About to be filled with three men at the same time—yet, treasured.

"Claim."

Teeth pierced into Luna, but this was not like a vampire's bite. It was a claiming bite. The one that meant forever. The pain dissipated quickly, and the bite seemed to make her feel…stronger. Immortality? Another of the men bit her. Then another. Her neck, arm, ankle…

Each bite stung on her skin, but a new wave of strength flooded through her.

They were making her stronger.

Daxton kept up the new, slower pace of his thrusting. Tilting her hips both provided a new, delicious angle for him to rub deep inside her and made it easier for Bastille's cock to sink a little deeper into her puckered entrance.

"Made for us," Bastille whispered.

Daxton grunted into each plunge. "Perfect."

"Love." Kobe stroked a finger over her cheek, and she cuddled into his touch, squirming to get closer. Her gaze locked onto his leaking cock.

"Love," the men agreed.

And she took Kobe's cock into her mouth.

CHAPTER 57

Two Years Later

"What would your people say if they could see their naughty little queen sucking a vampire's cock?" Bastille asked from the doorway of the grand castle bedroom.

It was rather early in the morning, but Daxton had already left their massive maroon silk-sheeted bed for light shifter "kingdom business." Sly and Kobe were passed out a couple feet beside her on the bed—always sleeping till close to noon.

All of them lived in the castle and royal bedroom together, bringing the two kingdoms—light and dark—together. The first year, it seemed impossible, as immortals clung to their old ways and prejudices. But the revolts were starting to dwindle under Daxton, Bastille, and Luna's rule.

When Luna had woken, Bastille's place beside her on

the mattress was empty and cold. Yet, she had smiled at the rumpled area he left behind. He typically visited the kitchen and brought her breakfast in bed, always trying to atone for his treatment of her back from the beginning of their relationship. No matter that she had spent the last two years telling him she forgave him.

Luna extracted her mouth from Nikolai's erection, holding herself up on her elbows to watch Bastille approach them with a platter of food. Nikolai's hard erection tapped at her chin, demanding her attention again as she loomed over his body on the bed. Her head faced the end of the mattress while Nikolai remained at the headboard of the bed as he splayed her thighs open and licked at her clit as his morning breakfast.

"Nikolai woke up hungry," she explained cheekily.

Bastille chuckled, light sparkling in his green eyes. Some days, the green appeared so much brighter than when she had first met him. No, not brighter—livelier. He remarked, "And we all know what a horny mess you become during his vampire bites."

She feigned an insulted gasp.

Meanwhile, Nikolai shook his face between her legs and growled against her pussy. The vibration from the sound distracted her.

Her arms and thighs trembled as the vampire doubled his efforts between her legs. Vampires had super speed for *every* part of their body. Thus, there was a hot, flattened tongue flicking against her clit with the speed of a frantic hummingbird's wings.

"Oh, fuck," she inhaled sharply, her hips bucking to Nikolai's mouth.

"I think you're getting distracted, Princess," Bastille cooed. He crossed his arms and leaned against one of the wooden pillars at the end of the bed. "Looks like Nikolai's doing all the work now."

She stuck her tongue out at Bastille before he suddenly appeared right in front of her, kneeling back on his legs on the mattress.

Her head was level to his crotch, but he directed her roughly with a, "Suck him off good, baby," and guided her head back down to Nikolai's engorged erection. She flattened the tip of her wet tongue against the aching head of his shaft. Nikolai's groan reverberated right through her pulsing clit.

As she wrapped her lips around him and sucked, he devoured her pussy with even more urgency. It was difficult not to get lost in the sensations. Hard to focus on bobbing her head and licking and sucking when he pushed her closer and closer to orgasm. The heat coiling and tightening inside her.

The first few months of being a prey with so many predator mates had been full of her heat—triggered by them. Eventually, her body lessened its pheromone production when it realized she was not going to leave these men and that sex almost every minute of every day, forever, was not maintainable. Much to her mates' dismay.

Noticing her distraction again, Bastille chortled and lightly pushed on the back of her head, sweeping her hair to the side as he watched her take Nikolai's cock in her lips. Bastille continued to apply more and more pressure to the base of Luna's skull until Nikolai's cock hit the back of her throat and she spluttered. Bastille was in the perfect position to observe as she looked up at him with watery eyes and moaned and gagged around the vampire's dick.

Nikolai's hips drove forward, nudging his length deeper in her mouth and throat. His satisfied grunts urged her on, as did his fervent lapping of his tongue between her legs.

"Fuck, you suck cock so well, lamb," Bastille purred to her, massaging his fingers into the back of her neck as she deep-throated Nikolai. "Swallow his dick."

She obeyed, her throat clamping down around his throbbing length. Nikolai groaned loudly, yet Sly and Kobe remained deep in sleep.

Bastille glanced over at them and snickered at something behind Luna's head. "You do realize, Kobe can smell his mate's arousal even in sleep? He's currently fucking the mattress." Bastille wished he had his phone to record the way Kobe slept on his stomach and grinded his morning erection into the bed. "Poor guy."

She bobbed her head faster over Nikolai, sucking harder and taking him as deeply as she could. Tears prickled her eyes, but she ignored them.

"*That's* it," Bastille praised her in that low, rumbly voice she loved so much. "Taking it so well." He rubbed a hand over the bulging crotch of his pants before ripping at the front of them.

Nikolai drove a finger into her pussy and curled it to rub her g-spot while still sucking her clit between his lips.

"*Ugahugah*," she moaned out around his length as she came onto his mouth.

"Enough," Bastille ordered, grabbed Luna by the hips, and redirected her body to face Nikolai's.

Bastille positioned her onto her hands and knees over

the vampire while Bastille lifted her, tilting her ass until his throbbing length prodded her wetness. His hand dug into her hair, pulling her head back roughly as he thrust inside her in one move.

Her passionate shriek at the sudden invasion woke Kobe from his sleep. The werewolf blinked his eyes open, glancing around and taking in the new scenery of Bastille fucking Luna from behind while Nikolai realigned his cock to her mouth.

"Look at how well our little slut takes her cocks in the morning," Bastille purred as he gyrated his length inside her. "So fucking wet. Practically dripping down her thighs."

A rumbling sound of approval came from Kobe as he leisurely laid back and stroked a hand over his dick, watching the show. Luna moaned as Nikolai breached her mouth once more, thrusting inside.

"Take him nice and deep," Bastille instructed Luna while she sucked off the vampire.

She moved forward until she gagged on him, sucking and choking and licking. She reveled in the way Nikolai's stomach muscles flexed and jumped when she did it.

Bastille's harsh, uneven breaths caressed her ear as he drilled his cock inside her tight pussy. Again and again. Rough. Hard. Fast. Taking his fill of her. His hand slapped down on her ass, and he groaned at the way her cheeks pinkened and jiggled for him. "Such a perfect fucking slut for us."

"*Mmmm*," she moaned around Nikolai's cock. Something about the vibration drove him wild. She watched, rapt, as a half-lidded blissed-out expression claimed his face. The vampire shot forward, bucking his hips with an erratic rhythm until he grunted, fisted her hair, and came with a loud groan.

At the sound of another male groan, she glanced over to see Kobe biting his lip and jerking himself off while he watched her swallow. She took her time, licking her lips as Kobe performed long, rough tugs on himself.

Bastille's hand came down on her ass again. The sharp sting of his palm changed to hot pleasure as he massaged the area. He kept pounding into her, spearing against the inner spots few could reach and tease quite like he could. He grated with each thrust, "So—fucking—good."

"I'm gone for fifteen damn minutes." Daxton's voice filtered through from the doorway of the grand bedroom. He shook his head, slipping the golden crown from his hair and placing it onto the table beside Luna's.

Bastille tossed a bored expression over his shoulder toward Daxton as he fucked Luna within an inch of her life. "Sounds like your problem."

Rolling his eyes, Daxton strode forward, already reaching for the buttons on his pants. "Did our little mate wake up needy again?"

"When is she ever *not* needy?" Bastille teased her by slowing his thrusts. She mewled her discontentment. "Thankfully, I'm here to give her greedy pussy what it needs. Why don't you go handle more 'kingdom business?'"

Daxton stripped himself in a matter of seconds, stalking to the bed. "If you're going to use that fucking mouth, use it on our mate."

Bastille smirked but tightened his grip on Luna's waist and turned them on the bed, so she faced Bastille and sat atop him. With his cock still inside her, he bent forward and cupped one of her breasts, kneading her tit and laving his smooth tongue over the pink tip and teasing it. "Mmm, there's that hard little nipple." When he began to suckle, her hips naturally rocked, grinding her clitoris on the base of him.

"That's it, baby," he purred to her as he squeezed her breasts, pinching the sensitive pink peaks. "Ride me. Take what you need."

She whimpered at the intense pleasure sparking through her as her hips slammed down over him. Her wet pussy contracted around him, and Bastille acted like her silken heat seared him.

Grunting, he helped guide her hips as she moved herself up and down his engorged length.

From behind her, Daxton kneeled on the mattress, running a hand over his cock. The swollen tip of his staff was an angry purple, as if it was enraged not to be inside her. "My turn," Daxton growled possessively.

Bastille cursed, continuing to drag her hips up and down, fucking himself with her pussy. "Then, share her. Take her ass, dragon. This pussy is mine right now."

"Bastille—"

He lifted his hips and began to thrust into her from below, bouncing her onto his hard cock. "My mate is riding my dick right now. I don't care that you've never taken her ass before." Bastille felt the beginnings of Luna's muscles tightening around him. "That's it, love. Come all over my cock."

Her head fell back as another orgasm swept through her, taking her away for a moment. Blanking out everything else but the rapturous spasms.

Bastille grated his words as her pussy clamped around him through her orgasm, "I don't understand why you refuse to fuck her ass. Is the 'good guy' proper dragon too good for it? Do you only want to fuck her in a way that will fill her with heirs?" Bastille slapped a hand over her clit, cupping her between her legs. "This is mine right now."

Daxton scowled as his hands fisted at his sides. "I don't…" His erection throbbed painfully for his mate. Red-tipped and leaky. Pre-cum already slicked him. "I'm not particularly concerned with making heirs right now."

"Stop playing the high and mighty card and take her ass," Bastille said. "You know you want to." He palmed the globes and split them, holding her open so Daxton saw the forbidden, puckered rosebud of flesh. "Do it. She loves it. Don't you, Princess? Don't you love being filled up?"

"*Yes.*"

Sweat beaded Daxton's forehead, and he swallowed hard as he watched her curves jiggle before him with each of Bastille's punishing thrusts.

"Don't you want to be filled like the perfect slut you are, baby?" Bastille asked her as he plunged himself into her again and again at such a toe-curling rhythm that she already felt something coiling low in her abdomen once more.

Bastille shifted a hand and dipped a finger to her ass. The digit dipped into her back entrance and at the tease of double penetration, Luna threw her head back and moaned.

Kobe groaned out as he jerked his cock faster, close to coming after watching his mate so overcome with ecstasy.

"Fuck, she's so tight here," Bastille whispered hoarsely

to Daxton, delving his finger further into her as he continued filling up her pussy. "You've never felt anything tighter than her ass. Take it, dragon. You know you want to."

Daxton's pupils grew into black, serpentine slits. His gaze zeroed in on where Bastille's finger sank deeper into Luna's ass.

Bastille spoke softly, "It'll feel so good wrapped around your cock."

One of Daxton's hands slid around her and sank to thrum at her pulsing clit between her and Bastille's bodies. He gathered her wetness on his hand before moving it to his own cock to slick himself with it.

"Luna, I think the straightlaced dragon is getting ready to fill your ass."

"*Mmmmm*," she moaned, writhing on top of him. She rolled her hips and arched her back in invitation. Slowly, Bastille painstakingly eased his finger from her, maintaining eye contact with Daxton from over Luna's shoulder.

Daxton narrowed his eyes on Luna's round ass as Bastille opened it for him. His cock was as stiff as the wooden pillars holding up the curtains over the bed. He had never entered her there. Though he'd never tell another, he often thought about it. About venturing inside her narrow channel. The unyielding tightness there.

"Do it," Bastille said.

Luna shifted back, displaying herself for him.

"Fuck," Daxton cursed under his breath and shuffled

closer to align his aching cockhead to her back entrance. He eased the tip in just a bit—testing out the sensation.

"Let him in, lamb. Relax and let him in."

One more inch entered her. Luna screamed and trembled as another orgasm wracked her.

Daxton ground his teeth, his jaw ticking as he fought for control to go slow. He pushed a little bit more of his length inside her tightness. She just kept *coming*. The orgasm never seemed to stop as she moaned and cried out and gasped.

He grunted at the erotic sight of her tiny hands clawing the sheets. Daxton hissed with each inch he moved deeper inside, his face contorting with pleasure-pain. He coaxed her with whispers of male satisfaction and soft words, even as Bastille counteracted it with dirty ones.

"You like being filled up by both of us at the same time?"

"*Yes.*"

Bastille smirked as he violently thrust his hips from below her. "The dragon already looks close to coming. Is her ass that good, Dax?"

"Fuck you," he exhaled through clenched teeth. Daxton's thighs shook from the pleasure of his cock being squeezed so tightly. *Never knew it could be like this.* His corded muscles strained; his chest heaved. He still had another three inches to push inside her.

By the time Daxton fully sheathed himself in her, Bastille slowed his thrusts to short rolls of his hips. Daxton knew what he waited for. Every time the men filled her at the same time, they moved to match their thrusts, providing her the most pleasure possible.

"Fuck, you being in her ass is just making her pussy even tighter." Bastille clenched his eyelids shut, trying to maintain control. "Fuck."

Daxton could feel the thin wall between his and Bastille's erections inside her. Luna, on the other hand, no longer seemed capable of speech.

"Grab the headboard and hold on, lamb," Bastille ordered.

Swaying, she obeyed, dazedly reaching out and gripping the wood.

"Ready?" Bastille asked Daxton.

Then, they moved. Every time Bastille slid inside her, Daxton pulled back, and vice versa.

A low growl rumbled the dragon's chest as they synced their thrusts. Luna erupted in begging mewls, unable to move or do anything but *feel* as she took their talented fucking. Bastille's fingers trailed up her spine before reaching her hair and tugging it back roughly. He nipped at her throat and drove himself into her.

Daxton's hands fell over hers on the headboard, pinning hers there and weaving his fingers through hers, interlocking them.

In minutes, the three were a wet tangle of hot, slippery bodies. With ragged breaths, Luna's body submitted to the alphas' wild, virile dominance. Desperate pants. She ground herself onto Daxton's dick in shameless yearning as tight spasms wracked her yet again.

"Good girl," Bastille cooed to her. "Taking us so well. So deep."

Daxton's heart raced in his chest, pounding so hard, he could hardly hear his own low, guttural grunts.

"You like her ass, dragon?"

"Love it," he shot back hoarsely.

Both men's muscles tensed, their balls heavy with seed as their mate came around them once more. Her tender inner walls contracted around them, and the pace of their thrusts grew unsteady.

"Feel those cocks inside you?" Bastille rubbed at her clit. Circling and pressing and tugging. "That's you taking what's yours."

She quivered between them, her nails digging into the wood of the headboard. The sound of their skin slapping together was so loud, it was a marvel Sly did not wake on the bed. "Can't take...anymore," she mumbled breathlessly.

"Yes, you can. You can take it. One more time, baby."

"*Bastille.*"

"Take my fucking cum, baby. Take it. Milk me with that perfect pussy. Yes, good girl—*yes*, FUCK," Bastille bellowed with pleasure as he slammed himself into her, spurting his hot seed. Even after he came, he continued numbly bucking into her in slow thrusts.

Daxton's abs and thighs shook as he came with an ear-splitting roar. He pumped his cock into her, spilling himself and fighting to find breath.

They all fell atop each other, shivering and clutching Luna as their heartbeats struggled to return to normal. All the while, Daxton gazed lovingly at her and stroked a thumb over her chin. Her expression softened at his tender touch.

"You an ass man now, dragon?" Bastille quipped then yelped at the returning punch Daxton delivered.

Luna ignored the small act of violence and reached her

arms over her head, stretching her limbs after her thorough bedding.

The dragon and basilisk grinned at each other, basking in mutual masculine pride.

"You guys couldn't have woken me up?" Sly's angry voice sounded from the far side of the bed, dripping with annoyance.

All of them looked over to the fox shifter who had been left out of the morning fun.

"You know what they say: the early fox gets the lamb," Luna muttered back, contentedly cuddling into her nest of men.

Upon seeing Luna's little smile as she slipped into a well-earned rest, the men curled in closer to her, all laying a hand over her flushed skin.

Protect. Pleasure. Love.

Their pretty little queen.

ACKNOWLEDGMENTS

As the first reverse harem romance novel I have ever written (the first of many), this book has a special place in my heart.

Thank you to the beta readers who offered feedback!

Thank you to God for not smiting me after I wrote several of these scenes.

Thank you to the reader! YOU! Thank you for picking this up and making it to the end! If you enjoyed it, I would LOVE if you would be willing to leave a review or help get the word out about this story to others who might enjoy it! I wanted to write something new to this genre and explore writing smutty scenes that my friends and families would never tie back to me! I hope you love it <3

Thank you to my mom, who did not get to read the last

few chapters because of all the group sex, but said "I like it" about the rest of this filthy book. Thank you for not bringing up the "slut" scene. Love you!

ABOUT THE AUTHOR

M. K. Kate decided to dabble in writing dark, edgy—and don't forget smutty!—paranormal reverse harem romance novels after watching too many spicy TikToks about monster romance. She seeks to put new spins on paranormal reverse harems and specializes in dirty-talking heroes and the sassy women who leave them tongue-tied. She also writes steamy romantic comedy romance novels under M. K. Hale, and "M. K. Kate" is her new alter-ego for all things filthy, kinky, and paranormal. "Pretty Little Prey" was her first reverse harem romance novel.

Follow her on social media: **@mkkateauthor**
    Join her newsletter:
    https://mkkate.weebly.com/contact.html

NEXT STEPS...

To keep up to date for when a new smutty reverse harem novel comes available, make sure to follow me on social media:

Instagram: @mkkateauthor

Or join my newsletter: https://mkkate. weebly.com/contact.html

If you enjoyed my writing, check out my steamy/spicy contemporary romantic comedy novels under the pen name "M. K. Hale!"

Instagram: @mkhaleauthor

Website: https://www.mkhale.com/

Coming Soon:

SUCCUBUS LESSONS: Smutty Paranormal Incubi Reverse Harem Romance Novel

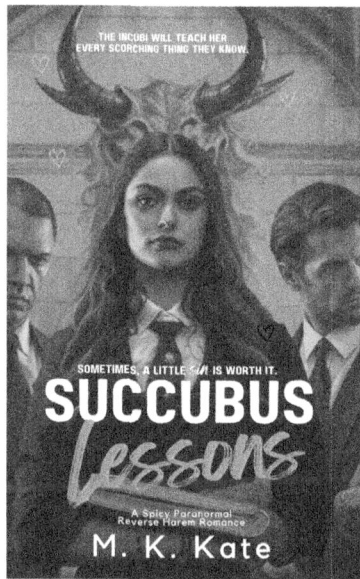

INCUBI MATES—SUCCUBI—ARE EXTINCT. EXCEPT FOR HER…

There are some incubi yearning to finally have a mate, and then there is Daemon. The leather-jacket-wearing sex demon has no interest in a "forever woman." Until he meets *her*.

Catholic university student and prim and proper virgin Kathryn

Bates swore to remain "pure" until marriage. But as she approaches her twenty-first birthday, she has been experiencing…cravings.

When she goes to the confessional on school grounds to repent for these new sexual urges, she has no idea a drop-dead gorgeous incubus sits on the other side of the confessional wall, raptly listening to her every sinful word. Kathryn has no idea that the velvety male voice, saying things like, *"Tell me what fantasies the devil put in your head, my child,"* belongs to a sex demon. She has no idea that, as she describes her wicked cravings, the incubus vows to seduce and corrupt her. *"You let the devil move your hand between your legs, and it felt good, didn't it?"*

SHE WON'T ESCAPE HIM.

When all-around deviant and incubus Daemon suggests she "rub out" her sins right there in the confessional, she runs, spooked. Daemon decides her Catholic university could use a new health teacher. And, of course, the new Professor Daemon Vurr must select Kathryn as his "volunteer" for the lesson on self-pleasure.

THE INCUBUS WILL TEACH HER EVERY SCORCHING THING HE KNOWS.

When her birthday reveals her to be a succubus, other incubi will fight for her affection. The straight-A student "good girl" fears submitting to her new role and, well, *appetite*.

NO ONE CAN RESIST THE SEDUCTION OF AN INCUBUS.

Sometimes a little sin is worth it.

CONTEMPORARY ROMCOM BY M. K. HALE

TIMESHARE BOYFRIEND: Steamy New Adult Beach Romantic Comedy Enemies to Lovers Novel

The love of a lifetime—two weeks at a time.

Reliving the same summer romance at an annual timeshare turns first love into first hate.

Evie Turner and Adam Pierce start off with the perfect summer romance, but when they reunite five years later, he acts like she is wet sand on the bottom of his expensive shoes. Hurt and embarrassed, Evie dedicates her two weeks at the timeshare each year to making him regret his decision. Throughout their young adult years, she tortures him—in a bikini.

After his words sting like jellyfish, she wants him on his knees, begging for forgiveness. Begging for her.

The girl in love with love. The boy who watches mob movies to remind himself that trust means betrayal. A clock of two weeks ticks away until they spend another three hundred and fifty-one days trying to forget each other. Until next year.

As the passion between them rises with the summer temperature, Evie can't help but feel his embraces are like a sunset: beautiful and temporary.

Above all, Evie must not forget one very important lesson: If he is hot, he can burn you.

Better get the aloe.

Printed in Great Britain
by Amazon